CROWN OF SHADOWS

Court of Midnight and Deception Book 1

K. M. SHEA

CROWN OF SHADOWS
Copyright © 2020 by K. M. Shea

Cover Art by Covers by Christian
Edited by Deborah Grace White

All rights reserved. No part of this book may be used or reproduced in any number whatsoever without written permission of the author, except in the case of quotations embodied in articles and reviews.

This is a work of fiction. Names, characters, places, and incidents are either the product of the author's imagination, or are used fictitiously. Any resemblance to actual persons, living or dead, or historic events is entirely coincidental.

ISBN: 978-1-950635-11-5

www.kmshea.com

In memory of Abo,
The best Night mare a girl could ask for.

CHAPTER ONE

Leila

I was on my way out the door from my parents' house on a humid spring day, eager to launch my long-cherished plan to become a Responsible Adult, when I glanced over at the horse pasture and saw it. A monster.

It was a skeletal creature that was only vaguely horse-like. Even from this far away I could see the bulges and indents of its bones. Its ribs and spine uncomfortably stuck out, and its neck was too thin and made its head look huge and blocky.

A fae creature if I ever saw one—which meant it was deadly at best and murderous at worst.

And it was standing about three feet away from Bagel, my pet donkey.

I dropped my manilla folder—which contained three copies of my resume that I planned to drop off at a small marketing company in downtown Magiford—and raced to the fence. I almost face planted when the dewy grass combined with my flats, which I had busted out for this hopeful occasion, made me slip.

"It's fine. It's fine—it's fine!" I smacked into the wooden horse fence. Shock was starting to numb my brain, so when I vaulted over the fence I vaguely noticed the white paint was starting to peel.

Once inside I slowed to a fast, tense walk—running up to the thing would probably triple my chances of getting trampled—and called out to Bagel in a raspy-but-hopefully-not-too-scared-sounding voice. "Bagel!"

Bagel peeled his lips back and smiled at me, completely unconcerned with the creature standing behind him that was totally capable of killing him.

I slowed down even more when I was almost within reaching distance of Bagel.

"Come on, Bagel. Let's go back to the barn and get some treats!" I said.

Bagel swished his bony tail, flicked his enormous ears, and didn't move.

The killer horse didn't seem worried about my floundering arrival.

It flicked its wispy tail—and its mane was just as thin and limp, though its black-ish coat looked crusty and dull. Pupil-less eyes that were a curdled yellow added to the animal's ghastly appearance, especially as it stared me down with a vicious intelligence that seemed natural to most fae creatures.

Bagel took a step closer to it.

"Oh, yes, I see you have a *friend*. But let's not annoy her and go back to the stables," I said with fake brightness.

The fae horse snorted at me, showing the red of its nostrils and pulling its skin taut. I could see the lines of its skull.

Bagel—the idiot donkey—hee-hawed happily at me, then grabbed another mouthful of grass.

I wiped my sweaty hands on my black slacks—even if I was

just dropping my resume off, I figured it would be most professional to dress for success. That's what all the articles I'd read on successful job interviews said, anyway. "It's fine. This is fine. I can totally get you safely out of here before your friend kills us both."

Bagel didn't look up from grazing, the gluttonous pig.

"I'm glad one of us is calm about this," I sourly said.

The fae horse took a step closer to Bagel, and my stomach flopped in my gut.

How am I going to do this? That thing looks capable of murder!

I studiously looked off to the side—trying to make myself appear unintimidating while still keeping the creature within eyesight in case it tried to harm Bagel. The donkey was the biggest pain on my parents' hobby farm, but I loved the fuzzy pain all the same.

That was how I saw the spiders.

They were gathering under the shade of the tree line that the pasture backed up into. They were a writhing mass of black, and each one was at least the size of a dinner plate with a bloated body covered in a sort of hard shell and hairy legs that had more joints than they should have. Their eyes—all eight of them—glowed an unnatural neon green, and ooze that was the same green color covered their front fangs, which were as big and thick as my thumbs.

I'm enough of an animal person that I'd venture to call some spider species cute. These spiders, however, were bloodthirsty fae creatures through and through.

What the heck? Are the fae slacking and letting their monsters slink from the fae realm into the human world?

I narrowed my eyes as I watched the spiders start to crawl away from the shade and move toward the pasture. At their size, they wouldn't have a problem taking out my mom's chickens, or even one of our cats.

"Nope! Nope. Not happening." I glanced at Bagel's unlikely companion—it was just as creepy but mercifully *still* even though

Bagel was now sniffing its thin tail. "Yep, the spiders are the bigger threat. It's time to prioritize!" I sprinted across the pasture and hopped the fence in record time. When I clattered into the barn the horses standing in the paddock neighed their morning greeting, but I ignored them and grabbed the big shovel I used to clean stalls and the can of wasp spray Dad kept by the garden supplies.

I stopped just long enough to kick off my useless flats and put on the spare set of paddock boots I always left in the barn, and then I was back out in the pasture before Bagel finished inspecting his friend's tail.

I tucked my slacks into my paddock boots, trying to give my legs more cover, and popped the lid off the wasp spray.

Should I use my magic?

As a half fae I had it, and I'd learned how to use it as a kid. But while I was decent with magic, I was not *fast*. And if one of those spiders got past me, I didn't know if I'd find it before it started terrorizing the barnyard.

The human—and the most efficient—way it is!

I peered over my shoulder at the fae horse, but it thankfully didn't seem inclined to move, even when I got between it and the tree line that shaded the spiders.

The spiders' oddly jointed legs made a clicking noise as they skittered in the shadows, crawling over what looked like a few dead animal carcasses.

I sprayed the underside of my shovel with the wasp killer, my stomach curdling with my nerves. A few of the spiders crawled toward me, their fangs parting in a sign of aggression.

That was enough to prod me into motion. "For the chickens!" I smashed my shovel into the two closest spiders and was incredibly relieved when I raised my shovel to see I had successfully flattened them. I'd been half afraid I wouldn't be able to kill them.

Two more rushed me, but I sprayed them with the wasp killer

—I'd have to tell the guy at the hardware store that the can really did have the fifteen foot reach it advertised.

The sprayed spiders stopped and started wigging out, waving their creepy legs and giving me enough time to smash them.

That became my pattern—spot a new target, spray it, and smash it.

I had to be fast. When I stopped to breathe, a spider actually reached me and tried to bite me. Thankfully, it couldn't get me through my leather paddock boots, and I was able to crush it before it moved up my leg.

It seemed like there was *no end* of the spiders. More came out of the tree line, rustling leaves and clicking their legs as they rushed me.

Sweat dripped down my spine and made my blouse stick to me as I smashed spider after spider.

How can there be this many? I sprayed one spider, stopping it instantly, then smashed my shovel down on another, shivering when I heard the disgusting crunch of its abnormal shell. *And why are they here?*

I crushed the spider I had sprayed, then wiped my forehead off on my arm. *I should tell Mom to hire a pesticide company.*

Another three minutes of spraying and crushing, and the spiders finally dwindled.

The ground was gross, and the air had a disgusting, bitter scent to it.

I planted my shovel in the ground and made a face at the gore. "One thing's for sure—I'm not letting the horses in this pasture until we get at least two rainstorms. Do you hear that, Bagel?"

I turned around to address the donkey, but he'd wandered off and was playing with water in the water trough up by the barn.

The fae horse-like animal, however, was where I'd left it. And scuttling toward it was a stray spider I'd missed.

I choked on my own spit as I snatched up my can of wasp

spray and wrenched my shovel out of the dirt, then ran after the spider.

It didn't seem like the fae horse saw it—it was too busy glaring at me, its ears pinned to its skull as it made a very hoarse, bark-like noise that sounded pretty ominous.

"Spider!" I panted as I ran toward it. "Watch out for the spider!"

I was catching up fast, but the spider was almost to the horse, its nasty leg joints clicking as it hopped a few steps.

I shook my can of wasp spray and tried to aim for it.

The can fizzled, and nothing came out—I had used the whole thing.

Snarling in irritation, I threw the can and narrowly missed smacking the spider, but it veered to the side, giving me just enough time to raise my shovel above my head and smash down hard.

I felt it crunch. When I lifted my shovel a leg twitched, but the thing was clearly dead.

The adrenaline that had propelled me across the pasture in record time left as abruptly as it had arrived. I had just enough time to dig my shovel into the ground and then lean on it for support.

"I've reassessed the situation. Mom needs to hire a pesticide company run by a *wizard*!" I wheezed and flicked my ponytail over my sweaty shoulder—so much for looking professional. "Or maybe we should just burn the whole tree line down. Talk about *creepy*!"

I shivered, but froze when I heard the muffled thump of a hoof stamping on the grassy ground. Slowly, I raised my eyes, and my stomach iced over when I finally noticed the fae horse had moved.

It was facing me head on, its eyes eerily shining as it tossed its head and showed the red of its nostrils. It pawed at the ground, and I swear the grass under its hooves turned brown and died.

Ah. It's mad.

Slowly, carefully I picked up my shovel. I'd have to abandon the can of wasp spray—it was closer to the fae horse than I was. Holding my breath, I took a shuffling step to the side.

The fae horse charged, streaking past me like a shadow. It neighed, but the noise broke off into a piercing shriek that could have broken glass.

I heard the tell-tale click of spider legs, and I spun around just in time to see the horse-like creature savagely attack a giant spider that had been creeping up behind me.

But this wasn't a plate-sized spider—oh no. It was much more horrifying, given it was roughly as big as a Saint Bernard.

A few of the smaller spiders scuttled around it. Probably the giant spider had laid its eggs in the tree line and I'd come outside just in time to find them after they hatched.

The spider stretched its fangs, trying to bite the attacking fae horse, but the equine reared up and slammed its front legs down on the spider's hardened exterior, forcing it to the ground.

The fae horse shrieked, revealing a mouth full of teeth that were much more jagged and sharp than any horse's, and clamped onto one of the spider's back legs. It whipped the massive spider back and forth—lifting it off the ground even though the monster had to weigh more than fifty pounds—then slammed it on the ground, crushing its own offspring.

It did this twice, and once all the smaller spiders had been killed and the mother was half dead, the fae horse stomped the spider's front end into the ground.

As I watched in shock, Bagel marched up to me and began inspecting my pockets, looking for the carrots I usually gave him and the horses once they were turned out for the day.

The spider's bloated abdomen deflated as it died, and its legs spasmed a couple of times.

The fae horse pawed at the dead spider, sniffed it, then made that weird, hoarse barking noise again.

"I guess this solves where all those other spiders came from," I said with numb lips.

I should call the neighbors once I get this cleaned up. They had trouble with the fae Night Court last fall. Maybe the Night Court is starting something again.

The fae horse finally left the dead spider and slowly came back to me, stopping a few feet away and swishing its tail as it watched Bagel twine around me.

I looked from the crumpled spider carcass to the fiendish looking horse, my brain still trying to catch up with everything that had happened.

This "horse" saved me from that spider. I didn't even hear it behind me—it must have been stalking me.

Cautiously, I pulled out half of a carrot from my front pocket. I fed a piece to Bagel, then slowly took a step closer to the fae horse and held out the remaining carrot chunk.

As a fae, I have some natural magic—magic that works even without the use of an artifact or magical item. It's the only thing I really like about my fae blood, because my natural magic happens to give me a good rapport with animals.

I was heavily banking on my natural magic—I could feel it stretching out to the frightening fae horse, but I didn't know for sure if it would work or not.

"Hello," I said as I might greet a person. "I'm Leila. Thanks for helping me."

The fae horse was still for a long moment that seemed to last forever, then it crossed the space between us and picked the carrot off my palm with a muzzle that felt similar to a horse's, but was somehow rougher.

"You're a good boy—or a good girl? Doesn't matter." I smiled as the fae horse slowly swiveled its ears, listening to the sound of my voice.

"How'd you get out here?" I kept my voice soothing and quiet. "Did someone dump you off?"

It had happened before. There were some seriously irresponsible people out in the world. All of our barn cats had been tossed out of cars out by the road before we took them in. Fae were pretty selfish and slippery supernaturals, so I could totally see them losing interest in their plaything and deciding to dump it off in the country.

I mean, there was no way this horse was wild. I live in the Midwest, halfway between Chicago and Milwaukee. We don't have wild horses around here.

I grimaced as I saw the individual ribs in its side. "You need to put on some weight. Your owner half-starved you." I fed Bagel another carrot, then offered another piece to the fae horse. "I'll get some hay for you—you deserve it after helping me out. Thank you."

The fae horse crunched on its carrot, and surprisingly followed after me as I headed for the barn.

It walked fast enough that it caught up and walked at my side, its head bobbing a little since it had a jolting walk.

I made myself breathe normally as I slowly raised my hand and eventually brushed its neck with one finger

The horse threw its head and shied to the side.

I calmly stopped, trying not to alarm it.

The fae horse arched its neck, but after a few moments passed it ambled up to me, blowing hot, almost sulfuric scented breath on my fingers as it sniffed my hand.

I held my hand up for better inspection.

Once the horse was satisfied it raised its muzzle, and pressed it to my temple.

I felt something...*strange*. I shivered without explanation, and I could have sworn I felt a bit of magic, but it was gone so fast I couldn't be certain.

The fae horse smeared its lips on me—probably leaving spit behind, but it didn't matter, there was no way I was going to drop off my resume looking like this—then it reclaimed its spot next to me.

"So much for becoming a Responsible Adult." I grimaced as I peered down at my gunk-spattered slacks. "But I have another set of business casual clothes. I'll shower to get the spider stink out of my hair, and *then* I'll go drop off my resume. I will own this—my entire life's goal!"

I pumped my hand in the air, but neither Bagel nor the fae horse seemed particularly impressed. Didn't matter—I was *determined* to live out my life in as human a way as possible.

That might sound like a ridiculously small life goal, but as a half fae, it was beyond most people like me. Fae loved to play mind games and push Court politics. I wanted a peaceful, stress-free life, so my greatest hope was to live like a human, get a regular job with insurance, vacation time, and every other beautifully mundane benefit. Crushing fae spiders was the most excitement I ever wanted to face.

I glanced at the fae horse, which was staying in step with me even though it was capable of zooming ahead. This time, when I placed my hand on its neck, the fae horse shivered, but it didn't react.

I pressed my lips together. "I don't think owning a fae horse counts as a life of excitement," I said. "Or really, we're not going to let it count. I'm going to get some weight on you, and you can live out a peaceful human life here with me."

The horse made a noise in its throat that sounded weirdly like a chortle, but it didn't even flick an ear when Bagel released his gusty, deafening hee-haw.

As I patted the horse, it didn't occur to me to be wary of it for any reason besides the possible physical threat it could have been.

I'd never seen a horse like it before, and with good reason. Almost no one outside fae Courts had ever seen a night mare before, so I had no way of knowing that—for me—its presence was a harbinger of the worst kind.

CHAPTER TWO

Rigel

I used a fragile sheet of rice paper to clean my dagger, wiping it free of dust and excessive oil as I waited in the shadows for my target.

A cat pounced on a mouse hiding in a fresh pile of wood shavings, one of the grooms picked up a leather saddle, which creaked as he carried it off, and the quiet tap of footsteps on stone announced two fae had arrived.

I looked away from my blade long enough to peer through a crack in the hayloft I had chosen for my position.

One of the new arrivals was one of the two stable managers. He whipped his baseball hat off and picked a leaf from his hair as he and his companion entered the shadow of the stables.

"It's as I've told you," the stable manager said. "We set the night mares loose every night, just as we have for the past two months. About a week ago, one of them didn't come back. Almost every morning since then, a new one has been missing."

His companion was a fae noble I vaguely recognized as a peon to the previous Night Court monarch, Queen Nyte. Or rather, he'd been her peon, before she'd lost all her sense and picked a fight with the most lethal vampire Family in the Midwest, who killed her for her numerous assassination attempts against their leader and his pet wizard.

The noble tilted his chin back and looked imperiously down his nose at the stable manager. "I cannot believe you are so inept at your job that you do not know *where* the night mares have gone."

The stable manager was a dryad, but the green hue to his skin was a sickly yellow-green rather than the usual healthy moss color. "We give them free rein—we have to. They won't go anywhere if we try to handle 'em, and we can't keep up with 'em once they set out."

The noble pressed his lips into a thin line. "If the night mares are congregating it means they've *finally* selected the next monarch of the Night Court." He convulsively tightened his hands before he got a hold of himself and pressed them against his white trousers. "The Night Court needs a ruler. We've been without one since late fall, and it's already May. The Night Realm..."

He trailed off, but I knew what he'd been about to say.

The piece of the fae realm that the Night Court owned was suffering without a ruler in place to keep the magic flowing.

They should have had a new ruler before the end of last year. But since the founding of the Night Court centuries ago, whenever the reigning monarch and their spouse died, the night mares chose the next monarch.

But the night mares had been ignored under Queen Nyte's rule and run wild. It had taken months just to capture them all, and just as long to convince the savage horses to *look* for the monarch.

"I don't know if they've found the monarch or not," the stable manager said. "They've been searching for weeks—much longer than they should have. The missing night mares may have just decided to stay free."

"A minimum of three night mares are required to choose our next monarch. How many are missing?" the noble demanded.

"Six," the stable manager said. "The most recent one failed to return with the rest of the herd this morning."

"Then it would seem they've found several candidates," the noble said. "Find them *tonight*. Failure will bring consequences you can't afford to pay." He swept from the stable with a storm in his face and pompousness biting at his heels.

I blinked, comfortably motionless.

The stable manager rubbed his face and groaned. He shed a leaf or two—revealing just how frightened he was—and went out the back of the stable, to the pastures behind it.

I folded up my used rice paper and slipped it into a pouch on my belt—I wasn't going to leave any sign of my presence behind.

I wasn't concerned about the Night Court's lack of a monarch. The Court had been in a downward spiral for decades. A new monarch wasn't going to solve anything—we were too far gone for that. Besides, it was our rulers who had gotten us into this position.

But I was interested in the next monarch candidate because I'd been hired to find and eliminate them.

Rather, *try* to eliminate them.

As an assassin, I had a perfect record. I'd never missed a target, and never bungled an operation. But given that my newest contract was to take out the next Night Court monarch, my chances of success were small.

As a fae I was forced into obedience to my monarch. The same kind of magic that kept all fae from lying also made it that we couldn't raise a hand against our rulers.

There were ways around it. One might be able to arrange an

accident, and the magic couldn't keep us from annoying our monarchs. But coups and assassinations were near impossible.

My only chance of eliminating this new monarch was to kill him or her before he or she was officially sworn in, activating the ancient magic that governed us.

I'd stated this when I initially refused the contract, but the contractor insisted that merely trying was enough to consider the contract fulfilled.

Fae aren't known for our generosity, which meant there was a fairly good chance this was a trap for me rather than an actual attempt to kill the next king or queen.

Which was why I took the contract. Traps didn't worry me—there was no one they could hire who was skilled enough to kill me. But it would always be more efficient to eliminate a threat I was aware of rather than blindly encounter one.

Besides, I had no love for the Night Court throne. The idea that a monarch could save us was a fairy tale. It made no difference to me if the candidate died.

I hadn't moved since putting the used rice paper away, but I heard the rustle of a rat, and looked down through the crack in the floor again.

Sure enough, the rat—my target—scurried down the stall aisles, moving to the far end of the barn, where he would pass just under the hayloft I hid in. He was sweating in his silken robes, and his complexion was waxy.

He was one of Queen Nyte's old officials—her steward, if I remembered correctly. He was as crooked as they came, and had lorded his position over others while funneling extra funds into his pocket and punishing anyone who didn't try to curry favor with him.

I wasn't killing him because of his sins. He'd angered a fae noble lady from the Autumn Court when he refused to repay her for a magical artifact he'd purchased from her. She hired me to kill him as revenge.

He should have known better. It was well known she'd inherited the artifact from her brother, who had "mysteriously disappeared."

That's the way we fae operate. We can't lie, but we twist and distort reality, struggling to amass power and taking what we like until it inevitably catches up with us.

It's a never-ending game, even though the players die off like flies.

I was soundless as I crept across the loft. When the crooked official scurried under the hay chute I was positioned at, I dropped down, landing directly behind him.

"*Mortem*." I breathed the name of my dagger. Its blade glowed a golden yellow color, and before the official even knew I was there, I stabbed him in the back of the neck.

The magic in the blade made it a simple thing to cut through bone and sever his spinal cord, resulting in a near instantaneous death.

All of the air in his lungs left with a gasp, and he collapsed to the ground, dead before I stepped back from the body.

I wiped my dagger off on his shirt then felt for a pulse, confirming his death. A few moments later I left the stables, keeping to the shadows where my magic and my dark gray clothes would cloak me.

I mentally mapped out my plans to contact the fae lady from the Autumn Court and begin tracking the night mares.

Killing had very little impact on me—I was just as much a villain as the fae I murdered.

But this game of power and dominance had been in existence for centuries. No one could escape it. It dragged us all down eventually.

CHAPTER THREE

Leila

My phone blasted my ringtone so loudly I jumped. I'd picked out a Lord of the Rings ringtone because I loved those movies, but it was pretty startling to have the Fellowship of the Ring soundtrack blast out of your butt pocket at a volume loud enough to wake the barn cats.

I fumbled with the phone for a moment before I managed to swipe and accept the call. "Hey, Mom!"

"Hi, Leila. I'll be home soon—I'm leaving the store right now. Would you tell Paul? I tried to call him, but he didn't pick up."

"Yeah, I think he's in his workshop. I'll let him know."

"Thanks. How has your day been?"

I grimaced. "I heard back from the marketing firm. They went with a different applicant."

"Oh, honey, I'm sorry. I know you said you really liked them when you interviewed with them."

"Yeah, but it's okay. There are a few online positions I can apply for. Otherwise I saw there was one at the Curia Cloisters."

I'd normally avoid the Curia Cloisters—it was basically the town hall for the supernatural community here in Magiford, which was pretty big since Magiford was considered the supernatural capital of the Midwest region.

It's not that I was against working for supernaturals, it just didn't mesh well with my goal of living like a human and remaining out-of-sight/out-of-mind to the fae community. They didn't usually let anyone with fae blood waltz around free, so I had to be pretty purposeful about where I lived and worked.

But I started looking for a full-time job in February when I was still in college. Now it was *May*, I'd finished my classes, and I *still* hadn't gotten a job. I was getting a lot less picky these days.

"That's a nice idea." She sounded kind of flat—which was pretty unusual for her.

"What, you're not going to tell me 'I told you so'?" I joked, trying to break the moment. "You told me last winter I should apply for something at the Curia Cloisters—in between times when you were showing me pictures of your friends' sons and trying to set me up on dates."

That got a weak chuckle out of her. "Wherever you end up, I know you'll be fine. I will *always* believe in you, Leila."

I briefly pulled the phone away from my ear so I could frown at it.

Mom was normally pretty sentimental, but not usually on the phone when she was driving home from the grocery store.

"Oops," Mom said. "I should go—I see Mrs. Brown out at her farm stand—I want to ask when the strawberry season will start."

"Okay—see you soon!" I ended the call and stared at my phone for an extra moment or two.

Mom has been acting off for the past few days.

My mom was always a super warm and sweet parent. But

recently she'd been hugging me a lot more, and watching me with sad eyes whenever she thought I didn't notice.

It was probably because since I had graduated college I was all "grown up" or something. She'd been harping on me about dating until about two weeks ago—which was a total waste of her time since I was way more consumed with finding a job and launching my Responsible Adult plan. But she'd stopped telling me to get out there and date the day the first fae horse showed up. Maybe she realized I aspired to become one of those old cat ladies, and figured I'd just do it with horses instead?

I finished cleaning out the horse stall I'd been working on and dumped out the dirty shavings, waving to all the equines as I mulled over Mom's sentimental actions. I went back into the barn just long enough to dump fresh sawdust in the stall, creating a mushroom cloud of dust that got me sneezing.

Dad hadn't noticed anything odd about Mom when I asked him about it yesterday, so maybe it was just the "grown up" thing.

Dad was just as warm and kind a parent as Mom—especially because I wasn't really his kid.

He was my step-dad, but he married my mom when I was about ten, and he taught me how to drive, helped me with my homework, and had been the best dad I could ask for—way better than my bio father, the fae degenerate that had gifted me with my fae blood. So, he was Dad to me.

Finished with the stalls, I stepped out of the shade of the barn and into the hot afternoon sunlight.

I rounded the corner of the barn and slipped through the wooden fence, stopping just by the water troughs.

Dad's horses were all clustered at the far side of the pasture, stamping their hooves and swishing their tails as they waited to be let inside again.

Bagel, however, was a spot of velveteen brown surrounded by six fae horses.

Wait...six?

"Oh, you dirty weasel." I sprinted down the length of the pasture, upsetting horses and ignoring Bagel when he hee-hawed to me.

I made it to the far side of the pasture where the tree line that the fae spider had tried to take over stood.

I boosted myself over the wooden fence and shot through a thin gap in the trees, popping out in a ditch right by the road.

I scrambled up the slight hill, my paddock boots slapping the asphalt when I reached the road. Shading my eyes, I looked up and down the road.

We lived pretty far out in the country, and were surrounded by cornfields and the giant estate that belonged to our next-door neighbors, the Drakes—the most powerful vampire Family in the Midwest.

Since there weren't many buildings around, I could see pretty far. There were no trucks or trailers on the road—not even a single car.

"Come on!" I shouted to the sky. "Why can't I catch the dirtbag doing this? There were five fae horses when I dumped the dirty stall shavings, and I only went back into the barn for a few minutes! Who can drop off a horse that fast?" I growled and took one last look—just in case I'd missed a truck or something—and then stomped my way down into the ditch and through the tree line.

Since the first fae horse had been dumped, more kept appearing. They showed up randomly. One had arrived sometime between night chores and when I went out to tell Dad dinner was ready. Another had been abandoned in our pasture when I'd gone to the feed store for more grain—I was going to get some weight on these fae horses even if I went broke doing it—and to drop off some more job applications.

"I'm going to find whoever is doing this, and I'm going to make sure they never own another animal again." I climbed over the wooden fence and dropped down with a huff. "I should get the Curia Cloisters involved. Whatever nutso is doing this is clearly from the supernatural community—probably a fae. Oh—or I'll file charges with the county and get humans involved! That will scare the supernaturals into doing something!"

The Drake vampires' presence should have been enough to scare off anyone from doing something stupid like this—the Drakes were known for their ruthlessness. And since Killian Drake had fallen in love with Hazel Medeis—the Adept of the wizard House Medeis, and a good friend of mine—they'd only become more respected. Though, admittedly, having petite Hazel and a bunch of hug-exuberant wizards running loose around Drake Hall did make them a tad less fierce.

Bagel and the fae horses had chosen to follow me, apparently, and were congregating at the end of the pasture.

As I walked through the herd, scratchy muzzles bumped me, and two of the horses crowded me, wheezing like asthmatic hippos.

"Yes, yes, I have treats." I patted the biggest one—I'd taken to calling him Solstice. He was a coal black color with oozing red lines in his coat that made it look like someone had stitched him together like a stuffed animal.

Solstice wheezed and rested his chin on the top of my head until I elbowed him in the chest to make him back up. He took his treat happily, as did Blue Moon, Comet, and Twilight.

I'd done my best to give them pretty names even though, as far as animals went, they were really ugly. Twilight was runty and such an off gray color he looked perpetually ill. Comet drooled red, but when I had the vet out to look her over, he swore up and down she didn't have any wounds or sores in her mouth.

All of the fae horses were as skinny and skeletal as the first mare that had shown up—I called her Eclipse.

Eclipse was last—or second-to-last thanks to our new addition—to come forward. She daintily accepted her treat, even though she looked as skeletal as the day she'd arrived a little over a week ago.

I stroked her neck with a frown. "I don't get it. You should have started putting on at least a little weight by now."

Eclipse turned her head to peer at the newcomer.

The newest fae horse was standing back a little. It showed its teeth, pinned its ears, then bobbed its head at me.

In a normal horse that kind of body language would have me cautiously backing up, but with the fae horses I'd learned it was almost like they didn't know *how* to be horses, so their signals were all off.

That's the only reason why I dug out a carrot chunk and stretched my arm out in front of me.

I let the new horse approach me. It came in faster than I would have liked, but instead of using its lips to scoop up the carrot, it licked my hand like a dog.

A quick check below confirmed my suspicions that I was facing a mare. She was slobbering like crazy and losing bits of carrot.

She—like all the other horses had when they first met me—pressed her muzzle to my forehead, leaving a smear of spit, then backed up a few steps.

I felt that elusive brush of magic play with my senses—I'd fast figured out the source was the horses, but it didn't seem malevolent so I was probably okay.

But this time was different.

The magic felt the same, but the impression of magic lasted longer, and I swear I felt cool night air fill my lungs, heard an owl hoot, and felt wet grass on my skin. There were stars in my eyes and moonlight on my skin, and then abruptly the feelings faded and I could see straight.

"That was weird." I studied the new mare carefully as I felt for my inherent animal magic—which oozed around me just fine.

I'd been intending to back up a step, but Bagel chose to ram into me at that moment, smacking me into the new mare's shoulder.

Mercifully, despite whatever abuse she'd endured, the mare didn't seem to mind being touched. She shivered, and her muscles jumped, but she didn't move or otherwise react.

I awkwardly patted her shoulder. "You'll need a name, like the others." I looked from her pale yellow eyes to her black coat—which had faint blushes of blood red hairs. "How about Nebula?"

The newly named Nebula flicked her ears, turned around, and walked off.

"It seems fine?" I asked Eclipse.

Eclipse was staring out at the open pastures, totally not listening to me. She pinned her ears, then coughed out the hoarse bark the fae horses used occasionally.

I'd come to learn this was an expression they used almost exclusively as a warning. Immediately I took a big step away from her, then jumped when there was an odd thrumming noise and something passed over my head. Something crackled and crunched, and a startled yelp escaped me.

The fae horses meandered around me without much concern, but I twisted around, trying to figure out what the noise was.

My jaw dropped when I saw the wooden fence just behind us. One of the boards of the top rail had a large hole in it. Whatever hit it had singed the wood, blackening it, and shredding it to splinters.

I felt a wispy sensation of fae magic brush my senses as I stared at the broken fence. "What the—"

This time I screamed when the thrumming noise passed over my head and I *saw* a magic bullet punch through the fence, showering the area with splinters.

Someone...someone is shooting at me!

CHAPTER FOUR

Leila

I bolted for the barn. "Bagel, Solstice, Eclipse, Comet, Twilight, Nebula, Blue Moon—come on!" I zigzagged through the pasture, trying to make myself a harder target as I tried to yank my phone and my magic artifact—a charm bracelet—from my pocket.

What's the emergency phone number for the Curia Cloisters? Why didn't I put it in my contacts list?!

I made it to the part of the pasture that was hidden behind the stable and slipped in a mud puddle. I flung my arms out to catch my balance, but dropped my phone in the process.

Fae grace and elegance my—

Something leaped from the barn roof and landed next to me—on the dry ground of course.

I toppled backwards, falling in my surprise. I started to scurry backwards, but when I looked up at my attacker, I found I couldn't move.

Black eyes of death stared at me from a face so handsome it could take your breath away. Even partially hidden behind a gray scarf that encased the lower half of his face, his long nose gave him an aristocratic look, and combined with his skin—a tawny copper color—and his hair—cropped stylishly short but a very eye catching silvery white color—it made him almost otherworldly.

He was a fae—the magic radiating from him was so strong I could feel it resonate in my teeth. But his clothes—leather arm bracers, black boots, fitted black pants, a sweeping dark gray jacket split up the back with a high collar—were also a dead giveaway of fae workmanship.

If I hadn't known any better, I might have thought he was one of the long dead elven warriors come back to life, but he had the whispery kiss of fae magic, and his ears were only slightly tapered like the fae.

But it didn't matter; his black eyes pinned me in place, and I knew he was here to kill me.

Terror held a scream in my throat that couldn't rip free. I stared up at him, paralyzed in fear. My fingers and legs were numb and didn't listen when I tried at the very least to pull myself backwards.

He stared at me with his dead, light-less eyes, and pulled a dagger from his belt. "*Mortem.*"

I tried to fish my charm bracelet from my pocket—one of the charms was stuck on the edge of my pants.

His dagger glowed white hot, and he flicked it in my direction.

The dagger caught on *something*—or it looked like it did, because the fae froze with the dagger barely hanging from his fingertips.

I blinked stupidly up at the fae, who was frowning at his dagger.

I saw him lean into the weapon, his muscles tense with exertion, and he clenched his jaw as he pushed.

His arm didn't move.

I gaped from the fae to his dagger. *What the heck? I don't see anything?*

And then I felt it—a faint pressure.

Veined with the cobweb sensation that fae magic gave me, I felt magic thrum around us, creating a slight pressure in the air.

At least, it felt slight to me—it must have been stronger to the fae. He gritted his jaw, and I could see the muscles of his neck tensing as he tried to resist it, but eventually it pushed him back two steps.

The fae horses casually joined us, flanking me like it was no big deal, even though the muscles in my arms were still shaking.

Blue Moon casually sniffed my phone, and I was so consumed with the hope that he wouldn't step on it, that I almost missed the fae's words.

"Queen," he said in a voice that was simultaneously smooth as ice and filled with rage.

"W-what?" I stammered.

His eyes were black holes in his freezing anger, and he dropped his chin for a moment.

Fae magic flared, and a stinging gust of wind blew dust into my face.

I curled an arm over my face to protect my eyes, and when everything settled the fae was gone.

"What just happened?" I stared at the spot where he'd stood—he hadn't even left boot prints in the dirt.

I glanced up at the fae horses. "Was that magic from you guys? I certainly didn't get a chance to cast anything."

None of the horses responded except Comet, who lipped the top of my head. I shivered, remembering the fae's cold, dead eyes. "He was definitely from the Night Court. Most fae from the Night Court have dark taupe, copper, or olive complexions like he did…I better call Hazel."

I boosted myself to my feet and was in the process of wiping muck off my phone when two cars gunned it down the driveway.

I squinted, and my heart—which hadn't recovered from my attempted murder—flopped uselessly in my chest.

The cars were a deep silvery color, and they both had the spotless, shiny look of luxury—which was at odds with the hobby farm, particularly as they parked just in front of the wooden pasture fence. But it wasn't until I spotted the beautiful woman driving one of the cars—gorgeous in an impossible sort of way—that I realized they were from the supernatural community.

"It's fine," I told myself as I quickly swiped my phone open and speed dialed one of my contacts. "Maybe they're following the almost-a-killer-creeper."

My phone dialed as the fae emerged from the cars, looking around them with their fine noses wrinkled in distaste.

They had to be fae with their slightly tapered ears and willowy limbs. And just like my would-be-killer, they were descendants of the Night Court—a fact made obvious by the crescent moon pins they wore affixed to their fancy clothes, and their ashen taupe complexions.

I relaxed my shoulders when my call was picked up. "*Leila! What's up?*"

"Hey, Hazel. Are you at Drake Hall right now, or House Medeis?" I asked. Since Hazel and Killian had become engaged, the pair split their time between the vampire hall and the magical wizard House.

"*We just arrived at Drake Hall today! Did you want to come over for dinner?*"

"Um, thank you, but no. But I could really use a little help right now."

"*Sure! What's up?*"

"A fae from the Night Court shot at me. I'm pretty sure he was trying to kill me, but he ran off when some strange magic intervened. Now I've got a couple fae walking across my lawn."

"*KILLIAN!*" The line cut off, ending the call.

I could swallow, now. If Hazel and Killian were on their way, I'd survive this—vampires were that fast.

A fae in a navy blue suit offered his arm to the beautiful woman who'd driven one of the two cars. She was wearing a flowered, bright orange dress that would have looked more appropriate at a fancy afternoon tea than visiting the countryside.

The other car held an older, distinguished woman who wore such a prominent frown she looked like a frog despite her fae beauty, and three guards who wore black and carried daggers and swords strapped to their waists.

They have to be chasing after the fae—why else would they bring guards? I'm Unpledged, but that shouldn't matter to them, even if they are from the Night Court.

Their presence made ice spread through my veins, and it wasn't until Twilight nudged me that I was able to recover.

"Hello." I walked past the edge of the barn, revealing myself to them. "Can I help you?"

I was grateful for the fae horses, who moved around me in a herd—suspiciously eyeing our guests. Comet sneered at them, and her red drool that dripped frightfully actually cheered me for once because all of the fae turned ashen when she aimed her coughing-bark at them.

One of the guards strode toward me, despite the shifty horses surrounding me. He lifted his sword and pointed at the wooden fence, mumbled a word, then chopped through the boards in one strike.

My jaw dropped. "That was our *fence*! We need that for the horses you inconsiderate—" I angrily swallowed my words, even though I wanted to shake my fist at them.

No, I don't want to argue with them, I want to get them out of here as quickly as possible. It's. Fine.

It didn't matter anyway. The fae ignored my outburst and were marching into the pasture with all the pomp and elegance they could muster.

This was why I didn't like dealing with the fae. They were incredibly *selfish*—and yes, I said that as a half fae.

The older, distinguished-appearing fae woman led them all. Her face twitched with disdain when she had to edge her way around a few piles of horse poop, but, hey, that's what she got for breaking my fence!

I loosely dropped an arm over Eclipse's neck when the mare stood next to me, an encouraging presence to me. "What brings you here?" I asked when the fae all stopped short of the fae horses and me.

"It cannot be you," the old lady said. "You are not even a full fae!"

"You're right," I said brightly. "Thankfully, I'm only half. But you still haven't told me why you're here, ruining our fences."

The old lady turned around. "You have misled us—our esteemed monarch could not *possibly* be half human!"

Esteemed monarch? What on earth is she talking about?

Suits—the fae in the navy blue suit—blinked. "I would not believe it either. However, doesn't the night mares' conduct prove it must be she?"

"It cannot be. We will have to release the night mares again. This will not be allowed," the older fae declared.

I called her older, but truthfully she didn't have many wrinkles—just a few lines at the edges of her eyes, which I'd bet were from scowling rather than smiling—and her gray hair was sleek and perfect.

Yeah, you could say the fae won the genetic lottery. Not only do they all have otherworldly looks and poise, but they age incredibly slowly and with a stupid amount of grace. I wasn't too sad about inheriting that trait, but my fae blood came with a ton of baggage since fae are opinionated and political, so I still wasn't a fan.

"How do we make them choose again?" Suits helplessly gestured to the fae horses surrounding me. "It took months to convince them to begin the search. If we refute their first choice it may be a year before they are willing to look again."

What the heck are they talking about?

Since the fae didn't seem inclined to answer me, I turned to Eclipse. "That's it—they're part of a cult, aren't they?"

The fae in the fancy day dress tossed her head, making her hair ripple flawlessly. "I refuse to believe it. The night mares searched for months, and *this* is what they find? This must be their revenge."

Nebula lunged at her, releasing a noise that started as a neigh and ended in that glass-piercing shriek all my fae horses could produce.

The woman screamed as she leaped backwards with an admirable amount of agility given that she was wearing high heels.

Apparently, this wasn't enough, because Solstice reared, his nostrils flaring red as he also shrieked.

My heart squeezed with love for my homely horses as the fae went running back across the pasture and threw herself into one of the cars, shutting and locking the door behind her.

"Such a good boy." I fondly patted Solstice on the shoulder.

"That's a confirmation that *two* have chosen her." The older fae woman peered down her nose at me. "But we ought to be able to make an appeal given her…*human* blood." She shuddered in open revulsion, and unknowingly hit my switch.

I like to think I'm a pretty chill person, but I was proud of my human blood. Heck, it was my fae half I wasn't thrilled about. And I wasn't going to put up with someone criticizing me for something I was proud of.

"Okay, that's it." I slid my arm off Eclipse and straightened up. "You barge in here, break my fence, insult me and take potshots at my horses without even introducing yourselves? You're awful—not to mention *unwanted*—guests," I said, speaking the magic words.

All supernaturals have natural strengths and weaknesses.

Fae are really gifted with magic and are able to twist and meld it for tons of different uses—for everything from wards to mind reading to temporary love potions.

Fae also tend to be faster and stronger than the average human—although they've got nothing on vampires in the speed department or werewolves and shifters when it comes to strength.

The fae are *powerful*. And yet, they're kept in check by some pretty iron-clad rules.

First off, they can't lie—they are physically incapable of it. Supposedly it has something to do with the way they use magic and their bodies process it, but I never really bothered to learn for sure.

Lying isn't as hard for them to get around as you might think—some fancy wordsmithing, a few vague sayings, and they can still manage to cheat and deceive people.

But the second big rule is etiquette. The fae are bound to lots of outdated rules of conduct. I think it's why they always prance around acting like old nobility from Europe.

The basic gist is that they have to obey and follow their monarchs—like lying, this rule is magic bound—but they're also supposed to be excellent guests and hosts. This is more of a cultural thing. Magic doesn't force them to do it, and they can get around it.

But you can still use it as a verbal weapon, which is exactly what I intended to do.

My accusation of their poor conduct made the fae stand tall.

"We," the older woman ground out, "are representatives of the Night Court."

"How surprising. What are you doing here?" I curled my hands into fists, dreading their answer.

"We are searching for our new ruler," Suits said.

And there we have it. The biggest mess I could ever ask for.

The previous Queen of the Night Court died late in the fall.

Since it was now May, that was a really long time to go without a monarch.

"And *why* would you be searching for a fae monarch on human land?" I asked.

The old lady pointed accusingly at the horses. "It is the night mares."

"What?" I asked.

"The night mares choose our monarchs. We've been waiting for them to choose for months," Suits said.

Night mares? Is that what they're called? I peered at my equine friends, who seemed entirely unconcerned with our fae visitors.

Solstice bumped my shoulder. I patted his head. "Why are they called night mares when I know that some of them are geldings?"

Suits rolled his eyes. "It's a title—not meant to be a description. It describes the type of animal they are."

"They could have just called them night horses," I grumbled. "I bet that they got named so one fae could tell a half lie to someone."

The older fae sighed. "And after our pleas, *this* is what they chose? A mutt?"

"We should return to the Court, to see what can be done to restart the selection process," Suits said.

"Yeah, good luck with that," I said. "But there's no way I'm letting you take these guys back."

Suits turned to me, the smooth skin of his forehead marred with a wrinkle of confusion. "What do you mean?"

I gestured to the horses around me. "They're skeletal thin and in horrible condition."

"Nonsense. It is merely that they have taken on the state of the Court," the older fae woman said. "As the Night Court is unwell, so are the creatures embraced in its bosom."

"Yeah, no. This is what happens when you don't *feed* them," I said. "And you can bet the Curia Cloisters are going to hear all about it. Until then, they stay with me."

The fae woman sniffed. "Empty threats. Guards—prepare for our departure."

A guard turned back to the fence and raised his sword at my poor fence again.

"*Don't you dare!*" I snarled.

The guard froze mid-swing.

I suspiciously glared at him, but relaxed when he didn't move.

"What are you waiting for?" the older fae woman demanded.

"I...can't," the guard slowly ground out.

Suits and the older fae swung around and stared at me, varying degrees of horror and terror flickering across their expressions.

"No, no it can't be possible." The older fae shook her head as she stared at the night mares. "They haven't bound a monarch in a century. They couldn't possibly bind us to you. It would send the Night Court on a path of destruction!"

Suits tugged on his tie, losing some of his prim-and-proper edge. "They chose. We're not needed—we can't do anything. She's already bound!"

I rolled my eyes at their theatrics—blissfully ignorant, or I probably would have been rolling around on the ground.

I wasn't exactly unfamiliar with fae. Since I was an Unpledged half fae there was always a chance one of the fae would decide I *had* to join them—and because the Courts have absolute jurisdiction over all fae, half or otherwise, it would have been hard to fight.

But I knew very little about the Night Court. My bio father was from the Night Court, and given how he had abruptly divorced my mom when I was a toddler, I didn't have a burning desire to get to know his Court.

The fae moaned for a few moments as my irritation grew.

"That's enough," I said, using the same, firm, no-nonsense voice I used when I was working with the Drakes' dogs. "You either explain, or you leave here knowing that you are never getting these horses back."

The older fae turned her attention to me, her anger making her expression cruel. "They chose *you*. How could they have chosen you? It was supposed to be Lady Chrysanthe—or someone proud and noble. Not a half *human*!"

"Get off this property, now," I ordered. "I don't want to see you again."

"We can't leave you," Suits pleaded.

"And why is that?"

"Because you're our new queen!"

"Though you don't deserve it, *human*," the woman growled.

That's it. I'm done.

I turned to the barn and stalked in its direction.

Ever since the spiders I'd taken to leaving at least two cans of wasp spray. I climbed over the fence, found them, and stalked my way back to the rude fae.

The guards, surprisingly, stumbled back a few steps.

"Wait, give us a chance to explain, Queen," Suits begged. "You need to come with us."

"Hard pass." I popped the lids off the spray cans. "And don't call me that."

"It's not a matter for you to decide." The older fae scowled. "We don't want you either. But it's out of our hands since you somehow courted favor with the night mares. You have no choice but to go with us to the Night Court."

Suits grabbed me by the wrist and tried to pull me across the pasture, but he severely underestimated the strength of a farm girl.

I dug my heels in, ripped my wrist from his grasp, and slammed him in the side of the head with one of the cans of wasp spray.

He toppled like a tree, groaning as he held his head.

I guess for all of their manipulations, fae don't fight dirty.

I raised the spray can I hadn't whacked on a fae skull. "Whoever tries that next is going to get a face full of wasp poison."

Suits slowly stood up and held his hands out. "We don't intend to harm you," he said in a classic case of fae wordsmithing.

He could have just said they *won't* harm me, but there was a good chance that was a lie, so he used the word *intend* instead.

"That's not good enough," I said.

The old lady glared at me. "You are a *viper*," she said. "Our Court will eat you alive!"

"Lady Demetria, this is not an appropriate time," Suits muttered. "Guards, if you would escort our new queen to the car, we must take her—"

"Oh, you *must*?" asked a sweet, clear, feminine voice.

Suits turned around—probably thinking to tell off the interrupter—but clamped his jaw shut when he saw who it was.

A male vampire—lethal with dark hair and eyes such a dark shade of red they were almost black—was cradling a petite blond who was just a little older than me.

She held a ball of crackling electricity in her hand, making her black wizard mark appear. The swirls of her mark crawled up the side of her face and down her neck.

The exact same mark appeared on the vampire's skin, telling the fae who they were dealing with.

Even if they had never seen this famous couple—unlikely, considering the Night Court's dodgy history with them—there was only one vampire/wizard pair in the Midwest: Killian Drake —Eminent of the Midwest Vampires—and Hazel Medeis—Adept of the wizards of House Medeis.

The tension and fear that had been building in my gut left me with one great whoosh. "Thanks for coming."

"Absolutely." Hazel wriggled until Killian let her go, but even when she landed she didn't release her fizzing magic.

"It's the neighborly thing to do," Killian said.

"Neighbor?" the older fae, Lady Demetria, apparently, croaked.

Killian raised an eyebrow. "Did you really come here to terrorize Leila, *not* knowing this land is next door to Drake Hall?"

The wobble in Suits's knees said they hadn't known at all.

"Now, let's get something straight," Hazel said. "You're going to explain what you're doing here and why you're manhandling our friend in the most *unembellished* way possible. Understood?" Her ball of magic stretched out, forming a sword made of magic.

Killian almost lazily withdrew a pistol from his suitcoat jacket, turning off the safety and racking the top of the gun, loading a bullet. Behind him, at least a dozen vampires—all dressed in black suits and every last one of them carrying a bare blade or a gun—lingered around the fae's cars.

Suits cleared his throat. "Understood." He glanced at Lady Demetria, but she was petrified and unable to do more than quiver. Reluctantly, Suits faced me. "Er, it is as we started to say—you're our new queen. The Queen of the Night Court."

"How?" I asked.

Suits gestured to the night mares. "After a monarch and their partner die, the night mares are released to search through all members of the Night Court and find the next ruler."

"It's not inherited by children?" Hazel asked.

"No." Suits deeply bowed to Hazel after quaking under Killian's red eyes. "In each new cycle, the night mares choose the next ruler. That ruler chooses their spouse, who may co-rule if allowed, and otherwise will rule if the monarch passes away before them. Their children do not inherit the title. Each time a royal couple dies, the cycle starts anew and the night mares find the next monarch."

"There are a few problems with that." I held up a finger as I started my list. "First of all, I'm not a member of the Night Court. I'm Unpledged. Secondly, as I said earlier, I'm half human. I don't ever recall a half human half fae ruler—in *any* Court."

"One does not strictly *have* to belong to the Night Court to be considered a candidate." Suits nervously eyed Eclipse as she pawed at the ground and gnashed her teeth together. "As long as you have blood from the Night Court, it's allowable. As for you being half fae…"

Comet snorted and reared up.

Suits flinched. "It seems it does not matter," he said lamely.

"Yeah, there's a third problem. I don't *want* to be your queen." I wriggled three fingers at him for emphasis.

Suits studied the ground with great care.

"Did you not hear her?" Killian asked with a dangerously pleasant voice.

"It's just…I'm not…it's not…" Suits gulped, then bent over in a bow to Killian. "She's already our queen."

CHAPTER FIVE

Leila

No. No way. I dreamed of being a Responsible Adult—not a flippin' queen!

"That's impossible," I said, my voice hardening fast. "You can't just arbitrarily decide to make me your queen without giving me any say!"

"It's the night mares," Suits insisted. "They bound you…" He trailed off when Blue Moon snorted and pawed at the ground.

"Is the Paragon aware of your little *expedition*?" Killian asked.

The Paragon was the most powerful fae in all of America. He didn't belong to a specific Court, and he was considered the national representative for all fae. Recently, he'd been hanging around in the Midwest.

"Ahh, to an extent," Suits said. "It was he who finally corralled the night mares, so we could prepare them to choose the next monarch. He is aware we would soon be conducting the search, but we did not specifically inform him that the night mares had found a candidate and we were coming to find her."

"Call him," Killian ordered in a tone that offered no alternative.

"Ahh, yes. Yes, we should." Suits frantically patted his suitcoat, eventually finding his cellphone. He tried to smile at us as he fumbled, searching through his contacts list. Eventually he dialed the right number, and I could hear the ringing noise that signaled he was making a call. He nervously switched the phone from one hand to the other, then brightened when the call connected. "Ah, yes! Greetings, Paragon—"

"*The number you are trying to call is not available*," a tinny, female voice recited. "*Please try again at another time.*"

Suits ended the call with a swipe and laughed nervously. "It seems he is not answering his phone at this time."

Hazel looked expectantly up at Killian.

"What?" he said.

"You try calling him."

Killian's eyebrow twitched. "You're joking."

"It's for Leila."

"He'll never shut up about it."

"It's for *Leila*," Hazel repeated. "She helped me when I needed it. You can put up with a clingy friend on her behalf."

I'd never interacted much with Killian—even though I considered the Drakes to be great neighbors. I mostly saw his First and Second Knights, who were his second and third in command. But I'd heard enough rumors that even I was impressed with Hazel when Killian narrowed his eyes and got out his cellphone.

When he dialed, the phone rang once before it clicked, picking up.

"*Killian! Such a pleasure to finally hear from you, bestie. I was beginning to think you'd forgotten how to use a phone in your dotage. How are you? Did you have a fight with Hazel? Is that why you're calling me? I am something of a romantic consultant you know.*" The speaker blared so loudly Killian actually held it back, away from his ear.

"If I had a fight with Hazel you'd be the last person I'd call," Killian said.

"*You said you wouldn't call me ever, too, and yet here we are! What did you do? Did you insult her House again? It's not wise to insult sentient magical houses.*"

Killian closed his eyes, resembling a parent counting backwards to keep their temper. "I'm calling because I'm standing on my neighbor's lawn, staring down a few psychotic fae who are claiming she's their queen."

"It sounds like a cult," Hazel shouted at the phone.

"I thought so too!" I said.

"*What Court are the fae from?*"

"Night Court," Killian said.

"*Ew,*" the Paragon said. "*Omw.*"

"What does that even mean—Paragon?" When his screen flashed, showing that the call had been disconnected, Killian wordlessly squeezed the phone, making its plastic case creak alarmingly.

Hazel gave me one of her sunny smiles. "The Paragon is on his way. Once he's here he can smooth everything out, I'm sure."

Suits exhaled in relief. "Yes, good. The Paragon can explain things." He actually offered me a slight nod and an even slighter smile.

I didn't like that—any sign of relief from these crazies was a bad thing for me.

Suits straightened his jacket, regaining his confidence with every passing moment. "We can escort you and the night mares to the Night Court estate and—"

"That's not happening," I interrupted. "I'll tell the Paragon I have no desire to be queen, and you can be off on your merry way."

Suits uneasily glanced at the night mares.

"If only it could be so," Lady Demetria grumbled.

Unfortunately, it was then that my mom pulled into the driveway.

She stopped the car, and I could see her eyes flick from the cars—fancy-dress-fae-lady was still inside the car, looking petrified as a few of the vampires had taken it upon themselves to circle and stand *on top* of the car she was hidden in—to the well-dressed vampires, to the fae standing in the pasture with me.

I scratched the back of my neck as I tried to figure out what I should say, but to my surprise she leaned back in her seat as if the display pained her, parked her car, then got out with a shaky smile.

"Is something wrong, Leila?" she asked.

"Yeah, there's been a huge mix-up," I said. "But Hazel and Killian are helping me figure things out."

"There is no mix-up," Suits said—he was starting to be a big pain. "You are our queen."

I scowled. "Could you please stop saying that!"

My mom clutched the shoulder strap of her massive purse. "I'll go get Paul." She disappeared around the corner of the house—heading for Dad's woodshop.

Seconds later, a black SUV with tinted windows pulled into the driveway, rolling to a stop just behind the fae's cars.

A back passenger door popped open, and an old man hopped out with a shocking amount of spryness.

The Paragon was the epitome of how a human would describe an elderly, aged fae. He had long, silvery white hair, a white mustache that drooped past his chin, spectacles with thin wire frames, and always wore a variation of silk robes. Today's robes were in muted forest green colors and were embroidered with gold leaves.

Since he was sort of my representative, I'd made sure to research him when I was first formulating my plan of surviving in the human world as a half fae.

He had a reputation for being remarkably good humored for a fae, and his short patience for his own people was legendary, which meant I loved reading about him.

The Paragon put his fists on his hips and beamed up at the cloudy sky. "What a fine day, is it not, Hazel, Killian?"

"It is," Hazel agreed. "Thanks for coming."

"Of course!" The Paragon paraded across the yard. When he reached the fence, he yanked his robes up—revealing knobby knees and skinny legs—and casually hopped over the fence despite his aged appearance. "It is always my pleasure to come to the rescue of my dearest friends!"

A wrinkle sliced across Killian's forehead. "Why did you arrive in one of *my* cars?"

"The fastest way here was to use my gate to your house," the Paragon said. "And though I will do much for you, I will *not* walk over here in this heat. One of your vampires agreed to drive me, and a delightful House Medeis wizard kept me entertained on the drive over."

"You have a gate that drops you on *my* property?" Ice formed at the edge of Killian's words.

The Paragon huffed. "Of course! Do you know what kind of a drive it is from Magiford out here? Annoying, that's what it is. I don't wish to waste my time! I invested in making a gate so I can pop over whenever I want."

"That's a great idea!" Hazel said.

"No, it is not," Killian growled.

Hazel pressed her lips together in thought. "Really? Because I think—"

"The Paragon is here for your *friend*, is he not?" Killian said.

"Oh, that's right." Hazel grimaced, then came to stand by me.

I was pretty tall for even a half fae, but I felt like a sky scraper as Hazel—a particularly petite wizard—didn't even come up to my shoulder. "Paragon," she began, glancing curiously at one of the fae horses. Eclipse and the others had backed off a little, giving us space, but they stayed clustered around us. "This is our neighbor Leila—she helped me the day I took back my House from Mason and is a good friend of mine. These weird cultist fae are bothering her."

"We are not from a *cult*!" Lady Demetria said.

"Wise and glorious Paragon." Suits, busting out his best manners for the occasion, bowed deeply to the Paragon. "We have found our new queen."

"And she's not cooperating," Lady Demetria added.

"Because I *can't* be the next Night Court ruler," I said. "I'm a *human*."

"Half human, half fae," Suits corrected—as if he was the expert on everything me.

"Doesn't matter," I said. "I don't want to be your queen."

"The night mares chose you?" the Paragon asked.

"They *bound* her," Lady Demetria interrupted and thrust her finger at me. "Her! A half fae!"

"You keep saying they bound me, and I still have no idea what you mean," I said.

"Ah," the Paragon said.

I turned to him, my spine stiffening with dread. "What?"

"Traditionally it takes a minimum of two night mares to select the next monarch." The Paragon smiled kindly at me, instantly putting me on my guard. "It's fairly common for three night mares to choose—which they do by congregating around the chosen fae, who is then anointed and sworn in as the official monarch. However, the night mares also have the power of King Makers."

I don't like the sound of that.

I glanced at my fae horses. "And what does that mean?"

"It means six or more night mares have to mark you." He tapped his forehead. "With their essences. They're creatures that are made of magic; it's a simple matter of shedding some of themselves on you—as I can see they have on your forehead."

I touched my forehead, recalling the way each horse brushed my temple when they arrived. Feeling oddly betrayed, I swung around to stare at the fae horses.

They avoided looking at me.

"And besides—you had *six* of them bind you. As soon as the sixth one marked you, their essence became strong enough to bind you to the Court—a process that would normally happen as part of a monarch's official crowning."

"And binding me to the Court means?"

"That you are already Queen of the Night Court." He gestured to the other fae. "They cannot harm you, and if you have enough resolve, you can control them."

"As you already have—when you stopped the guard," Suits "helpfully" piped in.

Mom and Dad came around the corner of the house in time to hear the Paragon's explanation, both of them looking a lot more worried and much less confused than I thought they'd be.

"Paragon." Mom bowed her head in respect.

Dad was a second behind in copying her, but I was mostly shocked that Mom knew who the Paragon was.

I didn't think they paid much attention to the supernatural community. I mean, I did. But that's because my general wellbeing depended a lot on who was in power. Unpledged fae like me typically don't last long. Usually a fae *has* to swear to a Court because otherwise they're easy pickings for any supernatural. When you belong to a Court, messing with a fae means you're involving their Court. Us Unpledged don't have that protection.

I'm pretty sure I survived only as long as I did because I lived next to the Drakes.

"Hello, and who might you be?" The Paragon smiled warmly at my parents.

"We're Leila's parents," Dad said.

The Paragon blinked as he studied my clearly human parents. "Aha. Is that so?"

"She's my daughter from a previous marriage," Mom said.

Lady Demetria sniffed. "And her father?"

"I'm her father. I adopted her." Dad's usual easy, warm smile was gone. Instead the slight downturn of his lips and his lowered, thick eyebrows gave him a watchful look as he moved closer to me.

He stopped to pet one of the fae horses or…night mares or whatever.

This elicited a mewl of alarm from Suits, but Comet—the night mare he was stroking—didn't even twitch a nostril.

"I see!" The Paragon's cheer was back. "What a quaint childhood here on a farm." He gestured to a few of my mom's black and white speckled chickens that had wandered over and were roosting on the lowest bar of the wooden fence. "Very idyllic, I'm sure."

"Who fathered her?" Lady Demetria interrupted, her chest puffed with self-importance.

Mom and Dad exchanged glances, and Mom's cheek twitched.

It struck me as a little weird—she hadn't ever given me the impression she hated my bio father, even though I wasn't shy about saying I did.

"He was a Night Court fae," I said. "What's it to you?"

Lady Demetria lifted her head. "If you have proper parentage then—"

"My parentage doesn't matter because I refuse the position of queen," I said. "Have a great afternoon, I could have gone without meeting all of you—except for you, Sir, er, Paragon—but such is life. Have a safe drive home, goodbye."

"Leila…" my mom said.

"I'm afraid it's not a position you can refuse," the Paragon said.

"Of course it is." I tried to keep the veneer of good manners—it wouldn't do to anger the Paragon when he was my best bet at surviving this. "You can't *make* someone become a ruler."

"Except you already *are* Queen of the Night Court," the Paragon said. "As I said, you've already been bound to the Court, and they are bound to your will."

No...no! I shook my head, unable to accept it. *They've overlooked me this long. This can't be happening!*

Naturally, the superiority-complex fae would say that means I only have half of the power of a fae because my blood is "sullied" or something stupid like that. But really what it meant was a lot of the fae limitations didn't apply to me.

I could totally lie—unlike all full fae—I was only half as rotten tempered, and I didn't need to visit the fae realm to stay healthy.

That was probably the most dangerous fae limitation, actually—in order to replenish their life force, fae had to visit the fae realm, which was a toxic soup of deadly magic *except* in the lands owned by the Courts—who kept the dark magic at bay.

It was why fae had to pledge themselves to a Court—to get access to the fae realm.

But I didn't need to visit it, and between squatting at the edge of the Drakes' property for safety and being only half fae, I was pretty safe.

My human blood has protected me for this long...

Eclipse bumped her head into my shoulder, using me as a scratching post.

I absently patted her neck and turned to my parents. "Mom, I..."

I trailed off, because Mom was crying.

There was a hopelessness in her eyes. She didn't think we could fight this.

"Then the night mares chose wrong." I turned back to the Paragon, losing my forced politeness. "It's just because I give them food and carrots—I'm not—"

"It doesn't matter *why* they chose you, Leila," the Paragon gently said. "They bound you as ruler of the Night Court. It cannot be undone."

I shook my head, unable to accept it. I'd worked endlessly for the future I wanted—for a *magic-less* life!

And now, I was suddenly the Queen of the Night Court?

It would be a disaster! I didn't know the first thing about running a Court—I just wanted to be *normal*!

Plus, the fae would hate me for my blood—probably hate that I hadn't even been raised as a fae—and that didn't even touch the general mess of regular politics!

Dimly, I knew there was a chance I would be killed because of this.

Hazel took my hand and squeezed it, but I stared unseeingly at the leaf pattern in the Paragon's robes.

"I understand," my mother said, shocking me.

"Mom—we can't accept this!" I started.

She ignored me and fixed the Paragon with a steely gaze I'd only seen her wear half a dozen times. It was her grimmest expression—the one she wore whenever things were bad and she knew we were in real trouble.

"But I want you to *swear* that you will help my daughter—that you'll show her how to be safe, and you'll teach her all she needs to know to survive and be happy—as long as she feels she needs your help," she said.

The barnyard was silent.

That was a pretty weighty promise—and fae don't take things like promises and contracts lightly. It's a part of their culture—like the whole guest thing.

Plus, Mom's demand was iron clad. It wouldn't allow him to conveniently "forget" to tell me anything, and it would tie him to me until *I* was satisfied.

There's no way he'll agree to it, but how did Mom even know how to phrase that?

Lady Demetria puffed up like a roosting chicken. "How *dare* you make such demands of the Paragon—human! He—"

"I'll do my best," the Paragon said.

My mom narrowed her eyes. "Make it a contract," she said in a cold, clear voice that shocked me almost as much as her demand.

I stared at her, stunned. This wasn't my mom who made me cookies when I got home from school as a kid. This woman was a warrior. And—human or not—she was going to fight for me.

Suits and Lady Demetria were practically shaking with anger.

The Paragon, however, glanced at the night mares. He studied them for several long moments, then swung his gaze back to my mom. "I swear I'll show Leila how to be safe, and I will teach her all she needs to know to survive and be happy as the Queen of the Night Court, as long as she feels she needs my help."

He had fitted a bit of a loophole in there—he'd said he'd help me as Queen of the Night Court, not myself. But I was still just shocked he'd made the promise.

Mom nodded, and the edge that had sharpened her disappeared as her eyes turned glassy with tears and Dad put his arm around her.

The Paragon awkwardly scratched the back of his head. "Arrangements will have to be made for you to move to the mansion that belongs to the ruler of the Night Court. I imagine there is much you don't know. We had best start immediately—"

"A week," I blurted out. "Give me one week here at home, first."

Lady Demetria huffed. "You are our queen! It is your duty to take up your position!"

"I'm certain this has been a surprise," the Paragon said. "We can give Queen Leila a week."

"But, Paragon!" Lady Demetria scowled at me. "Our Court is already in such a dire condition! We need our queen—"

"It's been months since Nyte died, and you survived this long," the Paragon said. "You can survive another week. She deserves a chance to prepare herself."

He glanced pityingly at Mom and Dad.

I, however, stared at the line of gun wielding vampires lining my driveway, the wheels in my mind turning.

"Yeah, thanks," I said.

I wasn't going to take a week to mope around the house. Heck no, I was going to use that week to learn to defend myself. Hopefully by begging some of the sharpshooting Drake vampires to give me a refresher course on handguns. (They had insisted I learn how to use a handgun when I first started training their dogs, but my skills had probably atrophied since they started teaching me.)

"This will also give the Court a chance to prepare a welcome for you." The Paragon tried to scratch his chin, but his fingers got tangled in his long mustache, and he grunted in pain when he tried to pull his hands free and instead yanked his head forward.

"I'm sure they'll welcome her with open arms," Killian said in a voice sharp enough to cut through cement as he stared Suits and Lady Demetria down.

That suitably cowed the pair, and brought another sort of stillness to the pasture.

"Right," the Paragon said. "Well, then, Killian—what say we retire and each get a pint?"

Killian pointedly glanced at the sky—which was still cloudy, but showed patches of bright blue. "I did not peg you as a day drinker."

"You thought I was referring to alcohol? Gross—no." The Paragon shivered in revulsion. "I meant ice cream! We can go to my private study—I have a pint of Sinfully Dark Chocolate and Caramel Peanut Cluster. Hazel, if you like I can have Aphrodite pick out a tea for you."

"No thank you," Hazel firmly said.

The Paragon jutted his lower lip out in a pout. "You never let me serve you tea anymore."

"That's because you *drugged* me the last time I did!" Hazel said.

Suits turned to the night mares. "Shall we attempt to bring

them back—"

The closest horse—Nebula—trumpeted her glass-shattering scream at him and reared up. I swear the red hairs mixed in her black coat glowed as she tossed her head.

"It seems the night mares shall remain with the queen." Suits rapidly backed up, stopping only when his back hit the fence. "We shall leave and begin preparations."

"I'm sure you will," Hazel scoffed. She peered up at me, concern darkening her usually bright face. "Are you okay?"

"No," I admitted as the Paragon continued to bicker with Killian, and the other fae cleared out. "But I'll have to be. Before these guys showed up, I had a face off with another fae."

"What?"

I tightened my ponytail, just to give my hands something to do. "Yeah, he tried to kill me, but magic seemed to stop him. I'd assume that's probably the magic that keeps a fae from harming their monarch, right? And now that I think of it, when my first night mare showed up that was when the giant spider spawned in the pasture. Do you think that was a coincidence, or could it have been someone trying to kill me?"

Hazel stared up at me, her face white. "*Killian!*"

Killian and the Paragon had me recite the scenes in excruciating detail—the fae hung around in the background, openly eavesdropping. They did, however, make a lot of squawking noises when I described the fae, weirdly enough.

In the end, Killian (read: Hazel) decided I needed guards, and they were going to include my parents' property in the vampires' patrols—even after I left. Just in case the fae decided to get creative.

I honestly wasn't as bothered by it as I should have been. But with all of these very sudden and unexpected swerves—which were going to take me the opposite direction from what I had planned all my life—I was having a little bit of a difficult time coping with it all.

"If you need anything, just call me," Hazel said, once I'd been thoroughly cross examined.

"Thanks. Actually, I do want to ask you about getting a sidearm refresher from the Drakes, but that can wait until tomorrow." It was hard to swallow when I looked away from Hazel and glanced at my parents.

Hazel stood on her tiptoes to hug me. "I understand. I'll call you in the morning."

She was gone before I even thought to hug her back, vampires flanking her as she marched up to the waiting SUV.

Killian followed her, and the Paragon trailed after him.

My unwanted fae invaders seemed inclined to hang around, until they realized that none of the vampires had left with Killian, and all of them were stationed in the driveway, bearing weapons of different sorts.

That got the fae piled into their cars awfully quickly, and as soon as they disappeared down the driveway and hit the road, the vampires bowed to me and then streaked off, returning to their land and leaving me, Mom, and Dad alone.

It had taken seconds to change my life forever. It seemed weird that "normal" could return so quickly...even if it was only temporarily.

"Oh, sweetie," Mom said, her voice crackling.

She and Dad swept me up in a hug, as if they could hold me together while my world fell apart.

"I don't think I can do this," I whispered. "Can I run?"

"You're the queen; they'll find you wherever you go," Mom sighed.

"You'll make it, Leila," Dad said with a confidence I wished I felt. "The Night Court has no idea what it's in for with *you* as its ruler!"

Mom agreed, but my mind screamed the truth.

Being queen? It was going to get me killed.

CHAPTER SIX

Leila

A week later, the Paragon came to pick me up.

It surprised me enough that he came himself—even if he had to keep his promise to Mom, he *was* the most powerful fae in America, and delegating was a thing. But after his phone call telling me he was on the way, I half expected he was going to bum a ride from the Drake vampires again. Instead, he showed up in a gleaming Porsche with a naiad chauffeur.

He helped me arm wrestle my giant blue suitcase and the two duffle bags I was taking into the trunk.

I gestured to the night mares who were standing with Bagel in the pasture. "I thought you'd bring a trailer to drive them back."

"Oh, they'll come back when they wish it." The Paragon opened the car door for me. "They'll probably show up when they work out that you've moved into the mansion." He hopped in the car after me, shut the door, and off we went, speeding in the direction of Magiford.

"Thank you for picking me up," I said after a few tense moments of silence.

"Of course." The Paragon casually straightened his thumb ring, which was topped with a huge sapphire that matched his purple-y robes.

I saw a wave of magic halo the ring, then expand, filling the back of the Porsche and creating a glittering bubble around us.

The magic felt whispery and soft, with a sort of sticky after-feeling, confirming it was fae magic.

Wizards, fae, and the other lesser known supernaturals that use magic can all sense magic.

Most frequently, you can taste or feel the differences in it—because each race uses magic differently.

I don't know how it is for most fae, but I can sense magic by the different sensations it gives me.

Fae magic is whispery with a slightly sticky residue—like a spider web. Wizard magic is a funny, tingling feeling—similar to the numbing sensation you get when you smack your elbow hard. I only encountered dragon shifter magic when I went to Tutu's Crypta & Custodia, which was basically the local bank/vault system for supernaturals and was owned and run by a dragon shifter. The magic there felt excessively warm with a dry heat—almost like a sauna.

"I apologize," the Paragon said. "I should have warned you first, but I activated a ward that will keep all sound within this bubble, and ruin any listening spells or devices that may have been planted in the car."

I glanced at the driver—who was outside the magic bubble. "I take it that means we have important stuff to talk about?"

"Precisely. I'll give it to you straight, kiddo. Showing my support for you—by picking you up like this—is about all I can do for you politically speaking. As the Paragon I can't be too obvious in my favoritism, or it will start a war," he grimly said.

I leaned back in my seat. "Why does that not surprise me?"

Fae, such competitive, pushy things.

"What do you know about fae politics?"

"Not enough to be comfortable going into this," I said. "And I know almost nothing about the politics of the individual Courts—I keep a closer eye on the supernatural community and the Midwest Regional Committee of Magic, though."

"Understandable, given who your neighbors are." The Paragon pursed his lips. "But it leaves you ill prepared for what you are about to experience."

"I know the gist of it." I shrugged uncomfortably and did my best to smile. "As a half fae, the nobles of the Night Court are going to see me as inferior, and they will do their best to take advantage of me as long as I'm around, and kill me as soon as they can."

"They can't raise a finger against you themselves," the Paragon reminded me. "A Court is bound to the will of their ruler. They cannot harm you."

"They can't plant the dagger in my back," I agreed. "But they can pay someone else to put it there."

"It's not quite so easy as that. It takes a great deal of conniving to achieve even that sort of betrayal, or the Night Court would have rid themselves of Nyte years ago. But your sentiment isn't wrong." The Paragon eyed me. "It seems to me you have a rather low view of the Night Court."

"I'm not a huge fan of fae in general," I admitted. "I don't like the mental gymnastics. But yeah, I would rather be on my way to any other Court besides the Night Court."

"As much as it pains me to say this, your natural reluctance will help you survive in your new life."

"That, and my stubbornness," I agreed.

Even though this was the opposite of everything I had worked for, I wasn't just going to flop over and give up. Heck no.

I would survive with the tenacity of a cockroach.

Because that's what this was going to be—a fight for survival.

And since it was my life on the line, there was no way I was going to lose.

I mean, I was pretty fond of living, but Mom had already had her heart broken by one fae. There was no way I was going to let this pushy Court hurt her again.

"Are you certain there's no way out of this?" I asked the Paragon one last time. "I can't believe there isn't some ancient bylaw made in case the night mares picked an incapable ruler—or even just a national law that could give me the right to refuse."

The Paragon shook his head. "No such law exists—to my knowledge. In any fae Court, once you are made ruler, you stay the ruler until the day you die. It's why coups among the various Courts can get...bloody."

I'd done some research in my week, so the news didn't surprise me, but it was still crushing to hear. I absently rubbed my aching chest. "Okay. Thank you." I glanced out the window—watching as cornfields and the occasional thicket of trees were gradually replaced with more and more houses. We were nearly to Magiford.

The Paragon pushed his glasses up to rest them on the top of his head. "When we get to the mansion, your Court is going to be waiting for you like a flock of vultures. It's technically tradition, but since you are an unknown entity to them it's your first impression on them, and their first chance to politically attack you."

"They sound friendly."

"The fact that you are already queen will help you," the Paragon said. "Even more so that it was the night mares who bound you—they haven't chosen a ruler that way in over a century. It's very rare and considered to be a great honor."

"It's an honor I could do without," I said.

I had spent more time with the night mares over the past few days—between my practice sessions with the Drakes who mercilessly drilled me until I could be called a fair shot—trying to sort through my mess of emotions. It just about destroyed me that they'd made me queen, but somehow, as I petted their dull coats and laughed when they lipped my hair, I couldn't bring myself to hate them.

The Paragon adjusted his ring, popping the bubble of magic that surrounded us. "Given that we have almost arrived, my offer is rather late, but are you comfortable? Do you want music on, or more air conditioning? I'd offer you tea, but I'm afraid to report that your driver has a lead foot—isn't that right, Azure?"

The naiad—gorgeous with her blue tinted skin and the faintest brush of opalescent scales across her forehead and dusted across her high cheekbones—didn't even blink in acknowledgment.

I, however, was majorly distracted by the bomb the Paragon had just dropped. "Wait, *my* driver?"

"Indeed. Azure is under your employment, and this is one of the cars that belongs to the monarch of the Night Court. As queen you inherit it all: the mansion in Magiford, the luxury condo in Chicago, the lake house in northern Wisconsin, the cars, the stables, the Night Realm and the palace there, everything in the treasury—all of it."

I stared at the Paragon, my brain already crashing.

"I made an inspection of your inheritance in the months between Queen Nyte's death and the day the night mares were set loose. I didn't want anyone squirreling anything away from you—as has occasionally happened in Courts with outside inheritance like the Night Court," the Paragon grimly said.

"I'm going to have employees," I said, a new kind of dread building in me.

"Yes, of course. You have your officials and advisors. But there are also the maids, the stable employees, a few accountants, gardeners, guards, and the rest," the Paragon casually listed.

"I'm twenty-two. How on earth am I supposed to manage all of them? Do I have an HR department?"

"HR? Goodness, no. They are under your rule."

"That's even worse." I rubbed my eyes and tried to keep my spirits up. "I knew I should have gotten my degree in business management instead of communications!"

The Paragon ignored my moans. "You will find that you can delegate. Your steward will be among the most important positions you fill as he or she can manage most of your house employees and act as a go-between for you and your Court officials. You'll also need to hire a director of security to train, organize, and recruit guards, which will take most of that work from you as well."

I opened my mouth to ask more, but the Paragon kept going, blocking me from asking any additional questions. "If you look outside, you'll see we are now on what passes as Night Court land in the human world. While this land here is technically under your rule, the individual houses are owned by the various fae and nobles that make up your Court—though I believe the apartment buildings belong to you."

Curious, I peered outside as we rolled down the road.

We passed a few apartment buildings that were constructed out of darkly colored bricks and dark blue siding with a fairly modern appearance. All of the apartment buildings had sprawling gardens attached, which stretched out between them. Not surprising—we *were* among the fae. I was a little animal crazy, but I was pretty tame compared to the rest of the fae, who were practically the hippies of the supernatural world.

A few blocks later and we were driving through what felt like a regular suburban neighborhood. The houses were cute and square with dark blue or gray siding, and an excessive amount of landscaping considering the fairly small lots.

The longer we drove, the bigger the houses and lots grew.

Soon, we were driving through McMansion-ville, and I was gawking at the beautiful houses and amazing gardens.

"The Night Court lands begin about ten minutes north of Magiford and cover a large, half circle area, with your property at the center. You, naturally, own the largest property—which includes the large amount of land that makes up the other half of the circle. Most of your personal land is contained in a wildlife preserve, a very small lake, and some sprawling gardens. You should be able to see the house shortly."

The road plowed through a thick patch of woods, and then opened up onto a pristine lawn that stretched around a massive mansion, which looked like it was doing its best to imitate a castle.

Constructed out of deep gray brick with three turrets and at least four chimneys poking above the slanted, almost gothic-like roof, it was obvious the architect had a thing for British manors. The medieval shape of the house, however, was overshadowed by the massive windows that stretched through every floor of the house.

Guess I won't be running around the place with bed head and my pajamas anytime soon!

The huge windows gave the home a more modern feel, as did all the fancy deck furniture placed strategically near the bits of the gardens that I could see.

But the beauty of the place was broken up by the massive crowd I saw spilling through the front doors of the house.

It seemed only the Night Court nobles were in attendance. Fae nobles appeared more humanoid, or picture-book, even, given their slender bodies, slightly tapered ears, perfect hair, and perfect skin.

While a fae Court was actually made up of a wide variety of fae—from trolls to pixies to brownies—it was usually the more humanoid fae that made up the nobles, and it was the nobles who most typically interacted with the human world because they were a whole lot easier to use for marketing and PR than a giant, wrinkly faced troll.

But the hierarchy also had to do with power. The fae nobles got their titles because they were the best at using artifacts and magic. Some of the common fae could only cast certain kinds of magic, and others were very weak.

I swallowed hard as the car rolled to a stop.

"Remember," the Paragon muttered as Azure the chauffeur slipped out of the car and circled around to open the door for us. "Don't show any weakness—they're worse than vampires who have scented blood."

The Paragon flipped his glasses back down his nose, slid across the seat, and was out of the car before I could respond.

I took a deep breath and forced myself to think of Mom and Dad.

I'm going to do this. I'm going to survive.

I put a smile on and slipped out of the car, standing next to the Paragon at the edge of the brick walkway before I looked out upon the stony crowd.

The fae were unnaturally still.

We were outside, and there was a slight breeze which should have blown through their hair or tugged on their clothes, but they were suffocating in their stillness.

They looked like a glossy magazine picture—so perfect in hair and dress that it was almost alien.

That was the difference between them and me: perfection. I was dressed in a nice pair of jeans and a cute lace top, and a few artful strands of my thick black hair were already slipping from the ponytail I'd pushed it back in.

The fae were dressed for a garden party, with the females all wearing dresses and skirts, high heels, and fresh flowers accenting their clothes, and the males wearing navy blue or dark gray suits with glittering swords secured to their belts. Not a hair moved on any of them, and the planes of their faces were equally frozen.

My smile wanted to die, but my stubbornness kicked in. I willfully relaxed my posture and made my grin grow a little.

The Paragon gave me an approving nod, then turned to

address the crowd. "Night Court, I give you your new queen: Leila Welkin."

I'm sure they meant their frosty expressions to be frightening, but it actually made them look like clothing mannequins as they stared at me with lifeless—but somehow still disapproving—eyes.

The whole stunt was intimidating—not because I particularly feared well-dressed people, but because it really showed just how many more of them there were than of me, and displayed the clear line between us.

"The night mares have bound her to the Court and made her queen," the Paragon continued, "but she will be publicly crowned before the end of the summer."

"She's *human*!" A beautiful fae who appeared to be about my age—which didn't mean much as fae aged way more slowly than humans—stepped out of the crowd, breaking their flawless formation.

Her button nose was scrunched with anger, and there was a slight flush to her olive complexion, but that didn't break the image of beauty she made with her blond hair floating in loose coils, her light pink dress that was a perfect fit and fell just below the knees, and her pink parasol trimmed with enough ruffles to strangle a doll.

"You have a skill of observation!" the Paragon marveled, not a hint of sarcasm lining the comment. "Yes. Queen Leila is half human, half fae."

The crowd collectively exhaled quiet murmurs that barely made their lips move.

Yep. They're going to be tons *of fun to hang with!*

The pretty fae curled her lips back in revulsion. "We can't have a *half* fae as our queen! It would bring shame to the Night Court!"

"It's a little late for that," I grumbled under my breath.

The Paragon cleared his throat to keep down a gurgle that sounded suspiciously like the start of laughter. "The night mares bound her," he said. "Her connection to the Night Court cannot be broken."

Lady Demetria stood next to the blond fae. She clutched a fluttering fan which hid her mouth, but I could tell by the way she leaned into the younger fae she was whispering to her.

"Perhaps, then, it is time that we change the tradition of letting the night mares choose, so a more suitable queen could be chosen," the blond fae said.

Oh ho-ho! This is who Lady Demetria wanted to be the next queen? I have to give her points for having the guts to come straight at me.

"It appears you are either daft of the mind or experiencing hearing difficulties. The night mares *bound* her. There will be no other ruler as long as Leila breathes. I suppose if you feel daring enough, you can float your idea past the night mares themselves. It would be such *fun* to see what they make of your opinion when they have been king and queen makers since the foundation of this Court in America."

That shut her up. The way she broke eye contact with the Paragon implied just how well she thought that would go over with the night mares.

The Paragon nodded in satisfaction.

"How, then, are we to face the other Courts with such a queen?" A male fae dressed in a dark green suit stepped up next to the blond's other side. "We are of the proud Night Court. Can we not expect to be led by a monarch of quality—not someone sullied by human blood?" His hair—braided on the sides and pinned to the back of his head—was perfect despite the humidity of the morning.

Sullied? My eyebrows wanted to arch upwards, but I managed to keep them flattened and my expression relaxed.

"The vice of humanity could cripple us more," someone else chimed in.

"The blood of humans *weakens* magic," Lady Demetria squawked. "It perhaps is responsible for the decline in magic that has plagued the supernatural community and threatens to ruin us. More ruin may visit us with a *half* on the throne!"

It hadn't escaped me how the fae excelled in speaking non-absolutes. Humans *perhaps* were responsible. My blood *could* cripple them. They were using vagueness as a way to get around their inability to speak outright lies.

Yes, magic was dying. It had been in decline for a long time—ever since the elves died out. But humans had nothing to do with it. These nobles were just using it as an excuse.

Do they really think they'll be able to make me cry just by rejecting me? Please! I want to be here even less than they want me here!

"Anyone who has concerns about your new queen is perfectly free to ask the night mares to search again," the Paragon said, his voice thundering above the outcries, silencing them with ease. "But Curia Cloisters law, the Regional Committee of Magic, and the national law are perfectly clear. There is only one Night Court in America, and Queen Leila rules over it since the night mares not only selected her, but bound her as well."

The crowd returned to its sullen silence, lips pursed in disdain and expressions taking on that airbrushed, plastic-y appearance again.

The Paragon almost inhaled part of his mustache when he scratched his upper lip, then turned in my direction and nodded his head. "Queen Leila, do you have any words you would like to say in greeting your Court?"

Oh, would I!

"Yes." I looked out into a crowd of seething hatred, armed with my brightest smile. "I wish I could say it's a pleasure to be here, but it's not, frankly."

That shut them up—mostly because they were too surprised to speak.

"Humans are taught that fae are elegant beings of culture and refined manners, but that's obviously not true anymore," I blithely continued.

"How could you say such a thing?" Lady Demetria shouted.

I put a hand to my cheek in such an obvious act of surprise the whole Court had to know I was being sarcastic. "After the welcome you just gave me? Very, very easily."

The crowd now stirred with a little concern as the fae whispered to one another.

"I suppose it's just as well—this way, we're *all* disappointed," I concluded. "And maybe that mutual disappointment will unite us."

I paused, and the desire to tweak their pride was too strong for me.

I don't want to let them know that their rules don't affect me, so I shouldn't tell them an obvious lie. But I also want to show them that I'm not going to be a pushover.

My smile turned into a smirk, and I lowered my eyes to half mast as I addressed my Court. "Finally, please allow me as someone *sullied* by human blood, to say it's the fae half of my heritage that I'm truly ashamed of," I concluded.

The crowd was in an uproar. A few fae ladies dramatically swooned, and I saw two pixies and a naiad zip off—probably to tell others how their new queen had just insulted the Night Court nobles.

Personally, I had to fight to keep in a cackle.

Shots fired! If you want to exchange insults, you'd be better off picking fights with someone who cares!

I smirked as the murmurs grew louder and louder. Although there was more than one red face, strained jaw, or veined forehead in the crowd, none of them reached for their magical artifacts or the weapons that they carried.

The Paragon was right—I really was bound to the Night Court. The will of magic had to be keeping them in check—it must have been what kept that rando night fae from killing me, too.

"Ah. Ah-ha-ha-ha," the Paragon uttered a canned laugh. "Isn't she funny? Thank you for your presence this morning. I shall show Queen Leila her new lands. Good day."

The Paragon zipped up the driveway, which curved around to the back of the house, taking us around the corner, which instantly muffled the outrage of my insulted Court.

"You are a new kind of crazy," the Paragon grumbled. Even though he was moving at a pretty quick clip for such an old guy, I was able to keep pace with him since I was just a tiny bit taller than him. "Or even worse, you are fearless! I said not to let them bother you—not that you should pick a fight!"

I shrugged. "Since they're never going to like me, it'd be better to show them that I don't *care* that they don't like me. Wouldn't it?"

The Paragon sourly scrunched up his lips. "They're bound to your will. You could have made them hold their tongues with the magic of the Court."

"I'm not going to be a tyrant."

"You're going to be *dead* if you insist on acting fearless and still stick to your moral code," the Paragon grumbled.

We climbed the stairs of a gorgeous patio, only to descend them on the other side as he led me into a tall garden walled in by huge hedges.

Just as the Paragon stepped through the wooden archway that marked off the garden entrance, I saw movement in the shadows of the castle-house.

It was the fae from my parents' place. The one who had tried to murder me.

CHAPTER SEVEN

Leila

He wore the same clothes—the long, dark gray jacket that let him blend in with the shadows, the leather bracers, and the smudgy gray scarf that covered the lower half of his face. But it was his eyes that struck me the most—as dark and lifeless as death.

"Paragon," I hissed urgently as I felt ice spread through my veins, making me cold despite the warm summer day.

The Paragon backed up several steps. "What do you—oh." He broke off when I pointed to the fae.

"That's the fae that tried to kill me."

"Him?" The Paragon grimaced. "Out of everyone in the fae kingdom, why *him*?"

"Who is he?" I asked.

"Lord Rigel of the Night Court, also known as the Wraith. Although he's a high ranking fae noble, he's an assassin by trade."

My heart thudded in my throat, but I felt it was my civic duty to break the tenseness of the moment. "How good of an assassin can he be if you *know* he's an assassin?"

"It's *precisely* because he's that good that he's known," the Paragon said. "He's one of the most dangerous fae lords in the United States—North America, even. It's an open secret that he's available for hire, but he's so good there's never any proof that it's him. His position as a high ranking noble in the Night Court leaves him politically untouchable."

Rigel didn't move, but there was something about him that threw all of me into high alert, and my heart beat faster and faster as his black eyes didn't look away from mine.

"But I saw him," I said.

"Did you physically *see* him shoot you?" the Paragon asked.

I tried to swallow. "No. He was on the roof of the barn then. But after he hopped down to the ground he tried to throw a dagger at me and some magic—the stuff that keeps fae from killing their monarchs, I think—blocked him from harming me. I think he was mad."

"If he showed himself, mad is a *vast* understatement."

"That's really comforting to hear." I was almost afraid to blink—would this nut attack me in broad daylight in front of the Paragon?

"Sadly, there's nothing you can do about him. With luck, whoever hired him to kill you did it on a long shot. As you discovered, he can't hurt you directly given that he's a member of your Court." The Paragon sucked his head back into the gardens and shivered.

"What about *indirectly* killing me?" I asked.

"It's a possibility, but it's not his style. Come on—you're safe with me, but I don't fancy you catching his attention."

I broke my standoff with Lord Rigel long enough to watch the Paragon scuttle farther into the hedge garden. When I looked back, the assassin was gone.

That's enough to keep me awake all night tonight!

I ran after the Paragon, but my very real fear was making it hard to breathe. "Care to tell me why you didn't think it was important to tell me one of my *lords* is a famous assassin?"

"Leila, there's *a lot* you need to know. That Lord Rigel is lower on the priority list should tell you just how grim things are," the Paragon darkly said.

I shivered when a leafy fern that leaned out into the wood-chip covered path we walked on brushed my jeans. "Are you sure we should just leave him? Can't he be arrested or something?"

"You could have him arrested, but Lord Rigel's assassinations are never personal. It's just business. By bothering him you risk making it personal, and there's a reason your predecessor—for all of her hatred of Killian Drake—never forced Lord Rigel to assassinate Killian, even though it was well within her abilities."

It still seems stupid to leave an assassin *running around.* I was so focused on this worry that when the Paragon abruptly stopped I almost ran the poor fae over.

"You're going to find, Leila, that becoming Queen of the Night Court is a matter of organizing the largest threats to the smallest. Due to his loner nature and being a member of your Court, Lord Rigel is no longer a prime threat. You have much bigger threats to face," he said.

"Like what?"

The Paragon mashed his thumbs into his eyes, then gestured for me to follow him.

At the center of the garden was a massive archway made of stone that had smoothed and turned a dirty black with age. Beautiful, looping metal work glided across the top of the stone. Half of it was a dark, onyx color, but there was a crescent moon shaped bit that was silver, so the archway gave the faintest impression of the night sky. A door stood in the center of the archway—dwarfed in comparison. It had the same beautiful metal work, but there was something unsubstantial about the door, and I couldn't say for sure whether there was anything solid behind it, or if it was just magic.

"This is a doorway to the Night Court lands located in the fae realm," the Paragon said. "There are several other ways in, but this is the easiest one to use, and will probably bother your stomach the least. Go ahead and open it."

I squinted at the sketchy door. "Do I need to say any magic words?"

"Nah." The Paragon casually swatted his hand at me. "You're the Queen of the Night Court. The Realm of the Night Court is yours—it will recognize you."

"You keep saying stuff like that, but I'm not sure I believe you." I cautiously reached out to touch the door handle—which was surprisingly cool given the summer sun hanging in the sky. "I don't feel any different. Even when the night mares marked me—or whatever it was—I felt something in the moment, but nothing has changed since then."

"Well, this will be some proof for you, then, won't it?" the Paragon smartly asked.

I pulled open the door, which creaked on hinges, and revealed an inky blackness that instantly cooled the air around us.

"Just remember to breathe," the Paragon advised before he brashly stepped into the black.

It rippled like water, and he was gone.

I was a lot slower to follow him, taking a deep gulp of air before I stepped through the door.

It felt like I stood on air, and the universe itself streaked past me—millions of stars moving so quickly they were tiny flickers of light in the endless black of space. It was rattling—I couldn't tell up from down, or even breathe.

The sensation lasted for only a second, but it left such a strong impression I staggered and almost fell on my face when I popped into the Realm of the Night Court.

My thoughts were slow and confused as my brain struggled to

process the sudden darkness—because we'd left behind the warm afternoon sun, and instead the night sky—dark purple swirled with a black-blue—stretched high above us, softened by the twinkling of stars.

"Welcome to the Night Realm," the Paragon said. "I've got some bad news."

"What," I started when I was finally able to rub more than a stray thought or two together, "could be worse than an assassin—oh."

While I'd never been in the part of the fae realm that belonged to the Night Court, I'd been in other pieces before. As a half fae I had to register, and that process was done at the Curia Cloisters in Magiford, and verified in the slice of fae realm owned by the Midwest Regional Committee of Magic. I had to renew my registration occasionally, so I was familiar with the overly gorgeous, sweeping architectural style of the fae realm—remnants of the days back when the elves had reigned and the fae had allied with and served the elves.

As a rule, the fae realm was always beautiful—at least the parts that were warded and guarded against the toxic wastes that pressed in on the claimed lands. There were always stunning gardens, beautiful songbirds you'd never see on earth, little waterfalls—things like that.

The Realm of the Night Court was the opposite.

The door had spat us out on a stone patio pressed into the back side of the Night Realm Palace. And while the silhouette looked beautiful, a second glance was much more telling.

The palace was decaying.

Even in the dimness of night, I could see the stone of the exterior walls were crumbling. The stone banisters and steps were covered with moss and pockmarked as if someone had taken a pickaxe to them.

The gardens were overgrown and filled with withered flowers, dry fountains, and bare bushes.

The air smelled stale and dusty, and only a few dim lights shone through what should have been sweeping doors made of delicate glasswork, but were instead cracked and hung uneven on their hinges.

"What...*why*...?" I couldn't find the right words as I swung around to gape at the Paragon. "How could this happen?"

"The segments of the fae realm often reflect the state of the Court that owns them," the Paragon said. "The same goes for the creatures that belong to the Court. The night mares appear starved, evil, and terrifying because that is the current state of the Night Court."

"How could it be this bad?" I stared at the ruined palace, my mind almost flatlining in disbelief. "The fae *adore* the fae realm. They could never let it get this bad!"

"I'd like to say you only have your direct predecessor to thank for this." The Paragon gestured to a toppled statue that was broken into chunks. "But I'm afraid the Night Court started to rot long before Nyte got her hands on it. The last few generations of Night Kings and Queens have been...less than noble. And with each new monarch it got worse."

"And none of them tried to reverse it?"

The Paragon shrugged. "Even if the fae wished to, it is the monarch who decides the fate of the Court. Their actions dictate the power the Court has. The Night Court has been in a steady decline of power for quite some time, but when Killian Drake revealed that Queen Nyte killed her first husband—the king who was chosen by the night mares—the Night Court lost all credibility among the other fae Courts."

I stared at a withered bush. "This is what you're talking about, then. This is the threat that's a whole lot bigger than a fae lord assassin."

"Unfortunately, it's only a part of it," the Paragon grimly said. "Come." He waggled his fingers at me and led me off the patio and out into the overgrown gardens.

He found two benches—they were stone and hadn't rotted out like the wooden bench pushed in front of a nearby empty fountain—then plopped down.

When I sat down on the bench opposite from him, the Paragon adjusted his sapphire ring, once again creating the sparkling bubble around us.

"No one can hear us?" I asked.

"Indeed." The Paragon took his glasses off and leaned forward, his eyes glowing with intensity as he addressed me in a voice that was a lot deeper than his somewhat dry and warbly one. "If you want the Court to survive long enough for the next generation or two, you will have to address this." He waved his hand at the palace. "It was an open secret that Nyte bankrupted the Court. You'll also need to do something about that. But neither of those issues should be your greatest concern."

For a moment I wondered if my hearing was off.

Bankruptcy and the Court's dead reputation aren't the worst thing I have to face?

When I could finally get my jaw working, my voice shook a little in a weird cocktail of disbelief and despair. "What could be more important than the realm rotting around me and bad Court finances?"

"Your life," the Paragon grimly said.

I paused. "I'll agree with that. You're going to tell me how to stay alive?"

"To the best of my abilities, yes." The Paragon rested his elbows on his knees and dropped his chin to his fist. "The most accurate description I can give you—and the easiest one to understand—is to say that you are entering an incredibly complex, multileveled game of power."

"Multileveled?"

"Hmmm. Here. This is you." The Paragon grabbed a clover leaf from the one spot of greenery near us, and set it down next to him on the bench. "The base level of this unfortunate game is your Court—the Night Court." The Paragon swiped a thumb-sized rock off the ground and casually tossed it on the clover leaf, flattening it. "The nobles will either try to gain your favor—not likely given your blood—or insult you until they figure out how to get rid of you. The nobles fight among themselves in all of this, and even if you manage to get the upper hand, I don't know that they'll ever stop fighting you."

"Sounds like a bunch of team players."

"If you can manage to solidify your Court and keep hold of your power as queen—a monumental task in itself—the next level and difficulty you face will be the game of power between *all* the fae Courts." The Paragon grunted as he picked up a rock that was just a little smaller than his head, and dropped it on top of the thumb-sized rock. "The Courts are locked in a never ceasing battle for power. They make alliances over tea and propose murdering their allies at hunting parties."

The Paragon stood, making his bubble of magic grow around us. "They thirst for power, because they mistakenly think it means survival in this time of dying magic. It makes them ruthless in a way that's hard to imagine. Your people will stab you in the back without a twinge of conscience. The monarchs of the other Courts would watch the Night Court and everyone in it die without remorse."

I stared at the rocks and, with a sinking feeling in my gut, rolled them off the bench, revealing the thoroughly squashed clover leaf that was now a smear on the stone bench.

"That's toxic," I said.

The Paragon sat back down on his bench with a sigh that sounded as old as he looked. "It is. I wish I could stop it, but on my own I don't have the power. I'm searching for a way, but..." He met my gaze, and his bushy eyebrows sloped in concern. "Even at my most optimistic I can't say I'll be able to enact it before your own Court—or the other monarchs—eats you alive. You'll have to play this game of power if you want to survive."

I rested my palms on the stone bench, grimacing when I felt dirt and grit smudge my palm. "And I'm supposed to try to win?"

"I don't know if 'winning' is possible," the Paragon said. "This game is much like a chess match with a hundred players all on one board. The truth is no one wins for long. The status quo is always changing, nobles are forever falling in and out of favor, and the Courts are always in opposition—though they may temporarily unite against a common enemy."

I heard scuttling, and through the dim light shed by the moon and the bright stars, I was able to see a creature that shouldered its way through the garden underbrush.

It was a griffin. Not the lion-sized, noble creatures from a picture book, heck no. Not in this grungy place! This cat-sized griffin looked like a combination of a raccoon and a pigeon.

It had the mottled gray wings, the extra round and empty head, and the unnerving orange eyes of a pigeon, but the rotund, fluffy body of a raccoon.

It was dragging a McDonald's takeout bag through the garden—I had no idea how it found that here in the fae realm—which it ripped open with its stumpy front legs that ended in creepy pigeon feet.

This place is bizarre.

I felt for the charm bracelet that dangled from my wrist—it was a magic tool my mom had gotten for me when I attended magic classes at the Curia Cloisters.

Unlike wizards—who channeled raw, wild magic through their bodies—fae had to use artifacts to wield magic if we wanted to do anything more than the innate abilities we were born with. Artifacts filtered the magic and let us use it to cast spells and charms, but there was a huge variety in artifacts—from modern, mass produced ones like my charm bracelet, to antique items that were made by elves or the occasional overpowered wizard.

The variety of artifacts meant there was also a lot of diversity in fae abilities. Not everyone was capable of wielding an elf-made artifact, but if you were, you'd be *insanely* powerful with the right artifact.

"How are you taking this?" the Paragon asked.

"It feels a bit unreal," I admitted. "But the backstabbing and power struggle doesn't come as a huge surprise to me. Although it seems like surviving will be harder than I thought."

"You do have some advantages—your friendship with Hazel Medeis and Killian Drake, foremostly. And of course, I shall try to aid you whenever possible as well." He hesitated, then said, "There is one more thing—which may lighten your load. Though I doubt you're going to like it."

I finally pulled my gaze away from the pigeon-raccoon-griffin—which had almost choked itself on a dried-out French fry. "What?"

"It's just one matter." He held his pointer finger and thumb the tiniest bit apart in a display.

"You can't *say* it's a small matter, which means it's big. What is it?"

"Oh, it's a tradition. A very old, required one that you'll have to follow now that you're the queen."

"And that is?"

"Ah. Yes. Ahem. Your marriage."

I relaxed slightly. "Oh, that's not a problem. I always figured I'd be fine being an old cat lady. I'll stay single and die alone."

The Paragon laughed nervously. "Ahaha, you can't."

"*What do you mean?*"

The Paragon grimaced. "It's part of the crowning tradition. The night mares pick the next monarch, the monarch is bound—usually by an acceptance ceremony, but you skipped that step since the night mares did it. The monarch then chooses his or her spouse, and the couple is sworn in together when the chosen monarch is publicly crowned."

My ears rang as I struggled with this newest complication.

It wasn't enough that I can't just have a normal life anymore, no, no. I also have to get shoved into an unwanted relationship that probably has a zero chance of being healthy and meaningful.

"The Night Court has the stupidest traditions I've ever heard of," I said. "And also ridiculously backwater. Have the rules been updated at all since the Middle Ages?"

The Paragon held his hands up in a foolish attempt to pacify me. "I'm aware of how distasteful it appears to be. But you can only be crowned after you marry, and you *need* to be crowned if you want to survive against the other Courts. The Night Court has to listen to you already due to the night mares binding you. The other Courts won't officially recognize you until you're crowned, and that will paralyze your efforts to consolidate power for yourself."

"I'm not even twenty-three years old yet. And you're telling me I need to choose a husband *right now*?" I rubbed my eyes and felt the stabbing sensation of a headache settling into my temples.

"It's not as bad as it sounds," the Paragon said.

"Really?" I drawled. "Marrying someone who is going to hate me for being human and also have a lot of political power isn't as bad as it sounds?

"You're *half* human," the Paragon corrected. "And when you focus on the forced marriage part, yes, it's going to sound pretty bad. But this will play into the power game—for your benefit. Marrying will help you control the Night Court better—if you choose your husband carefully."

I dropped my hand. "Oh?"

"If you pick someone with the sort of connections your people admire, it will make your job as monarch much easier. Though I would personally recommend you select someone with as few deep social connections as possible. It will split their loyalties."

"It seems risky to split my power with another fae when you *just* finished telling me how toxic we are." My groan scared the pigeon-griffin, who abandoned his McDonald's bag to scurry under a bush.

"Oh, that's another positive," the Paragon said in an unnecessarily upbeat voice. "*You* are the monarch chosen by the night mares, not him. You get to decide if you want to share power with him."

That confused me enough to beat back my growing dread. "How does that work?"

The Paragon shrugged. "You're the queen. You decide if your husband is going to be a mere consort or a true king. As the selected monarch, you can change your mind at any time—you can even demote him from king back to consort if you choose. Some monarchs only give their spouse the power to rule after they die—that's what happened with Queen Nyte. That's probably why she killed him, now that I think of it."

I tried to dust off my knowledge of the dead queen. "She remarried—did she have to?"

"No. She chose to—and her new husband could only ever be called her consort. It's only the monarch selected by the night mares that has the ability to share their power."

A sigh leaked out of me. "The other Courts don't have this rule, do they?"

"No," the Paragon said.

Yep. I reaaalllyy wish I was anything besides half night fae.

"But, as I said, these rules were laid with the foundation of the Night Court here in America," the Paragon said, opting to continue the history lesson. "Because it used to be one of the most powerful Courts. Unlike the Winter, Autumn, Summer, and Spring Courts—one of which exists in each region—or the Seelie and Unseelie Courts—which are found locally—your Night Court is the only one in existence in America. And because of its power, the founding king created these rules as a sort of power balance. Otherwise the Day Court—which is also the only one in existence here in America—was the only other Court with a similar amount of clout."

That seems suspiciously thoughtful for a bunch of fae. I don't buy it.

"Given how naturally linked the Day and Night Courts are in power, when the Night Court agreed to these laws it naturally checked the Day Court's power as well," the Paragon added. "To keep it, however, the laws were written into the very foundation stones of the palace. You can't fight them, Leila, but you can use them to your advantage."

"Let me guess." I narrowed my eyes. "This *founding king* was the same guy who decided night mares should choose the new ruler?"

"Yes."

"Wow. I have never so passionately hated a historic figure before," I said.

The Paragon laughed uneasily. "He is venerated despite dying centuries ago—and he was extremely powerful and wise to adopt these laws as natural checks."

"Wise, is it?" I slapped my thighs a few times, trying to pin down exactly how I felt about this seemingly endless downward spiral. "Yep. Okay. My life is already a burning dumpster fire. What could a political marriage do to make it worse?"

"It could be better than you are expecting. Monarchs before you have wed for political reasons, and forged a sort of warm friendship between them and their spouse," the Paragon said.

That actually didn't sound too bad. *But*! What were the chances of that actually happening?

Based on my reception today, I'd say slim.

I wiped my hands off on my jeans. "How much time do I have before I'd be expected to announce who I'm marrying?"

"Ideally, you'd be crowned in early August, and marry before then. You can make your decision on short notice. With your fleet of servants ready to work, it's a relatively easy matter to put a wedding together in a number of days," the Paragon said. "Though I would hope you might announce your engagement well before, giving you enough time to make your wedding day appropriately beautiful and romantic."

"It's a political marriage," I said. "How romantic could it possibly be?"

"I know." The Paragon gazed off into the shadowy depths of the garden. "I wish there was another way. But you have to play this game of power, or you won't survive."

Living is my priority, I reminded myself. *And maybe if I survive long enough, I can change some of their outdated laws. My Court would probably get behind that, given that they got stuck with me.*

The Paragon adjusted his ring, disassembling the bubble of magic.

I let out the breath I was holding—if he was dropping his magic, that meant he had no more bombs to drop on me. This was bad, but at least I knew where I stood—in a burning pit.

"That's the worst of the news," the Paragon said, confirming my guess. "From here on you can begin to build your own path. Today you'll get settled, and tomorrow I expect you'll be asked to choose your steward—they'll be your right hand in all of this."

I also stood up and retrieved the trashed McDonald's bag. "Any tips on who to choose when I can't trust anyone?"

The Paragon shook his head. "I'm afraid not. Don't let yourself be swayed by sob stories. Instead, question everyone—and watch carefully for any vague or misleading words they use."

"Cool, I always wanted to play detective in a struggle to preserve my life. This should be thrilling." I wadded up the bag and followed the Paragon as he led the way out of the abandoned gardens.

He chuckled. "I think you'll do better than you expect, Leila. I suspect your sarcasm will help you slice through all the lies your Court will try to feed you."

"I hope so," I said grimly. "Because I don't have any other options."

CHAPTER EIGHT

Leila

As the Paragon predicted, I was shown to my room in my new mansion.

I'll admit, the room was a giant perk—not enough to make up for the whole everyone-may-try-to-kill-me thing, but the massive bed, with the bathtub that was practically the size of a small pool, did a lot to improve my mood.

I didn't sleep a lot—all of the ugly truths the Paragon had dropped on me didn't exactly lull me off to sleep, and despite his dismissal I still was pretty worried about *the Wraith*.

But I used my sleeplessness to my advantage and went over some of the financial records the Paragon handed off to me earlier in the day.

I thought the Paragon had been speaking figuratively when he said Nyte bankrupted the Court. Nope! Of course not! We had literally no money left, and the Court was up to its neck in debt.

Around two in the morning I started making a list of some of the expenses I'd have to jettison—the luxury condo in Chicago was going to be the first thing to go as soon as I found someone trustworthy to sell it—but while I felt productive, it wasn't exactly a mood lifter.

Thankfully, my mood vastly improved after a sunrise swim in my bathtub and eating a protein bar and apple—some of the snacks I'd packed in the two duffle bags I had filled with food and brought with me.

Not surprisingly, I was all the way to the stables—a luxurious building that was nicer than my parents' house with a fancy vaulted ceiling, cobblestone flooring, and individual skylights over every horse's stall—before anyone realized I was up.

"Queen Leila!"

I'd been staring up at a beautiful glass tea set—yes, a tea set in a *barn*, and the teapot and the cups all looked spotless, which had to be magic—that was carefully arranged on a wooden serving tray that appeared to be bolted to the wall as a decoration of sorts. But at the sound of my name I peered down the stable aisle in time to see a flabbergasted dryad drop the pitchfork she was holding and bend herself in half in a hasty bow. "I—this is—"

"Good morning." I tried to sound warm and inviting. "Sorry for showing up unannounced—if that's a thing?"

The dryad didn't get up from her bow. Her brown hair—which was threaded with beautiful green leaves—hung down and covered most of her face. "I am entirely at your service, Queen Leila. The stable is yours to see whenever you wish."

"Okay, thank you." I studied her, trying to figure out how to get her to stop bowing to me, which felt ridiculous. I decided to go for bluntness. "You can stand up."

"I wouldn't presume, Queen Leila."

"It's fine!" I breezily said. I meandered around the disbelieving dryad and walked deeper into the stables, making my way toward the fancy stalls. "The night mares live here now? The Paragon mentioned they were wild for a while, but..." I trailed off as I stared at the wondrous creatures that peered out at me from their stalls.

The dryad popped out of her bow and scurried after me. "No, Queen Leila. The sun stallions are kept here," she supplied.

Beautiful horses—some a stark white color that had the intensity of the afternoon sun, some the same beautiful gold color of sunrise, while others the red shade of sunset—nickered invitingly to me.

Flames in hues of blues and orange flickered in their manes and tails, and their eyes were a bright, blazing white that flashed with the same intelligence I could see in the night mares. Everything about them reminded me of the sun, and even the daylight that poked through the skylights seemed to almost bend around them.

"Aren't you handsome?" I slowly approached the first stall, which housed one of the smaller boned horses. It hung its head over the door of its stall and nickered at me.

When it stretched out its neck in a clear invitation, I stepped even closer and stroked its muscled neck. "Are they all stallions?" I asked.

The stable worker cleared her throat. "No, the name is something of a misnomer—like the night mares. All of the sun stallions here are geldings and mares."

The sun stallion I was petting lowered its head and breathed its warm, horsey breath into my face. Something inside me relaxed. "I'm guessing they're from the Day Court?"

"Indeed. Sun stallions are a rare breed of fae horse that are guarded and cared for by the Day Court. They are extraordinarily difficult to buy due to their rarity, the level of care required before the Sun King is willing to part with one, and the general demand for them among fae nobility," the stable worker said.

I stared up at the chandelier that hung over the aisle—yes, a *chandelier* in a *barn*. I was starting to understand why the Court was broke. "What you're saying is that they're really expensive," I said.

The dryad hemmed and hawed behind me, which was as much of an answer as I needed.

A quick count said I was the owner of eighteen sun stallions.

If the Day King required chandeliers and skylights in a stable to sell his horses, I was pretty sure these animals were individually pricier than a top-of-the-line, luxury car.

I sighed as the sweet-tempered sun stallion rested its muzzle on my shoulder, but forced myself to turn to the dryad with a smile. "I'm sorry for being rude and not asking this earlier, but what's your name?"

The dryad started to bend over in another bow—which I would have thought would be awkward since she was quite a bit taller than me, but despite her long limbs she had the sort of swaying grace of a weeping willow tree.

I held a hand up to stop her before she got into a full bow. "Please, bowing isn't necessary."

From the way the subtle green hue of her skin was turning yellow, I was pretty sure she was going to start shedding some of the leaves in her hair from all her anxiety. "I'm Dawn, Queen Leila. My brother, Dusk, and I manage and run the stables."

"Great." I smiled at her, trying to appear as friendly as possible. "You're exactly who I need to talk to. As much as I regret it, we're going to have to sell the sun stallions."

Dawn's mouth dropped. "Pardon?"

"Queen or not, it's silly to have *eighteen* horses on top of the night mares. Where *are* the night mares, anyway? I know six of them are still with my parents, but I was under the impression there were more of them."

"I'm afraid I don't know, Queen Leila. They tend to be fairly autonomous."

"I don't know how autonomous they really are considering

how they look." I frowned a little. "I want them stabled and cared for."

"Then...you're certain?"

"About selling the sun stallions? Absolutely. As long as you can find them good homes where they will be well cared for."

"That won't be a problem—anyone who wishes to sell a sun stallion must use the Day Court as a broker. They will find the best home possible..." Dawn picked up the pitchfork she'd dropped earlier, her forehead wrinkling deep with concern.

"I'm sensing a 'but' at the end of that sentence, and not a horse one." I winked at Dawn, but she totally ignored my joke and tightened her long fingers—which were knobby like a twig—around the handle of her pitchfork, too scared to say anything.

She's not telling me everything. What do I ask to ferret out the truth?

I glanced up and down the line of horses. "Is there a problem with some of the horses that will make them more difficult for the Day Court to resell?"

Dawn's grip on her pitchfork made her knuckles turn white.

"Which horses—or horse?" I asked.

The stable manager reluctantly led me deeper into the stable, stopping in front of a stall near the center.

A large sun stallion stood inside. His white mane and tail were threaded with blue tinted flames. His coat was a glossy copper color, but it seemed to have an iridescent blue and green sheen to it—like a telescope photo of a supernova.

"This is Fax," Dawn said.

Fax came to his stall door, his ears perked.

"Hello, Fax. You're positively gorgeous, aren't you?" I cooed over him as he sniffed at my clothes.

"He is of a rather advanced age," Dawn said. "I'm certain there would still be interested buyers, but they might...push him more than he can handle."

"Okay. Then we'll keep Fax."

Dawn's bones audibly creaked as she snapped her head to gape at me. "Really?"

"Of course," I said. "We don't abandon our pets just because they're getting old."

When Dawn exhaled, she seemed to settle—like a relaxing horse. "Very good, Queen Leila."

Fax was so cute, I couldn't help myself, and I very daringly kissed his nose.

Fax responded with a pleased nicker.

"Yes, you're just the sweetest thing. I think you'll do well with the night mares. Are there any other older sun stallions?"

"No. Fax is the oldest—he was purchased by the previous king. Queen Nyte and her consort bought all the rest more recently," Dawn said. "But, are you sure you do not wish to retain one or two of the best sun stallions? They are great boons during Court hunts and races."

Hunts and races? What the heck are these fae monarchs doing all day long?

Slightly disgruntled that the other Courts apparently had plenty of time for relaxing while I was stuck cleaning up the trash heap that was the Night Court, I made a negative noise at the back of my throat. "I'll just ride the night mares for any official event."

"The *night mares*?" Dawn gasped—I had a feeling I'd blown her mind this morning more than she'd encountered in the last year based on all the gasping and gaping she did. I wasn't sure if that was a good or a bad thing.

"Yep. They're sweeties. Is your brother around? I'd like to meet him—"

"Queen Leila!" A guy with the legs of a goat and the upper body of a man—a faun—scrambled into the stable, his goat hooves tapping across the meticulously cleared cobblestone floor. "My apologies, the kitchen staff were unaware you had risen early. Your breakfast will be ready immediately."

"No thanks," I said, "I don't need it."

The faun—who was wearing a crisp white shirt, a black vest, and a dark, purplish-blue-ish bowtie bowed. "Then we will prepare your morning tea."

"Thank you, but no. I don't want that, either," I said.

When the faun's doe-brown eyes almost popped out of his head, I added compulsively, "But I appreciate the thought."

"But, but you'll need your morning tea. The candidates for your steward, companion, and director of security are being gathered," the faun said.

"Great! I'll come meet them."

"After breakfast?" the faun asked.

"No. I don't want anything to eat or drink," I said firmly. "Why don't you lead me to wherever these interviewees are?" I was halfway up the stable aisle before I remembered myself. "Sorry, Dawn—I'll come back later to meet Dusk! Thank you for the help—and for handling the sun stallions!"

Dawn had been resting her hand on Fax's neck, but when I looked back at her she folded over in a bow.

Ugh, I'll have to do something eventually to stop all this bowing. I shivered a little as I left the stable and popped out on a walking path that led back to the mansion.

The faun hurried after me, his legs going twice as fast to keep up with me, since I was over a head taller than him. "But, surely you need to eat *something*, Queen Leila. You refused to eat last night as well!"

Yep, and I was intending to do that for a long time.

That old story that you shouldn't eat or drink anything a fae gives you? Totally true. Fae had an easy time bespelling food and beverages. I was pretty sure that food made in the fae realm also had a magic quality about it which could be potentially dangerous, but since it seemed like the Night Court operated almost entirely in the human world, I wouldn't have to worry about that just yet.

Regardless, it was safe to say I wasn't eating anything here. It's why I had packed bags of fruit and snacks.

"I had some food packed from home," I said vaguely. "So, where are we going? I want to meet my potential employees."

A half-strangled wail escaped from the faun's mouth before he caught it and reeled it back in. "This way, Queen Leila."

The faun led me across the irritatingly perfect lawn and inside the mansion.

It seemed like he led me through a dizzying maze of rooms—I hadn't explored the place much the previous night since the Paragon's bad news had just about "funned" me out—before we reached what appeared to be an over-the-top, lavish meeting room.

An egg-shaped table made of carved wood and topped with granite squatted in the center of the room. The wood paneling on the walls seemed to depict the phases of the moon and a wolf-like creature chasing after it, and the floor to ceiling window at the far end of the room was half covered by a stiff and heavy curtain made of dark blue fabric.

The only other ornamentation in the room was an unassuming brownish-red clay teapot, which sat on a little shelf and was positioned under a spotlight.

"Queen Leila, these are the applicants for the position of steward." The faun bowed—this time to the fae who were seated around the table.

All of them were fae nobles—which didn't really surprise me considering my steward, second only to my unwanted-but-forced-on-me-husband, would be one of the top officials in the Court.

My early morning Google session had taught me that the position of steward was twofold. First, they were in charge of the personnel of all of my properties, and secondly they were a government official who was capable of representing me in political situations. A lot of the Court official stuff—communications with my people, taxes on my nobles, laws, and gathering reports on current topics/events, etc—passed through the steward before reaching the Court monarch.

Basically, they were my second in command. And I was supposed to choose my steward from a group of fae that were convinced they were better than me and were probably going to do their best to fudge my efforts. (Particularly when they found out I was going to sell as much as possible to make up for all the budget deficits.)

I scanned up and down the table, noting the perfect hair, tapered ears, and bronze skin that was the mark of a full blooded night fae.

I tugged on the lace hem of my shirt—a cute, silk blue shirt that I liked because it really brought out the purplish-blue of my eyes—and approached the first applicant. "Hey there! Let's cut to the chase: do you like humans?"

The applicant, a handsome fae with a dazzling smile, flashed his dimples at me. "Some may find humans intelligent and—"

"Yep, you don't. Thanks, but I'm looking for an applicant with different qualifications." I stepped up to the next candidate. "How about you? Do you like humans?"

This applicant, a beautiful female with blond-brown hair, glanced at the handsome fae, whose face had twisted with anger at the fast dismissal. "Is it important for a *fae* steward of a *fae* Court to like humans?" she asked.

I gave her a pitying look. "You need to work on your implications—he was a lot more convincing than you were." I gestured at the still angry first candidate. "Thanks for stopping by, but I regret to say I don't feel this position is a good fit for you." Another step and another applicant. "Surprise question: Do you like humans?"

"Yes."

"Splendid! A follow up question: are you applying for this job with the intention of harming or hurting me?"

The applicant fish mouthed for a moment, shocked by my blunt question.

"I, I," she said, unable to answer with a lie.

"Ohhh, you were close, but the correct answer is: No. Thanks for applying, though. Good luck next time. How about you, are you applying for this position with the intention of harming or hurting me?" I asked the next applicant, a male.

"You are the Queen of the Night Court," he countered. "I can't physically hurt you."

I stared at him for a very long moment and wondered if he really thought I was that stupid that I only meant physically. "Have you seriously not watched the way I've laid everyone before you flat for their wordsmithing? You had longer than them to prepare something. One star—very disappointing. Sorry, but no. I'm looking to move this Court in a different direction. Next!"

One of the female fae jumped from her chair, her slender frame taut with fury. "You cannot conduct yourself in this way."

"Oh, can't I?" I batted my eyes at the irate fae. "I was unaware there was a higher power than me in this Court."

"It lacks tact and elegance," one of the male candidates sneered.

"Oh no." I dramatically clasped my hand to my heart. "Not *that*! How will I function without tact and elegance?" I chuckled to myself, then settled on the next applicant. "How about it? Do *you* like humans?"

Silence answered me.

I was about to move on to the next candidate, but there was something that made me look at the applicant.

She was different from the others. Her ears were like mine—not tapered at all—but she still had the blessing of fae beauty with her heart-shaped face, button-nose, and high cheekbones.

Rather than the typical bronze skin of the Night Court, her skin was a warm shade of gold. Her hair was pretty different, too.

It was a lovely shade of a dark, ashen brown, but it was extremely short for a fae—just a bit longer than chin length—though it was perfectly curled with no amount of frizz my jealous eyes could see.

She's part human. But someone might have sent her hoping to score some sympathy.

I hated that I even had to think that, but—as the Paragon told me—I was an unwilling participant in a game of power.

My pause gave the applicant enough time to reply. "Yes," she said. "I like humans and enjoy spending time in the human world."

Behind me someone scoffed.

"Are you applying for this job with the intention of harming or hurting me?" I asked.

"No," she said.

"Then why are you applying?"

She hesitated, but her gaze went beyond me, to the other applicants.

I turned around, frowning when I saw none of the fae I had dismissed had actually left. "Since you seem to require *elegance* in order to understand anything, allow me to express it differently: I have found the lot of you lack certain areas to both your personality and your moral compass that make you unpleasant for me to spend any length of time with. Thank you for exiting this interview in a manner befitting of your station."

"You can't be serious," the male fae—the sneerer—said. "I'm the eldest son of Lord Vyalnt!"

I smiled and clapped my hands together. "And I have no idea who Lord Vyalnt is! Which, unfortunately for you, means I don't care. At all."

A few of the irate applicants started to leave, and I turned my attention to the remaining three I would have left to talk to after I finished chatting with the part-human-part fae. "I'm going to ask you the same questions. If you don't like humans, want the job because you're plotting against me, and can't tell me why you're applying, there is no sense in staying."

Two of the applicants—a male and female fae who looked more frightened than angry—exchanged glances, then stood up and fled.

The third—a smug looking male fae I recognized as the friend/cohort of the blond fae who had started the heckling when the Paragon had introduced me—smirked and settled into his chair.

"Yeah, no," I said. "I remember you *quite* well. It's not happening. Buh-bye."

The final applicant narrowed his eyes at me. "Soon you will learn this was a mistake—to treat us so poorly."

"Because based on the way you all responded, I'm *sure* I missed out on becoming life-long besties with all of you. Goodbye—and better luck next time!"

He finally left, and when I glanced at the faun who had escorted me here, he bobbed and bowed. "I'll just wait outside."

He disappeared through the door, leaving me alone with the remaining applicant.

I studied her for a moment, trying to get a feel for her. "You're part human?"

"Half, Queen Leila." She inclined her head in a nod of respect to me. "My name is Skye—I'm the granddaughter of Lord Thales."

When I kept staring at her, she added, "He is a member of fae nobility."

"I can't say I find that shocking. Tell me, Skye, why do you want to be my steward?" I plopped down in one of the chairs and rolled closer when I discovered it was on wheels.

Skye's lips twitched.

"You don't want to tell me?" I spun my chair so it faced the door, and was opening my mouth to send her on her way, but she spoke before I could.

"Your questions are designed to strip the applicants bare."

I swiveled back in her direction. "And you find that inappropriate?"

She wasn't wrong.

I had spent the earliest hours of the morning trying to figure out what questions I could ask so I didn't end up with a backstabber as a steward.

"No...I can understand why. But no fae will willingly reveal themselves like that. It's against all our instincts and everything we've been taught. To be open is to be weak. It gives your enemies an advantage and makes you an easy target."

I drummed my fingers on the granite table-top. "Then how would *you* go about getting a job candidate's reassurance that they won't backstab me at the bidding of their family?"

"I would ask each candidate who they would be most loyal to. The trick is to allow the candidate the chance to remain veiled, but have the motivation *you* want your employees to have."

Oh, she's good. I whistled, impressed by her thought process. *But a tad optimistic. Just because I'm queen doesn't mean anyone is going to be loyal to me—even the ones I hire. Which means I just need to come up with a motivation that I can work with.*

"I can swear that I will be loyal to you, Queen Leila," Skye said.

I smiled to show I appreciated the gesture. "Thank you for saying that, but you *are* half human. I know you can lie to me."

Skye looked slightly puzzled. "Do humans commonly lie?"

Her question felt genuine. The light in her eye was questioning, and she hadn't smothered her reaction like a fae usually would. But seriously, how could she not know?

Her face cleared, her confusion smoothed away by a solemn expression. "Regardless, you are correct. As a half fae, my vows don't mean as much. But as a pledge of my loyalty I will reveal that I am here at the request of my grandfather."

"He's plotting against me?"

"Not at all. But his line is one of the smallest noble houses. If I became your steward, it would bring us honor and prestige," Skye said.

"And he asked you because he was hoping I'd be softer toward a fellow half human?" I guessed. She didn't react, so I was probably right on. "Were you primarily raised by fae?"

"Yes," Skye said. "My father was human, but he died when I was young. My mother and I moved in with my grandfather, then." She paused, then added. "I received a fae education, as well as a general human education at my mother's insistence. I have the training necessary to fulfill my duties."

She's lived among nobles, and she obviously understands how fae society works. I don't trust her—not this soon, anyway. But as long as I stay on my toes, it should be okay. She doesn't feel off to me.

For a moment I paused, and the impossibility of what I was trying to do threatened to collapse on me.

I'd been here for *one day* and I already felt tired. But, hey, hopefully that was the sleepless night talking!

Hmm, which probably means my director of security is the most important position I hire if I ever feel like sleeping again.

"Okay." I slapped my hands on the table and stood up. "Welcome to the team, Skye."

She stared up at me. "You're hiring me?"

"Yep."

"To be your steward?"

"That's the position you were applying for, right?"

"Yes..."

"Great. Then your first task as steward is to make an online job application ad for my new director of security." I strolled outside the meeting room and was pleased to find the faun waiting outside. "You're still here, perfect. I've hired my steward, who is next?"

"Ah, this way, Queen Leila." The faun swayed in a dance-like bow and hurried down the hallway.

Skye left the meeting room and followed us, typing away on her smartphone with a speed I knew I couldn't match. "You wish to place an online *ad* for the position of director of security?"

"Yep. I'll need to hire a supernatural, obviously, but the Curia Cloisters does have a specialty jobs for hire section on their website. You can start by posting it there." I studied the mansion decorations with fascination as we walked.

Apparently I was slow on the pickup. I was just starting to realize everything in the place was decorated with dark shades of blue and purple, with streaks of black and accents of silver.

"You mean to open the position up to the other fae Courts?" Skye asked.

"No," I said. "I mean to hire anyone but a fae."

Skye didn't say anything as she tapped away on her smartphone, stopping without looking up when the faun hesitated in front of a large door.

"In here, Queen Leila, are the applicants for the esteemed position of companion," the faun said.

I tilted my head. "What?"

"Companion," the faun repeated.

"What does a companion do?"

The faun grabbed at his bowtie and started to look a little sweaty from his nerves. "They are your companion?"

"A companion will attend socials with you, aid you with your wardrobe, see to your needs, and provide any entertainment you may need," Skye helpfully supplied.

"Kind of like a personal assistant?" I asked.

"Of a sort," Skye said. "Your companion will devote herself to your needs."

"Yeah, sounds like a personal assistant. It's fine—I'm sorry, what did you say your name was?" I asked the faun.

"Eventide, Queen Leila." The faun nervously bowed again.

"Nice to meet you, Eventide. Okay, unleash the candidates!"

Eventide and Skye stared at me.

I sighed, dying just a little inside due to the general lack of humor among the fae. "I'd like to meet the applicants for the position of companion."

"Yes, right away!" The faun scrambled to open the door. "Queen Leila," the faun announced to the room.

They'd gathered the companion applicants in a fancy sitting room—the type I'd only seen before in Drake Hall. The wood floors and fancy rugs—which were dark blue decorated with silver star patterns—probably were each worth as much as a car, but I was pretty sure it was the hand painted wallpaper—a deep, subdued blue with swirls of purple and black and dustings of silver and gold creating star-studded galaxies—that was the most pricy thing about the room.

Like the previous room, this one also had teaware on display. Four shelves fixed to the wall housed a silver teapot, sugar container, and a tiny pitcher I assumed was for cream, as well as three different sets of porcelain tea cups that all depicted blue or purple flowers surrounded by gold swirls. Each piece was lit by glowing orbs of magic.

I'm starting to sense a pattern with all of these tea accoutrements. That does not bode well for me as a coffee drinker.

Crowded inside, sitting on the furniture—which looked plush, but based on the stiff way everyone was sitting it must have felt as comfy as stone—was a wildly diverse group of candidates.

Two dryads, a naiad, a sylph, three sirens, what I thought was a female dwarf, a brownie, and a banshee all stood up and bowed to me.

I leaned closer to Skye. "Do the less powerful fae usually fill the position of companion?" I whispered.

"Yes," Skye murmured. "It's a position traditionally ear marked for such fae because it gives them a direct line to the ruling monarch."

Surprise! More politics!

"Thanks, that's good to know." I strolled in, making a show of looking around, when in reality I was considering Skye's earlier advice.

What motivation can I use since loyalty is off the table?

"Right." I clapped my hands a few times, buying myself a few moments. "Who, here, is applying for this position because of money? Please raise your hand."

CHAPTER NINE

Leila

One of the sirens, the brownie, and the sylph all raised their hands.

"Great," I said. "Everyone else can go."

The fae gaped at me for a moment, but gathered up their things and left with *much* more elegance and style than any of the spoiled nobles had.

Next to me, Skye shifted. Her expression didn't give anything away, but she'd stopped tapping away on her phone.

"I know you said to ask for loyalty, and there may have been someone in that group that genuinely wants to see the Night Court improve," I explained. "But loyalty is fleeting. I want something that lasts forever."

"The desire for steady employment?"

"Nope. Greed." I grinned at Skye, then turned my attention to the three remaining candidates. "You're here for money—what do you mean by that?" I asked.

The siren slightly bowed her head. "I desire whatever money I receive as compensation for my position."

Okay, that was neatly worded enough that she could be referring to bribe money—which means it's a solid no for her.

The Sylph was next. She straightened her blouse then smiled at me. "I am intrigued by humans, whom I have heard possess generous spirits. I would happily serve such a person."

Pretty sure she thinks I'm an idiot she can sweet talk money out of. Not the worst motivation, but hopefully the brownie is better.

I smiled emptily and turned to the brownie.

As it is with all brownies, she was smaller—about waist high—and had thin, willowy limbs.

"And what made you apply for this job?" I asked.

"The offered salary," the brownie bluntly said.

I perked up at her plain words. "*Only* the offered salary?"

The brownie peered at me with shiny brown eyes, slightly magnified by a pair of classy cat-eye glasses. "Yes?"

"What else attracted you to the position?" I asked.

"The size of the salary," the brownie said.

"You already said that."

"You asked them about their motivations." The brownie nodded her head at the other candidates. "I'm telling you mine. It's the salary, the size of the salary, and the holiday bonuses."

Annnndd I'd found her. This was *exactly* who I wanted to hire. Someone who was money minded rather than shifty—like the sylph and siren.

"What's your name?" I asked.

"Indigo, Queen Leila." She curtsied, pulling her skirt wide with the motion.

"That's a pretty name. Indigo, welcome to the team!"

"What?" The sylph drew back, her airy powers making her hair flutter in her disbelief.

"Sorry, that was pretty poor leadership." I gave the sylph and siren my business look. "I am gratified that you applied for the position, but we'll be going with someone else. Thank you for your time."

"But she's a *brownie*," the sylph said.

Ahhh yes, the Paragon was right.

I needed to win the power game in my own Court—so people stopped questioning me about my food choices and hiring habits.

It's fine!

I propped one fist up on my hip. "Yeah. And?"

"A companion is supposed to represent the best of us common fae. A brownie companion will make our Court a laughing stock at multi-Court socials!" the sylph said.

"Yeah, and I'm concerned about what the nobles spend their time actually doing all day since there's apparently all this time for socials, but we're not solving that problem today. Thanks for applying. Goodbye." I turned my back to the sylph and smiled at my new companion/assistant.

It wasn't that I didn't understand what the sylph was alluding to—she was talking about the second level of this power game.

But the fact was if I didn't get my Court under control, it didn't matter how little the other Courts thought of us, because I'd be *dead*. For now, surviving my own people was the highest priority—starting with picking employees that weren't going to betray and/or possibly harm me.

The door creaked as Skye opened it for the upset applicants.

"Eventide?" I called.

The faun scurried through the door. "Yes, Queen Leila?"

"How many other people am I supposed to hire today?"

"Oh, yes. Um, your director of security."

"That's it?"

The faun discreetly checked a tiny notepad he whipped out of a pocket of his uniform. "Yes. You will eventually need to decide on an advisor, but no one has volunteered for the position as of yet."

"Great—we're done, then. Like I told Skye, I want an ad

placed through the Curia Cloisters for the director of security position. Is there anything I have to do?"

The faun shut his notepad. "Your new companion and steward need to be briefed—they will take over handling your schedule. You have an appointment with a tailor this afternoon for your new wardrobe, but your companion will help you with that."

"Cancel the tailor," I said.

"B-but Queen Leila! You need...that is to say..." The faun wrung his hands and eyed my cute but very human lace shirt I was wearing.

Skye was better dressed than me in her slacks and flawless dress shirt.

Ugh. As little as I like it, something tells me the way I dress is going to be part of the power game. But that's fine—I just have to figure out how to do it in the cheapest way possible.

I grimaced. "Reschedule for later this week, please. I know I need clothes, but there are a few things I need to iron out first."

Eventide relaxed so much he looked like he might pass out in relief. "Yes, of course. It will be as you say." He bowed three times for good measure. "I will return after rescheduling the appointment to give your new staff their work phones and pass along to you the numbers you'll need for your head housekeeper, gardener, and the like."

"Great—thanks, Eventide!"

The faun left looking like he needed a massage or something to lower his stress levels, the poor guy.

I squared my shoulders and studied my new employees.

Indigo was squinting at me behind her cat-eye glasses, her slightly upturned nose scrunched in suspicion.

Her thick, russet colored hair was pulled back in a ponytail, and her skinny frame was covered by an oversized blue sweater—which seemed a little strange given that even though the air conditioning was on, it wasn't *that* cold—and a simple but neat, gray skirt that covered most of her knobby knees.

She reminded me a bit of a pony with her thick hair, small stature, and big temperament.

Skye was the other end of the spectrum with a pleasantly blank expression, slightly plain but flawless clothes, and her adorably curled bob. Although she didn't look suspicious, I could feel her reserve stacked around her like a brick wall.

"I sort of already said this, but thank you for applying for your positions, and congratulations. I hope we get to know each other quite well," I said, rattling off the standard welcome speech I'd heard in training for the various retail positions I'd held as a high schooler and college student.

When they both bowed their heads, I continued. "As part of your welcome, I want you both to know that should you ever be offered a bribe, please know I will always pay higher."

Indigo's jaw dropped, and Skye's eyes widened slightly.

"Queen Leila?" Skye asked.

I shrugged. "I'm not stupid. Nobles, probably even fae from other Courts, are going to offer you money and ask you to do things. When this happens, come to me, and I will *always* pay more than them."

"You are our queen," Skye started. "Our loyalty—"

"Is definitely not with me," I interrupted. "I might be human, but I know about the constant political upheaval in Courts. I know about the betrayals, the underhanded dealings, and the bribes. Even if I hadn't known before, getting targeted by the Wraith was a pretty solid indicator of what life in the Courts is like."

"The *Wraith* tried to kill you?" Indigo squeaked.

I waved a hand at her. "He didn't know the night mares had bound me as queen so he wouldn't be able to. It's fine. It's not like he was the first person to try, either. I'm pretty sure a giant spider was sent after me as well, back when only Eclipse was around and I was just a candidate to be queen."

Indigo—her eyes bulging—looked to Skye, who now had faint creases in her forehead that hadn't been there before.

"I'm not asking for your undying loyalty or faithfulness," I continued. "I just want to be able to guarantee your continued service."

Really, I wanted to *buy* their loyalty, but that sounded pretty slimy to say and would speak a little too loudly of how I felt about being queen. Plus, it might offend them.

Thankfully, they seemed more shocked by my conduct than put off.

"Do we have an agreement?"

"That if we are offered incentives or bribes, we'll come to you and you will offer a better deal?" Skye slightly shook her head, as if she couldn't believe her own paraphrase.

"Yes, exactly!" I beamed. "I think we're going to get along great."

Skye bowed. "I am honored to be your steward."

Indigo pushed her glasses up her nose, then curtseyed. "And it's my honor—and delight—to be your companion!"

Some of the tension I'd been holding in relaxed. I wasn't alone anymore. I didn't trust Skye or Indigo, but at least I could count them as allies. And I needed them, badly. I didn't know the first thing about the Night Court, and that had to change.

This little plan of mine was going to cost me, but I'd ditch the Chicago condo and cut where I had to if it meant I knew the two people I worked most closely with wouldn't betray me.

"Yep, I feel pretty confident no one is going to recognize this as a human clothing brand." I inspected myself in the mirror, admiring the dress—which was a dark, blue-ish gray color with a navy blue lace overlay.

It was a lot fancier than anything I'd normally wear, but with all the socializing the fae did, I'd come to realize that a wardrobe change was needed after all. However, with the power of the internet, and by harnessing Indigo's brilliant mind, we'd hatched a plan that saved me the cost of having an entire tailor-made wardrobe. I didn't even want to think how much that would have cost.

Instead, I bought my clothes online with a lot of advice from Indigo—who had a better idea what kind of clothes I needed as well as an eye for fashion—from human retailers. We then cut off the tags, and paid the tailor to custom fit them to me.

Which, have you ever wondered why off the rack clothes seem to perfectly fit glamorous celebrities? Yeah, it's because they pay a tailor to take them in.

So I had a wardrobe that wouldn't disgrace me—particularly because my nobles would never recognize human brands even if I was waltzing around with a jacket covered in brand patches—and for a fraction of the price!

Indigo studied the dress and leaned closer to inspect the fabric. "It's a suitable tea dress."

I found the book on manners Skye had gotten for me to read up on—she obviously didn't have very high hopes for me because it had a lot of illustrations and was written for kids. "Or maybe a coffee dress?" I suggested.

"A coffee dress? That doesn't exist," Indigo said.

"Don't the nobles ever drink coffee together?" I asked hopefully.

In all my secret trips to the kitchens—I was still on my "don't-eat-what-fae-have-made" diet and had to sneak my food—I'd never managed to find a coffee maker, to my disappointment.

"No." Indigo wrinkled her nose in disgust. "Tea only. Fae grow specialty tea leaves you cannot find outside of the fae realm and have flavors beyond reckoning."

I took my kids' manners book and skulked over to a chair, readying myself to read about "Good Manners Mandy" and

"Uncivil Sandy." It was a *fascinating* read, I promise. "Only if you like tea," I grumbled.

Indigo hung a pair of slacks the tailor had fit for me in my walk-in-closet—which was about as big as my bedroom back at my parents' house. "What did you say?"

I was saved by a knock on the door.

Indigo scurried to open it, her russet hair—which was shoved up in a bun today—bouncing on the top of her head. She poked her head outside, then flung the door open. "It's Skye."

"Come on in, Skye," I called to my steward.

Skye entered, her head slightly tilted down as she bowed. She looked like a high rolling CEO with her business suit—which had the familiar Night Court crescent moon embroidered over a pocket—and carried a smartphone and tablet, both of which chirped roughly every ten seconds.

"Queen Leila, I have an update for you."

I set my book down. "Did someone finally offer to be my advisor?"

Skye shook her head. "No. Not yet."

"Ahh, okay." I took in a deep breath of air and puffed my cheeks as I thought.

In the few days that had passed since I hired Skye and Indigo, they explained that an advisor was an official Court position, granted to fae who were exceptionally intelligent and capable of helping the ruling monarch make good decisions.

Basically, he or she was an experienced expert I could consult if I needed advice. It was an incredibly influential position...and no one had applied for it yet.

I'm pretty sure no one applied at first because they didn't know how to best appeal to me, and after what Skye said about my questions being unspeakably rude when I was interviewing the steward candidates, I'm pretty sure that really miffed them, and now the nobles were paying me back by refusing to help.

Oh, they'd cave eventually. But when I finally did start

receiving offers, I had no idea how I was going to choose someone that didn't intend to manipulate me for their own purposes.

"I have, however, interviewed the candidates answering the online advertisement for the director of security position, as you instructed," Skye said.

"And?"

Skye pressed her lips together—flattening them. I'd come to learn that this, and the crease on her forehead, were her two only real tells of displeasure. "I regret to say that there was only one candidate I found worthwhile, and I do not know that you will approve of him."

I grabbed an apple—swiped from the kitchens—which I'd kept in a duffle bag. "Why wouldn't I approve of him?"

Skye glanced down at her tablet. "You expressly wished to hire a wizard."

"Yes."

"He's a werewolf."

I cringed. "And he was the best candidate?"

Skye swiped through some screens. "He has the best background, experience, and moral discipline. Several wizards applied for the position, but most of them were underqualified. The one candidate I had hopes for proved to be incompetent during her interview."

I chewed on my lip as I thought.

I'd wanted a wizard as my director of security because wizards are naturally immune to most kinds of fae magic. That would be a seriously big help in trying to keep me safe while I played the fae's game.

"Should I post the position to the Curia Cloisters website again?" Skye asked.

"Not yet—I should at least meet him first. Where is he?"

"I took him to the stables—as you instructed I should do if I found a worthy candidate."

"Okay, let's go meet him. Come on, Indigo." I marched out of my room and veered down the hallway.

I still hadn't slept great since becoming queen, so I'd spent my nights walking the mansion when reviewing finances got too depressing. Which meant I was getting more familiar with the layout.

"Do you need to change?" Indigo bounced at my side, her glasses nearly sliding off her nose.

"Nah—the dress is machine washable." I tossed my apple up in the air and caught it. "Anything I should know about the position, Skye?"

Skye spent the several minute walk from my room down to the base floor of the mansion and then out back to the stables describing the various duties a director of security would have.

It really made me sad there were no good wizard candidates, and by the time we reached the so-expensive-I-was-still-cringing-stables, I was leaning more toward posting the ad again.

Together, my steward, companion, and I clattered into the stable aisle, eliciting noises from the horsey residents.

About half of the sun stallions were gone, but my bony, dull-coated night mares had taken up residence in the empty stalls, and they were the ones who called out to me. They *tried* to sound cute—they really did. But instead of nickering warmly like Fax, the old sun stallion I was keeping, they seemed to almost growl.

Their noises made the young man standing in the center of the aisle turn around to face us and bow in one smooth movement. He'd probably heard us when we'd been walking across the lawn, given his werewolf hearing.

"Queen Leila, might I present Chase Washington of the Northern Lakes Pack," Skye announced.

"Hello, Chase." I smiled.

"Queen Leila," Chase said.

He was a few years older than me—maybe on the edge of thirty—but werewolves age slowly, so I could have been wrong about that. I mean, they don't age as slowly as fae, but magic seems to preserve supernaturals. Age was always an iffy thing among our kind.

His warm sepia-brown skin tone made the cutting yellow color of his eyes—a mark of his werewolf heritage—that much more startling. His black hair was very precisely cut—short on sides and slightly longer on top with just a hint of dense curls—and he wore a business suit for our meeting.

Like most werewolves, he had an impressive set of broad shoulders, and I could see the shadow of defined muscles in the way his black suit fit him.

"It's a pleasure to meet you, Chase. Tell me about your skills." I smiled at him as I edged closer to the stalls, angling for the one Eclipse had claimed for herself.

"I'm versed in various forms of martial arts, I have extensive firearm training, and I served as a marine in active duty for six years," Chase said.

"Any leadership training?" I propped my arm up on the edge of the stall, smiling when Eclipse joined us.

Chase slightly bowed his head to Eclipse and didn't appear at all bothered by her frightening appearance. "Yes. I am one of the top ranked wolves in my pack, and I have experience leading both civilians and shifters..."

He listed his work experience, but I wasn't too concerned about that. Skye said he was competent. For her to say that he had to be good.

I was far more interested in seeing how the night mares reacted to him.

Eclipse was doing her best to beg my apple from me and was mostly ignoring him—that wasn't a bad thing, though.

Suits—the guy who had shown up with Lady Demetria and the others when they found me—had stormed the stable once to object when he heard I was selling the sun stallions, then left immediately, screaming, because Twilight almost kicked him.

In fact, the longer we stood by Eclipse and the longer she didn't react, the more I suspected Chase had to be a stand up sort of guy.

"That's really impressive." I finally gave in and gave Eclipse the apple. She slobbered over my hand in her version of thanks. "Skye said you were from the Northern Lakes Pack. That's in northern Wisconsin, right?"

"Yes, Queen Leila." He straightened up and stood with his hands clasped behind his back.

"Which means you are leaving your pack?"

Magiford straddled the state line between Wisconsin and Illinois and was hours away from the Northern Lakes Pack territory. Werewolves lived with—or at least *near*—their pack, which meant there was no way he was remaining part of the Northern Lakes Pack.

"No, actually. I've received special permission from my pack Alpha, and from the Pre-Dominant, to apply for this position and take up residence in Magiford but remain a member of the pack."

I almost put my slobbered hand on my hip in my surprise before I caught myself. "The Pre-Dominant?" The Pre-Dominant was the highest-ranking werewolf in the region. For her to be giving her approval to Chase was a pretty big deal.

"My pack has a higher-than-average number of wolves with alpha capabilities," Chase said. "It's not a problem due to the strength of our pack, and all of us would follow our Alpha no matter what. The Pre-Dominant approached our pack and asked if several members would be willing to relocate and find strategic positions." He hesitated, then added, "Given the events of the past year, it's become obvious to us werewolves that we need to make greater strides in working with other supernaturals."

Which was political speak for saying that the vampires and wizards getting along splendidly due to Killian and Hazel's romance was scaring the pants off the werewolves, because it meant the vampires and wizards could team up on the Regional Committee of Magic.

See? Sometimes it *did* pay to be more aware of local politics than whatever dramas the fae had most recently invented to amuse themselves.

I tapped my hands on the stall door and glanced at Eclipse.

She blew her sulfuric smelling breath at me. I tried to discreetly tilt my head in Chase's direction.

Eclipse just swished her thin tail and stared at me.

When I made a face at her she finally took my unspoken hint and reached over the stall to nudge Chase.

He glanced at the mare, then gently patted her neck.

Eclipse grunted at me, checked my hand for any additional apples, then retreated into her stall to blow smoke at her haynet.

His non-reaction made me narrow my eyes and openly study him.

Chase wasn't what I wanted. He was a werewolf, and still susceptible to fae magic.

But as a werewolf he'd have some advantages. Werewolves were agile—not like the vampires, but in strength they could beat vampires every day. They—most shifters, really—also were extra perceptive with better eyesight, hearing, and smell.

What I really need in a director of security is someone competent that I can trust. I can trust Chase Washington.

I felt the truth of that statement all the way to the bottom of my gut.

"Okay," I nodded.

"Yes?" Chase stood straighter yet, resembling a finely sculpted block of marble.

"Chase, I'd like to offer you the position of director of security," I said. "I'm not going to lie—it's dangerous work, and I don't think my nobles are going to give you a welcome that overflows with warmth."

Chase gave me a slight bow. "I understood the possibilities

when I applied for the position. Thank you, Queen Leila. I vow to see that you are safe—both among your own people, and when in public."

"Thanks. It's the 'among my people' part that I'm most concerned about," I said blandly. "We'll provide you with a room at the mansion and all of that—Skye?"

"Yes, I can handle the details and introduce Mr. Washington to the guards who will be under his command."

"Please, it's just Chase." Chase gave Skye a charming smile—which, I was impressed to see, didn't even make her blink.

"Thanks, Skye. And welcome, Chase. I hope you enjoy your employment here." I was edging my way down the aisle, hoping to run into Dusk or Dawn, but Indigo was two steps ahead of me.

"Queen Leila." She propped her hands up on her hips and locked her knobby knees. "You've got an appointment this afternoon with an accountant, and you *need* to eat a proper meal—no more of these plastic-smelling protein bars or beef jerky."

I sighed with enough angst to make a TV soap opera star proud and followed the brownie as she led the way out of the stables. "It's fine," I said.

"You say that too much."

"It's my catchphrase! Every queen needs one."

Indigo gave me "the look," which she leveled at me whenever I was being cheeky and she wanted to blast me but remembered at the last second I was technically her queen.

The look consisted of her eyebrows lowering to give her a particularly unimpressed expression, matched with her mouth screwing up as if she had just sucked on a lemon. It was fun to know I was so charming I could inspire the expression!

"What you need is a cup of tea," Indigo decided once we reached the shadow of the mansion.

I snorted as I followed her inside. "Oh, heck no." I had to pause and blink, the brightness from the sun half blinding me now that I was in the shade. "I'm not drinking any tea. I'll make an online grocery order first."

"If you have special dietary needs tell the kitchen and they'll send someone out," Indigo said.

"No, I don't want anyone touching my food."

Indigo might have pushed the matter, but we rounded a corner and almost plowed into a crowd of nobles.

Yeah, that was one thing I was having a hard time adjusting to.

Since I was the queen, the whole Court revolved around me. As a result, the lower floor of my new home was a common place for nobles to laze about.

Totally weird.

And yeah, their presence irked me—not because I minded them being there as much as I found it stupid they apparently had all this free time to just stand around and gossip.

"Queen Leila, how pleasant to see you out and about." One of the nobles smiled and approached me, but the angle of his lips was more predatory than welcoming.

"Good morning." I glanced down at Indigo to see if she could help me get out of this, but she'd retreated a few steps so she was standing a little behind me, her eyes lowered and her hands gripping the bottom of her cable knit sweater—today's was purple.

No help there. I'll have to get us out of this on my own.

"You have such splendid timing. My name is Lord Argyos, and I was just discussing with my fellows how I should introduce you to my son. I'm sure you'd find him delightful." He took a step nearer, making him uncomfortably close. "He'd be a perfect marriage candidate."

I blinked three times as I reviewed what he had said in my brain just to double check I wasn't completely off base.

"Oh dear," he sneered. "I seem to have confused Queen Leila. Or were you merely surprised my noble house would deign to align itself with you?"

Because Lord Argyos was recommending his son, I was almost

positive his family was *not* great or noble, but I smiled anyway as the handful of nobles at his back twittered with laughter.

"No, not at all," I said when they quieted. "I was merely marveling at your parenting instincts. I was unaware it was a fae custom to go around offering your children in marriage. But it doesn't matter, because now isn't the best time for me."

I moved to step around him, but Lord Argyos managed to move with me, blocking me from passing as his smile grew an angry twitch to it.

"Really, I must insist. You have failed to socialize with anyone since your arrival several days ago. It might be good for you to meet someone close to your age—it would be good for the future of the Night Court as well," he said.

I eyed the fae noble, unimpressed.

If life were fair, Mr. Pushy here would look like a woodchuck that fell in a grease vat, but no. He was fae—which meant he had flawless skin, long, flowing hair with not a strand out of place, and the long, lean body models would kill for.

"As I said, now isn't the best time," I repeated, my voice hardening. "I haven't even attended a formal social event yet. I'm not thinking about who I'm going to marry."

"You just need to meet him. He is *charming*," Lord Argyos said in a way that made me certain his son was probably really skilled at love potions—or something similar.

Mental note: stay way far away from this basket case and his kid.

"No thanks. I'm busy—step aside," I said.

Anger burned in Lord Argyos's eyes. "But I insist."

I heard footsteps somewhere behind me, and I moved, intending to put my back at a wall. "I said no."

"You ought—"

"What's this, pressuring *my* darling daughter? I'll not have that."

CHAPTER TEN

Leila

Both Lord Argyos and I turned to face the intruder on our confrontation, who had come up behind me.

A fae noble who appeared to be maybe in his mid-thirties grinned invitingly at both of us. He had the fashionable long hair of the fae, but his was such a dark black color it almost had a hint of blue to it, and he had it pulled back in a ponytail.

His clothes were more of a fashionable human style than the classy, stuffy theme the fae adopted with his black slacks, dress shoes, and light blue dress shirt. He'd casually rolled his sleeves up to his elbows, and a pair of aviator sunglasses perched on top of his head.

All in all he was your typical handsome fae, but there was something about him I just didn't like on sight.

"What's this you're saying, Lord Linus?" Lord Argyos asked.

The new arrival—Lord Linus—slapped Argyos on the shoulder, making the other fae stagger slightly. "I'm saying I'll meet your strapping young lad first, to see if he's worthy!"

"And who are you?" I asked as dread made my stomach flop in my gut.

No, it couldn't be.

Lord Linus grinned broadly at me. "Why, I'm your father, my sweet daughter!"

Unfathomable anger ripped through me, and I struggled for a moment, trying to keep a roar of rage in.

Lord Linus took the opportunity to neatly send Lord Argyos on his way.

"*You?* The father of our queen?" Lord Argyos snorted. "We really are all doomed if she's at all like you."

"I assure you we're nothing alike," Lord Linus said. "But I never liked you to begin with, so I'm still wishful that you take yourself and your minions elsewhere—someplace we are not."

Lord Argyos's cronies were murmuring between themselves—probably trying to decide if this obviously crazy guy really was my father.

It had to be a lie. He must be using a loophole so he could say it. There was no way he could abandon my mother years ago, only to pop up once he found out I was queen.

"Go on. Shoo!" Lord Linus flapped his hands at Lord Argyos and his cronies. They retreated about halfway down the hallway, stopping frequently to look back at us.

"Now, as for you, my darling daughter..." Lord Linus turned around and flung his arms wide. "Why don't you greet me, your father who has missed you all these years, with all love and joy—"

For the first time in my entire life, I saw red.

I'd never been this furious before.

I'd always hated my biological father, but in this moment I *despised* him. How dare he sweep in as if I'd been anxiously waiting for him—as if *he* wasn't the reason that I'd never seen him—and, most maddening of all, as if he was my dad, and not Paul.

WHAM!

With instincts I didn't know I possessed, I grabbed a massive beeswax candle off a wooden stand on a side board and slammed it upside Lord Linus's head.

The cylindrical candle snapped in half, and Lord Linus made a pained gurgle and staggered a few steps.

"Daughter?" he tried once he could finally speak again.

I dropped the bottom half of the candle, and it took several long moments before I was able to unclench my hands from the fists they'd curled into. "*Never* call me that again." I stormed off before he could answer.

Lord Linus waited for a moment, then trotted after Indigo and me. "But that's what you are—my daughter."

I pulled my phone out, found my mom's number on my speed dial list, and called her.

"Leila—don't you want a tearfully fond reunion?" Lord Linus asked as he trailed behind.

I ignored him and listened impatiently to the ringing of my phone. I scowled at Lord Argyos when I passed him and his friends in the hallway.

They were all watching the unfolding drama with unabashed glee, snickering and laughing with one another.

Finally, Mom picked up. "*Hello! You're calling me early today,*" she said with her usual sunshine.

"Mom, what's the name of the fae you married?"

"*You're referring to your biological father?*"

I barely held in a growl. "Yes."

"*Linus. Actually, Lord Linus. Did he come visit you? He said he was going to.*"

"You've *spoken* to him?" I asked, incredulous.

"*Well, yes. I thought he should know you'd been chosen as the new Queen of the Night Court since it* is *his people you're ruling*," Mom said with a rare bit of wryness.

"You've been in contact with him? Why?"

"While I gave you the option of pursuing a relationship with him, he still wanted to know how you were. He is your father—"

"No, he is *not*," I stressed. "Paul is my dad. He's my only dad. This kook here is in no way a father to me. He's…" I turned around, and when Lord Linus smiled at me, it physically hurt to recognize that I did look a lot like him.

My black hair had more of a purple shine to it, but we were both tall and built leanly. Most condemning, though, were his purple-ish eyes—which I had never seen on another fae except when I looked in a mirror.

But he looks like he's barely thirty-five!

"Here. Hold on a second." I impulsively minimized the call and opened up my camera application. I snapped a shot of Lord Linus, who smiled obligingly, then sent it off to my mom. "Is that really him?"

"Hold on a moment, let me check." Mom was quiet for a few moments, then she said, *"Oh my."*

"It's not him?"

"No—that's Linus. He looks good—I don't know if he's aged more than five years since we met! Tell him he looks great."

I could barely believe what Mom was saying.

She didn't sound love addled or hurt, just a friendly sort of factual.

How could she be friendly to the fae that had abandoned her with their toddler?

"Oh, I heard that!" Lord Linus brightened. "Hello, Bethany! Thank you for the compliment," he shouted at me and my phone.

I turned my back to the obnoxious lord, and hurried down the hallway, taking the shortest route to the nearest staircase. "Why didn't you tell me?"

"Because I knew you'd tell me not to."

"Then why would you still tell him?"

"Honey, you're the Night Queen." My mom's voice lost its bright shine and turned serious. *"There are going to be nobles going after you*

with everything they've got. Linus, absentee as he might have been, doesn't want you to die. You're his daughter, and he does care for you in his own complicated way."

"Yeah, sure. I believe that," I drawled.

"*I know you resent him for how he treated us, but you don't have many allies right now. Linus knows how the Courts work. He can help you.*" She paused, then added with a hint of wryness, "*And if all else fails, use him as a shield and hide behind him if someone tries to hurt you.*"

I laughed, and something in me relaxed. "I wish you would have warned me."

"*You'd have done everything in your power to stop me. And I am your mother, Leila. I want what's best for you.*"

We said our goodbyes, and I reluctantly hung up just before I reached the first major staircase—which was carved out of obsidian rock.

I turned around and scowled at Lord Linus—who'd followed behind the whole way. "What do you want?"

"Only to help you, my darling daughter—"

"I already told you, don't call me that."

He shrugged and slid his hands into the pockets of his slacks. "I'm here to volunteer my services—and knowledge." When he glanced at me this time his purple eyes seemed sharp, and his smile was slightly crooked. "You need an advisor."

"I do," I acknowledged. "But there's no way I want you filling that job. Who knows when you'll just *abandon* your position?"

Lord Linus's selfishness must have known no boundaries. He didn't flinch at my jab, just laughed. "Having a flight-risk advisor is better than having none at all. Or didn't you know—most monarchs have a handful of advisors. You don't have any—has anyone even offered yet?"

I shrugged. "It's just a matter of time—they'll want to start trying to control me and use me for their own ends."

Lord Linus spread his hands out in front of him. "Except who would be a better choice than your own father?"

"You are *not* my father," I said bluntly. "My dad's name is Paul, and he lives out in the country with my mom. You are a total stranger. I have no reason to trust you—particularly given your past actions."

Lord Linus shrugged. "I'm no more a stranger to you than anyone else in our Court. And as little as you like to claim your blood, the fact is I am the last of a powerful fae house. As your advisor, I can help you. Your steward may know what needs to be done to keep your mansion functioning, and your companion can dress you appropriately, but *I* have personal relationships and know the dirty underside of the noble houses. I can help you rule."

No, absolutely not. This guy obviously has no morals, or he wouldn't have abandoned Mom and me. Who knows what his angle is—he might be here just because another noble is making him. And—

"All I would ask for in return is a little financial compensation," Lord Linus continued.

I narrowed my eyes. "What?"

"Times are difficult for the Night Court," Lord Linus said. "Most of the nobles are struggling. And perhaps I have had a moment or two of folly…"

"What are you talking about?"

Lord Linus shrugged. "Fae socials are dead boring. To lighten the atmosphere it is common to wager a bit of money on cards or a game or some such thing."

Oh my gosh. It's not enough that my Court is deep in debt, my biological father is a gambler. I shut my eyes and tried to think of happy things—my cute night mares, my pool-sized bath tub, my giant arse bed…

If I let him run around loose, he's going to cause me more trouble. And if I'm paying him and he desperately needs the money at least that will keep the power balance. He won't be able to hold his position as my bio father over me.

"It's confirmed." I rolled my neck back and stared up at the ceiling. "Fae are regency era wastrels and rogues."

"What was that, Queen Leila?" Indigo asked.

"Nothing." I sighed and scowled at Lord Linus. "I accept your offer of becoming an advisor. *But* I am going to strictly monitor your finances and actions, and you're staying in the mansion." *Where Chase can keep an eye on you and I can keep you leashed.*

Lord Linus bounced up and down on the balls of his feet. "Splendid! The old family home needs some repairs and, er, furniture. And the utilities were all turned off…"

I rubbed my temple. "Just how *deep* in debt are you?"

Lord Linus airily laughed. "I'll just find your steward so she can assign me a room—you hired Thales's granddaughter, didn't you? No matter, I can ask one of the servants." He paused in a doorway just long enough to turn around and wave to me. "I look forward to spending more time with you, daughter!"

"I said don't call me that!"

I was too late; he was already waltzing through the door, totally ignoring me.

I felt exhausted as he disappeared. "He's got to be neck deep in debt."

"To the gills, I reckon," Indigo agreed.

I groaned and sagged against the stair banister. "Just my luck."

Indigo shuffled her feet. "Do you need anything?"

I lethargically stared at a painting of a delicate fae dancing around a tree. "Yes. A latte—or a burger. Maybe a grilled steak."

"I'll place an order with the chef."

"No! Sorry, I was kidding." I rocketed upright and gave Indigo the strongest smile I could muster.

Indigo suspiciously peered up at me. "The chef would be gratified to cook you something. The whole kitchen is in an uproar because you won't eat."

I shook my head. "No. I—"

My stomach took that very inopportune time to rumble with enough strength I felt it in the back of my throat.

Indigo raised one judgmental eyebrow at me.

"I'll just go back to my room for a snack," I said.

"Would you like tea?"

"No, thank you."

Indigo put her fists on her hips. "If I bring you a water bottle and a bag of peas or something, will you eat it?"

"If they're unopened, yes."

Indigo nodded, making the bun of her thick hair bob. "Fine. I'll go get you something—and risk angering the chef further. I'll bring it up to your room." She marched off, her shoulders stiff with resolve.

"Thank you, Indigo!"

She waved, and slipped through the same door Lord Linus had.

I smiled fondly and climbed the first step of the stairs. I glanced around the room once more, freezing when I noticed something at the edge of the room.

My brain didn't have enough time to identify Lord Rigel, the Wraith, before he stepped out of the shadow cast by the staircase.

His eyes, black and soulless, were trained on me. Today he wasn't wearing his fancy jacket or scarf, and I could see his annoying aristocratic features including a long, perfect nose, high cheek bones, and a strong jaw.

I didn't see any weapons on him—but he still wore leather bracers over his long sleeved, charcoal gray shirt.

Hopefully that meant he wasn't here to kill me?

My nerves sloshed unhelpfully around my stomach as he approached me.

He stopped about ten feet away and didn't bow or incline his head to me unlike every other fae I'd met. Instead he looked me over from head to toe. "No screaming today?" he asked in a voice that was simultaneously rich and almost smoky.

I shrugged—or I *tried* to shrug. It took a second attempt to make my shoulders move. "You're not the scariest thing in the mansion." I was impressed with myself because my voice didn't shake.

The Wraith nodded. "You're right." He glanced at the door Indigo and Lord Linus had disappeared through and showed no inclination to move.

"Do you make it a habit to just lurk in the shadows, or is that part of your aesthetic?" I blurted out, my nerves removing the filter between my brain and my mouth.

He shifted his gaze back to me, and I deeply regretted speaking. "Call it an occupational hazard."

I waited, but he didn't leave. "Are you here to try killing me again?" I boldly asked.

The Wraith blinked. "You are my queen. I cannot raise a hand against you."

"That doesn't mean you won't attempt it," I said. "Why are you here?" I asked.

The silence stretched just long enough to make me start to sweat before the Wraith answered. "Curiosity."

I think his honesty is the most terrifying thing about him, I realized. *All the other fae feel like they have to thinly veil their hatred. But the Wraith is so powerful, he doesn't care what I know.*

I cleared my throat. "Curiosity about…?"

He stared at me.

"It's a legitimate question," I said. "There's a lot for you to be curious about. In fact, I wish there was *less* for you to be curious about."

He turned away. "I'll see you again, Queen Leila."

"I'd rather not," I grumbled.

He must have heard me because he turned to look back at me, his eyes extra dark and soulless.

I'll admit it. I was weak.

I leaned against the stair railing when I could feel that I was teetering a little under his gaze, but I refused to fully give in to my fear, so I gave him the most obnoxious, joyful wave that I could, nearly dislocating my arm in my fake enthusiasm.

The Wraith blinked, then glided out of the room with an unnatural soundlessness.

I felt all the air leave my lungs with a collective exhale, then plopped down on the stair.

That was terrifying. And just think, I have all of this and more to look forward to for the rest of my life.

I shook my head, dislodging the pessimistic thought from my mind. "That's not a help," I muttered to myself, needing to hear the words out loud.

I stood up and brushed my dress off, then made myself climb the stairs and head back to my bedroom to wait for Indigo.

I wasn't going to be beaten. Not by my Court, not by the Wraith, and not by myself.

CHAPTER ELEVEN

Leila

"And who is this?" Skye flipped her tablet around, displaying a picture of the beautiful blond fae who'd made the outcry when the Court first saw me.

"Lady Chrysanthe." I rested my hands on the delicate wooden table I was seated at, feeling a bit like a kid in school, even though I was sitting in a stupidly lavish sitting room. "Lady Demetria's granddaughter, and one of my haters."

Skye nodded and flipped the tablet around to select her next target.

She'd been quizzing me on nobles ever since I'd hired her, but the day I had my run in with Lord Rigel the Wraith she'd increased the memorization sessions significantly because the Paragon had contacted me to organize my first fae social as a royal —which was going to be held in two days.

"Lord Argyos," I said when she flipped her tablet back around.

Lord Linus—who was lounging on a couch and drinking a fae

alcoholic beverage, snorted with laughter. "No chance of forgetting him."

I shot him an impatient look. "Why are you here again?"

"I'm your advisor." He aimlessly dragged a finger through the air. "I'm here to advise!"

I rolled my eyes but turned back to Skye.

Before my steward could select the next noble, there was a rap on the door, and Indigo poked her head in.

"Great news!" Her eyes shone as she scurried inside, an excited spring to her step. "The Day King is here!"

I frowned. "What? Why? Did one of my loitering nobles invite him?"

It seemed I was the only one who was concerned about his presence. Skye actually stood straighter, her delicate features flashing first with surprise and then her golden cheeks getting a pink hue. "The Day King is here? To meet with Queen Leila?"

Lord Linus actually hopped to his feet. "Excellent! Solis is a good sort. Leila, you need to go down and greet him!"

"He's requested an audience with you, Queen Leila," Indigo said.

"This is an excellent opportunity." Skye clapped her hands together once. "King Solis is the best tempered monarch in our region, and the Day Court is a place of warmth and beauty. If you can make a favorable impression on him, it will do much for your reputation. That he's visiting you before you've even been publicly crowned is a great honor."

"Okay," I agreed.

The word was barely out of my lips before Skye and Indigo whisked me out of the room and escorted me through the mansion, with Lord Linus following on our heels.

I'd read up some on the Day King, King Solis.

He was beloved by his people and had a good reputation among the other Courts. He was adored, however, by humans.

Not that I blamed them. He was the Day King. I'd caught

glimpses of him when attending a party at the Drakes', and he was handsome in a celebrity kind of way, and seemed pretty charismatic.

That's why I was prepared when Skye and Indigo practically shoved me into the sitting room where the Day King was waiting.

He was as handsome as humans made him out to be with braided hair the same warm, golden color as the morning sun, and the timeless beauty of a fae. He looked like he was maybe in his early forties due to some fine lines around his eyes, but they seemed to give his face a sort of warmth and realness that most fae—with their flawless skin and stoic expressions—lacked. In reality, he was probably a lot older than his forties, given that my own biological father appeared to be in his mid-thirties.

The Day King stood when we entered the room, revealing that he was actually taller than me, and making his robes—made of gold and red silk—rustle with the movement.

"Queen Leila of the Night Court," Skye bowed first to me, then swiveled and bowed again to my royal visitor. "King Solis of the Day Court."

King Solis smiled, making him even more dazzling. "Queen Leila," he said. "It is my honor."

"The honor is all mine, King Solis." I evaded an end table that held a stoneware tea set that was glazed jade green, and made my way to the star patterned chair directly across from the wooden chair he'd been sitting in.

Now that I stood closer to him, I could see he wore a gold circlet studded with red and orange gems threaded through his hair, and the crest of the Day Court—a rising sun—was embroidered into his robes.

"Thank you for seeing me today." He sat down in the chair, somehow able to make it seem throne-like even though it was unadorned and simple in design. "I'm sorry for dropping in with no prior notice."

"I'm a new...queen," I said—I still wasn't quite able to say the title without stumbling over it. It still felt foreign, and like a lie. "I'm highly gratified you deigned to visit me at all."

King Solis smiled slightly, but didn't comment on my honesty. "I actually wanted to thank you."

Surprised, I furrowed my brow. "For what?"

"Fax," he said, naming the older sun stallion I'd elected to keep. "My steward told me you were selling all but the oldest sun stallion and submitted the deals through us to broker a proper buyer."

He met my gaze, and the honesty and warmth in his eyes was shocking. "He said you'd chosen to keep Fax, and that your stable managers said you wished to provide him with a comfortable home for the remainder of his life."

"He's in great health—he still gets ridden and exercised," I said.

"Yes, but I'm aware he's of the age where he shouldn't join in on the races—possibly even the hunts," King Solis said.

Just how many races and hunts do the fae hold?!

"And I know some Courts would be unwilling to have the expense of keeping a sun stallion if it could not be shown off," King Solis added.

"Yes, well, I take pet ownership as a serious charge—and he seems to get along great with the night mares. I'm happy to provide a home for him."

King Solis leaned back in his chair. "I'm glad as well. It seems like the Night Court finally has a good queen."

"I'm not certain my subjects would agree with you there," I said plainly—it wasn't like the entire fae race didn't know my human blood horrified my nobles.

"As you said, you are a new queen. You need time to grow into your role," King Solis said. "But I am greatly encouraged."

I blinked—a little surprised by the king's warm but frank manners, which went against everyone else I'd met in this mess. "Encouraged?"

"The Day Court and Night Court are inescapably linked due to our shared natures," King Solis said. "We're the opposite faces on the same coin. When the Night Court suffers, so does the Day Court. And the Night Court has not been well for...some time."

It's pretty telling how bad things are when a king from a totally different Court is concerned for you.

I pressed my fingertips together as I carefully considered my next words. "I didn't know the Day Court and Night Court were dependent. I always admired the Day Court when I was a kid."

I'd actually spent years wishing my fae blood came from the Day Court and not the Night Court, but I didn't need to unload on him like this was a therapy session.

"The Day Court is, thankfully, thriving now. But I'm aware things could get worse." He waited until I met his gaze before continuing. "If you should need any advice—or a word from someone experienced—I should be honored to guide you."

"Thank you." I smiled at the king. "I appreciate it."

King Solis frowned slightly, furrowing his forehead so his golden eyebrows knit together. "In fact, I suppose now is as good a time as any to warn you. In late July we'll have the annual Magiford Midsummer Derby. During which, you'll meet all of the Court monarchs in the Midwest. Make sure you stay clear of the Autumn King." He slightly shook his head. "He can be a poor sport."

That big of a jerk, is he?

I resolved to ask Skye about the Autumn King—and what the heck the Magiford Midsummer Derby was—as King Solis stood.

"But I've taken enough of your time." He twitched his robes straight and graced me with another smile as warm and mellow as sunshine. "Please allow me to say again that I am delighted with the dedication you have shown Fax—and that you are the Queen of the Night Court."

"Thank you," I said. "I hope together my stable manager and

your people can find the rest of the sun stallions wonderful homes."

I reached the door first and opened it, revealing Eventide—who was quivering a little—Skye and her tablet, and Lord Linus—who had gotten himself a paper straw with watermelons on it and was sipping at what was probably his third refill of his alcoholic beverage.

When Eventide saw King Solis he threw himself into a deep bow. "P-please excuse the interruption, King Solis, Queen Leila."

"No worries, Eventide. We're finished." I turned around to the king. "Can you find your way out, King Solis?"

"I can show King Solis to his car," Skye volunteered, offering a little bow to both of us.

I smiled. "Great, thanks, Skye."

King Solis winked. "In that case, good day to you, Queen Leila."

Lord Linus slurped his drink as he reached the bottom of his cup. "See? Charismatic as money he is."

I ignored Lord Linus and smiled at Eventide. "Did you need something, Eventide?"

The faun blushed a little and gave me a shy smile. "Only to inform you that your online grocery order has arrived."

"Grocery order?"

I hadn't seen Indigo until she spoke—she'd been perched on the edge of the marble base of a giant deer statue, glued to her phone.

"Yes, my food!" I pumped an arm in the air. "Thanks, Eventide!"

Indigo pushed her glasses up her nose and scowled as she followed me to the kitchens. "You ordered food from a grocery store when you have a kitchen staff?"

"Yep!"

Indigo looked like she wanted to say something, but she pursed her lips and held it in.

I glanced at her, but rather than try to tease her thoughts from her, I doubled my pace.

I wanted to get my food before it sat out very long, giving anyone the chance to enchant it.

I was sure Indigo and everyone else thought I was nuts, but I figured prevention was worth it. Maybe once I had a better rapport with my people, I could eat without being afraid—I was starting to feel a little bad about this, anyway.

Actually, I felt like a monster when Skye asked me to teatime the previous day and I just had water while she and Indigo drank tea and glanced longingly at the refreshments that they had to refrain from eating if I did.

Baby steps. I just met a nice fae king—something I didn't know was possible. We'll count this as a win. Which is something I need, given that my first social is coming. I hope it's not a disaster.

They wouldn't try to humiliate me in front of the Paragon again, would they?

Either way, I was about to find out.

―――

THE NIGHT of my first official social as Queen of the Night Court, my stomach pretty much never stopped doing somersaults in my gut.

Azure—my chauffeur—drove me to the location of the social with Indigo riding in back with me and Skye sitting up front lobbing last minute names at me.

She'd worked with me the entire time I got ready—all while Indigo had threaded black pearls through my hair and then pinned it in place, and even when the diligent brownie had stuffed me into my dress and shoes for the night.

Apparently I had to match my night themed mansion, because she'd selected black shoes, a black clutch, and a beautiful dark blue dress with a black lace overlay and black pearls beaded around the off the shoulder sleeves and neckline.

I was pretty chuffed about the clutch. Hazel Medeis had told me how she once beat off a wizard with her clutch. I'd chosen to stuff mine with the can of bear mace Dad bought me when my college gym class/self-defense instructor recommended it, and my charm bracelet that served as my artifact so I could use magic in a pinch.

I knew Chase and his newly hired guards—he'd fired a bunch of the old crew who had served Queen Nyte—were going to be stationed around the restaurant. But it was really confidence building to know you were carrying bear mace, which was capable of taking down a grown fae!

The car rolled to a stop, and I opened the door before Azure could hop out and do it for me. Indigo reacted with a grunt, but Skye never stopped talking.

"And as for Lady Korinna—"

"I shouldn't mention the store she runs on Main Street since Queen Nyte once visited and ruined a display, then later raised a fuss about a noble working for a living—talk about *stupid*. Instead I should invite her out to the mansion and imply I would appreciate her thoughts on the stable since she is an accomplished horsewoman," I said.

"Yes. Although you should perhaps refrain from mentioning the stable almost exclusively holds night mares now," Skye said. "And what of Lady Lysandra?"

"Avoid her like the plague since she has a thing for Lord Linus and probably isn't going to forgive me for being born." I shivered and looked around as if saying his name could summon Lord Linus.

He was here tonight—I didn't think he'd miss the chance to publicly remind everyone whose daughter I was. Plus, since the food and alcohol were free, he would have been here with or without me.

"Excellent. You've done well. Let's go in." Skye motioned for me to lead the way inside since Azure had dropped us off right at the curb.

"Okay—thanks, Azure." I twisted around long enough to wave at my chauffeur—which still felt bizarre to even *think*.

She bowed her head to me, bringing out a shimmery dark blue hue in her aqua colored hair.

I smiled at her, then stepped through the gateway of the wooden fence that surrounded the restaurant.

It was a beautiful Italian restaurant that was fairly large and overlooked one of the lakes that squatted in downtown Magiford. They had a pretty garden with a bunch of outside seating that was illuminated by twinkling fairy lights and beautiful lanterns.

Based on the delicious smells, the buffet had been set up outside since the weather was nice and mild—warm, but with a cool breeze that rolled in off the lakes.

My stomach growled at the scent of basil and garlic. *I should be able to eat here, right? The fae aren't making the food, the restaurant is, and it's human owned and run.* I pressed my clutch into my stomach as if I could forcibly make it shut up, but it only growled louder.

"Ahh, there she is—the woman of the hour!" The Paragon strolled up to me. He was wearing his typical robes, but I was most drawn to the gray baby sling he was wearing, and the pink, hairless head that popped out of the top.

"Hello, Paragon." I dipped my head in reverence. "Thank you for organizing this dinner for my Court and me." I tried to look him in the face, but my eyes kept getting drawn back to the animal sitting in the sling.

It took me a few quick glances before I realized it was a pink skinned, hairless cat peering up at me with a wrinkled forehead.

"Yes, yes, of course! It's my pleasure—you have been plunked down in the middle of things. But the only reason I could do this without ruffling any feathers is because of the Day King, you know! When word got out I was doing this, he took the other monarchs to task and said you deserved it since you were half human and still adjusting to your own kind, much less your new station. He told me he found you charming when he visited my personal study the other day—he likes to do that a lot, and he doesn't shut up." The Paragon squinted at me. "I hope with you around he'll stop fretting that the Night Court is going to bring about the destruction of the Day Court, too."

He seemed to expect an answer, so I ripped my fascinated gaze from the yawning hairless cat—its expression making it closely resemble a goblin. "Yes, I'll do my best."

"Oh, listen to me, gabbing on when I ought to introduce you. Queen Leila, this is my dearest darling, Aphrodite."

"Hello, Aphrodite." I held out my hand, and Aphrodite sniffed it before rubbing her forehead against my fingers. Her skin was a weird sensation. "Do you often bring her to social events?"

"No—she's a magical cat, you know. Very choosy about who she wishes to associate with. Naturally she doesn't want to come to most socials. When I told her about you, however, she insisted. I knew you'd be delighted to have her bless you with her presence!" The Paragon beamed.

It's always reassuring to meet someone who is even more of an animal nut than I am. It makes me realize I'm really not so bad after all.

"She's very beautiful," I said.

"Thank you! It's refreshing to meet someone who can see that!" The Paragon huffed. "But as much as Aphrodite and I enjoy your company, we must move on—there are still a few last-minute details we must see to. We won't be long, though!" He wiggled his fingers at me and wheeled off, barging through the crush of fae that were slowly meandering into the restaurant.

Rather than push my way inside, I moved to the edge, nodding and greeting the lords and ladies I recognized from Skye's quizzing and picture games.

"What's this?" Indigo muttered under her breath as I slowly

edged closer and closer to the buffet. "Are you actually considering eating *hot* food?"

I grinned at my companion. "Shocking, isn't it? But I think the food here will be safe."

"Indeed, it will be," Skye said.

"And if it can get you over your paranoia, that's all the better," Indigo said.

"What was that?" I asked.

"Hmm? I didn't say anything." Indigo innocently adjusted her sweater—she was wearing a cute black one matched with a flowered skirt tonight.

The food was a call that I couldn't ignore, tugging me forward as I salivated like a dog.

When I finally rounded the hedge that partially screened the buffet from the seating area, I almost ran into Lady Chrysanthe and Lord Myron—the dark haired friend of hers who had tried applying for the position of steward, most likely at her suggestion. A few other young fae nobles were with them, but they were clearly the ringleaders.

"Queen Leila." Lady Chrysanthe looked like she'd stepped out of a magazine advertisement with her sleek navy blue dress and heels that were one of those designer brands I didn't know the name of because I'd die before I spent that much money on shoes when I could instead buy a latte twice a day for about a year.

"Lady Chrysanthe and Lord Myron, good evening." I smiled slightly, following the polite protocol Skye had *deeply* impressed upon me. "Thank you for coming to this celebration."

"Queen Leila," Lord Myron said reluctantly—as if it pained him. He was a mixture of fae fashion and human history with his long hair pulled back in a braid and his patterned silvery vest and pocket watch that looked more historical than modern.

"It's such a shame." Lady Chrysanthe made a show of looking around the tiny inlet of the garden. "Normally the Queen of the Night Court's first social would be in the Night Palace with all of its splendor, rather than a small and unsophisticated location." The tilt of her lips was cruel as she smiled at me. "But perhaps it's fitting for you. It's a good match to you, because you aren't a real fae."

Lady Chrysanthe's minions twittered with laughter and hid their smiles behind raised hands as they whispered to one another.

Skye inhaled sharply, hinting that this was a pretty low insult, which made me alter my reaction.

"I know, right? I'm *so glad* I'm not, too." I rolled my eyes and gave Lady Chrysanthe and Lord Myron an off-tilt smile that I knew was more relaxed than a typical fae smile. "I wake up every morning filled with gratefulness that I'm only half fae! I imagine that's why my life is as good as it is—or was." I frowned. "My luck has changed a lot for the worse the past few weeks—obviously."

Lady Chrysanthe stared at me, her hand frozen from where she'd brushed her fingers against the white chrysanthemums tucked into her hair. "Are you an idiot?" she asked.

"Nah. I just don't care what you think. At all. Or ever." I winked at her and raised my hands to perform a cheesy rendition of jazz hands.

Lady Chrysanthe blushed pink in her anger. "You're going to deserve every ounce of misery you get," she growled—don't get too impressed. She sounded like a hissing kitten more than the angry tiger I suspect she was aiming for.

"Wow, judgy, are you?" I tapped my clutch on my hip as I made a show of looking contemplative. "Have you ever gone to therapy? Because I feel like a therapist could have a field day with all your anger issues."

Fury flashed across Lord Myron's face. "You dare to insult a member of fae nobility?"

Yes! This is the question I wanted!

I studied him with practiced nonchalance. "Are you saying I shouldn't, when you tried to insult your queen?" I smiled sharply.

"And note—I said *tried*. Because my human blood is never something I'll be ashamed of, unlike my fae half."

Lord Myron's flash of fury was threatening to settle into his face, and their crowd of followers had grown quiet with their anger, but it was Lady Chrysanthe—practically shaking with anger—who spoke. "You might think you're clever, but remember who you rule over. None of us are cowed by your attitude—it only serves to anger us more. You don't deserve your position, nor are you capable of fulfilling it."

"You're right," I agreed. "And yet, the night mares chose me over all of you. What does that say about you?"

A strangled silence settled over us—even the minions didn't make a noise.

Lady Chrysanthe turned her back to me. "Myron, we're going!" She marched through the crowd of her followers, rounding the hedge and rejoining the rest of the party attendees.

Lord Myron gave me a murderous look, but followed after Lady Chrysanthe and the rest of their party.

I sighed happily. "It's fun to rile her up."

Indigo watched the spoiled nobles leave with a speculative look.

"What is it?" I asked.

She bowed in a quick curtsey. "Nothing, Queen Leila."

I reoriented myself, following my nose around a few bushes before I saw the heaven that was a stuffed buffet table. "It's not nothing—you looked curious."

"I was merely impressed with your fortitude, Queen Leila," Indigo said.

"My fortitude?"

"I was also impressed with your conduct," Skye said. "You were calm but measured in your responses. Most would have taken serious offense to Lady Chrysanthe's words."

"Oh. Well, it's not like she said anything I wouldn't have expected—or anything that was worth getting upset over. And besides." I grabbed a plate and greedily scanned the table. "If I threw a fit, I knew you'd make me reread that book about 'Good Manners Mandy,' Skye. Did you know almost every line in that book rhymes? It reads like a Doctor Seuss book from your nightmares."

"I would never ask you to reread it, Queen Leila," Skye shook her head, and for the first time since I'd hired her, I saw the corners of her lips twitch. "I'd have you peruse the sequel, which follows the adventures of 'Polite Paul' and 'Rude Randy.'"

I froze, and even the tantalizing smell of Italian food couldn't drag me from gaping at Skye with horror. "Are you telling me there's a *series* of these books?"

"One for every possible mishap, yes."

I groaned. "That's awful. You should tell Chase—he can use them as punishment for any wrong-doers." I turned back to the buffet and pinned my clutch to my side with my elbow as I tried to decide what to go for first. I froze when I peered down to the end of the line and saw heaven: the dessert table.

I swiped up a cannoli, practically slobbering as my stomach rumbled. "Bless the Paragon for hosting the party here." I closed my eyes in mental preparation—as excited as I was, I couldn't scarf my food down—then took a big bite of the cannoli. The crunch of the rolled pastry and the smooth sweetness of the cream filling were delicious enough to make me hum in appreciation.

And then I felt the whispery brush of fae magic.

Oh, no.

My throat closed, and I couldn't breathe.

CHAPTER TWELVE

Leila

I tried to open my mouth to spit the cannoli out, but it felt like my teeth were glued shut.

It was spelled. What do I do?

I dropped my plate, and it shattered on the ground.

"Queen Leila?" Skye asked.

I fumbled with my purse, ripping it open and holding it upside down.

The bear mace fell out with a clank, my silver charm bracelet falling on top of it.

I dropped to my knees—my lungs were starting to burn, and the sweet cream filling was melting in my mouth and dripping down the back of my throat, but I couldn't clear my airways.

"What's wrong?" Indigo asked.

I grabbed my charm bracelet, then stared at it in horror.

I couldn't open my mouth, and I needed to speak to activate my bracelet and cast a dispel charm.

My throat clogged. My heart beat like a drum in my ears.

"Queen Leila?" Skye repeated.

I reached up and grabbed her hand, then pointed from the cannoli to my mouth.

"...I'm sorry?" Skye frowned, thoroughly puzzled.

"Something's wrong with the food." Indigo dropped to her knees next to me. "She's not talking."

Skye, her forehead wrinkling, twisted her ring which was topped with a pink diamond and muttered under her breath.

Fae magic swirled around the ring, wispy but bright as it sucked the wild magic out of the air and twisted it into something Skye could use.

My vision was blurring and black around the edges.

Skye crouched and held out her hand to me.

The whispery feeling of fae magic intensified, then abruptly faded, as if it had snapped.

I opened my mouth and spat out the bite of cannoli, coughing and gagging as I tried to clear my throat and breathe without inhaling my spit.

Several long moments passed before I finally managed to take in a gulp of air.

"Thanks," I gurgled.

"Happy to be of service." Skye watched me with a worried expression while she and Indigo peered at my face.

"I can't believe it!" I coughed and wiped my mouth off. "I was almost Snow White-ed. With a cannoli!"

Indigo was crouched next to me, her face tight with worry. "I'll get the Paragon."

"No!" I coughed again, grimacing at the new raspy feeling in my throat. "No," I repeated in a much quieter tone. "Tell Chase and get this food removed and checked, but don't tell *anyone*."

"Queen Leila, someone tried to kill you at your first official social function. This is very serious," Skye said.

"I know, but that's also why we can't let anyone know." I could finally breathe enough that my heart was slowing down, though the air still tasted faintly of the sweet cream filling.

Ugh. I don't know if I'll ever be able to eat another cannoli ever again.

"My first event, and my Court nearly succeeded in offing me?" I shook my head. "I don't know if it's feasible to ever get a good relationship with my Court, but *that* kind of opener is going to make them think I'm easy prey. No—we have to act like it didn't happen and see who is angry as a result."

Indigo and Skye exchanged looks.

"As you wish, Queen Leila," Skye said slowly.

I nodded and tipped my head back—thankful to be able to breathe again.

I thought I was taking this pretty seriously, but I guess not seriously enough. I can't cower from them and let them walk all over me—or I'll never survive long-term. But what can I do?

I glanced down at my charm bracelet. *Practicing magic would probably be my best option. I'm so-so at it, but if I want to survive I'll need to get a lot better. Preferably good enough to make charms that don't need words to activate, as it seems I'll be needing those.*

Indigo stood up and brushed off her skirt.

"One more thing," I said.

She bowed to me. "Yes, Queen Leila?"

"I don't want to hear another word about how upset my chef is," I said. "I almost died because I took a risk. I'm not going to be shamed for being proactive when my life is on the line."

Indigo's forehead wrinkled. "I'm sorry."

I waved my hand and stood up. "It's fine." I smiled, trying to appear at least a little friendly. "I just don't want to hear about it again."

Indigo bowed, then hurried around the corner of the hedge, disappearing from sight.

I sighed and brushed my gown off, looking for spots of dirt.

I survived my second assassination attempt. Now I just have to get through this party without letting anyone find out.

Chase proved that hiring him was possibly one of the best ideas ever.

He handled everything like a pro and had the food quietly removed before instructing the waitstaff to restock the buffet. He also pulled all the security camera footage and packaged up my half-chewed cannoli and sent one of his people—a fae—off with it to see if the magic used could be traced. He also personally accompanied Skye, Indigo, and me, and did all of this without raising any suspicions from the partying fae.

"You're a gem, Chase." I raised the water bottle—which he'd delivered to me unopened—to him in thanks.

It had been about two hours since the party started. The near brush with death put a real dampener on my appetite, so the smells were actually making my stomach turn, but I was thankful for the water.

Chase gave me a brief, professional smile. "I do my best, Queen Leila," he said before he got back to surveying the area.

We were seated off to the side, under the branches of a weeping willow that screened me off from the fae who'd been stopping by to get a view of their half human queen.

Thankfully, they'd become disinterested with me and were now busy talking amongst themselves. Lord Linus was laughing with a set of slightly older male fae, while Skye was mingling with a few of the less hostile lords and ladies I might actually stand a chance befriending. I'd told Indigo she could go eat, so it was just Chase and me at the moment...until the Paragon swooped in.

"Leila—there you are! How can you hide here when this party is all for you?" He pushed branches aside and peered at me. "Come, come. I have someone I want to introduce you to!"

The Paragon held out his hand, and when I took it he tugged me out of my chair.

"Who could be left to introduce me to?" I obediently followed him through the crowd. "I've met so many people, Skye felt safe leaving me alone."

"Ahh, yes, your steward is very diligent—I wanted to mention to you she was a good pick. Oh my, sorry, Aphrodite!" The Paragon, standing on his tiptoes to see above all the guests, almost stumbled into a bush, barely avoiding it in time to save his cat from getting poked.

He staggered around the bush, trying to regain his balance. "Ah-ha! There you are, Lord Dion—ew." He stopped abruptly, having interrupted a conversation.

I stepped around the Paragon, wondering what could have made him pause, and I was pretty sure my heart fell all the way down to my left foot.

The Paragon had pushed his way to two fae lords who were standing by one of the decorative lanterns, sipping beverages from crystal chalices.

One lord was classically handsome with crimson red hair which was cut short but partially covered by the black fedora he wore. His fashion style was more human—although his black tweed suit matched with the fedora had more of a vintage than modern feel to it. If all my name memorizing served me correctly, his name was Lord Dion.

But Lord Dion's fashion sense only caught my attention for a moment. Because the second fae lord was none other than Lord Rigel, the Wraith.

The Paragon made the noise of a balloon leaking air.

Can I duck out? I'm pretty sure Skye's manners books wouldn't approve, but chatting with a confirmed assassin who tried to kill me doesn't sound good for my health. Maybe he was the one who bespelled the food?

The red-haired lord stood straighter when he saw the Paragon. "Paragon." He smiled—a disarmingly mischievous grin with a glimmer that brightened his eyes. "I see you have returned."

"Yes, and I probably wouldn't have if I knew you intended to chat with someone else," the Paragon said. "Queen Leila, please allow me to introduce you to Lord Dion." He put his body between me and Rigel, but he was shorter and skinnier than the lean fae lord, so he didn't block much of my view.

"Queen Leila, it is a pleasure to meet you." Lord Dion smiled gallantly. He took my hand and—like a prince from a storybook—kissed my fingers.

Sounds romantic, right? I can't say I liked it considering I'd almost gotten offed like a fairy tale princess just a few hours earlier. I'd be happy to leave prince charming and poisoned apples/cannoli in the books, please, kthx.

"Good evening, Lord Dion." I spoke extra slow to buy myself some time to remember what Skye had told me about him.

I didn't need to bother because the Paragon took it upon himself to rattle off his personal history. "Lord Dion is the pride of the Night Court!" he said. "He runs a law practice in Magiford that serves both supernaturals and humans, he attended a human university, *and* he is the head of his family since his father passed away some years ago."

Why does the Paragon sound like he's a proud parent?

"You're a lawyer?" I asked.

Lord Dion laughed—an infectious sound. "Indeed, I am. You'll have to excuse my pride, but I dare say I'm skilled at it since I inherited a fae's way with words."

"I can imagine."

"Oh, please let me introduce you to my close friend, Lord Rigel." Lord Dion glanced at the Wraith with a rueful smile.

Today Lord Rigel was still wearing black boots, but to jazz it up for the occasion he'd switched to gray breeches and a black long-sleeved shirt.

Yeah, the color variety in his wardrobe was stunning.

My smile probably showed more teeth than necessary. "Ahh, yes, Lord Rigel, is it? Such a pleasure to officially meet you."

"Queen Leila." Lord Rigel sipped from his fancy chalice. "It is remarkable to finally be introduced to you."

"Oh, I'm sure. Our first meeting was *such* a surprise." I smiled at the man who tried to kill me and was tempted to tell him it was not as exclusive of a club as he might think, but I wasn't tipping my hand about anything. *Especially* to him!

"For all parties involved." Lord Rigel stared at me over the edge of his cup, his black eyes still as soulless as they had been in our previous meetings.

"And are you friends with Lord Dion?" I asked.

Lord Rigel shrugged, but Lord Dion threw an arm over his shoulders. "Of course we are! We've been friends since we were kids." He winked at me. "These socials are wretchedly boring if you don't have anyone to drink with. But with you as our queen, I expect that will change."

Lord Rigel swirled his cup. "Most likely in more ways than one."

"You know, Lord Rigel, your positive, can-do outlook is downright inspiring!" I bubbled, sounding excited and cheerful just because I knew it would irritate the assassin.

Hey, if I was stuck talking to him and making the clock tick down on my lifespan, I was at least going to have fun doing it!

"And you seem to have a remarkably changed opinion of me since our first meeting."

"As I told you last time we chatted, you're no longer the scariest thing I have to deal with."

The Paragon had sucked his neck into his shoulders as he watched us go back and forth, but he apparently had worked up the gumption to interrupt, because he jumped forward. "I told Lord Dion about your fondness for the night mares, Leila."

"Your devotion to them is admirable." Lord Dion's smile and pleasant voice were a stark contrast to his deadly friend. "I've heard you are selling all but one sun stallion?"

"Yes. Fax is staying—the night mares are incredibly fond of him," I confirmed.

"Lord Dion loves all types of animals!" the Paragon bragged. "He's very thoughtful toward creatures."

I took a sip from my water bottle as I watched the Paragon. "I see."

He sounds like a neighborhood matchmaker—wait...is that what this is? Does he want me to choose Dion as my husband?

"In case you're not keeping track, he's a fae lord, a lawyer with a successful practice, he loves animals, he's single, and he's handsome to boot! What a catch, right?" The Paragon winked at me.

Wow. He's certainly not trying to be subtle about it.

I took another swig of my water so I didn't have to answer.

Lord Dion laughed. "You can't talk about me like that, Paragon, or she'll have such great expectations for me I'll never be able to meet them." He flashed that smile of his. "And I would never want to disappoint Queen Leila."

Ahhh, he's in on this.

I glanced at Lord Rigel and was surprised to see that his eyes *could* hold something besides death: boredom.

His eyes were still a fathomless black, but the soulless look had faded due to the obvious boredom flickering across his face.

That's something to tuck away and remember later.

"You sound like a very inspiring person, Lord Dion." I finished my water because I'd been using it as a delay tactic for talking, so I looked around for a recycling container.

"Not at all, Queen Leila." Lord Dion gently took my bottle from me, his smile devastating. "I merely love my Court and wish for what's best for it."

And that's why he's willing to get saddled with a half human. I tried to smile back, but some of my bitterness might have leaked through. *I guess I can't complain. He's actually been decent, and I don't think the Paragon would recommend him like this if he didn't have a track record of it. I'd been hoping I'd be able to avoid thinking about the required marriage part of this job for at least a few more weeks, though.*

I opened my mouth, intending to say something, when someone crashed into me.

"*Paragon*," Lord Linus drawled. "I told you—no dragging my daughter off to secret meetings without me! Who knows what sort of *stuff* you'd get her involved in?" The dark haired fae peered at Lord Dion and Lord Rigel with suspicion. "Aha!" He pointed at Lord Rigel. "See?"

It's 100% confirmed. Lord Linus is a blockhead.

"I've told you *clearly*, Lord Linus, that you are not to refer to me as your daughter." I don't think Lord Dion and Lord Rigel could hear my teeth cracking as I gnashed them together, but the Paragon must have from the wide-eyed look he gave me.

"Oh, posh. Yes, Saul is your dad, but you're still my daughter—or we wouldn't be standing here!" Lord Linus said.

"His name is *Paul*."

"Yes, my apologies—Paul. Got it! I'll remember next time." He grinned at me, not at all chastised, then turned to Lord Dion. "Since everyone here is a dead bore, what say you, Lord Dion, to a game of cards? Perhaps a little wager, to make things interesting?"

I'm going to kill him.

I hefted my clutch and considered bludgeoning him or whipping out my can of bear mace. "*Lord Linus*."

The fae lord glanced guiltily at me. "Whoops. Sorry, daughter. I'll behave." He slightly shook his head, making the ponytail he kept his dark hair tied back in sweep over his shoulder. "So. What are we talking about?"

My throat ached dully as I made myself smile at Lord Dion. "It was a pleasure to meet you, Lord Dion. But it seems Lord Linus and I need to find my steward."

"Of course, Queen Leila." Lord Dion bowed slightly. "I look forward to meeting you again."

I glanced at Lord Rigel. "Next time you decide to visit the

mansion, Lord Rigel, I would appreciate it if you wore a bell or something."

"I'll keep that in mind."

I grabbed Lord Linus by the arm and dragged him away from the duo.

"Why are we going to find Skye?" Lord Linus asked. "She is a likable girl, but she strikes me as being a bit too proper for a good party. Makes things boring."

"We are going to find her because you need a babysitter," I growled.

"You know," the Paragon said, surprising me because I hadn't realized he followed us. "The day you were made queen, Killian told me you had guts, but I feel better now. You've got the fae spirit all right!"

Both Lord Linus and I frowned at the eccentric fae.

"You'll do quite fine," he predicted. "Just consider Lord Dion as your marriage partner—he's one of the few unspoiled and good ones. Toodles!" He waved to us and disappeared in the crush of the crowd.

My head started to hurt in addition to my throat. Weak, I gave in. "Chase?"

"Yes, Queen Leila?" The werewolf stepped out of the shadows, his yellow eyes gleaming in the dim light.

"Where is Skye?"

"Right this way, Queen Leila."

"Thanks." I followed after my director of security, names and information tumbling through my brain with every fae I passed.

That settles it. Someone tried to kill me tonight, I'm being set up for an arranged marriage, and Lord Linus is annoying!

Tomorrow, no matter what, I'm going to get myself some coffee!

"I'm glad it went well, sweetie!"

I juggled my phone to my other hand as I peered into the stall Twilight had taken over. He was hiding in the back, but when he saw me he perked his ears and walked through a skylight sunbeam to reach me. "Yeah, me too. I thought for sure there'd be a brawl—I was kind of hoping Lord Linus would get himself punched out. But the worst anybody did was sneer at each other."

I patted Twilight on the neck and ignored the prickle of my conscience.

I had decided not to tell Mom or Dad about the attempt on my life. It would only worry them, and for all of his sleuthing, Chase and his people hadn't been able to figure out for certain who had bespelled the food. Apparently the buffet lay just out of range of the restaurant's cameras, and they hadn't been able to pin down the magic—although they did confirm the spell was customized just for me. It wasn't dangerous for anyone else to eat.

Whoopie! Right?

"One second, honey. What?" Mom shouted directly into the phone. "Oh! Yes! Paul says you looked beautiful, and thanks for texting us the picture of you in your dress."

"Of course!" I moved down the stable, pausing to pet Fax since he had his head draped over his stall door. "I should probably go, though. Love you, Mom."

"Love you too, honey! Goodbye!"

The call disconnected, and I slipped my phone into a back pocket of my jeans, then stopped in front of Comet's stall to kiss the mare on her scratchy muzzle. "Okay, I'm out. I just wanted to check on you lovelies to make sure everyone is doing good."

I did a quick visual sweep of the stables—all of the sun stallions were gone now, except for Fax, obviously. My six night mares had claimed stalls as soon as they opened up, but mine weren't the only night mares, because over the past few days new night mares had appeared. Now, we were up to twelve.

I made my way back up the stable aisle, pausing when Eclipse bobbed her head invitingly at me. "Chase?" I called to my director of security—he was speaking in a lowered tone with Dawn, but when I called out he swiveled to face me with very precise and crisp movements.

"Yes, Queen Leila?"

"Can we head out yet?"

To celebrate the victory of surviving my first social—and because Skye and Indigo had the day off—I was busting out of this joint to pursue the worthiest of goals: coffee.

Specifically, coffee at my favorite café in Magiford, which was human owned and human run, so I'd be safe ordering there. That's why part two of my plan was to buy my weight's worth in breakfast sandwiches.

I was sick of eating jerky, protein bars, and raw fruits and veggies. It got old after the second week of it.

But I couldn't go out alone anymore, so I asked Chase to come with. I'd been hoping he was a coffee fan—no dice, I was still the sole coffee lover in my mansion—but he agreed to come with me anyway.

Chase bowed slightly. "I will notify Azure to pull the car up around the front—"

Eclipse screamed and banged on her door, making the hinges creak ominously.

"Hey, hey, what's wrong?" I soothingly stroked her neck as she pushed her head into my chest.

Since she seemed fine, I started to walk away.

This time Eclipse *and* Solstice screamed—their calls loud and piercing and very not-at-all-horse-like.

Chase thoughtfully studied them, slightly tilting his head in a very wolf-like manner.

Dawn rubbed her hands together, then asked in a voice loaded with tension, "Do you think they want to come with you?"

"Nah!" I laughed. "Why would the night mares want to go with me to get coffee?"

CHAPTER THIRTEEN

Leila

Turns out, they wanted to go with me to get coffee.

About half an hour later I was mounted up on Eclipse, squinting even though I wore sunglasses, as I studied Solstice—who was riderless but wearing a leather halter for our jaunt—and Chase—who was riding Fax.

The helmet I borrowed from Dawn was squeezing my head a little, and everything felt a little *off*. Eclipse was so skinny the saddle sat differently on her, but her movements were a lot smoother than I'd prepared myself for.

"Are we sure this is going to work?" I asked.

"Absolutely, Queen Leila." Dusk fed Solstice a chunk of carrot. "One of the reasons why the night mares are revered is because of their ability to make their own fae gates. They can walk into the Night Realm and then create another gate to drop you straight into the human realm. You just have to think of where you want the new gate to drop you."

"Yeah, but as much as I love my beauties, I don't know how well they're going to deal with all the noises and sights of downtown Magiford." I glanced nervously down at Eclipse, who was standing placidly.

Dusk brushed a leaf that was drooping over his right eye back into his hair. "It will be fine, Queen Leila."

"I don't want them to make a gate to the café and then get scared because they hear a car horn," I said.

Dawn joined her brother, and the two stood shoulder to shoulder. "In truth, Queen Leila, the time when the night mares were most likely to...*express* themselves is when you first mounted Eclipse." She glanced from Solstice to Eclipse, then added, "I don't believe Dusk or I have seen anyone ride the night mares since we were kids."

That explains why they were nervous when I first hopped on.

"They're long lived, have been ridden into battle, and have roamed the human realm at their leisure for the past decade," Dusk said. "They'll be fine."

Eclipse swished her tail, and Solstice rested his chin on my foot.

"Okay. I guess I'll have to believe in them." I twisted in the saddle to offer Chase a smile. "Are you ready for this?"

Chase grinned—he'd loosened up a bit since hopping on Fax. "Yes, Queen Leila."

Thankfully Chase already knew how to ride horses—don't ask me how that happened, because Chase didn't tell me in the scuffle of getting the horses ready—and Dusk and Dawn had assured me Fax could have a screaming child draped on his neck and the placid gelding wouldn't react.

"Right." I centered myself, then looked down at Eclipse's bony neck. "So...Eclipse...you want to do the thing?"

"Do the thing?" Dawn repeated, sounding shocked with my impressive wording.

"*I* don't know what to call it—"

I cut myself off when I felt magic—not the whispery-but-sticky sensation of fae magic, but the same magic I'd felt when I first met the night mares and they pressed their muzzles against my temple. It was faint, but strong—like the light of a distant star.

A hum—which may or may not have faintly reminded me of a lightsaber—made the air throb, before a stone archway and metal gate identical to the one in the garden assembled in front of us.

The door swung open, revealing the misty black interior.

"Ah. Yes. This doesn't at all seem like a bad idea," I said as Eclipse walked toward the door.

I hurriedly turned in the saddle to address Dusk and Dawn one last time. "I have my cellphone. I'll call you if I need you to come pick us up with the trailer!"

"Think of where you want to go," Dawn urged me.

"Gotcha!" I faced forward and thought of King's Court Café.

Riding through the gate on Eclipse was a far more pleasant experience than when the Paragon had sent me through solo.

I didn't experience that terrible sensation of not knowing up from down. Sitting on Eclipse's back with my legs pressed to her sides, I could feel her warmth and the leather saddle.

The darkness held more swirls of blue and purple, and instead of light streaking by, when I looked out I swear I saw *stars* glittering in a beautiful ocean.

And then Eclipse stepped into the Night Realm, popping us out in a grassy field just next to the dilapidated castle.

Think of King's Court Café, think of King's Court Café!

I hurriedly turned my thoughts to the pleasant and cute café—taking care to picture the café's building and drive through, because I did *not* want the night mares dumping us inside the café.

King's Court was pet friendly, but I was pretty sure that invitation didn't extend to horses inside the café.

Eclipse gave me about two seconds to breathe in the cool but stale night air of the Night Realm before snapping another stone archway in place in front of us.

More stars and clouds, and we were out, stepping into the parking lot King's Court Café shared with the nearby buildings.

"Wow." I blinked—my eyes were struggling to adjust from the craziness of moving from light to dark and back to light again. "That was a ride."

I turned Eclipse in a circle and craned my neck while looking around.

Yep, we were downtown all right.

King's Court was named after the little side street it crouched on, King's Court Drive. It was just around the corner from Main Street, which was the heart and soul of Magiford. From this angle, you could see Royal Beach—a small greenspace and a tiny public beach the city maintained along with the boardwalk that encircled almost all of the two lakes that rested along Main Street.

The closest lake, Fairy Lake—and no I'm not making this up, that's really the lake's name—sparkled extra under the intense summer sun.

I could smell the pastries from the French-style bakery just a few doors down, and even though it was mid-morning, the gelato store had a steady stream of customers coming in and out.

A car with a paddleboard tied to the roof slowed to a crawl when it saw Eclipse and me.

I waved and tried to look as nonchalant as possible—which I realized might not be convincing considering I was sitting on top of a murderous-looking fae horse.

I heard the totally-not-a-lightsaber-hum behind me, and turned Eclipse in a circle just in time to see Chase, Fax, and Solstice emerge from the gate, which sputtered shut behind them and disappeared with magic.

"What do you think?" I asked Chase.

He surveyed our surroundings. "I don't believe there are any threats, but I will remain vigilant."

"No—I meant of Magiford!"

"Oh. It's sufficiently tourist-y to maintain a healthy local economy."

I was about to slap my hand to my face, but the serious werewolf continued.

"Back at home we had to invest heavily in making our town a popular tourist destination to maintain a healthy and happy city. I am glad Magiford has done the same. Their efforts show—the city is quite adorable."

"Yeah—I've always loved living near Magiford," I agreed. "But I'll be the first to admit there is some manipulation at play. Since it's the supernatural center of the Midwest, the Curia Cloisters spends a lot of money helping maintain downtown—I think it's so they can manipulate things a little and show how beautiful and picture-perfect things are when humans live with supernaturals. But it's a fun place to live."

Two cars almost collided in front of us because the drivers were gawking at Solstice, Eclipse, and Fax. Pedestrians had stopped and had their cellphones out—most likely taking pictures of us.

I better get going—I'm not really sure I'm cleared by the Curia Cloisters to parade the night mares downtown, anyway.

"Okay, I'll go get my coffee. Are you sure you don't want anything, Chase?"

Chase somehow managed to bow, even from on Fax's back. "Yes, Queen Leila."

"Okay, great. I'll be right back—come on, Solstice!"

King's Court Drive was thankfully empty, so Eclipse and Solstice were able to walk shoulder to shoulder, their silver shod hooves clattering on the pavement.

I stood up briefly in the stirrups to fish my wallet out of my jeans, then stopped the night mares at a speaker.

The speaker crackled, before a voice greeted me. "*Welcome to King's Court—what the!*"

The voice cut out briefly, but continued, slightly muffled.

"*Rhonda! Rhonda, we've got a rider of the apocalypse in the drive through!*"

Oohhh, that's right—I forgot they have a camera pointed at the drive through.

"Actually, they're really rare fae horses called night mares!" I tried to sound extra friendly as I waved to the little camera that was pointed at us.

"*Calling them night mares doesn't sound much better than a rider of the apocalypse. It sounds like they could kill you in your sleep,*" the café employee said suspiciously.

"Uhhh…"

"*Are your buddies Pestilence, War, and Famine getting ice cream up the street?*"

"My friend is riding the sun stallion at the front of the café."

"*What? Where—WHAT?*" The speaker blared with the volume the employee shouted. "*We've got an angel horse up front and demon horses in the drive through! That's it, the world is going to end. I knew I should have applied to work at the kayak stand!*"

"Their names are Eclipse and Solstice." I draped myself over Eclipse's neck, giving her a half hug.

"*Pretty names don't change the fact that they look like they stepped out of one of those messed up surrealist paintings.*"

I sat up straight. "Hey, that's mean—they're adorable!"

"*Mmhmm, as adorable as sharks.*"

A new voice crackled over the speaker. "*Landon, what are you shouting about?*"

Even though the speaker horribly mangled the voice, I still recognized it. "Hi, Rhonda!" I waved again for the camera.

King's Court was my favorite café in Magiford, and when I was in college I stopped in once a week while on my way to classes. That was how I met Rhonda, the owner.

"*Give me that.*" There was another loud crackle, and Rhonda's voice was louder and clearer. "*Leila, it's been too long! I saw the article in the Curia Cloisters' newsletter that you'd been made Queen of the Night Court."*

"Article?" I absently patted Eclipse's shoulder when she shook her head, getting rid of a fly and jangling the bridle.

"Yeah, it talked about how you'd been chosen and that you were a local girl and one of our own. They had one of your high school pictures with it."

"My high school pictures? I must look like I'm about ten!"

"I thought the braces were a cute touch."

I groaned and hung my head—talk about a way to make an impression.

Rhonda laughed. *"What can I get you, Your Majesty?"*

"No teasing, Rhonda, I can't take it today. I want my summer usual—a medium iced caramel latte with whipped cream. And then two bacon and egg breakfast sandwiches—no, three."

"Okay. Anything else?"

I glanced at Solstice.

Even though he just had his halter on and he wasn't tied to me or Eclipse, he was being a perfect boy, standing still and in line with Eclipse. It was pretty cute because he dwarfed her with his massive size.

"Do you still sell fresh fruit?"

"Yep!"

"I'll take three apples then. And make that four bacon egg sandwiches."

"Gotcha. If you move up to the window Landon will get your bill settled and make your latte. I'll get on your sandwiches."

"Okay, thanks!"

My stomach rumbled as my night mares politely walked up to the window, and I debated adding a fifth sandwich to my order, but as hungry as I was, I probably wasn't going to be able to eat more than three. The last one was for Chase—even if he didn't want anything, I would feel horridly guilty eating in front of the werewolf.

"Landon," a gangly teenage boy with a thick dusting of freckles and bright blond hair that sprang up in unruly cowlicks, was waiting for me at the window.

He narrowed his eyes as he pushed the window open. "They're not *zombie* horses, are they?"

"They really are fae horses—they can do magic," I said.

Eclipse "smiled" at the boy, which involved peeling her lips back and revealing teeth that were too jagged—and too numerous—to belong to a normal horse.

Landon took my credit card from me. "Mmhmm. They can do *death* magic, I bet." He ran it through the machine and handed it back to me. "You're a fae monarch—the new Night Queen?"

"Yep."

"Then what are you doing getting a latte and food from a human café?" he asked.

"*Landon*," Rhonda growled from inside the café.

Landon hunched his shoulders, but I laughed. He disappeared from view for a minute, then reappeared, holding a small brown paper bag and my iced latte. "Three apples for your demon horses and angel horse."

"Landon," I called before the teenager could dart away again. "I'm getting my latte here because the fae don't drink coffee—there isn't any in my new home."

Landon's eyes bulged. "Not even a coffee maker?"

I took a sip of my latte and hummed with pleasure at the slightly bitter drink swirled with creamy sweetness. "Not even *instant* coffee."

Landon made a gagging noise. "My apologies, my queen! Stop by with your demon horses any time—I can make you my specialty drink. I call it the All Nighter!"

I laughed, and noticed Chase had directed Fax around to the side of the building so he could keep an eye on me.

I waved to him, then almost hit myself with my apple bag

when I saw the people blatantly trying to take selfies with him and had to swallow my laughter.

Really, I couldn't blame the humans.

We supernaturals tried really hard not to publicly invade the human realm much—we wanted them to think we were safe and not a threat.

The downside of that was they didn't see many vampires, werewolves, or other supernaturals, and they didn't get to experience fun stuff like petting a sun stallion.

I wish we could change that.

"I've got your breakfast sandwiches here, Leila." Rhonda edged past Landon, passing me a second paper sack. "Are they treating you okay in your Court?"

I juggled my bags and latte. "Probably as good as could be expected."

Rhonda frowned. "That doesn't sound encouraging."

I shrugged. "It's the fae."

She pursed her lips slightly and folded her arms across her formidable chest. "Maybe, but you're you." She winked. "Give 'em all the trouble you've got, girl."

"I'll try."

Rhonda cackled. "You'll win," she predicted. "They'll regret the day they cross their lovely new queen."

I laughed as I nudged Eclipse into a walk. "Thanks, Rhonda."

"Of course—and if anyone asks, tell them your favorite café is King's Court!"

"Naturally!" Eclipse and Solstice picked their way across the parking lot, stopping when I pulled them to a halt just a bit short of Chase and Fax.

"I got you a breakfast sandwich, Chase." I held the bag up and shook it a little.

"I said I didn't need anything." Chase watched a woman who was trying to take his picture and nudged Fax so the sun stallion turned his rear to the lady.

"Yeah, but you're a werewolf. You're *always* hungry. Plus I was going to feel guilty eating in front of you. Should we head back home?"

"Yes."

"Um, excuse me?" Surprised, I peered down, where I found two college-aged girls standing on the sidewalk. "Could we take a picture with you?"

I blinked in surprise—I figured they'd want Chase's picture, but not mine. "Um...sure?"

"Thank you!" The spokesperson for the two turned around and held her phone back as the duo arranged themselves so they were in frame along with Eclipse and me.

"You're a fae warrior, right?" the second girl eagerly asked.

"Nah, nothing like that," I said.

"She is Queen Leila of the Night Court," Chase said.

Both of the girls looked at me with dropped jaws. "You're a *queen?*"

"Reluctantly, yes." I tried to give the duo a cheerful smile.

"Oh wow—we're taking our picture with royalty!" the chattier one squealed.

"Smile!" the other one said.

Once they finished, they thanked me, performed a few adorably bad curtseys that were still better than anything I could do, and were on their way.

"That was fun," I said as we turned the horses back into the parking lot, preparing to head back home. "I wish more of my role as queen involved fun stuff like this."

"In a week you'll be participating in a Court-wide ride," Chase pointed out.

"Yeah, but it's not the same." I sighed, and my stomach took that opportune moment to rumble.

Chase glanced in the direction of my stomach. "Perhaps we ought to head home."

"That sounds great." I rearranged my bags, trying to balance them on my saddle, hold my latte, and grip the reins with one hand. "But while I have you alone, I wanted to ask you for a favor."

A favor—those were dangerous words to say to a fae. Favors meant minute shifts in power, and fae were famous for being able to manipulate something small—like answering a simple question—into something as big as a blood debt if you weren't careful.

Since Chase was a werewolf, he was the only supernatural on my staff I was comfortable talking to like this.

Chase glanced at me, his golden eyes glowing. "I am yours to command."

"I'd like you to investigate Lord Linus," I said. "I know you looked into him when he first came to the mansion, but I want to know more. Specifically, I want to know who he owes money to."

Chase nodded. "His debt is a dangerous liability."

"Exactly," I said. "One I'd like to get settled as quickly as possible."

"I will look into it."

"Thanks, Chase. I appreciate it."

"Of course." He bowed slightly still on horseback, and his eyes lingered on Eclipse. "You know, Queen Leila, there will be one upside to next week's ride."

"Oh? What's that?" I took another sip of my iced latte and almost shut my eyes in pleasure.

Chase offered me a very slight but thoroughly mischievous smile. "You'll be riding the night mares—which most of the Court fear greatly."

CHAPTER FOURTEEN

Leila

"I feel betrayed," I said.

Today's social event was a Court-wide ride held in the nature preserve in my backyard—which was fun. For the occasion, Indigo had stuffed me into a pair of white breeches, knee-high black boots, a floral pattern dress shirt that suspiciously reminded me of a teacup pattern, and a navy blue dress coat.

I didn't mind the breeches and boots, but I very much minded the coat—which was unbearably hot in the summer sun—and the neck of the dress shirt was closed with a golden moon pin that was jabbing me in the throat.

Skye gathered up the reins of her calm, chestnut colored mare. "You were the one who insisted on wearing a helmet."

"Because I have good self-preservation instincts!" I complained. "It's not my fault the rest of my Court are more concerned with their aesthetic and like to thunder around on horses without proper protective headgear!"

I scowled as a few nobles cantered past.

They were wearing more traditional fae garb—tunics and flowing dresses, neither of which were very practical to ride in—and laughed as they held onto their bows and crossbows and had quivers of arrows strapped to their backs.

Skye gave the night mare I was riding—I'd chosen Solstice today—the side eye. "I'm not saying your helmet is a bad thing—just that your wardrobe had to be adjusted to match it."

"I think it's a smart idea to wear a helmet," Indigo said from the back of a shaggy pony that faintly reminded me of her with its thick forelock and hair. "Since you *had* to choose the biggest brute of the herd to ride."

"I trust Solstice—which I need when I'm around my Court." I sniffed as I threaded the reins through my fingers. "And he's excellent for intimidation purposes."

"I won't argue that," Indigo muttered.

Sweat trickled down my back, and the afternoon sun beat down on me with not a cloud in sight.

"This is going to be such a *fantastic* afternoon," I said. "I can just tell."

"This is good practice for the annual hunt all the monarchs attend in the fall." Skye peered out over the nature preserve. There were all kinds of dirt trails that wound around the lake, a few marshy spots, and an open field, while other paths dove off into the forest and a bunch of tree-lined lanes.

"I'd much rather be practicing magic," I sighed. I hadn't had much time to myself ever since I went to King's Court, so I hadn't gotten to practice my magic much more, and that made me nervous.

I wanted to practice because I wanted to dust off all those warding skills and dispel charms I'd learned because now *I finally needed* them! And yet here I was, riding in a coat in the heat of summer with the very people I needed protection from.

I frowned. "Considering I'm supposedly a queen, it seems like I rarely get to do what I want."

Indigo's pony snorted, and birds chirped and sang with enough enthusiasm to be heard over the thundering of horse hooves. "Quite so," Indigo agreed—she also wore a helmet like me, but Skye was letting her get away with wearing a hunter green sweater with tan breeches and black boots.

Why does she wear all these sweaters in the middle of summer?

"You'll get to choose your royal artifact in the next few weeks," Skye said. "We just have to wait because there are preparations to be made—and an official ceremony to hold."

"Really?" I perked up in the saddle. "I would have thought they'd make me wait until I was crowned!"

Skye shook her head. "No, you need your artifact in order to be officially crowned."

More fae thundered past—giving us a wide berth when Solstice pawed a hoof on the grassy ground.

"Huh, well that's something."

The sound of high-pitched laughter rounded a bend in one of the tree-lined trails, then Indigo screamed.

I turned just in time to see an arrow pierce the ground so close to Indigo's pony that it scraped the poor thing's leg.

Her pony shied, and Indigo nearly slid off its back. It pranced a few steps, its nostrils quivering as she tried to calm it.

The laughter grew louder still, and I turned Solstice in time to see Lady Chrysanthe lower her crossbow.

Her minions surrounding her giggled, their gauzy dresses floating around them as their beautiful, delicate horses showily tossed their heads.

"Indigo, are you hurt?" I asked.

Indigo hopped off her pony and inspected his leg. "I'm fine," she said in a voice that was shaky with fear. "I don't think my pony is hurt too badly, but I should take him back."

Using my legs, I swiveled Solstice around to face the snake-ish fae ladies. "Skye," I said in a lowered voice.

"Yes, Queen Leila?"

"Send for Chase—tell him Indigo needs an escort back to the stables." I didn't take my eyes off Lady Chrysanthe as she leaned over the side of her horse to say something to Lord Myron.

Meandering behind them rode Lady Demetria, another elderly fae lady, and two lords. They were smirking openly, as if Indigo's fright was amusing to them.

"Yes, Queen Leila." Skye slipped off her horse and made a call on her cellphone, speaking in a quiet murmur.

I glanced down at Solstice.

Just how much can I trust him?

Solstice chewed angrily on his bridle bit, then curved his head around so I could see the eerie yellow of his eyes.

I felt a spark of my fae magic, and I knew from deep in my blood that he'd stand as long as I asked him.

I nodded to him, and he swung his massive head back around to the front.

"Lady Chrysanthe," I called out to her in the strongest voice I could muster. "You shot at my companion."

"I would apologize, except she's just so dowdy looking, one could mistake her for an animal." Lady Chrysanthe smirked as she tossed the braid of her hair—today she'd tinted it a light purple that matched her loose, sleeveless dress—over her shoulder. "You can hardly blame me." She adjusted the white chrysanthemum tied around the tail of her braid and glanced at Indigo, her unearthly beauty making her almost ugly combined with her words.

I clenched my jaw. "You frightened her and hurt her mount."

Lady Chrysanthe picked at the purple flower chain that served as the belt to her dress. "She's not injured, and the pony can walk just fine. But wasn't it deliciously hilarious?" she asked her groupies.

Yep. Now is a good time to reveal my ace in the hole—and teach them to never harm my people again.

I dropped my reins and started unbuttoning my coat.

They all twittered in laughter.

"She nearly fell off her mount—if it could be called that," Lord Myron laughed. He'd gone full-blown Jane Austen fashion for the day with high waisted white breeches, a blue hunting jacket, and a black top hat that almost covered the low ponytail he'd pulled his long hair back into.

"You must forgive these youngsters, Queen Leila." Lady Demetria wore an enormous bonnet-like hat that was covered in flowers and bobbed with every word she spoke. "They get restless in their excitement—such is the spirit of the hunt."

"Indeed," Lady Demetria's female companion said.

"Hear, hear," one of the lords said.

I pulled my pistol from my shoulder holster. I already had a magazine in it, but the safety was on and the chamber was empty.

My movements were hidden by Solstice's massive neck as I very carefully pointed the gun over his side, aiming it at the ground.

Just as Josh Drake had endlessly drilled me in the week before I came to the mansion, I calmly pulled back on the top of the handgun, racking it and filling the chamber with a bullet.

I switched off the safety and looked up just as the fae ladies stopped the worst of their laughter.

Lady Chrysanthe had stupidly drawn near enough that Solstice might have been able to kick her mount if he really tried.

That's why I didn't waver as I raised my gun and shot at Lady Chrysanthe.

I'd purposely aimed to miss her, but the bullet *may* have passed a wee bit closer to her than I planned—so close, in fact, that it stirred the fabric of her dress on her shoulder.

Lady Chrysanthe screamed.

Like, hysterically.

I'm pretty sure they heard her screams all the way back in the apartment buildings near the neighborhood entrance.

Her horse understandably freaked. It reared, and her groupies and minions scattered as they also struggled to control their horses.

In fact, all the horses in the area—except Solstice and Indigo's pony—spooked.

"Lady Chrysanthe," I shouted over her screams and the worried neighs of the horses. "I would advise you in the future *not* to target one of my people. You'll find it will have a poor effect on your health."

"Are you insane? She's just a companion!" Lady Chrysanthe screamed. Her eye makeup was just a tiny bit smeared, creating a crack in the image of her perfection.

I batted my eyelashes. "What do you mean? It was just a mistake—and your reaction was...how would you say it? *Deliciously hilarious.*" I held her gaze, letting my fury escape so my voice grew dark with an unspoken promise.

Solstice did his part to add to the image. He snorted, and puffs of smoke drifted from his nostrils before he broke off in that piercing cry that could make your blood freeze in your veins.

Lady Chrysanthe went quiet, but she mashed her lips together so tightly they were white with strain.

"Never harm one of my people," I repeated—I wanted to make sure I drove the point home as I raised my gun again. "Understood?"

Lady Chrysanthe scoffed, but I saw the fear in her eyes.

She'd keep bullying me, but at least she had learned her lesson.

"Queen Leila!" Lady Demetria's cheeks shook like an angry bulldog's, and her hat had come off in the scuffle. "That was extremely inappropriate!"

"You shot at a noble—with a *gun*!" Lord Myron's face was tight with anger as his horse wildly rolled its eyes and pranced—frightened, this time, by Solstice.

"Yes." I held up my gun, looking at it with mock contemplation—I'd already switched the safety back on, but they didn't have to know that. "I decided it would be smart to bring a *gun* to a bow and arrow fight." I smiled widely at him. "Call it a side effect of my fae blood, but I've never been overly fond of fair fights."

"Y-you!" Lady Demetria was too angry to talk.

The lords and ladies bristled with anger, but as I watched them with half lidded eyes, they could do nothing more than turn their horses in tight circles and shout at me.

I had won this round—they couldn't outright hurt me, after all. I'm sure that's why Chrysanthe targeted Indigo.

I'd pay the price eventually. They just needed time to plan ahead and get around the magic that kept them from harming me by making it seem accidental.

But it was worth it. I wasn't going to let anyone hurt my people.

"Queen Leila!"

I twisted around in the saddle just as Chase and two guards—riding in a golf cart that the werewolf was flooring—and, surprisingly, Lord Linus riding a black horse, came careening down one of the trails.

Chase skidded the golf cart to a stop, spraying dirt and making the horses spook all over again. "I got Skye's texts, but we heard a shot." His yellow eyes flicked from the nobles to me, and he narrowed in on the gun in my hands.

"What kind of crazy person is wielding a gun out here?" Lord Linus demanded, his eyes flashing.

"That would be me." I secured my gun in my shoulder holster.

"Oh." Lord Linus relaxed, losing the slight edge I'd seen briefly in the set of his shoulders. "In that case—good shot!" He gave me a loose smile and a thumbs up.

"Lord Linus—how could you encourage her?" Lady Demetria shrieked.

"She is my daughter and, importantly, the queen," Lord Linus said. "And some debts are too big to get rid of on one's own will…"

I rolled my eyes with disgust, then turned around. Indigo and Skye were both staring at me, their eyes wide and faces smooth with shock.

"What?" I asked.

"You just shot at Lady Chrysanthe," Indigo said.

"Yeah," I said. "I *was* there, you know."

"But…you—" She shook her head, and her cat eye glasses skidded down her slightly upturned nose.

I shifted back to Chase—who was sending out a text message. Probably to his people to update them on the gunshot. "Chase, can you help Indigo and her pony get back to the stables? The pony was injured in an *accident*."

"Yes, Queen Leila." Chase gave me a bow before he took over, packing Indigo in the golf cart and tying the pony to a complaining Lord Linus. With his brisk efficiency, he managed to get Lord Linus moving, and he followed behind with the golf cart.

By this time, Lady Chrysanthe had moved on with her people, so Skye and I were alone.

"Shall we get moving?" I asked.

Looking a little windblown—and maybe even a little ill—Skye nodded. "Yes, Queen Leila."

I pointed Solstice in the direction I thought we'd be least likely to meet someone, and nudged him forward.

"Where did you learn to shoot like that?" Skye asked.

"The Drakes."

She briefly held her stomach, but she said nothing more as she reined her reluctant horse closer, and we walked off.

I uncomfortably shifted in the saddle. "Remind me to give you, Chase, and Indigo an increase in your salary," I said.

Skye rubbed her stomach one last time, then straightened up. "Whatever for?"

"Call it hazard pay," I said.

Skye knitted her eyebrows together and still managed to look elegant and professional in her confusion. "We were aware of the risk when we accepted our positions."

I answered with a shrug.

I liked Skye and Indigo, but I didn't want to spell out my actions to her.

With fae it's important to make sure you aren't indebted—you *never* want to owe them a favor, because it can get pricy fast.

Increasing their pay was the easiest way I had to make sure we were balanced—but I couldn't even *tell* them that because there was a possibility they might be able to use that knowledge to claim I owed them somehow.

I hate the way I have to second guess everyone just to survive in this cesspool. Fae culture is the worst.

CHAPTER FIFTEEN

Rigel

"She *shot* at Lady Chrysanthe! With a *gun*!" Dion pulled on his hair, then draped himself over his horse's neck to complete his dramatics. "The Paragon wants me to marry the equivalent of a wild animal."

I loosened my reins—since Dion seemed mostly interested in dramatics at the moment, there was no point in riding off. He was annoyingly persistent enough that he'd just ride after me, wailing at the top of his lungs.

"Are you opposed to the Paragon's plan?" I asked.

Dion peeled himself off his horse. "Not really. She doesn't seem unpleasant—and I'd be marrying her for the sake of securing the Night Court's future. It's just when she does stuff like shooting at people, I don't know that I can handle it."

"I suspect you should be more worried about surviving our Court than your potential wife turning on you," I said.

"Probably. It's just...she's *wild*." Dion sighed, then peered in my direction. "What do you think of her?"

I thought for a moment of our previous meetings.

In the never-ending struggle we fae engaged in for power, Queen Leila upset the status quo by ignoring traditions, speaking bluntly, and reacting openly rather than veiling her actions like a real fae would.

She was sending ripples through the whole game—something I hadn't seen before, and something I wasn't sure was good.

The fae's thirst for power was unavoidable. Given her conduct, Queen Leila would never win it. The question was, how many would she take down with her when she fell?

"She's unpredictable," I finally said. "Which can make her dangerous."

"That is the understatement of the century." Dion smoothed his hair, already returning to his façade of handsome, smiling courtier. "I'll just have to teach her. She seems reasonable."

"On the one occasion you spoke to her."

"What, and you've seen her so many more times than me?" Dion shot me a look.

I kept my silence—Dion didn't know I'd tried my hand at killing our mad queen before I knew she was bound to the Court. And if Queen Leila wasn't going to reveal that, I saw no reason to tip the game of power one way or another.

Of course, I'd seen her several additional times since then, but then I'd have to explain *why* she had the tendency to hiss at me like a cat.

"Although, now that I think about it, she *did* say when we met at the party that it was nice to finally be introduced. What do you think she meant by that?" Dion, in his irritating wit, raised both of his eyebrows at me, waiting for a response.

I heard a voice around a bend in the trail, and I held up a hand to silence my longtime friend.

"—good neighbors—the best, really. I miss Hazel, she's hilarious, and—oh." Queen Leila and her steward rounded the corner, stopping when they saw me.

The steward bowed graciously. "Lord Dion, Lord Rigel, good afternoon."

Queen Leila, perched on top of the biggest night mare I'd seen—who looked like he was slashed through with glowing lines of red dotting his body—seemed to be warring between a look of politeness and open distaste.

Yes. She's the only one with the guts to openly shoot at someone. I can only imagine the reaction provoked.

For a second, I wished I had been present to witness the act. Queen Leila was *funny* in her anger.

I stared the new queen down, but it seemed that she wasn't in the mood for any rude sayings today. She was hastily turning her massive beast around.

Dion turned on his charm, oozing likability and flashing a grin that had multiple ladies in the Night Court cooing over him. "Queen Leila—you look lovely today."

"Thank you, Lord Dion." She twisted around in the saddle with the familiarity of someone used to it.

It wasn't surprising—I'd seen her parents' farm.

It was interesting, though, that when she placed her hand on the night mare's rear to stabilize herself, the giant creature didn't budge.

I suppose they bound her because they like her.

"It's a splendid day for a ride," Dion said.

Our queen squinted at him. "I'm not sure I agree to that. It's hot. I'd get rid of my jacket if I could, but I have been informed it's necessary." She cast a side look at her steward, who—aware that she ranked lower than Dion and me, even with her new position—had her eyes downcast, fixed on her hands.

"Would you care to ride with us for a spell?" Dion asked.

"Ah—no." Queen Leila gave him a mini salute. "Sorry. Wouldn't want to intrude on this festival of manliness." She narrowed her eyes at me and sucked her head into her shoulders in wariness.

A muscle in my chest twinged with her unexpected hilarity—she looked like an angry turtle.

Oh, yes. I really wish I had been there to see her shoot at Lady Chrysanthe. It must have been highly amusing.

Dion laughed, using every ounce of his charisma to appear charming. "Queen Leila, you wound me."

"If this is a festival of manliness, I imagine you'd fit in," I said.

Queen Leila's suspicion crusted over, and her vibrant purple eyes were little slits. "Oh?"

I prepared myself for a good show, because I was about to push one of her buttons. "You have the boldness for it, given you can shoot at one of your own courtiers. Is that not extremely manly?"

Her eyes flashed, and her open scorn was vibrant and colorful among the usual guarded fae reactions. "The ability to fight back isn't limited to males—you just have outdated, backwater beliefs, you hulking mountain goat!"

"You're right," I agreed. "Your actions surpassed gender distinction. You are in a class of your own: stupidly bold."

Queen Leila made a choking noise.

"Rigel," Dion growled between clenched teeth. "Queen Leila, I apologize—Rigel is not used to dealing with such magnificent women as yourself. Many would find your firearm-related capabilities admirable."

"I question that, given I only shot at Lady Chrysanthe about half an hour ago and you two already know about it," Queen Leila said. "Unless you have a secret passion for gossip, Lord Rigel?"

"Ahaha." Dion used the fake laugh he trotted out whenever he was trying to smooth a situation over. "Gossip is such an *ugly* word. Do let us return to civilities and polite language—"

"The screams were hard to miss," I said.

"Ahh, Lady Chrysanthe does have a lovely set of lungs," Queen Leila said.

"Quite," I agreed.

Dion and the queen's steward stared at us both for several moments of silence. Dion, particularly, gave me the stink eye.

I stared back at him.

While I'm not sure our queen's blunt way of speaking will have a positive influence on the Court, I'm going to enjoy it as long as she's around—or as long as that particular quirk survives. Once she realizes we're bound to her will I imagine it's only a matter of weeks before she has us dancing to her orders like puppets.

It was an idea I did not look forward to, though I was relatively skilled at evading royal orders. But the thought alone was enough to make me push another one of our half human queen's buttons.

"You brought a gun to a hunt?" I asked.

"Yep." She gave me a bored look. "Because I, unlike the rest of you fae, apparently, live in the twenty first century."

"It hardly seems sporting given the rest of us are armed only with bows or crossbows," I said.

"Oh please." Queen Leila snorted. "If you were feeling particularly motivated, you could kill someone with a toothpick."

"*Queen Leila,*" the steward said in a voice that quivered with fear. "Perhaps we ought to ride on?" The steward lost some of her poise and looked distinctly sick with fear as she glanced at me.

"The toothpick would be unnecessary," I said. "Nor would a gun."

"Whatever!" The night mare started walking off on its own accord, but Queen Leila clung to the back of the saddle so she could shout to me, "I'm not the one who is an openly acknowledged assassin—talk about bad business practices!"

"Queen Leila," the steward said in a tight, quiet voice. "You cannot *speak* like that to Lord Rigel."

"I totally can! You just don't want me to." Our entertaining queen stuck her nose up in the air. When the night mare moved into a smooth-flowing trot, her body gracefully moved with him, even though she couldn't possibly see anything like that.

Yes, she is quite amusing when she's angry. Like a puffed-up kitten.

"It's fascinating, but she doesn't seem to fear you. I don't know if that's admirable or not, though. Even Queen Nyte knew enough to avoid you." Dion glanced over at me. "You really enjoy winding her up, don't you?"

I laid a hand on my mount's shoulder when it pawed the ground. "She has entertaining reactions."

Dion turned his horse in a circle. "That's all?"

I shrugged. "I am attempting to provoke her to see if I can uncover her thought pattern—it would help me ascertain the Night Court's future."

"And?"

I watched the giant night mare disappear back around the bend they had come from. "If she has a pattern, it's not one I understand."

"What do you think that means for the Court?"

I paused—as amusing as the new queen was, my main concern would always be how she would upset our precarious balance.

She hasn't found her place yet, but when she allows herself to act freely, she's like a night mare—fierce and overwhelming. A queen like that leading a Court where a whisper can change the whole power structure?

I nudged my horse forward. "Nothing good."

CHAPTER SIXTEEN

Leila

"Okay." I rolled my shoulders back and planted my feet. "Try now."

Comet flicked her extra thick tail, smacking some of the yellow dapples brushed into her coat, then charged.

I whispered to my charm bracelet, *"Flore."*

When it flared to life, I spun magic through it, creating an iridescent purple-ish-blue ward on the ground. Once I finished the last thread, a magic shield flared to life, encircling me in a protective shell just before Comet reached the threshold.

The whole process took about ten seconds—I was improving.

"Yes!" I pumped my fist in the air, then dropped my shield. "I may not be able to do anything at all offensive-focused. But a year of practice like this, and I will make shields like a boss! Thanks, Comet."

I kissed Comet's scratchy muzzle and petted her, grimacing

because her neck was *still* bony even though Dusk and Dawn had put the night mares on a high fat grain that was supposed to help them gain weight.

Comet flicked her ears and accepted my love—lipping my shoulder a little to communicate her own feelings.

"You're too sweet! Thank you—thanks to all of you for the help!" I addressed my little night mare herd, who were all watching and taking turns when I needed someone to play the role of attacker.

My six night mares were present, as were a few of the more wild stragglers.

Their presence was incredibly reassuring in the eerie quiet of the Night Realm.

I shivered a little and glanced at the sky—which was the only beautiful part of the crumbling castle grounds.

"What do you think, Indigo?" I let go of Comet and turned to the brownie—my only non-equine companion at the moment.

Indigo was perched on a crumbling stone bench, her legs dangling, and her arms braced on the bench. "I think they love you," she said.

"Aww, that's cute!" I grinned at her, then spun around in the soft light of the night sky.

At the moment, the moon was full, giving me a better look at the castle than I had when I first came with the Paragon.

It must have been gorgeous at some point. While it had the structure of a true castle, most of it had been constructed with glass walls, built to overlook the now ruined gardens, and the giant lake beyond it.

"Hey, Indigo. Did they build the mansion where they did because the landscape reminded everyone of this place?" I asked.

"Maybe a little, but I don't think it was a high priority," Indigo said.

"What? Even though the mansion and the Night Realm both

have lakes?" I peered out at the dark expanse—streaked with moonlight at the moment—that marked out the enormous lake.

Indigo hunched her shoulders. "Most assuredly the *lake* didn't matter. The lake here in the Night Realm has been heavily avoided due to the pesky urban legend that a large sea monster lives in it."

I gaped at her. "For real?"

She shrugged. "Rumor has it. No one has been too keen to test it."

"Ugh, knowing the Night Realm it's totally possible." I peered in the direction of the lake again and shivered.

And with my luck, it'll be a monster that hates humans. Guess I won't be taking a dip in there anytime soon!

I loved animals, but swimming in the Night Realm in a lake rumored to have a monster? Yeah, that would be the definition of stupidity.

I leaned into Comet for comfort as I saw one of the pigeon-raccoon-griffins nest in a dead bush.

I wouldn't normally choose to spend free time here, but when I told Skye and Chase I wanted to practice magic, Skye told me the Night Realm was an excellent place to do it—because no one would see me here since the fae had almost entirely vacated the realm.

I should get back to practicing—or go back to the mansion and get back to work.

"Why did you do it?" Indigo abruptly asked.

I scratched my side as I reviewed the last few minutes of my life. "Make the shield?"

"No." Indigo stiffened her shoulders and her eyes were unusually wary as she adjusted her glasses. "Why did you shoot at Lady Chrysanthe?"

"Because she almost hurt you—I mean, she did succeed in hurting your pony. You're one of my people, and I'm not going to let others harm you."

"But you said you didn't want our loyalty. What value was there in warning her off like that?"

I crossed the courtyard, joining her on the other side. "I said I didn't *expect* your loyalty—I never said I didn't want it." I didn't really know what to do with my hands, so I settled for propping them up on my hips—fae grace, hah! Why get that trait when I could have their sparkling personality?

"I don't expect," I continued, "because I'm half human, and the likelihood of anyone really swearing themselves to me is about nil."

"But if you don't expect loyalty, why did you do that? Is there something you are seeking in return?"

Aw crud, I forgot about the stupid fae balance/not wanting to be in someone's debt, thing. I pulled my elastic ponytail holder, yanking out a wad of my hair with it. "Nah. Whether or not other people are loyal has nothing to do with my own loyalty."

"But it doesn't benefit you." Indigo curled her small hands into such tight fists, they trembled.

"Sure it does," I said. "I feel better about myself, and I don't want to turn into a slimeball like Lady Chrysanthe or Lord Myron. I win all around."

Indigo stared at me, something big but inexpressible in her eyes.

"Look, I'm a human," I said.

"You're half fae."

"Maybe by blood, but in the way I was raised, I'm fully human." I winked and gave her a cheesy grin, but she didn't react. "Ahem. Anyway, I'm fully convinced that humans are one of the best races because of their great capacity to love. Sure, they can be just as awful as us supernaturals, but they're *open*, and the vast majority of them will respond with love if you reach out first. I want to keep that aspect, because if I become cold and hard like the rest of the fae nobles, life will become unbearable in a totally different way. I'll protect my people. No matter what—and without expecting anything in return, or thinking that you'll be in my debt."

Indigo was apparently unmoved by my little speech, and kept staring at me.

Nothing like pouring your heart out and getting silence back in return. Talk about awkward! I turned back to the night mares—Nebula was investigating the pigeon-raccoon-griffin, making it squawk this awful, chittery noise.

"Guess it's time to get back to practice," I said.

"I'm into human pop culture," Indigo blurted out.

I rapidly blinked. "Sorry, what?"

Indigo yanked off today's cable knit sweater—which was a charming red—revealing the t-shirt underneath, which was emblazoned with a Lord of the Rings slogan about hobbits and second-breakfast. "I love Star Trek, Lord of the Rings, Harry Potter, Disney, Star Wars, Doctor Who, all the Godzilla movies, superheroes—all of it. I wanted the salary of a companion because I really wanted the money to buy books, movies, and memorabilia. My family disapproves because they think all of that stuff is silly, unrealistic, or makes a mockery out of our community, but I *love* human entertainment culture!" She'd spoken so fast she was panting by the end of her explanation.

I could only watch in surprise and think how awesome it was that she managed to smuggle her geekdom into boring socials by wearing her unassuming sweaters.

"I haven't told anyone outside my family because the fae look down on human culture. They hate it, actually," Indigo said.

I gurgled a little. "You don't say? I never would have guessed."

"But I want you to know, because I'm loyal to you, my Sovereign."

Huh, I haven't heard that title before.

"I know you might not believe me, but I swear to follow you

for the rest of my life." Indigo hopped off the bench and planted her hand over her heart. "Whatever I can do to help you—whatever you want me to do, I'll do it." She paused, then added, "And I'm sorry. For not believing in you, when you believed in me."

I studied my companion, hardly daring to hope.

Could I really find a friend here? Someone that I don't have to continually second guess?

Indigo started to bow.

"Nope, nope, nope—not that," I said.

"I beg your pardon?"

"You said you'd do whatever I want, right? Then no more of the bowing."

Indigo tilted her head. "No *bowing?*"

"It makes me feel awkward, and I haven't done anything to deserve it." I hesitated, then added, "Besides—friends don't bow to one another." I held out my hand.

Indigo hesitated, then took my hand in her bone-crushing grasp and shook it with a firmness I envied. "Friends, then."

"Thank you, Indigo. I really value your offer—what is it?"

Indigo had gone white as snow, and was staring at something behind me.

I swung around, and my heart dropped, flopped off my stomach, and skidded its way down to my left foot.

Standing at the edge of the courtyard, close to the night mares, were two different creatures.

One was wolf-like in form—except its head would hit me about at my waist, and it was covered in black fur that was somehow simultaneously wet-looking, and blurry, as if the creature couldn't come into focus. The creepiness of its form was only increased by its burning crimson eyes and its massive *teeth*.

The other animal was a giant cat. Like, we're talking mountain-lion size. It looked really unhealthy because it was panting, and its red and gray fur was patchy, letting me see the gaunt lines of its body because it was just as skinny as a night mare. It also had yellow eyes—chances were both of these creatures were something Night Court exclusive, goodie—and teeth large enough to make my throat ache. Its enormous paws were accented with massive claws—which were spattered with red.

"What are those?" I whispered as Indigo and I slowly backed up.

"The wolf-like one is a shade. The cat is called a gloom." Indigo jumped on top of the bench she'd been sitting on earlier. I scrambled to do the same—not like I thought the extra height was going to make much of a difference.

Both the gloom and the shade could pounce on us with those teeth and claws before we even started screaming.

"They're creatures from the Night Court?"

"Yes. That's why they have this appearance."

My skin broke out in goosebumps as the gloom screamed—for real, it sounded like an injured goblin.

Shadows moved, and several more of the shades and glooms stalked out from behind the night mares.

I peered behind us, and was grateful for the dead hedge at our backs.

"Why are *you* scared?" Indigo hissed—apparently with this newfound loyalty her good manners were coming off, too. "You have natural magic to connect with animals!"

"Maybe, but I don't make it a habit to try communing with animals that could *kill me*!"

"What are you talking about? You hang over the night mares like they're sweet ponies!"

"Because they *are* sweet ponies—they're coming this way!"

One of the glooms and one of the shades sauntered closer to us, crossing the courtyard, and stopping at the halfway point.

Several long moments passed, and my heart beat so rapidly I could hear my blood flow in my ears.

Eclipse, the leader of my little night mare herd, also crossed the courtyard, stopping next to the monstrous creatures.

She doesn't seem alarmed by them, and I'm confident enough in her love for me that I'd say she doesn't want to see me hurt. Maybe...they won't hurt me.

Cautiously, I stepped off the bench.

"Are you really going to risk it?" Indigo asked. "Shades and glooms can—and have—killed! At least the night mares are somewhat domesticated—but the shades and glooms haven't been in the Court for over a century!"

"I trust Eclipse," I said.

Indigo muttered under her breath about "crazy, brainless humans," and I heard a familiar chime when she unlocked her phone.

I kept my gaze on Eclipse and slowly crossed the courtyard. All of my instincts screamed at me to run to safety, but the breezy feeling of my own natural magic grew.

This is the one thing I'm good at—handling animals. I've always been cautious, but I believe in my magic, and in Eclipse.

I stopped short of the creatures and held out my palm.

The shade took a few steps—this close I could see its fur was still blurry, but distinctly matted—and sniffed my hand. Its dry nose brushed my fingers, and then it licked me with a slimy tongue.

My heart stuttered, but I felt my magic, and noticed when the shade started wagging its tail.

I slowly reached over its head and petted it.

I nearly screamed when it abruptly moved in and pawed at my foot with one of its two front paws—which were a gray color.

"Good boy," I stupidly offered, but it leaned into me with the delight of a dog getting pets.

The gloom screamed again, which made me jump and kicked my heart up another notch. But I offered my hand out again.

The gloom sniffed it like a house cat might, then rubbed its cheek against my palm.

The shade's fur was thick and full—if not a little greasy feeling. The gloom's fur was sleek but strangely gritty feeling.

I relaxed as the gloom started purring, a deep, throbbing noise that came from its chest and rattled my bones as it leaned into me.

I finally dared to look away from it, and glanced at the other glooms and shades lingering with my night mares.

I did my best to offer them a smile, though for a moment I could have *sworn* I saw movement far behind the night mares, and a glimpse of silver hair and dark eyes.

Is that Rigel? What's he doing here?

Twilight turned around to see where I was looking, and the gleam of silver was gone.

If it was Rigel, he'd moved on.

I glanced around the courtyard, but none of the animals seemed upset. I turned a little and called back to Indigo. "We're good."

"Are you sure?"

I glanced from the shade—which was still wagging its tail—to the gloom rubbing its face on my pants. "Yeah. It's fine."

Indigo reluctantly climbed down from the bench and slowly crossed the courtyard, watching the animals rub against me. "I will say that for all your brashness in dealing with fae, you are excellent with animals."

"Or maybe the animals have always wanted to be like this, the fae have just been ignoring them."

"No, I don't really think that's it." Indigo stared at the gloom's paws and gigantic claws.

I grinned, but let it slip from my face and sighed. "I should get back to ward practice—for offensive and defensive purposes."

Indigo squinted at me. "Wards can only be used for defensive purposes."

"Maybe—I bet there's a creative way you can use it to smash someone." I winked, then froze when I heard a rumbling noise.

My fingers were buried in the gloom's fur, so I felt the cat tense up.

"What's that?" I whispered.

Indigo grabbed my arm—this time her eyes swam with despair. "That's the ward surrounding the Night Court. It's failing!"

CHAPTER SEVENTEEN

Leila

"What?" I wildly turned in a circle, but we weren't anywhere near the ward that marked off the border.

"The fae realm is shrinking—all the Courts are trying to deal with it. But most monarchs can subsidize the ward's power and lessen the shrinking effect. Since we haven't had a ruler in months, the Night Court has been rapidly shrinking."

I started to swear, but cut myself off—there wasn't time for that. "What can I do?"

Indigo shook her head. "You can try to add your power to the ward, but—wait—you haven't been trained for it!"

I ignored the warning and wriggled my way onto Eclipse's back. "I have to try. Eclipse, let's go!"

At my urging, the mare swiveled in a tight turn, then lunged into a canter.

I was riding bareback—which was fun, but not in the night

and while racing through a dangerous fae realm—and bridle-less—which I had never done before.

Go me, getting all of these "fun" new experiences.

Eclipse streaked through the realm. Everything was a dark blur, and my eyes teared up.

I clung to her back, terrified that if I fell off I'd seriously hurt myself. We were moving *that* fast.

I could hear the calls of the other night mares—they must have followed us. Based on the occasional awful scream, it seemed the glooms, and probably the shades, were coming along as well.

But above all of that—even above the wind streaming past my ears—was the terrible rumbling of the failing ward.

Eclipse had worked up a sweat by the time we reached the ward—even though it was a lot cooler here in the Night Realm. I wasn't sure how long we'd run, but my fingers ached from gripping her mane, and my legs were starting to cramp from squeezing her sides when she slowed to a trot and then a walk.

I impatiently rubbed my eyes, trying to clear them.

We stood in a meadow, which was divided in half. The half I stood on was clear and glittered with moonlight, although the grass was mostly weeds and looked pretty shriveled.

The sliced off half was a hazy black. The grass had died there, and the only remaining evidence that trees had ever been on that side were a few dead stumps. The air moved weirdly, too—it danced like heat above pavement on a hot day.

A pale yellow barrier of magic divided the areas. Fae symbols and letters forged of glowing magic were burned into the ward, and they flared as the toxic magic on the other side of the barrier pushed against it.

Blue Moon trumpeted at the wall, and Nebula pawed the ground with a hoof and tossed her head. It seemed like for now it was just me and the night mares. The shades and glooms hadn't caught up yet.

I shook my wrist, the familiar bangles of my charm bracelet providing minimal reassurance as I gazed at the wall. "*Flore!*"

My charm bracelet glowed, and I pulled magic through it. "Let's hope I'm doing this right!"

When I was a kid and attended classes to learn how to use magic, I'd learned a bit about combining spells with other fae.

I was *betting* this was a similar idea—I could add my power to the structure of the spell. The trick was adding it correctly so I didn't *break* anything.

I thrust my arm out in front of me—my palm flat—and willed the spun magic to join in the ward by filtering it in through a few specific symbols.

My magic—the same purplish color as my eyes—glowed as it entered the ward, adding a purplish patch to the ward.

I could *feel* the ward. It was ancient, and immense. As I threw more magic at it, I could see the complex spell work behind the barrier. And I felt it sputter, and weaken.

Eclipse abruptly made a sharp turn, and cantered off.

I yelped and would have slipped over her side, but she crow hopped, throwing me back into place.

"Wait—I can do more!" I shouted. The rumbling noise was so loud, I couldn't even hear myself. It was like being stuck in a giant clock.

Eclipse tossed her head and cantered into a shadowy forest filled with trees that had lost most of their leaves.

She slowed to a walk and turned around as the other night mares ran past us, looking back at the barrier.

I clutched her thin mane as the barrier—immeasurably old and powerful—was pushed across the meadow.

It was a horrifically slow crawl. And every inch it gave up blackened and died once it hit the toxic air past the barrier.

Slowly, the barrier shrank, and the toxic outer realm ate up the entire meadow.

The ward stopped—making the ground shudder—just short of the forest the night mares and I were hiding in.

I couldn't seem to catch my breath.

The Paragon said the fae realms were shrinking, but I never thought it would be this bad.

My eyes lingered on the bright magic symbols.

How am I supposed to solve this, if magic this powerful can't hold up anymore to the toxic outer realm?

I started shaking, so I draped myself across Eclipse, greedily sucking up her heat.

"Why did you choose me to be queen?" I asked. "I can't do anything about this. I was proud because I could lift up a shield faster—I can't rebuild a ward."

Blue Moon affectionately lipped my shoulder, and the glooms and shades appeared in the shadows of the forest, their eyes glowing in the dim light.

I shut my eyes and pushed my face into Eclipse's bony neck.

I can't do this. There's no way I'm going to win—not my Court, not the stupid fae war for power, and certainly not this fight for the realm itself.

Eclipse's muscles rippled as she stamped a hoof.

But they chose me. I have to try.

———

"You enter the treasury through this door, find the artifact that resonates with you, then continue to the door on the far side of the chamber where Indigo, myself, and the Court will be waiting for you to complete the ceremony and claim your artifact," Skye said. "Do you understand?"

"Yep," I said, purposely popping the p.

Indigo plucked at my skirts, straightening them for me.

For this very official occasion, she'd selected a midnight blue, off the shoulder gown with lace sleeves and little crystals sewn into the torso so it resembled a twinkling night sky.

They hadn't shoved a crown on my head yet—today I was wearing another silver circlet—but I was starting to wonder if there was a rule that required long sleeves and skirts to make the monarch as uncomfortable in summers as possible.

Probably. I bet it's that darned original king's work.

"How strongly will I feel the pull of the artifact that resonates with me?" I asked.

Skye had gotten herself a leather case for her tablet, which she flipped over it and gripped like a clutch as she frowned in thought. "That's difficult to say, as only royals have experienced the process. When I researched the process, it seemed to be a very strong, unmistakable pull. When you touch it, you'll know."

"*'You'll know,*' typical magic description," I grumbled. "Thank you for researching this so thoroughly."

Skye shrugged. "I had plenty of time while you were practicing magic and reading fae history books."

"Ahh, yes, I was very happy to graduate from 'Good Manners Mandy' and move on to more serious topics," I said. "Though I wish you had not given me the children's textbook version."

"Were you offended by the reading level?"

"No. The pictures were *awful*! They need to get a better artist," I complained.

A smile briefly warmed the edges of Skye's lips. "Good luck, Queen Leila. I look forward to your triumphant ceremony." She bowed, then swept off, leaving me and Indigo alone.

I sighed and raised a hand to rub my eyelids.

"Don't you *dare*." Indigo prodded my skirt. "It took me too long to get your eyeliner right—I don't want you ruining it."

When I cracked a smile at my companion she sniffed, then added, "You'll do fine, my Sovereign. I know you're worried about your magic, but in truth I think you've practiced more than a lot of nobles bother to."

"Maybe," I said. "It just seems better to brace myself—every official social situation I've been in has had a disaster in some form or another."

"No one can set a trap for you," Indigo said. "Only royals are allowed in these chambers—magic kills any regular fool who is stupid enough to try otherwise. It's a safe location. And the artifact resonates with *you*. They're impartial judges—you won't face any hatred for your blood."

I nodded, my spirits lifting a little—I'd been feeling a little low ever since the Night Realm shrunk a few days ago, and had been dreading this, but Indigo had a point.

"You're right," I said.

"Of course I am." Indigo put her hands on her hips. "Now, go pull your sword from the stone!"

I paused, my hand on the door. "Do they really have one of those in there?"

"I meant it figuratively." Indigo shook her head. "Stop freaking yourself out. Besides," she turned and started down the hallway in the same direction as Skye had. "You don't really care what all of those fussbudgets think, anyway!"

I grinned at the brownie's back and watched until she disappeared around the corner, before I reluctantly pushed open the rather unassuming door that was dust covered and had a few cobwebs draped around its frame.

The treasure room was deep in the heart of the castle in the Night Realm—it was a ceremony that couldn't be moved to the human world because, as Indigo had said, only royals were allowed inside.

Given the state of the castle, I'd prepared myself for a crumbling room with tarnished, decaying treasures.

But when I stepped inside, I found a space untouched by the passage of time.

Gold globs of magic flared to life, lighting up the chamber. A spell, written out in symbols, wrapped around the exterior of the room—it cast the light, served as a defense spell, and had a few other pieces to it that were too advanced for me and written in a language I didn't understand.

Inside the room were enough treasures—and of rare variety—to match a small country's gross domestic product. See? I'd been studying up *a lot* on ruling a country, er, Court.

There were baskets of giant gems; rows and rows of weapon stands filled with swords, halberds, staffs, bows, and more; trays of necklaces, bracelets, rings, and earrings studded with massive jewels; beautiful, ornately made instruments ranging from a violin to a golden flute to a lyre; huge shelves stuffed with magical tomes that were bound in dyed leather; and less regular artifacts, like a compass that smelled strongly of the ocean, a teacup made of solid gold, and an armoire filled with masks in different shapes and sizes.

The air smelled like metal, wood polish, and—weirdly—of dew. There wasn't a single cobweb or speck of dust to be seen anywhere.

The door closed behind me with an ominous thud, and I stood in the entryway, waiting for the pull of an artifact.

And I waited.

And waited.

Oh my gosh. I'd bet a lifetime supply of my favorite coffee that I'm going to be the first fae queen who doesn't have an artifact resonate with her.

I paced back and forth, peering anxiously around the room.

Maybe I need to go in deeper? So more of the artifacts feel me?

It sounded like an excuse, but I really, really didn't want to be the first queen without an official royal artifact.

I desperately walked up and down the rows of treasures, my stomach sloshing with each step I took.

I stared at the door I was supposed to go out—it had an ornate moon carved into its wooden surface. "It's fine," I said.

"Totally fine. I can work with this—I'll have to. Besides, it makes sense—I am human."

And then I felt it.

Faintly, magic brushed against me.

It wasn't a pull—it wasn't even a tug—it was just a barely-there feeling.

Desperate, I followed the feeling, which led me up to one of the baskets overflowing with jewels.

I picked up the first few on the top—a giant opal, then a ruby the size of a tennis ball. Neither reacted.

I worked my way down to the very bottom of the basket, pulling out precious gems of every color and size, until I reached what looked like a glass prism.

It was about the size of my thumb—just a little bigger—and had a pointed top, while the base was a little rough, as if it had been snapped off a bigger gem.

It was well polished, and when I held it up, it cast little rainbows across the room, and I felt the magic strengthen into a very slight tug.

It certainly didn't feel strong enough to be called an unmistakable pull, but when I touched it, I did feel...*something*. It wasn't like I felt the artifact itself, but more like I could better sense the wild magic that floated in the air through it.

It's about what I expected. I curled my hand around the prism. *I'm such an oddball here, of course I would end up with a small, unimpressive artifact.*

I mean, I wasn't thrilled—with all of this evidence stacking up I really had to wonder what on earth made the night mares think I could even be a decent queen—but a small artifact was better than no artifact.

I dutifully piled the gems back into the basket—since no one could come in after me, if I left it here it would stay a mess for my successor, which would be rude—but it wasn't until I'd made my way over to the exit that I had a happy realization.

"Oh, but this means I'll be able to fit it in my purse or pockets! Now that is some awesome convenience. Yep, it's fine!"

Cheered, I pushed the door open. As soon as a slit of light from the outside entered the room, the globs of light winked out.

I slithered out of the opening—I got the feeling I wasn't supposed to let anyone see the inside—and when the door clicked shut behind me, I felt magic thrum to life.

I'm pretty sure if anyone tried to go inside, the door wouldn't open.

I smiled brilliantly for my Court, and tried not to look too gleeful.

It was going to be oodles of fun to show them my tiny artifact!

I was pretty sure Lady Demetria was going to throw a fit and then maybe pass out from the exertion of it if I got her wound up enough.

Was it likely they were going to redouble their efforts to have me offed once they saw this? Absolutely! But you have to take joy in the small things—like annoying one's Court—or life won't be worth living.

With all the pomp I could muster, I held out my glass prism. "I have found my artifact!"

The fae nobles—and a bunch of representatives from the common fae—had gathered together like a judgmental choir and were seated in comfortable chairs—which looked distinctly human-made, understandable since two of the magic lights in the room weren't working and the rug laid over the stone ground was moth eaten.

As one, they looked at my artifact, and I was not disappointed with their reactions.

"This cannot be." Lady Demetria stood up. "We cannot have such an inept, powerless queen that her artifact is a *prism*!"

"We'll be the laughingstock of the other Courts!" Lady Chrysanthe—her dress color and hair tint today were a pretty purple—managed to create a tear or two, which she dabbed at with a handkerchief.

"There, there, Lady Chrysanthe," Lord Myron murmured to her. "Your concern for the Night Court is touching—you work on its behalf."

I was pretty impressed I kept a straight face after that one.

Of course a number of fae protested—including the pixie representative—and the room was ripe with grumbling and horror.

It wasn't all fun, though. A few reactions nearly made my smile sputter out and reminded me just how unworthy I really was.

I saw Skye, standing off to the side, see my prism, and discreetly pull a little metal mint tin from her pocket in the ongoing kerfuffle. She removed a chalky tablet from the tin and chewed it. Based on its large size and the way she crunched it, I was pretty sure it was a chewable antacid.

Yeah, I was *that good* of a monarch that my steward had taken to carrying around tins of antacids to munch on.

Maybe I need to increase my staff's hazard pay again...but we're still broke!

Indigo furrowed her forehead, but when she saw me looking, she smiled hugely. Lord Linus—his expression serious for the first time since I'd seen the annoying clinger—rubbed his jaw, and the edges of his eyes crinkled in worry. Chase, standing next to him, looked warily around the room, his golden eyes glowing.

I am in trouble.

I glanced back at the audience, and I almost missed him, but since he was possibly the only one in the room not murmuring to his neighbor, I did a second glance and spotted Lord Rigel.

CHAPTER EIGHTEEN

Leila

He was standing in the shadows—of course—but his silver hair gleamed against the copper tone of his skin. Unlike everyone else, he didn't look bothered by my artifact. In fact, everyone else was whispering to one another—Lord Dion, standing next to him, seemed to be exchanging a few whispers with a dryad—but Rigel met my gaze.

In that moment, I could have *sworn* I saw him quirk an eyebrow at me, but I blinked, and he was back to looking soulless and dark.

The "ceremony" was over pretty quickly—I just had to recite this dusty speech every monarch gave about having the power to protect the Court, blah, blah, blah.

The last piece of tradition that I had to observe was to stand at the door at the back of the room as everyone exited and walked past me.

Supposedly it was so they could congratulate me, but mostly I just got icy looks, or veiled hostility.

I did my part—standing there like a posable doll with a smile that never dropped.

Even when Lady Chrysanthe stopped in front of me, my expression didn't change.

"You are a disgrace to our Court," Lady Chrysanthe hissed. "I cannot *believe* the night mares chose someone like *you* over more qualified candidates."

"What, like you?" I drawled.

Lady Chrysanthe tucked her hair behind her ear, nearly upsetting the purple chrysanthemum fixed there. "You think you're clever with all of your witty retorts, but all it does is prove how little you understand us, and how much you don't belong. You'll never have the Court's loyalty."

I shrugged. "Doesn't bother me—I never thought any of you were physically capable of *being* loyal. And you're right, I don't belong—because I'm human."

Lady Chrysanthe shook out her skirts—for the ceremony she'd gone with a more traditional fae garb of a gown made of a light fabric that drifted around her like a cloud. "I predict that you're going to *ruin* us."

Lord Myron—who apparently followed Lady Chrysanthe's fashion cue and was wearing green robes today—gently touched her elbow. "Come now, Chrysanthe. Perhaps it won't be so—for the Court will always have you."

Lady Chrysanthe gave him a beautiful smile, and the pair swept off.

I leaned back so I could mutter at Skye and Indigo, who stood behind me. "Are we taking bets if those two end up becoming a thing? Because they've got the whole 'friends-to-more-than-friends' vibe going on."

"Actually, before your arrival in Court, Lord Myron and Lady Chrysanthe were merely acquaintances," Skye said.

I turned around for that bit of news. "Are you serious?"

"Quite." Skye adjusted her hold on her tablet. "The pair became more friendly shortly before the night mares were released to find you. Previously, their families have been at odds."

"They united over their mutual hatred of me?" I finally turned back around. "Huh, I never thought my presence would harken romance. Now that gives me warm feels!"

"I don't know that either of those two are unselfish enough to really love another," Indigo said.

My polite smile became real. "Indigo—such fire! Good for you!"

More fae filed past. A few did stop to give me curious looks or reluctant congratulations, but for the most part the room emptied *fast*.

Among the last to leave were Lord Dion and—drifting behind him as if he were worried I was a communicable disease—Lord Rigel.

"Congratulations, Queen Leila!" Lord Dion gave me a sweeping bow and a handsome grin. He'd donned gray robes for today—maybe the traditional clothes were a requirement for attendance?

"Thank you, Lord Dion," I said. I reflexively glanced down at the prism, which I had pinched between two fingers.

"It is very beautiful—and the size strikes me as convenient," Lord Dion said.

I knew he was just being friendly and charming because of the Paragon's plan—there was no way he didn't know he was the Paragon's choice, heck, the Paragon almost certainly told him so he would be extra charming. But I was pretty gleeful about that particular feature, and I didn't care if the comment was just sucking up.

"It is, isn't it?" I held the prism up for his admiration. "I can easily carry it in a purse, but I realized that if I have to wear sleeves even in the dead of summer for reasons I can't fathom, I could even tuck it up my sleeve!"

Lord Dion's smile shifted slightly—I think I was getting a glimpse of his true grin. "That's a brilliant idea—I don't think most monarchs are able to secretly carry their artifacts. Some of them aren't quite travel size." Back came on the charming façade as he leaned closer. "And, if you are able to secretly carry it upon your person, it would be a great reassurance to your safety!"

"Yes, that is a concern," I said.

Off to the side, Lord Rigel soundlessly shifted his weight. His black eyes were still lightless, but today that bored look seemed to crust his body language.

"Don't worry, Lord Rigel," I called to the assassin. "You'll always be special to me, since you were the first person to try to kill me."

That got some reactions.

Lord Dion—still admirably able to keep his politeness on display, asked in a deceivingly calm voice, "Rigel, you tried to *assassinate* the queen?"

"Queen Leila!" Skye's voice was an interesting combination of a whimper and a hiss.

Rigel stared at his friend with his soulless eyes—but all traces of boredom were gone, muwahah!

"It was nothing, Lord Dion—it was so long ago it's all in the past." I gave a few fanciful waves, then winked at the red haired fae when he turned back around to face me.

Lord Dion slightly inclined his head. "You are as forgiving as you are beautiful, Queen Leila. The Court is lucky to have you."

I was pretty impressed he was able to say that—it felt like there was a lie somewhere in there, but I couldn't figure out how he'd gotten away with saying it. "Thank you, Lord Dion. Your way with words is quite impressive."

Lord Dion laughed. "You must take me for a jokester, but

everything I have spoken is the truth! Nonetheless, I have taken up too much of your time. Good day, Queen Leila." Another bow, and he was strolling away.

Interestingly, Lord Rigel didn't follow him.

He was watching me, his expression back to that haunting, dark look—the only expression he wore besides boredom. Although, I noticed that unlike everyone else he was wearing his usual dark shirt and boots combo.

It feels like the fae put clothes on and off like costumes for a part they mean to play for the day, except Rigel. He never pretends to be anything but deadly and wild.

"Hey, Rigel. Thanks for coming," I said.

Skye made a quiet squeaking noise, and Indigo actually kicked me through my skirts.

Rigel blinked. "You aren't bothered by the appearance of your artifact."

I glanced down at the prism, then shrugged. "Nah."

He slowly nodded. "You intend to flaunt it to upset your naysayers."

I was a little surprised that *Lord Rigel*, of all people, correctly guessed what I was going to do. *I wouldn't think his chosen work would require people skills. Maybe he's just that observant?*

I studied the lethal but handsome lord, unable to pin down exactly what I was feeling.

He stared back at me, and I made myself smile. "I'd prefer to call them haters, but sure. I mean, it's not like the appearance necessarily reflects the artifact's ability to refine magic."

He blinked again. "You are a strange queen."

"Yeah, well your career path is illegal," I said.

Another kick from Indigo actually stung enough to make me jump a little.

"Rigel?" Dion called from farther down the hallway. "Are you coming?"

Lord Rigel stared at me for a few heartbeats, then glided off with all the grace a fae should possess.

Indigo waited until the assassin left the hall before she dared to speak. "Has he *ever* bowed to you?"

"Nope," I said.

"Queen Leila." Skye sounded strangled and at the last tether of her nerves. "Did Lord Rigel truly try to kill you?"

All the fae had left, and it was just us and Lord Linus and Chase who were speaking together—or really Lord Linus was speaking, Chase was babysitting him to make sure he didn't run off to find someone to play dice with as he had tried to when the fae first started arriving for the ceremony.

I turned around to face my companion and steward. "Rigel tried to off me right before Lady Demetria and the others found me and informed me I was queen. Unfortunately, he was about five minutes too late—Nebula had already shown up and bound me to the Court, so he couldn't hurt me."

"And you didn't think to *tell* us this?" Skye asked.

I tapped my chin. "Well, since he can't outright hurt me it didn't seem to matter as much as some of the other lords and ladies. I told Chase about him, though."

Skye pulled her tin out of a pocket—this close I could see it was pink and emblazoned with a few silver stars. She flipped it open, revealing an assortment of tablets.

"Are those antacids?" I asked.

Skye selected the chalky, chewable pill she'd eaten when I first revealed my artifact, and popped three of them. "Unfortunately."

I winced. "Sorry, Skye. I don't mean to drive you to acid reflux."

"Your food getting bespelled, or the Wraith attempting to kill you, are not your fault," she said.

"No, but I'm betting me shooting at Lady Chrysanthe was the nail in the coffin that made you decide to start carrying antacids around."

Skye look startled for a moment, then smiled a little, relaxing.

"But really, everything is fine with Rigel. He's not trying to kill me—and he's had plenty of chances to."

Skye crunched her pills. "It's never fine where the Wraith is concerned."

"Probably," Indigo agreed.

"But he can't kill me anyway," I pointed out.

"No, but the attempt resulted in something nearly as bad," Skye grimly said.

"And what would that be?"

"He's *noticed* you."

"In conclusion, do you have any questions about the first American King of the Night Court?" Skye asked.

I was surrounded by three books—the children's textbook with pictures, a recreation of a diary kept by a fae lady during the original king's time, and a book of sonnets and songs written about her.

"Nope. You had me read over him pretty thoroughly before today's lecture." I tried to sit up straighter in my chair.

"That's because he's a hero to our people—and widely adored!" Lord Linus briefly puffed up his chest. "Although he's not popular with the Day Court, given all the restrictions he adopted naturally affect them."

"Due to our shared nature as night and day, right?" I asked.

"Correct." Skye stacked a few books and put them back on the shelves.

I can't say I disagree with them. He's the bane of my existence, the reason why I have to get married, and why I couldn't turn down being queen and miss this entire mess. What a jerk.

We were in what Skye referred to as my personal study, but what I thought of as a library.

The room was rectangular shaped—it was very deep with one massive window—but it was two stories tall with a staircase and walkway that led to the upstairs bookshelves.

The ceiling had a painting of the night sky—Skye told me it was enchanted so supposedly the painting changed with the seasons—and almost every inch of wall space was covered with massive bookshelves.

The center of the room had several dangerously comfortable couches, a big desk for me, some filing cabinets, and extra tables and chairs.

I peered at the kids' textbook and tapped a painting of the original king. "What happened to his artifact? I didn't see it in the treasury room, and it's pretty unusual."

If the pictures were accurate, the original king used a massive staff topped with a crescent moon that was bigger than my head. Stars clustered around the top of the moon, and there was a gem of some kind at the base.

"The original king's primary and secondary artifacts, weapons, and armor are all preserved for public viewing, and are not held in the treasury," Skye said.

"They're on display in the Night Realm castle." Lord Linus plopped down on a couch. He set his head on the arm rest, and scooted so he could look at me upside down. "Hey, we should check them out sometime—it'd be a great bonding experience!"

"Not interested." I frowned at him. "What are you even *doing* here?"

"I'm your advisor. I'm here to advise." He lifted a hand into the air and gestured without wobbling in his precarious situation.

"I invited him," Skye said. "Your...interaction with Lord Rigel made me realize that although I have taught you the names of the fae nobility, I haven't taught you much on their common alliances and interactions. Lord Linus will know much better, given his lengthy experience."

"Yes! I'm the fae expert!" He gave me a thumbs up. "Granted, I've spent the last two decades traveling a lot, but I kept up to date on all the gossip!"

"If you have time, Queen Leila, I do recommend you see the original king's weapons," Skye said. "They're very inspiring to see."

"I'd like to, but it will have to wait." I stretched my arms out in front of me and groaned. "I've got a phone call with my realtor—he found a buyer for the Chicago condo—and then I'm going to run some numbers with the accountants. I also need to talk to Dusk and Dawn about the stables this afternoon, and whether or not we need to try to care for the shades and glooms, and tonight I need to practice magic."

"Yes, you have been very diligent with that." Skye put another book away. "Are you afraid your security is not enough? We could tell Chase to increase hiring."

"Nah, it's fine," I said. "I'm actually not practicing for my safety. Well, not much. I'm practicing some, but I've switched over."

"Oh? What, then, are you so diligently working on?" Lord Linus sat upright for the occasion—despicably, his hair fell perfectly into place, and there wasn't even a wrinkle on his shirt.

"I'm practicing barriers and wards," I said. "Next time the Night Realm starts to shrink, I can bolster our wards."

"Ahhhh," Lord Linus nodded. "Yes—that's very smart."

Skye slowly picked her tablet up, her eyebrows knitting together.

"Is something wrong, Skye?" I asked.

"No, Queen Leila. It's just..." She hesitated, then met my gaze. "I'm reluctant to bring it up because I'm aware you are learning more, managing more, and doing more than any monarch of the Night Court has in the past two generations, but there is your marriage to think about."

"Ah, right." I leaned back in my chair. "I haven't thought about it very much."

"You have until the end of summer—which is when you *need* to be crowned," Skye rushed to add. "Before then we have the Magiford Midsummer Derby at the end of July—which is fast approaching."

"I need to look into that too, but I'm more concerned about my marriage. It's not really a decision I want to make last minute." I stared at the tea set displayed on one of my bookshelves. My library was a room in a fae household; obviously it *had* to have something tea related on display, but I actually really liked looking at this set. The teapot was silver and was a lot taller than other teapots I'd seen, and the cups were beautifully shaped glasses with gold flourishes and swirls painted on them.

The swirls on the cups were particularly soothing to stare at, so I kept my eyes fixed on them as I continued. "I don't need to be quizzed on the members of my Court anymore—I think I even have the leaders of the common fae down. Let's scratch the quizzes and use the time scheduled for it to start looking over possible candidates."

"It will be my time to shine!" Lord Linus declared.

I glared at him. "*You* are the last person I would consult on a good marriage partner."

He blinked innocently at me. "Why?"

"It's because you even have to *ask* that, that I know you're despicable," I said.

Lord Linus managed to keep up his innocent look despite my harsh criticism.

I wonder, is he really an idiot? Or just pretending?

Lord Linus sighed. "I heard about this—daughters rebelling against their parents. Don't worry, Leila—I'll always love you! Which is why I'd like to bring up the discussion of my *pay*." He flashed his white teeth at me. "I'd like an advancement, thank you."

Yeah, he's just an idiot.

I tilted my head back and stared up at the painting on the ceiling.

"Are you all right, Queen Leila?" Skye asked.

"Yeah. It just feels like I'll never be able to catch up. Like I'm going to die, buried by work." I rubbed my eyes. "I need to find a husband, learn how to bolster our realm barrier, get myself crowned so the other Courts don't get any ideas about us, deal with whoever hired Rigel to kill me and whoever bespelled the food—assuming they aren't the same person—cut spending, keep learning how to manage the Court…"

My throat squeezed, and it was hard to breathe. "I don't think I can do it."

"You're doing quite well, Queen Leila," Skye said.

"Yeah, but doing 'well' isn't going to solve all those problems." I straightened up in my chair and tried to motivate myself to stand—I had too much to do to sit here and feel sorry for myself.

"It's important to remember these problems were not your creation. Thus, none of it is your fault, thus, it's also not your fault if you can't solve it!" Lord Linus said with the assurance of someone who had used this excuse before.

I rested my chin on my hand and stared at him. "*You're* one of my problems—do you know that?"

He ignored me. "What you ought to do is go visit your mother. Nothing can soothe you like a hug from your mother!"

Because the advice was coming from him, I was initially tempted to ignore it, but he actually had a point.

"That's not a bad idea—I haven't seen her since I moved in."

Lord Linus folded his arms across his chest. "It's as I've always said—you inherited your genius from me."

"Really? Because I think it's more like the saying that even a blind, deaf, ancient squirrel unable to smell will occasionally find a nut," I said.

"I'm pretty sure that saying doesn't use all those descriptors," Lord Linus said.

"Maybe not, but they apply in your case." I stood up and rolled my shoulders back. "But this decides it—I'm clearing my schedule for this Saturday, and I'm going home to see my parents."

CHAPTER NINETEEN

Leila

I spent an unbelievably peaceful day with my parents—arriving early enough to eat breakfast with them, where I proceeded to pound down enough food for three people.

Most of the time was filled with eating—that was mainly me—drinking coffee—also just me—and chatting with my parents.

I helped Dad clean out stalls—there is something really therapeutic about doing work with your hands after you've been penned up doing office stuff for weeks on end—and by the time the blue sky was darkening and the clouds were streaked with pink from the setting sun, I was sitting out in a lawn chair that overlooked one of the horse pastures, nursing a cup of decaf coffee.

The birds were singing extra loud as they returned to their nests for the night, and a few lightning bugs started to glow, tracing spinning pathways through the air.

Bagel was pushing his face through two of the wooden boards

in the fence—which had been repaired since the fae thoughtlessly sliced through it.

I sat on the edge of my seat and caressed his velveteen nose.

"You know, I think he misses those horses of yours." Dad propped his arms up on the fence and affectionately rubbed Bagel's forehead.

I almost spat out my mouthful of coffee. "The *night mares?*"

"Yeah, he liked them a lot. He pined after them once they took off after you."

I shook my head at the fuzzy donkey. "You have messed up priorities, little man."

Dad laughed, then leaned down to kiss me on the top of my head. "I'm proud of you, Leila."

I peered up at him. "Where did that come from?"

He shrugged. "You've been busy with your Court, but I can tell in your texts and your phone calls that you're doing your best. You don't even try to hide that you can't stand most of your people, and you had to give up all your plans for the future that you'd worked hard toward, you know, being a mature adult and all."

"Responsible Adult," I said.

He chuckled. "A responsible adult, yeah. Despite all of that, you still do your best for your Court's sake." He smiled with all the love and affection he'd given me every day since I met him when he started dating Mom. "You're special."

I snorted. "Yeah, special like Bagel-the-idiot."

"Maybe a little like Bagel, but neither he nor you are idiots." He squinted down at me. "Not many animals could love those night mares of yours. But Bagel can, and you can. I don't think you understand how special that is."

I clutched my coffee cup tighter. "Thanks, Dad."

"Of course." He ruffled my hair, then looked back at the barn. "I better give the horses their hay for the night. I'll be back—don't run off while I'm gone!"

"I'm not going anywhere," I promised.

As he headed out to the barn, Mom joined me, plopping down in the chair next to mine and passing over a slice of my favorite German chocolate cake.

"Thanks!" I eagerly dug into the thick slice. "I've missed your cooking *so much*."

Mom gave me an amused look. "I think you miss eating regular food is the reality."

"Can't be helped." I took a sip of my coffee to wash down the flavor of the sweet, coconut frosting.

Mom watched me devour my cake for a few moments. She stood up to pet Bagel—the donkey leaned eagerly into her hand. "Do you feel any better?" she asked.

I was only halfway done with my cake, but I set my fork down for the moment. "Yeah. I enjoyed the break—and getting to eat was amazing." I sipped my coffee—my parents had made my favorite flavor, chocolate blueberry, for the occasion. "I'm not looking forward to going back."

I'm dreading it, actually. Today just reminds me how little I like the fae.

"Have you asked Linus for help?" Mom sat back down on her chair, scooting it around to face me. "He told me he's your official advisor."

That little tattle-tale—I can't understand how she can stand to talk to him!

"No, I haven't asked him for help," I said. "I don't like him. I wouldn't have even made him advisor, except if I hadn't I think he would have wandered off and gotten himself farther in debt from gambling or drinking or whatever it is that he does."

"He can be very capable."

"He doesn't *act* like it," I grumbled. "He runs around and is generally annoying. I don't like that I'm half fae, but knowing I inherited *his* blood makes it worse." I meant it as sort of a joke, but Mom didn't smile.

She studied me with very soft but sad eyes. "You're unhappy."

I shrugged and went back to my cake. "I'm a human that's been forced to run a fae Court. I don't know anything about the Night Court, and I'm struggling to keep up with the nobles, stay alive, and learn what I need to so the Court itself can survive. They have all these rules…" I trailed off and stared down into my coffee cup before I took a swig of it, then finished the cake off.

I was about to stand up and go back to the house to load my empty plate in the dishwasher—or maybe to get myself another slice of cake, who knows?—but Mom reached out and set her hand on my arm.

I looked into my mom's eyes, which were warm with love.

"Honey," she said, her voice soft but kind. "You're wrong."

I blinked. "What?"

"You aren't human," she said bluntly. "I didn't even *raise* you as a human. You are half fae. You've known magic since you were little, you observed supernatural politics as a teenager. When the Drakes hired you to train their dogs, they chose you because you are *half* human and *half* fae."

I settled back in my chair, surprised by her fierce words. "Yeah?"

"It's time you stop acting like—as you said yourself—a human ruling over fae."

"…what?"

"Sweetie, you're special. And I'm not saying that just because you're my daughter, but because of your blood." Mom leaned across the gap between us and set her hands on my cheeks. "You can do magic like a fae, you're *beautiful* like a fae, you have the stronger senses of a fae. You. Are. Fae. But," she let me go and held up a finger. "You can lie like a human. You aren't bound to the typical fae rules of conduct. And—most importantly—you were raised out of the political game most fae are born into. You've lived in a world they can't even fathom. You. Are. Human. You're *both*—and that's your greatest strength."

"Yeah, but what does that have to do with me being queen?"

Mom narrowed her eyes. "Because you're acting like a human who has to be like a fae queen, when you're neither."

I could only gape in shock. Mom had that edge back—the one she used to pin the Paragon into place.

"Stop going along with their plans just because it's the way it's always been. Stop thinking of yourself as helpless when you have all of the advantages they have, and extras! You need to rule how *you* want to—you can shape the Court how you want to! If you're sick of its festering underbelly, change it."

Not a single thought was able to form in my mind, I was that surprised.

"You can continue this way if you want, of course. But—Leila—you're going to be Queen of the Night Court for the rest of your life. This isn't some temporary job."

I clutched my mug to my chest, but she was right.

I had focused on surviving the way the fae wanted me to. I didn't play up the strengths I had that they didn't. I'd let them drag me into their game, and protested by being snippy with them, when in reality I could just change the game.

"You're right, Mom," I said.

"Naturally—I knew this day would come eventually. You were always so proud to be considered Paul's daughter we both worried it would make you reject your blood." She took my cake plate off my lap.

"Dad agrees with you?" I asked.

"Of course, but whenever he tried to encourage you to embrace your fae blood more, you'd do the opposite and dig in your heels and insist you're human." Mom briefly scowled. "He always did dote on you too much for your own good."

I laughed.

"Sweetie, all I want for you is that you make a life for yourself—as queen—that makes you happy. What do *you* want?"

I stared at Bagel. "I don't want to scramble around in the power games that they play. I'm sick and tired of them."

Mom rattled the dish as she started for the house. "Then make it so they can't play those games. Use your humanity—and knowledge of the human world—against them."

Bagel gave a loud hee-haw that made his entire body move when he sucked in air.

Slowly, I smiled. "Okay. I think I know how I'm going to start."

I'M PRETTY sure everyone back at the mansion knew I was up to something when I called Azure to tell her she didn't need to come pick me up that night.

But none of them could have expected the fun I was about to unleash on them.

As I drove through the neighborhood, passing the apartments, houses, and eventually the mansions, the loud rumble of my truck drew people outside.

My mansion had a really well-lit driveway. It was easy to pull the truck around the circle, even with the trailer hitched up to it.

Trailers aren't loads of fun to drive, and I hadn't driven Dad's much, but I was determined to see my plan through. I just drove reaaallly slow around the corners and avoided backing it up.

Eventide—in his white dress shirt and dark vest—was the first to greet me. "Welcome...home...Queen Leila?" He looked from me to the trailer.

"Don't worry about this—Dad is coming to pick it up tomorrow morning." I patted the side of the trailer, then walked around to the back end to open it up.

"Did you need to bring it for something?" Eventide scratched at the base of the small goat horns that popped up from the mop of his thick, curly brown hair.

"Oh, *yes*." I was practically glowing with smugness. I swung the doors open and hopped inside. It was dark, but I was familiar with the trailer, so I was able to move the necessary bars, click and unclip the right ties, and lead out what I'd brought back.

Eventide clutched the bottom of his vest. "Is that...a *donkey*?"

Bagel stopped at the end of the trailer to happily hee-haw out to his new abode.

Surprisingly, I heard happy shrieks drift from the direction of the stables—the night mares must have heard him.

"Might I enquire what's going on?" I heard Skye's voice, and Bagel and I hopped off the trailer in time to see my steward, companion, and Lord Linus stroll down the front sidewalk.

When they saw my furry friend, they stopped dead.

"You brought a *donkey* back with you?" Indigo asked.

"Yep! This is Bagel." I patted him on the neck, and he peeled back his lips to smile at my friends.

"Why?" Indigo asked.

"Because he's my pet. I'm queen, I shouldn't have to go without him."

I turned to Skye—I'd thought she'd have lots of objections—but she was too busy opening her antacid tin and crunching pills to say anything.

To my surprise, Lord Linus strolled closer then squatted down next to Bagel and started stroking him.

Bagel preened under the attention.

"He's cute," Lord Linus said.

"Thanks."

The screams coming from the direction of the stable were getting louder.

I better take him back there before they break their doors down.

"There should be room for him in the stables." I tugged on Bagel's lead rope. "But I still need to tell Dusk and Dawn—"

I jumped, and I heard bitten off curses and startled yelps

behind me as a familiar stone archway and gate popped into existence.

Solstice, Eclipse, Nebula, Comet, Twilight, and Blue Moon charged through the gateway, prancing across the perfect lawn.

Bagel bellowed out a greeting—which they enthusiastically returned.

Eventide yipped and scurried backwards as the night mares charged down the driveway, tossing their heads.

Only Lord Linus stayed with me and Bagel as the night mares circled around us, affectionately sniffing and wheezing at us.

Bagel brayed happily as Blue Moon nosed his cheek.

"I can see your night mares love him," Lord Linus mildly observed.

I was pretty shocked when he nonchalantly reached up and patted Blue Moon's neck once he stood up.

"Come on, Bagel. Let's get you over to the stables."

Bagel hee-hawed. His loud, booming bray echoed across the mansion grounds.

"Your nobles are going to *love* that noise," Indigo said.

I tossed a grin at her over my shoulder. "Oh, I really hope so!"

I ROLLED my prism around my palm, practicing pulling magic through it and pushing it into the magic wards that were about a car length away. "Right," I shouted.

There was some scuffling before my six night mares turned to the right as one long line.

"Good boys and girls—you're so smart!" I cooed to them.

I cast one last look at the ward and tried to pull more magic through my prism—I was having a hard time figuring out how much power it could handle—but when I pulled enough to physically feel it in my hands, I cut off my connection and shoved it into the ward.

The ward rippled, but gave me no indication if my magical boost was at all useful. I was guessing not—when I had asked Skye about the ward, she mentioned I'd be able to visibly see my magic spread across the ward, and I didn't think she was talking about a puddle-sized amount like I was looking at right now.

I need to get better at this. But there is something about my artifact—I can't feel it quite like I can my charm bracelet.

Brushing my hands off on my breeches, I crossed the field—tripping on a root poking out of the ground that I didn't see due to the Night Realm's perpetual darkness.

"Whoever decided the Night Realm should be dark all the time was incredibly short sighted," I grumbled.

"Historically the Night Realm has regular day cycles—if the Court is balanced," Lord Linus said.

I glanced curiously at him. "Have you ever witnessed it in daytime?"

"Yeah, when I was a kid—but even back then our days were pretty short. Once the new monarchs were crowned about twenty years ago, the sun never rose in here again." Lord Linus had managed to grub his way into a tiny bit of my good graces because he seemed to genuinely like Bagel, and he didn't whimper whenever the night mares surrounded him.

Today, he'd wormed his way into coming to the Night Realm with me by offering to hold Bagel's lead rope as I practiced magic.

But I still didn't like the guy all that much.

I gave the fae a sharp nod, then turned my back to him and squinted through the darkness. "Right again."

The night mares, still moving as one, turned again.

"Now left!"

The night mares turned accordingly.

"You're so good! Come on in!"

The night mares trotted up to me, encircling me so I could easily pat each of their necks and kiss their muzzles.

Lord Linus watched us as he rubbed at an itchy spot on

Bagel's neck, making the donkey melt into him. "I get why you're practicing with the ward. But what's up with the night mares?"

"Why am I teaching them verbal commands?" I asked.

"Yeah."

I smiled and rubbed Twilight's forehead. "Because I like them, and I've decided I'm going to make them a bigger part of my Court—because I want to."

And because maybe, just maybe, I'm thinking about entering the Magiford Midsummer Derby with one of them.

I expected Lord Linus to protest—maybe trot a complaint out about tradition or something—but he just nodded. "Okay, then."

"You're not going to protest?"

"Why would I?"

I smiled when Blue Moon rested his chin on my shoulder. "Because it goes against tradition?"

"You're Queen of the Night Court," he said. "You don't have to follow tradition. *I* don't think you should even have to get married to be crowned, but does anyone listen to me? No!"

I waited for a deeper explanation, but it seemed he was content to partially sidestep the issue. "Technically I'm not even training them right—I'm supposed to use the words gee and haw for turning, but I couldn't ever keep those terms straight, and it seems stupid when the night mares can understand most of what I say anyways."

"So?" Lord Linus frowned a little when Bagel smeared green spit on his shirt, then shrugged. "You could ride your night mares through the mansion hallways and I wouldn't care. I'm just pleased you're talking to me without sneering—for once."

What is up with this guy? I narrowed my eyes and clenched my prism tight. *His airheaded ways are too real to be an act—especially because fae don't* act. *They veil, cheat, and betray, but they do all of that with stoic expressions. They don't act stupid for fun. Is he really an idiot?*

Lord Linus caught me staring at him. "What?"

"Nothing."

He grinned. "No, no, don't retreat now! You felt it, right? Our father-daughter bond! You're finally willing to accept all my paternal love!"

Yeah, he's definitely an idiot—or he would know to read me better.

Lord Linus sighed happily. "I'll have to tell Chase! I'm sure he'll be thrilled to know our relationship is deepening!"

"No, it's not," I said.

"It is! It absolutely is! You just went five full minutes without insulting me or scowling! Where's my cellphone? I should take a picture to commemorate the moment."

Disgusted, I turned away from him.

That was when I caught sight of the gloom, standing at the base of a tree, flicking its tail.

"Hey there, beautiful. Did you want something?" I held out my hand.

The gloom bounded across the meadow, fearlessly twining itself through the night mares' legs and rubbing its head against my hand.

Its purr was a deep, rusty sound I could feel in my fingers as it leaned into me.

Lord Linus whistled. "Your mother told me your magic made you good with animals. It was pretty obvious from the way the night mares adore you, but I confess, I didn't think you were strong enough to bring in the glooms."

The gloom was desperately leaning into me, as if it wanted to soak up every little bit of contact that it could.

"Good kitty." I winced when I stroked its back, feeling its bones through its skin on the patches where it was missing hair.

An eerie howl—similar to a wolf's but more jagged and sharp—sliced through the air.

I had to nudge Nebula aside so I could see the shade standing behind them.

It was a barely decipherable black blob—I could barely make out its outline since the Night Realm didn't have a full moon tonight, but its head was easy to spot because its orange eyes disturbingly glowed in the dark.

"Perfect timing. Come on, kitty-cat. Guys, could you move?"

The night mares dispersed, letting me walk closer to the shade.

I stopped about halfway to it and crouched down. "Are you here to say hello?" I asked it, even as the gloom leaned into my shoulder and purred.

The shade wagged its tail, then cautiously slunk up to me. I offered it my hand, and it nosed me—its nose unnaturally dry and scratchy.

I need to get a vet out here.

I petted the shade. "You're a good puppy, aren't you? Yes you are!"

It sat down like a dog at an obedience class, its ears perked and tail thumping on the ground.

"But I'm glad you're both here." I addressed the gloom and shade together. "Because I wanted to ask—do any of you want to come live with me?"

CHAPTER TWENTY

Leila

"Queen Leila, we need to discuss—" Skye strode into my library, but her arms shot out and she gripped the doorway when she saw the four glooms and seven shades sitting around me and Chase.

"What? What is it?" Indigo pushed her head into the space between Skye and the door with a scowl, which shifted immediately to surprise as her eyes grew as big as moons.

"Indigo, Skye—perfect timing!" I smiled. "I'd like you to meet our newest additions to the mansion!"

I waded through the shades and pointed to each animal as I named it. "We have Bob, Larry, Barbra, Mary, Tom." The shades flicked their ears as I said their names.

I paused in front of the last two—the biggest shade of the pack, and a smaller one that had adorable gray front paws. "And this is Kevin and Steve—Steve is, in fact, a girl. I just didn't think to check before I started naming, and now she won't answer to anything *but* Steve."

"Steve?" Skye repeated, staring at the shades in a way that said there was going to be a shopping trip for more antacids in her future.

"Yep. Then for the glooms we have Fluffy and Patches over here, and then Whiskers & Muffin." I rested my hand on Muffin's head—she had a cute little swirl of red fur on her forehead while Whiskers had excessively long, white whiskers.

Indigo stared at my new menagerie. "I'm assuming there is a reason why you gave the shades the most bland, human names ever, and the glooms all sound like pet cats?"

"I spent a *really long time* on my night mares' names—I wanted to give them beautiful names that would make people see their beauty." I clapped my hands together. "That didn't work. I figured this time I should concentrate on using their names to lower their potential fear factor a little. I don't know if it worked. What do you think, Chase?"

The werewolf rubbed his jaw as he stared down at Whiskers, who was leaning into him and purring. "I think I might prefer a higher fear factor for the sake of security." He absently patted Whiskers's back as he pulled out his cellphone.

"I was introducing them to Chase, so they'd know to go to him if they see anything weird or dangerous," I said. "But I should probably introduce them to you, too."

Indigo sucked in a deep breath that made her puff up like a hedgehog, then stiffly marched deeper into the library.

Skye took a few steps and paused—I think out of confusion and not fear based on the way she furrowed her eyebrows. "You believe they can understand such things?"

"Oh, for sure." I nearly fell over when Kevin and Steve crowded my space, asking for more pets. "My natural magic is the one part about my fae heritage I'm confident in, and it's a bit of a cheat code that makes whatever animals I work with smarter. But even beyond that, the fae creatures are way more intelligent than your typical pet dog. They're a cinch to work with—once they trust you."

Indigo was still puffed out with fear as she thrust her hand out to Steve. "Nice to meet you."

Steve sniffed her hand, then leaned her massive head forward and licked Indigo's cheek, her tail wagging wildly.

Indigo made a strangled noise. "Their breath is *awful*." She squeaked when Whiskers—bored since Chase was busy—sniffed her back and then leaned into her. Since Indigo was smaller, the shades were taller than her, and the glooms were nearly eye height.

"Do you think they could be taught to watch for certain individuals, or pick up distinctive smells?" Chase squatted down and took Fluffy's picture.

"Yeah, but not right away," I said. "It's going to take them some time to adjust to living here and not in the Night Realm."

"Living *here*?" Skye asked with extra politeness in her voice.

Chase nodded, then addressed the cat. "You're Patches?"

The real Patches tapped her paw on Chase's shoulder.

"My apologies, then you must be Fluffy?"

Fluffy purred and twitched his whiskers.

Chase tapped away on his cellphone. "I'll make certain to send their pictures to my men."

"Thanks, Chase." I sat on the arm of one of the comfortable couches.

Chase bowed slightly, then moved on to taking the shades' pictures.

"You said we needed to talk about something, Skye?" I asked.

Skye squared her shoulders. "Yes, Queen Leila." She glided forward, stopping respectably short of the animals. She held out her hand, and both Kevin and Muffin meandered up to her.

Kevin licked her hand while Muffin twined around her like a house cat.

Apparently, they like all of my people. That's a relief—but maybe I shouldn't rely too much on their opinion. They liked Lord Linus a lot, which doesn't demonstrate good judgment.

Irritated, I pushed away the memory of Lord Linus rubbing Kevin's belly while the big shade twitched his paws in glee.

The glooms and shades opened up a little path for Skye, who took it, then set her tablet down. "We have two matters to discuss. Firstly, you must decide on your personal seal."

I frowned. "My what?"

"Your personal seal." Skye flipped her tablet around to show me. "The Night Court has an official seal that is used for any official statements, papers, alliances, etcetera, that need to be posted to other Courts, to the Curia Cloisters, or to other supernaturals. It stands for our Court—and by extension your will." She tapped a picture of a seal—a crescent moon and a few stars—pressed into navy blue wax.

"However, you need a personal seal to use on all internal documents—any statements you might give specifically just in the Court, anything that needs you to bear witness like passing estates on to children, tax documents, basically anything that will stay in our Court but needs to be marked so the citizens know it comes from you."

I plopped down in my leather office chair, which wheezed out air. "It's *just* for internal stuff? No one outside the Night Court will see it—including other Courts?"

"Correct. Given Court loyalty—and the...competitive spirit between Courts—no one outside the Night Court would ever see this seal, given that it would mean they are looking at important internal documents." Skye swiped on her tablet, showing a new display of seals, all pressed into wax blobs. "Here are examples from past rulers."

The seals varied greatly from fierce—a scythe slashing through a full moon—to beautiful—a flower in front of tiny stars. There was even one with a gloom on it—although it didn't look as underfed or have patchy fur like mine.

"Okay." I thoughtfully leaned back in my chair.

Skye bowed slightly. "I expect you'll need a few days to think it over."

"Nah." A grin crawled across my lips. "I know exactly what I want in my seal."

Ohh, this was going to be fun.

Skye pulled a stylus out of a pocket in her suitcoat and took her tablet back. Once she got to a new screen, she held her stylus above the tablet in preparation. "Yes?"

"It's a creature from the Night Realm," I said.

Skye nodded as she started to write on her tablet. "An appropriate choice. What one?"

My big grin made my cheeks hurt. "For my seal, I want a pigeon-racoon-griffin."

"You want one of *those* trash pickers?" Indigo yelped. "But they're disgusting—they're vermin!"

"I know. That's why I want it," I said.

Skye's eyes widened slightly, but she wrote it down.

"You've lost your mind," Indigo flatly said.

"Nope—I have a really good reason for it." I wanted to look cool and set my feet up on the edge of my desk, but it was a *really* nice desk, and my parents raised me better than that, so I leaned forward and rested my elbows on it instead.

"I've finished with the photos—I'll explain things to my people immediately," Chase interrupted. He bowed to me, nodded to Indigo and Skye, then beat a hasty retreat like a man who knew something was about to go down and he wanted no part of it.

Indigo had her hands propped up on her hips and didn't even acknowledge Chase's flight. "What kind of idiotic reason could inspire you to pick out the realm vermin as your seal?"

"Because every last noble is going to *hate* it," I purred.

"But it's not going to stabilize your position, or increase your reputation," Skye said.

"Yeah, I'm aware of that. And I don't care anymore."

Skye almost dropped her stylus. "W-what do you mean?"

"This game that the Paragon told me about—the way I need to win over my Court and establish a strong front of power? I'm not interested in it."

"Queen Leila." Skye sat down in one of the chairs pulled up to my desk for the first time since I interviewed her. "What do you mean? You have to play for power—there is no other way."

"You don't *think* there is another way, because there's never *been* another way," I corrected. "And there's also never been a half human…half fae on the throne before."

"I'll bite." Indigo hopped into the other chair, draping her arm over the side to pet Kevin. "What are you up to?"

Muffin made her way over to me and leaned into my chair. I petted her—a warm comfort as I tried to figure out how to explain everything.

Indigo is mine—I know she'll stick with me. I think Skye will. I hope she will. But I have to tell them either way. I can't keep my closest people in the dark.

"I've been too reactive," I said. "I respond to insults, attempts on my life, and attacks on my people. I'm sick of just sitting around waiting for stuff to happen in order for me to really do anything."

"If you were more aware of the intricacies of fae life, it would be easier to respond," Skye admitted.

"Yeah, except I'm not. And I don't think I ever will be—I don't *want* to be. The fae are screwed up." I stroked the red spot on Muffin's head. "But I'm done being reactive. It's time for me to go on the offense. But I'm not going to do it the classic fae way—no murders, no insults, no social snubs or stupid ploys like that. I'm going to troll my Court."

"Troll?" Skye asked.

"Since they're offended by me, I'm not going to hide what makes me different. I'm not going to conform to their picture of what a queen should and shouldn't do. I'm going to name my pets whatever I want. I'm going to put a pigeon-raccoon-griffin on my seal to show them just how little I actually care what they think, and I'm going to rip this current system apart."

Indigo adjusted her cat eye glasses. "That's what bringing your donkey here was—the first shots fired in this new campaign of yours."

In my surprise that she'd caught on already, I stopped petting Muffin. The cat shoved her head under my hand, restarting my brain. "Yes."

"And what do you hope to accomplish by this?" Skye asked. She didn't seem upset—surprised, yes, and maybe curious. But she hadn't gotten her antacids tin out, yet, which was a good sign. "And do you mean to do the same with the other Courts?"

"The Night Court thinks they can yank me around—I just want to show them that they can't. I don't know about the other Courts, yet. I've only met King Solis, and something tells me he's not the norm."

"No, he's far dreamier and kind hearted than the rest of the Courts." Indigo sighed in appreciation.

Skye tapped her stylus on her tablet, then nodded. "Very well."

I blinked, surprised. "You're just going to accept it?"

Skye shrugged. "I am your steward—I do what you tell me. It's in the job description. Besides, you have proven your desire to do what is right by your struggle with your studies and your desperation to improve your magic. Truthfully, I don't understand what you mean to do, but I am confident enough that—based on your past actions—you don't seek to get everyone killed."

"No," I agreed. "Just ruffle some feathers."

"Yes," Skye hesitantly agreed. "Which is something the Night Court, perhaps, needs right now." She cleared her throat, then looked down at her stylus. "I will see to it that several sample sketches are drawn up for your seal."

"Thank you, Skye. Was there something else you wanted to ask me?"

"Yes, about your marriage—have you given it any thought?"

I groaned and let my head fall and thump my desk. "Not much since you last mentioned it." I peeled my forehead off the table and made myself look at her. "Is there anyone besides Lord Dion who is at all remotely trustworthy?"

"Trustworthy is not a word I would often use to describe any fae, Queen Leila," Skye said.

"You can say that again," Indigo muttered.

"I have taken the liberty of making two lists of the top candidates depending on your choice. A list of fae from less powerful families—which means they won't be able to pressure you into anything, but are likely to use your position to aid their climb to power and will be unable to help you should you need it—and a list of candidates from more powerful families—which means they will certainly aid you should you need it, but they will also pressure you to rule in a way that benefits them."

"Ohhh, I bet family dinners are going to be fun," I said. "Which list is Lord Dion on?"

Skye slightly pursed her lips. "Neither, actually. I believe that's why the Paragon chose him. He's more neutral—while his family is neither powerful nor weak, he is personally well liked by the Courts, considered quite competent, and has strong ties to the Paragon thanks to his work outside the fae community."

Ah. That's why the Paragon chose him. He's the least ruthless match up, but then the Paragon could pressure me if he liked.

The Paragon didn't strike me as the type to do so—he was pretty famous for trying to avoid work, actually. But marrying someone who was most loyal to the Paragon didn't sit quite right with me, either.

It's not like there are any other options. No one in this awful community is a true neutral. They wouldn't survive.

It occurred to me, then, that there was perhaps one *deadly* neutral lord in my Court.

"Just for curiosity's sake—and I know he's not on the lists, but if he were...which list would Lord Rigel be on?"

Skye shifted her tablet and thoughtfully tilted her head. "Again, neither list."

"Really?"

"He's the only one in his house," Indigo said. "His parents and older brother died under *'mysterious'* circumstances. Mind you, less than a month after their funeral was when he launched his career as an assassin."

"Because everyone fears Lord Rigel—and because he is the only member of his line—he has been able to remain outside typical Court politics," Skye said.

"Yeah, because no one wants to get on *the Wraith's* bad side," Indigo grumbled.

Skye cleared her throat and tucked a curl of her chin-length hair behind her ear. "I'll email the lists to you, if that is acceptable, Queen Leila?"

"Yeah. Yeah, it's fine." I forced a smile. "Thanks, Skye."

Skye nodded and stood up, pushing her chair back a little. She was picking her way through the shades when I called after her.

"Skye, who would you recommend?"

Skye passed through the wall of animals before she turned around, her expression contemplative. "Logically, Lord Dion would be the easiest partner," she said. "He will cause the least trouble, and won't actively scheme against you since he is a friend of the Paragon's."

I narrowed my eyes, hearing something in her voice. "But?"

She hesitated. "I'm not certain he would be the best spouse. He would remain loyal and friendly. But I suspect he wouldn't quite know how to react to your fire—like the majority of the fae."

To my fire, huh? I don't know that I can afford to be sentimental like that, but it still makes me happy Skye notices and thinks about these kinds of things.

"Thank you, Skye."

She bowed. "Of course, Queen Leila." She strode from the room—all beauty and elegance despite the cat and dog hair that graced the legs of her slacks.

I leaned back into my chair and groaned. "Am I crazy, Indigo?"

"Yeah," Indigo factually said. "But that's okay. Your Court is filled with a bunch of psychos. They could use your brand of crazy."

I laughed. "Thanks."

Indigo shrugged and shed her sweater like she tended to do now when it was just the two of us. Today she wore a yellow Hufflepuff shirt, which she fidgeted with. "My Sovereign?"

"Hmm?"

"I wanted to offer my help, if you think you need it," Indigo said.

"Oh!" I perked up. "Really? I actually do need some help, and I'm fairly certain you're the only one in my Court who can help me."

Indigo pushed her glasses farther up her nose. "With what?"

"This." I pulled out a catalog of horse equipment and clothes for riders. "I need, like, three of this helmet—in this size." I tapped the helmet I'd circled with a red marker.

Indigo took the magazine, but her forehead was more wrinkled that the clothes sitting at the bottom of my closet. "Why do you need me to get them?"

"Because I'm *guessing* based on how much merch you buy online, you have Amazon Prime, right?"

"Yes."

"Perfect! That means free shipping—and I checked, it's the

same price on Amazon as it is in the catalog!" I clapped my hands in glee.

Indigo peered down at the glossy catalog page. "Are you seriously having me order this just so you can save a few bucks on shipping?"

I scowled. "You have no idea how deep in debt this Court is. Every dollar counts!"

"Then why are you getting new helmets?" Indigo asked. "I thought Dusk and Dawn found one for you."

"Yes, an older one with no head vents. It makes me get as sweaty as a pig, and I'm pretty sure it's been sitting around for a long time. Who knows if it will actually protect my head when I fall?"

"You take head damage very seriously," Indigo said. "I would have thought you'd trust your night mares more."

"I trust my night mares. I just don't trust any of the fae nobles, unless they are unconscious," I corrected.

"I see," Indigo said.

"Do you mind getting it? I can get you the money right now."

Indigo breathed out, making her cheeks puff. "Sure. I'll order them tonight."

"Thank you!"

I was trying to remember where I'd hidden my wallet, when Indigo continued.

"I'm happy to do this for you, but when I offered my help, I had something more specific in mind."

"Oh?"

Indigo tugged on the hem of her Harry Potter shirt. "Yes. I was thinking that since it seems like you trust me these days?" She looked up at me for confirmation.

"I do," I assured her.

"Maybe, so you don't have to eat protein bars and jerky all the time..." She sucked a big breath in. "I could cook for you!"

I blinked. "I'm sorry, what?"

"I know you don't want to eat anything made by a fae—and after the night at the restaurant I totally understand why. But I'm still concerned about your health, and it doesn't seem fair that you have to run on such terrible food. I was thinking that I could make your meals. We could keep your food in a locked fridge, and as long as I make it and we banish everyone from the kitchens while I'm finishing so no one can do something to it, it should be safe."

I leaned back in my chair, making it creak, and stared dumbly at Indigo.

"I'm not an amazing cook or anything," she blurted out. "But I think I'm okay—better than just *beef jerky*, anyway. And I can only really cook human foods—my mom loves it, that's how I got introduced to human forms of entertainment."

I wasn't just shocked, I was speechless. I couldn't help but close my eyes and think. *I could eat again. No more choking down fruit snacks for breakfast, or eating an entire cucumber for lunch. I could have food. Cooked food.*

I'm not an emotional person, but I'll admit that my eyes felt hot, and I knew if I thought about it much longer I was going to start crying.

Ever since coming to the Night Court my sleep hadn't been great, and my eating habits were worse. I felt half defeated just waking up in the morning. But if I could eat again...

Maybe I could teach her how to make coffee.

"That is, if all of this is okay with you? And I haven't offended you?" Indigo's voice was small now, and I realized in my unsurpassed joy I hadn't done anything to show just how excited I was.

I almost lunged across the desk. "No—I think it's an *amazing* idea. A thoughtful idea! It's just—no one has been this nice to me since I arrived." My throat tightened. "And I really, really just want to eat *anything* cooked."

Indigo's eyes were moon-like, and she sucked her neck into her shoulders under my passionate enthusiasm. But when I finished speaking, she offered me a smile. "I'm glad. I was thinking last night when I decided I was going to offer this that it's not a common role for a monarch's companion. But you're not a common monarch, and I want to support you however I can."

I grinned at her. "Even when I'm planning to rile up my nobles?"

"Especially then." Indigo rolled her eyes. "Please. The fae might have adopted stuff like cellphones and the internet, but in a lot of ways they're back in the dark ages. I *hope* you make them upset—they're waltzing around like a bunch of regency heroines."

"Ah-ha!" I pointed at Indigo. "I think so, too!"

Indigo sniffed angrily in agreement. She jumped when Steve put her head on Indigo's lap, then cautiously patted her.

"Since you're with me in this, I'm going to let you in on a little secret." I was so excited, I could barely sit still in my chair. "You know that Court event next week that is supposed to be held at some fancy—and expensive—restaurant?"

"Yes?"

I chuckled. "I've canceled that reservation and rented out a different location."

"Where?"

CHAPTER TWENTY-ONE

Rigel

"*Mini golf?*" Dion gaped up at the sign hanging over the location of our Court social. "Is she for real?"

I shrugged. "It seems congruent with her twisted sense of humor."

"We're fae," Dion said. "Does she really expect the nobles to play *mini golf?*"

I glanced at my friend. "I was unaware you were such an avid hater of miniature golf."

"I'm not—I've actually played it before, and it's pretty fun. But can you picture the likes of Lady Demetria or Lord Thales?" Dion rubbed his forehead and sighed.

I turned back and looked in the direction of our cars. "Are we not attending, then?"

"No, we're going in." Dion grimly squared his shoulders. "I need to convince her to marry me, and *you* are my moral support, Rigel. Come on."

We went inside, and the new queen had very cunningly set Lord Linus up as the official greeter responsible for explaining the game and giving everyone equipment.

Lord Linus had always been a Court favorite, and given that he'd managed to avoid making enemies—although he had inspired a lot of gossip given his travels across the human world, much less the fact that he'd married a human and now, apparently, fathered our new queen.

It was an easy thing for him to sweet talk fae ladies into taking brightly colored golf balls, and hand off ridiculously small golf clubs with a wink to his fellow lords.

He got Dion and me through the doors in record speed, ejecting us into the strange world of mini golf—a swathe of fake greenery and plastic with unnatural bright colors that assaulted my eyes.

I stared at the black ball Lord Linus had given me—very original of him—then glanced at Dion. "If you try to make me play, I will kill you."

Dion laughed uneasily. "Fear not—I'm not *that* confident in our friendship. Come on."

The mini golf course was a confusing swirl of holes accented with animal statues, miniature architecture, and blue pools of water that likely contained all the filth of humanity.

Weirdest of all, however, were the fae walking through it.

Certainly, some of them were reacting as Dion thought they would and were standing on the sidelines, whispering to each other with pinched expressions.

But many individuals—*most* of the lords and ladies, in fact—were stalking through the course, clutching sheets of paper and tiny pencils, and swinging their clubs with a great deal more enthusiasm than I'd seen most of them muster up in months.

"I say—did you try hole twelve? It has a water wheel—very difficult."

"*I* finished it in two shots! But I had trouble at hole eight."

"The one with the giraffe statue that's missing a leg?"

"Yes! That's the one—I swear upon my family's house the missing leg affects the wind speed in that area. Such a cheat!"

Dion craned his neck, but apparently was unable to see his target. "Give me a second, Rigel." He hopped on to the base of a smiling hippo statue and peered around.

I was left to stare at a group of ladies comparing score cards with smugness.

What is happening to them?

I felt the muscles of my forehead pull slightly in my temptation to frown in confusion, but I instantly smoothed the expression from my face.

"I see her." Dion jumped off the statue. "Come on—she's near the tenth hole." He led the way through the crush of the crowd—paths miraculously opened up whenever anyone glanced at us and saw me—and bounded up the stairs built into the hill and nestled between some poorly grown bushes.

"Queen Leila! How happy you look this evening," Dion called to her.

The Queen of the Night Court was wearing a dark purple, lacy sundress and clutching a silver travel mug as if someone might rip it from her. She was also carrying one of those purse-things she seemed to be forever holding, and when she saw Dion she carefully smiled at him—probably taken in by his dazzling charm.

"Lord Dion—it's always a pleasure to see you!" she said. "Could have done without you, Rigel, but it is decently enjoyable to see you in the middle of a mini golf course."

I blinked. "Fascinating. I was just thinking how this...*interesting* place suits you."

Dion ignored our verbal spar and continued with his planned seduction. "The pleasure of seeing you will always and forever be mine, Queen Leila, for you bring joy everywhere you go."

I don't understand how he's able to say ridiculous things like that without gagging.

The queen must not have been paying complete attention to Dion—she didn't giggle and swoon like most fae ladies would have. Instead, she chortled to herself and smacked her thigh with her purse-thing. "Oh, I would dearly love to hear if today is one of those *joyous* times!"

"Did you not move today's event to this bright place in hopes of inspiring joy?" Dion tactfully asked.

Queen Leila snorted like a horse. "No. I moved it here because I thought it would annoy everyone! But they're taking my challenge seriously—which is a lot more satisfying than I ever imagined."

"Your challenge?"

She gestured to the course. "Anyone who gets a higher score than me will receive something from the Night Court Treasury."

Dion stared at her. "Really? Are you that skilled at this game?"

"Not really, but I've appointed Chase as my representative, and he's a regular snake at this."

Curious, I glanced at her director of security. The werewolf—his eyes gleaming—hadn't looked away from me since I had arrived.

Someone has inspired that famous werewolf loyalty...

"He has a perfect score," Leila continued. "The most someone could do is tie with him. But it doesn't matter—no one has a hope of even coming close."

"Why not?" Dion asked.

Leila took a sip from her silver travel mug. "None of you have played mini golf before. Already the course has lost two lights, a pot of flowers, and one employee—and it's only been half an hour. It's going to be carnage by the time the day ends."

"Queen Leila." The steward came tapping up the steps, a look of concern crossing her face.

Leila lost her air of glee. "Is something wrong?"

"Somewhat. Lord Iason accused Lady Lysandra of cheating at the fifteenth hole. They're clogging up the use of that hole, and now Lord Gaios is threatening a duel to clear Lady Lysandra's golfing reputation."

"I swear." The queen shook her head. "The fae could make drinking water into an insult-worthy competition. Chase?"

"My men are on their way there." The werewolf had his cellphone up to his ear and looked unmovable—I suspect he wasn't going to leave her side as long as I was around.

A smart wolf—but unnecessary. I canceled the contract. A frown briefly twitched at my lips. *My first failed contract—why do I suspect she would be proud to be such a distinction?*

"Excellent." Leila clapped. "I apologize, Lord Dion, Lord Rigel, but it seems my presence is needed elsewhere. Enjoy mini golf—or at the very least, the show."

She winked with enough charm to match Dion—though she was a bit too mischievous to be seductive—and was hopping down the steps, her director of security following close enough behind her he was nearly stepping on her heels.

The queen glanced back at her employee. "By the way, Chase," she said. "I meant to compliment you on your hidden talent of mini golf."

"It's not that surprising, Queen Leila," the werewolf said as I began to lose their voices to the swirl of sound surrounding us. "Several humans live in my pack, and one of them in particular would frequently drag us to the mini golf course in town."

"Ahh, the mystery has been solved," I heard the queen say before the rest of her words were lost among the noise of the place.

Dion shook his head as he watched her go. "I know we fae are supposedly mercurial. But she takes unpredictability to a new level."

I shrugged. "Something for you to look forward to."

My oldest—and only—friend twitched his shoulders back. "She's nice enough, I'm sure we'll get along. Come on—let's go mingle before I come back and try talking to her again."

CHAPTER TWENTY-TWO

Leila

I was shocked the mini golf excursion was going over so well. I figured less than half of the fae would play, but—shockingly—the majority of them were having a go at it.

Skye and—as reluctant as I was to say it—Lord Linus were responsible for a lot of the event's success.

Skye smothered any potential outbreaks of ugly behavior, while Lord Linus's high spirits and tendency to float around with smiles and winks made his good humor infectious. (That, and he seemed to enjoy shocking his fellow fae with his skills. He wasn't nearly as good as Chase, but he was decent enough. Apparently he'd played mini golf while traveling.)

But. The natural downsides of having Lord Linus around were still at play.

"An admirable shot, Lord Linus." A fae lord gave him a nod of respect.

"Thank you, thank you." Lord Linus winked at a young fae

lady—the fae lord's daughter. "Let's just say I was inspired by the beauty surrounding me."

The fae lady laughed and tapped her club on the ground.

I sipped my coffee I'd bought from King's Court Café on the way to the golf course and tried not to barf.

Sure, Lord Linus looked in his mid-thirties, but he *was* my biological father, and the fae lady appeared to be just a little bit older than me!

While the fae lady stepped up with her pink golf ball, Lord Linus edged closer to her father.

"This event has been quite amusing," he said. "And so unpredictable as to who will actually finish with the required low score."

"Indeed—though I do fear what will happen if the other Courts hear of it. It will sink our reputation even lower than it already is," the fae lord said.

"Maybe, maybe. But in the meantime, we ought to enjoy ourselves. Shall we make a wager?" He jostled the fae lord with his elbow, but I had heard enough.

And that's it.

Intent on blocking the irresponsible lord's mischief, I sidled away from where Chase was giving a fae lady a few pointers on the next-door hole, and stepped up to Lord Linus. "Good evening, Sir, Lady. Lord Linus, I am sure someone needs you."

"But I—"

I wedged my clutch into my armpit and grasped his elbow and tugged him away. "What was that? You'd love to help? How perfect!"

Lord Linus groaned like an inconvenienced teenager as I dragged him off. We climbed the slight hill to the highest part of the golf course, where the giant statue of a giraffe—three-legged, because I'd rented a classy place—was situated.

I released him and retrieved my clutch from my armpit. "What have I told you, Lord Linus?"

"No gambling." He'd recovered his spirits and was grinning at me. "But isn't it the spirit of the event?"

"No," I firmly said. "No one gambles over mini golf."

"No one *you* know," Lord Linus said. "You don't know the right sort of people."

I stared at him. "You're probably right. And you know, you'd have a lot of time to hang out with them if you suddenly became unemployed!"

Lord Linus laughed. "You did inherit your mother's spirit. Very well, I shall bow to your wishes and keep my fingers clean tonight. Ta!"

He was off before I could stop him, waltzing off like a social butterfly to laugh and gossip with anyone that looked at him.

He makes me exhausted. I adjusted my sunglasses with a deep sigh. *Why do I get the feeling this is how a parent feels when trying to raise children?*

I took a swig of my coffee for fortification. Even though I was now much better fed—because it turned out not only was Indigo an excellent cook, she made awesome dishes inspired by human pop culture, like lasagna inspired by the Garfield comics and shawarma from a superhero movie—I still lacked coffee because she refused to make it. Even worse, she told me it was sacrilegious to drink it since I was a fae and fae drink tea.

I turned in a circle, looking for Chase. He had been adamant in the pre-event briefing session that I stay near him given events of the past two Court socials.

I wasn't going to argue—I didn't feel like getting poisoned or shot at—but he was difficult to find in such a crowd.

I hope we haven't filled the place past the fire safety code.

Something behind me creaked, and I turned around to see the giraffe statue tipping over...in my direction.

I swear everything moved in slow motion.

The statue sliced mercilessly through the air, and although my brain screamed at me to run, it took my legs a few precious seconds to respond.

I ran, but I could tell I was too late. The thing was going to land on top of me.

I was wearing my charm bracelet, and almost automatically I activated it and spun wild magic through it, throwing up a shield in record time.

I automatically raised a hand—as if I could catch the statue—but there was a massive thump, and it never even touched my shield.

Chase had caught it at the shoulders. The muscles in his arms were bulging with effort, and his lips were peeled back in a wolf-like snarl as he struggled to hold it.

"The queen!" Lord Dion shouted. He cleared the top step and rushed to help Chase.

Realizing I was gaping at them like an idiot, I ran down the paved walkway, getting out of range—though I kept my shield up.

Once I was clear Chase—with the help of Lord Dion, and guards who had quickly convened on us—let the statue fall to the ground with a thump I felt in my feet.

"Leila!" Indigo came hustling up the walkway, pushing past whispering fae lords and ladies.

I held up my hand—thankfully everyone was far enough away that they wouldn't be able to see it shaking—and forced a smile. "I'm fine," I announced to my Court. "But it seems the tally for broken things grows. I'm not going to get my security deposit back because of you all," I teased.

A few fae laughed nervously, but mostly they stared at me. I'm not sure if it was with disappointment that I hadn't been squashed or just general apathy.

"Leila."

Grateful for the distraction, I turned to Lord Linus, who was coming up a different pathway with Skye.

"It's fine," I said in a lowered voice.

"It's *not* fine," Skye firmly said. "Someone just made an attempt on your life!"

Lord Linus didn't even say anything. He just rubbed at his mouth and walked in a tight loop.

"You're right, but no one was up here with me," I said. "I turned in a circle while I was looking for Chase. I was alone. I have no idea how they pulled it off."

"It was set up to look accidental, that's for sure," Indigo said.

"Queen Leila," Chase called.

I picked my way to the werewolf, jumping over small shrubs and walking through the landscaping since he was crouched by the fallen giraffe's feet.

He pointed to the metal plates that were fitted around the giraffe's three surviving feet. "Someone removed—and in some places cut—the bolts that secured it to the ground. It looks like a golf ball hit—there I think—loosening the plates enough so it tipped a little, then naturally fell in the direction of its missing leg."

I was going to ask how he knew a ball had hit it, but when he pointed to the spot on its neck it was pretty obvious—the golf ball had burned through the statue's paint.

I edged around the statue and touched the bald spot. "Feels like magic. Fae magic." I flicked my fingers, trying to get rid of the sticky feeling.

"Smells like it, too," Chase confirmed.

Lord Linus crouched down. "I don't get it. Leila is queen—they shouldn't be able to hurt her like this."

"If they can make it into an accidental death, it seems the magic won't stop it," Skye said. "Given the experience at the restaurant."

"The amount of work it takes to set something like that up is incredibly difficult, though, and they shouldn't be able to pull it off with this frequency," Lord Linus argued.

"Maybe we're looking at this wrong?" Indigo asked.

"I don't see how." I tapped my chin in thought. "I'm pretty clearly the target." I paused and looked at my free hand.

Why is it empty?

I glanced at my other hand, holding my clutch, and slapped my thigh. "No!"

"Queen Leila?" Skye quizzically asked as Chase took a phone call.

I ran around the giraffe, stopping with heartbreak when I saw my travel mug tipped over with my precious coffee splattered on the ground. "My coffee."

Skye heaved a sigh with relief, then started patting her pockets—probably in search of her tin of antacids.

Indigo shook her head in disgust. "Serves you right for partaking in that sacrilegious drink!"

"You're just ignorant," I said. "Your eyes haven't been opened to the glories of coffee."

"I'm fine with that," Indigo said. "In fact, I'd prefer they stay shut."

Lord Linus had been glancing out at the Court, and seemed tuned out of Indigo's and my play fight. He ended it by awkwardly patting me on the shoulder. "I'm glad you're safe, pumpkin. But it's getting crowded up here, and I see a lord I owe—er, I should mingle." He winked, then glided off.

"*Pumpkin?*" I snarled at his retreating back.

He waved, and I was half tempted to pick up my fallen travel mug and pitch it at his head, but Chase forestalled me.

"The man I set up at the security cameras called." He returned his cellphone to the holster on his pants belt—a very dad-ish gesture of his.

I whistled in appreciation. "Whoa—you had someone stationed there? You're thorough."

I'm so glad I hired Chase instead of a wizard. He's worth his weight and his wolf form's weight in gold!

"The camera caught the ball that hit it. He was able to trace it back to the hole where it was putted," Chase continued.

I straightened in surprise. "Really?"

"Yes." Chase's voice turned grim. "The fae who hit it was with Lady Chrysanthe's group."

I leaned back on my heels. "Ahhh. Why does that not surprise me?"

"My men are taking the fae aside for questioning," Chase said. "You should head back to the mansion."

"Nope," I said. "Not going."

Chase rubbed the back of his neck. "And why won't you?"

"You don't have to put a brave front on," Indigo said. "You said you wanted to break the way the Court operates."

"I do," I acknowledged. "But this is a lesson I've learned living on a farm. You *don't* turn your back on an animal you can't trust. I need to stay."

Chase sighed. "Very well. But you're going to have guards stand with you while I talk to the fae."

"Sounds good. Thanks, Chase."

He nodded, then started barking orders at his men that were taking photos of the giraffe feet and sweeping the area.

Four of them split off, discreetly moving into place around me.

Skye eyed them, then bowed to me. "I'll see what reconnaissance I can do."

Indigo picked up my silver travel mug. "And I'll get you another beverage—*not* coffee!" She shook my mug at me with such a fierce look I couldn't help but crack a smile.

"Thank you, both of you," I said.

Another shake of the travel mug and a bow, and they were off, leaving me alone with my guards.

I made a point of mingling around the top for a few minutes—I spoke to Lord Dion for a while, and some of his acquaintances—but around the time my Court's interest had finally waned and they were returning to their games, I escaped out of the hot sun, and moved closer to the entrance shaded by trees—with my guards, of course.

I took my sunglasses out and fished my prism out of my purse, noting with disappointment that my can of bear mace wouldn't have done much against the statue.

I pulled the bear mace out as well and was studying the bottle, when I *felt* something behind me.

I popped the lid off my can and had my finger on the spray part, when I realized I was staring into the unimpressed eyes of the Wraith.

My movement caught my guards' attention, and they all turned inward, grappling with their weapons when they saw him.

My heart stuttered for a few beats, but I smiled at my guards. "It's fine," I told them. "Lord Rigel isn't going to hurt me."

I wonder how I know that.

I wouldn't trust the fae to stand at my back, but somehow I instinctively knew he wasn't standing here with the intention of killing me.

Probably because he would have already made his move by this point.

The guards exchanged uncertain looks, but I flapped a hand at them. "It's fine—isn't it, Lord Rigel?"

Lord Rigel stared at me for several long moments. "You have an interesting definition of 'fine'," he said.

I noticed it wasn't the reassurance I asked for, but my guards did turn back to scanning the course—though they kept their weapons, all of them artifacts that glowed with magic they had gathered—out and ready.

I reluctantly capped my bear mace and stuck it back in my clutch. "What do you want?"

Rigel said nothing, he just stood next to me like a handsome statue.

I rolled my eyes and meandered up to the suspension bridge at the entrance, which crossed a little pond of water that looked about five inches deep, but the water color was questionable, so it was hard to judge.

Rigel followed behind me and even stood on the bridge with me as I peered over the side.

"Why did you arrange for the social to take place here?" he finally asked.

I pressed my prism to my heart. "I'm shocked."

Rigel blinked.

"That may be the first non-antagonistic thing you've said to me! Wow, this is a *special* day."

"Why?" Rigel repeated—which was about equivalent to yodeling out his insistence, for him.

"It's a human thing," I said.

"And?"

I was considering my reply, but Rigel beat me to my next thought. "You didn't bring us here because you're helplessly attached to human ways—though that might be what you're attempting to lead the Court to believe."

"And how do you know that?"

"Because you're too purposeful to be that dream-addled," Rigel said. He kept staring at me, which was a little unnerving.

I held onto the wooden railings of the bridge and tried to size him up. "Why do you care why I brought everyone here?"

"Because you're the Queen of the Night Court," Rigel said. "And I like to be aware of all the players in the game."

I made an annoyed noise in the back of my throat. "You're one of those 'fae life is a game of power' people?"

"*All* fae are one of those people," Rigel said. "Have you witnessed anything that contradicts such a view?"

"No, but I think it's precisely because you all share that view that the stupid game continues, and crushes more and more fae as part of it."

Lord Rigel fell silent, which made me nervous. Worriedly, I glanced over at him.

His black eyes didn't have the dead look to them, but they didn't look bored, either. They looked...different. "You all," he said.

"What?"

"You said you all. That implies you don't share the belief, as does your original reaction."

"Oh, I believe there's a game all right," I assured him.

"And?"

"And what?"

"What do you intend to do in it?"

I intend to crush it.

I kept my mouth shut. I didn't want to blurt my plans out to Rigel, but I suspected he was *not* the fae I should trot out my ability to lie and use it on. "I don't see why I have to tell you. In fact, you tried to kill me. Logically, I *shouldn't* tell you."

"It was just business—nothing personal," Lord Rigel said.

"Yeah? Well *I* found it personal." I glanced at our guards. One of them was openly staring at me with wide eyes, her warm olive complexion turning pale. The others were all doing better about pretending not to listen.

Several long moments passed, but I jumped to my feet when a bubble of magic surrounded Rigel and myself. It took me a second to realize it was the same sound-proofing spell the Paragon had used.

Oh, heck no. He's going to kill me in this silence zone. Not today! Nope!

CHAPTER TWENTY-THREE

Leila

I took a step toward the edge of the bubble, but Rigel stopped me in my tracks.

"I canceled the contract."

I paused and turned around. "*What?*"

"I canceled the contract that hired me to kill you."

"But...everyone told me you've never failed before."

He shrugged. "Everyone also said there would never be anything less than a full-blooded fae on any Court's throne."

"Touché. Care to share who commissioned the hit?"

Rigel stared at me.

I shrugged. "I had to try!"

My guards had jerked to attention, but at Rigel's announcement I smiled and waved to them to show I was okay.

The guards exchanged a few hand signals before one settled in to watch Rigel and me and the others went back to scanning the surroundings.

"I take it now you want me to tell you why I held the social here?" I guessed.

Fae aren't known for their generosity. They expect equivalent exchange.

Lord Rigel fell back on his old goodie behavior and stared at me.

"I'm going to *require* a verbal answer for this one," I drawled.

"I want to know how you intend to play this game of power."

I snorted. "Buddy, have I got news for you—I am *not* telling you my entire strategy. That's not worth knowing the contract was canceled!"

"It's obvious you're hoping to change the game," Rigel ignored me and continued. "You held a social here—correctly assuming that the foreign setting would challenge the Court and shake them out of their usual behaviors."

Huh. I would have thought he'd vastly underestimate me, not totally miss how little I actually care about how the Court feels.

"You have sold the sun stallions and brought in the night mares to disconcert the Court because it underlines how the night mares—a creature of the Night Court that symbolizes our power—have been neglected, and you have given the wild glooms and shades ridiculous names to accomplish the same as well."

"HAH! I knew I saw you that night I met them!" I pointed a finger at him. "But that's a solid miss."

Lord Rigel narrowed his dark eyes. "Then what are you trying to accomplish? You dare to shoot back at a fae that bothers your companion—"

"—shooting at Indigo is *way more* than bothering her!"

"But you don't immediately eliminate a threat against your life."

"Yeah, because *due process* is a thing! I'm not gonna let heads roll without evidence!"

"You act strong when your life is in danger to impress your

Court, but then make your personal seal the vermin of our realm?"

Oh-ho-ho, we've got ourselves a nosebox here!

"You are wildly unpredictable, and you're acting in an unstable way that could topple what little balance of power we've managed to achieve in the Court," Lord Rigel said.

Never mind. He's just obsessed with this stupid game of power.

"As best as I see it, you are either wholly oblivious and an idiot in your humanity, *or* you so deeply despise fae that you intend to destroy us."

"Hey, now. I don't *dislike* fae. I just find you all excessively annoying."

"Queen Leila," Lord Rigel said in a tone of voice I was pretty sure most people didn't survive hearing.

I blew out a breath of air. "You're overthinking things, and trying to connect my actions in patterns that a fae would move in."

"You are not a naïve human."

"No."

"Then that makes you a threat, because the way you plan to play the game—"

Something in me broke. I don't know if it was the irritation of all the fae pressing me to try to see the world in the broken, horrible way they saw it, or if it was the sheer frustration that the Night Court was so backwards no one could even fathom escaping these politics.

"I don't want to *play* the game," I shouted. "I want to *destroy* it!"

Lord Rigel fell silent, but he'd pushed me into talking.

"I am *sick* and *tired* of all these time-consuming, energy-wasting politics the fae play, when the Night Realm is crumbling around us, the Court is in debt up to its ears, and the fae want to use stupid, sneery little insults to try to score a point over one another? Who has time to care about that?"

"While your motive is...noble, you can't break out of this game. It's been going on for centuries, and no one has successfully been able to stay out of it," Lord Rigel said.

"I never said I wanted to break out—I said I wanted to *end* it," I growled.

"It's the same thing."

"*You* are a fae, and you've escaped the game!"

"It might appear so, but how do you think I got everyone to avoid me?"

I paused.

Is he—no. No, he can't be saying he became an assassin to keep everyone away? I just figured it was an example of his terrible morals.

I set my jaw. "I don't care. I'm going to end this game. I don't know if it's because I'm half human, or because I'm only half fae, but I can see that these stupid ploys are going to be the end of the Night Court if someone doesn't change something. And if there's one thing I'm good at, it's bringing change to this stale Court."

Lord Rigel shifted, briefly ringing the alarm bells in my mind. "I don't think you can do it."

I leaned against the railing of the bridge. "And I don't think you've truly seen fae cunning crossed with human ingenuity yet— especially if you think humans are idiots."

Lord Rigel briefly touched his arm bracers in a way that made me think there was a hidden blade in them. "I suspect it will be apparent very quickly whether or not you can win. After all, events like today will never stop if you can't bring the Court to heel."

AKA, he thinks I'll get myself killed if I don't start playing the game. Whatever.

Aloud, I said, "It's fine."

"You tend to say that a lot—typically when it *isn't* fine."

"I'm still alive, aren't I? It's fine," I insisted.

Lord Rigel turned, and the magic bubble popped. "It is to be hoped, for your sake, that you are right."

He left as silently as he had arrived.

I shivered a bit, watching when Lord Rigel reached Lord Dion and exchanged a few words with his friend.

The red haired fae lord smiled at him, but brightened even more when Lord Rigel looked back at me. He slapped the Wraith on the back, then started in my direction—probably continuing his plan to win me over for marriage.

And that's the best option I have—a fae who will marry me for the good of his Court. What's the likelihood he's not going to be thrilled with my 'destroy the game' goal?

I looked from the incoming Lord Dion to the rest of the Court.

But I don't think there's a better option...is there?

My phone rang—its Lord of the Rings ringtone slightly muffled in my clutch.

I hurriedly ripped it out and picked up the call when I saw it was from Chase. "What did you find out?"

"*He didn't do it,*" Chase said, sounding disgusted. "*We found the ball—it was bespelled. The fae that actually hit the ball never knew about it.*"

"And you can't track whoever placed the spell."

"*Correct. We do know it was a fae spell, though. Unfortunately, we can't confirm if it came from within your Court or a different one.*"

"Yeah, that's expected." The kind of supernatural you were affected how the magic felt or tasted, but that was it. You didn't leave a particular signature on it or anything, and it couldn't be traced back to individuals. "I'm betting it's someone from my Court—though I'd love to know how they're getting around the magic."

"*Even without proof I still have suspicions. Since they were present, we questioned both Lord Myron and Lady Chrysanthe. Both were able to say they didn't try to kill you.*"

"And as fae they can't lie."

"*In theory. But I'm almost certain it's one of them.*"

"Lady Chrysanthe, probably. She seems to take the greatest offense to me," I sighed. "She was in the group I saw at the restaurant, too."

"*It's quite probable.*"

I sighed.

"*Your orders?*"

Lord Dion was almost on me, now. Hurriedly, I turned my back to him and rushed to say, "Keep investigating. But we can't make any formal charges yet."

"*As queen, you don't need to formally charge anyone.*"

"Maybe, but as little as I like my Court I don't want to be a tyrant. Thank you for your work, Chase."

"*Of course, Queen Leila.*"

I made myself drop my grim look as I turned around to smile at the charming fae lord.

Even though I felt defeated, I was determined.

I don't care what Lord Rigel says. I'm going to end this pointless game.

DAYS PASSED, and the end of July was nearly upon us.

I had three events I had to survive: picking who I was going to marry and surviving that marriage, the annual Magiford Midsummer Derby—which was for fae only and I was supposed to choose representatives who raced on behalf of my Court—and my crowning.

I intended to enter the race myself, and I had been training the night mares for months, so that was probably the least worrisome event, even though—according to Skye—the outcome of the race would greatly impact the standing of the Night Court.

No, what kept me up at night was picking my future hubby.

The week of the race, I was up late, going over the detailed rules to the race while cuddled up with Kevin, Steve, and Whiskers out in the stables. Our pile up was apparently too hot for Muffin, who was snoozing in front of Nebula's stall.

I smiled and watched the mare lower her head over the door of her stall and lip the cat's head. I sucked in a breath and tried to focus on the documents, but my eyes were tired, and everything was turning squiggly.

To think, I once thought the greatest tragedy in my life was that I couldn't get a job and launch my Responsible Adult plan. Hah!

"Queen Leila?"

I leaned forward, slightly upsetting Steve, who was curled around my back. "Skye? What are you doing up this late?"

Today Skye was wearing a pencil skirt and a pastel yellow shirt, but to my surprise, she sat down in the middle of the aisle despite her business clothes. "I'm well aware you've been staying up late."

"Did Chase tell you?" I play scowled. "Considering he's *my* director of security he certainly doesn't hesitate to leak information to you and Indigo!"

"It's because he's such a good director of security that he does so." Skye tilted her head in thought for a moment. "That, and his werewolf nature which drives him to protect you—even from yourself." She shifted her dark gaze to me. "You're reading up on the Magiford Midsummer Derby?"

"Yeah. I figured I better make sure I don't break some random rule that the other rulers use as an excuse to hate me. It says each Court that enters must enter a minimum of six horses, but it says nothing about the required number of riders—that seems weird to me."

"Ah, I believe that rule was made because a number of the local seelie and unseelie Courts that are normally too small to enter would try to ride double and put an inexperienced rider with an experienced one that would control the horse, thus doubling their rider count, allowing them to enter."

"You can't race while riding *double*!"

Skye shrugged. "You cannot win. But it's vital for any Court that wants to increase its reputation to at least enter. Only those who place near the top increase their Court's *power*, however, which is why the regional Courts struggle greatly to win and overcome their rivals."

I glanced down at my papers. "Huh. Interesting."

Skye brushed something off her pencil skirt. "I assume it is the prospect of your marriage that keeps you up?"

"Yeah." I put my papers down and scratched behind Kevin's ears. "I've been trying to puzzle it through for weeks, but I think it'll have to be Lord Dion."

"You sound reluctant."

"It's because I am," I admitted. "I feel like marrying him is just a survival tactic—not that we'd truly be fantastic together or because I specifically think he can help me with my goals and plans for the Court. But no matter how many times I've thought it over, there's no one else."

Silence stretched between us.

Skye delicately placed her hands on her knees. "Do you wish to set a date to make an official announcement?"

It's not like someone who is exactly what I want is going to pop out of the Night Realm like magic.

"Yeah. How about in a few days? There's no sense putting it off until the end of summer when I have no other options besides Dion. Oh, but do I need to warn him?"

"Not necessarily." Skye said. "In fact, it is strongly encouraged that the monarch does *not* ask their marriage partner ahead of time."

"Why not? So everyone can witness the humiliation if the other person says no?" I paused. "The other person is *allowed* to say no, right?"

"They are." Skye leaned backwards when Whiskers sat up and inquisitively shoved his long whiskers in her direction. "The silence was often adopted to hold back any political ramifications that other nobles might enact, but I suggest you don't tell him…in case you change your mind at the last moment."

"An escape route? Skye—aren't you cunning!" I smiled at her and studied my animals. "In that case, schedule the announcement for Friday."

"Very well." Skye hesitantly patted Whiskers on the head with the very stilted motion of someone not used to animals, then stood. "I'll make the arrangements."

"Thank you, Skye. You're priceless."

She bowed, and turned on her heels.

"Hey, Skye?"

"Yes, Queen Leila?" She turned back around and smiled at me.

"Can you think of anyone else we might be missing?"

She slightly pursed her lips. "The Day King, perhaps?"

"Eww! Heck no. He looks older than Linus—which means he's *got* to be older than him! And I am not marrying someone older than my biological father."

Skye smiled. "Lord Linus would be greatly encouraged to hear that you referred to him as your biological father."

I rolled my eyes. "Thanks for the thought, Skye, but that is a hard pass."

"As you say, Queen Leila."

I sighed, listening as her footsteps clicked down the stable aisle.

My marriage has a huge potential to help me destroy all of these petty alliances and power moves. But Lord Dion has an alliance with the Paragon. And while I like the Paragon, that somehow doesn't feel right either. Hah, I never thought what would disappoint me most about my marriage is who my husband's friends are!

The evening of my engagement announcement, my stomach had taken up the delightful hobby of practicing flips in my guts.

I stared with a twist of fascination and horror as Skye climbed into the fancy, wrought iron gazebo that had green vines twisting up its sides. "May I have your attention?" she called to the crowd of fae that had invaded the mansion's gardens that evening.

She kept talking, but I didn't hear it. My heart was thumping too loudly for her voice to cut through. "I'm going to be sick," I whispered. I was hiding behind a bush trimmed to resemble an English teapot and was thankfully out of my Court's eyesight at the moment.

"No you're not," Indigo said. "You're just nervous—unless you're serious?" Her forehead furrowed. "But I was very careful to only make bland foods for you for the past two days—just in case."

"That's why you made potato soup and rice gruel? Aww, Indigo, you're too thoughtful!" I tried to smile, but I couldn't tell if I was or not. My whole body had gone numb.

The fae meandered down to the end of the gardens where the gazebo was, whispering to each other as they gathered beneath the darkening sky. Today they were putting on their "refined" act, which meant they were dressed like British royals. Now that I'd figured out how their costumes changed with the image they wanted to convey, it was a lot easier trying to figure out what games they were playing. I'd bet today they were proper and powerful because no one had a legit idea who I was going to choose, so they needed to cover their bases.

"It's fine." I rolled my shoulders back and tried to listen to the crickets to calm my churning stomach.

We had to hold the announcement outside because it was the only place big enough for the crowd that had come today—a bunch of the common fae were here, too.

Indigo had actually introduced me to her parents—who were

incredibly pleasant brownies with warm smiles and not a single cross thing to say. I peeked down at Indigo.

She scowled at me. "What?"

Yep. No idea how their pleasantness combined created her.

"I still think we should have held the announcement earlier in the day," I grumbled. "Holding it at twilight means we had to haul a bunch of lights out here and have all the servants use their magic to create those light orbs. Talk about inefficient."

"Chase certainly tried to back you up—though I think he was more concerned about ill-wishers being able to hide."

I laughed, but the sound was flat and nervous.

Indigo reached up and gently touched my elbow. "Are you okay?" she asked. "I don't think I've ever seen you this nervous."

"It's because before this I haven't had to pick who I'd spend the rest of my life with—and, more importantly, who is going to be my closest ally."

"Ah, yeah, that's a good point." Indigo squinted at the wide array of fae. "To be honest, I figured you'd pull another one of your shenanigans out and surprise us all. But Lord Dion is a solid candidate. Plus, I'm pretty sure you'll break him in under a month."

I couldn't respond as I stared out at the fae. All of the nobles were present—looking bored and vaguely offended even though I hadn't addressed them tonight.

The common fae openly looked back and forth between Skye —still making her announcements—and me.

I saw a few I knew from the various Court functions I'd gone to—a family of highly respected pixies, the representative from the trolls, a few centaurs, a mermaid had even come for the occasion—she was sitting in the giant fountain in the center of the garden courtyard.

Why is everyone staring at me? I jerked my gaze to Skye, who gave me an encouraging nod.

"Is it time?" I whispered to Indigo.

"Yes." Indigo's forehead wrinkles grew. "Do you need help?"

"Nah. I can walk. Thanks, though." I tried to smile at her again, then climbed down the stairs of the little stone patio we'd been standing on, and took the pathway through the fae that magically opened up for me.

I think I get why Skye insisted I wear gloves tonight even though it's not really in style. My palms are so sweaty, I could fingerpaint. I wonder if Indigo picked out a mermaid style gown because I can't run easily in it?

For today's auspicious occasion, I'd been poured into a gown that flared at the knees. It was such a deep blue color it was almost black, though it had silver trim around the bottom of the skirt, and the neckline was designed to look like glittering stars.

Don't trip. Don't trip. Don't trip. I glanced up and happened to catch Lady Chrysanthe's eye.

She glared at me, then leaned into Lord Myron and whispered.

The look Lord Myron gave her was...odd. It was sneery, and if I didn't know better I'd say I had seen this expression before—when he was looking at me. It didn't matter; as she spoke, his expression smoothed over, and he grinned at her and said something back.

Their little exchange reminded me, though.

I'm not going to let the fae know how much this stupid engagement thing bothers me. Least of all Lord Dion—I don't want him pouncing for power if he thinks he can take it.

For a moment my heart was crushed.

I can't be safe or free in a single part of my life, can I? No, I have to be pushed in from all sides and be ever-aware that even my husband will try to play this stupid power game. Particularly when he finds out how much I mean to change about this rotten place.

I reached the gazebo and climbed the few stairs into it. Giant spotlights were pointed at it—because we couldn't go for elegant —and cheaper—mood lighting. Gosh no.

Naturally, my Court would want to see every detail of my unwanted engagement in clear lighting.

Skye's forehead puckered with worry. She started to reach out, hesitated, then returned her hand to her side. "Just make the announcement of your fiancé," she whispered. "And this will be over."

The slight smile she gave me brimmed with sympathy. Then she bowed and made her escape, leaving me alone under the hot lights and the expectant stares of my Court.

I forced a smile and nodded in greeting. "Thank you for coming to this important event, where I announce my chosen husband."

The crowd seemed to inch forward, pushing against me with their sheer will. I swear the individual faces I could make out were all drawn with anticipation and greed.

"After giving this *unusual* and clearly *outdated* requirement some thought," I started. And yes, the rip on the marriage thing was entirely necessary! "I have chosen he who will rule with me, share the burden of power, and safeguard our people. And it is—"

I glanced at Lord Dion—he was easy to spot with his bright red hair. He was, of course, standing with Lord Rigel. Lord Dion gave me a charming smile, but Lord Rigel's eyes were half mast, barely disguising his open boredom. At least there was one member of my Court who didn't care about political movements!

Wait.

Everything in my mind sharpened, and I stopped breathing.

Wait. Lord Rigel doesn't have any political connections. Lord Dion is his only friend, he's the only surviving member of his family, and since he's an assassin everyone leaves him alone.

Rigel has no ties to any power except his own.

I stared at him, and I felt something dangerous in my chest: hope.

CHAPTER TWENTY-FOUR

Leila

What I really wanted was a shell to stand around and play the role of husband. I didn't want anyone sticking his oar in trying to tell me what to do—because no fae would *willingly* agree to break the game of power like I intended to.

I wasn't looking for love, or help, or protection.

I just wanted someone who would leave me alone—and maybe not kill me as a major bonus.

He believes in all the power plays, but only because he thinks the pattern can't be broken. He did try to kill me, but he said he canceled the contract, and he can't lie. But is just canceling the contract a clear enough action to gamble my entire life on? I mean, he's an assassin.

I licked my lips, and was only distantly aware that the crowd was starting to stir at my long and awkward silence.

Can I do it? Do I have the guts to make an assassin my consort?

The possibilities made my brain buzz, and I knew I had made

my decision when I ripped my gaze away from him, thinking, *Skye is going to have to give Chase some of her antacids.*

I cleared my throat and smiled again. "And my chosen husband is Lord Rigel."

When I glanced at the Wraith, I saw to my delight that I had managed to elicit another response in him: shock, I think?

He straightened up, and his lean and usually relaxed body was stiff as he stared me down.

His dark eyes didn't look dead at all, oh heck no. Now they very much had a certain light to them—whether it was the aforementioned shock, or building rage, I couldn't tell.

Please, please let me survive this decision!

Lord Dion at his side dropped his jaw and gaped at me—along with the rest of the Court.

No one moved—not even to twitch a muscle. The only noise in the gardens was the hum of the spotlights and the chirp of the crickets.

There was a scuffle near the back of the crowd, and when I looked I saw Chase with a hand slapped over Lord Linus's mouth. The fae lord's eyes were as big as moons, and Chase seemed unable to stand still or straight as he gawked at me. A clatter near the front drew my eyes to Skye. Her hands were arranged in the position they'd normally be when she was clutching her tablet, except it must have slid out and fallen to the ground.

Yep. Clearly my people thought I'd lost my mind. I swung my gaze back to my potential fiancé.

"Lord Rigel? What is your response?" I held out my hand.

Please say yes!

Air leaked out of me, and my lungs seemed unable to suck it back in as the moment stretched on forever.

A year passed before he moved, and it took my shocked brain several seconds to process the fact that he was coming toward me.

He climbed the stairs to the gazebo and stopped at my side.

When he moved again I *almost* winced—afraid I was about to get payback for my most definitely unwanted request.

Instead, my heart stopped when Rigel took my hand in his, and turned to face the crowd with me.

"Is that an acceptance?" I whispered.

Rigel didn't even look at me. "Yes." His voice was loud enough for the Court to hear.

"*Hah!*" Lord Dion broke out in a loud, amused honk, but he immediately smothered his reaction and switched to a smile and an enthusiastic clap.

He was still fighting a grin as the rest of the Court joined him—though they lacked the enthusiasm and were clearly going through the motions with their polite golfer clap as their brains tried to catch up with this unexpected twist.

Rigel didn't look at me as he said at a volume I could barely hear over the shocked applause of the Court, "I assume you have a reason for this?"

"Oh yeah," I assured him.

"You will explain it to me—*in detail*—tomorrow."

"Gotcha!"

The crowd grew louder—they were still applauding at the same level, but now they were also murmuring to one another like a cloud of hornets.

And based on the glittering eyes, stiff expressions, and raised chins, I was betting the nobles weren't happy. The common fae still appeared mostly overcome by shock—though the troll's confused but thunderous claps were the loudest in the area.

I gave Lord Rigel a thumbs up and a wink when he finally glanced at me.

This close I think I could safely categorize the expression in his eyes: puzzlement.

I managed to baffle the Wraith. That's gotta be an achievement!

"You don't love me," he stated.

I inhaled my own spit and choked. After about ten prolonged seconds of coughing, I assured him. "*No!*"

His expression cleared—he seemed to feel better about it—and Skye slowly approached the base of the gazebo. "If you would step forward, Queen Leila and...Lord Rigel. I will arrange a receiving line so the Court can...wish you both well and give you its congratulations." Skye kept giving me a meaningful look during the lulls in her sentences.

Lord Rigel dropped my hand like it was a dead fish and glided down the stairs. I was a step behind him—moving more carefully because I still wasn't great with heels.

Once Skye arranged us to her satisfaction, she stepped to the side to converse with some of the guards, who started motioning at the fae like an airport employee directing landing airplanes.

Indigo joined Lord Rigel and me, looking markedly less disturbed than anyone else on my team as she scooted around to stand behind me.

"Congratulations, my Sovereign, and to you, Lord Rigel," she said.

I peered back at her. "You seem remarkably chipper."

"Of course!" She sniffed up at me. "I was really worried for you. But this is exactly the sort of thing I would expect from you normally. I'm glad you're still doing fine."

"Gee. Thanks."

"Now smile!" Indigo poked me in the lower back for emphasis. "And enjoy this moment. Because everyone is going to be *furious* that you've outfoxed them again!"

"Are you *insane?*" The Paragon planted his feet and set down the baby car seat he'd been carrying. It was about six in the morning, and he'd obviously just woken up based on the fuzzy blue slippers he was wearing, as well as his blue bathrobe that was dotted with overweight, gray cats.

Given how late the celebration "festivities" had lasted the previous night, I was still in my fancy dress—although I yanked off my gloves with enthusiasm. "What do you mean?"

"Marrying *him*!" The Paragon poked a finger in Lord Rigel's direction. "What else—besides a loss of all intelligence—could inspire you to marry an assassin?"

"Perhaps you shouldn't be quite so strong in your words, Paragon?" I suggested.

Lord Rigel didn't look upset. He'd settled against a wall where his dark shirt let him blend in with the early morning shadows.

Still. He *was* one of the deadliest fae in America.

And I just got myself engaged to him. Shock was settling in, but I didn't regret my decision.

The anger of the nobles had actually convinced me I'd taken the best route by choosing Lord Rigel.

The Paragon scoffed. "*I* have no reason to be afraid of your new beau. Even if he is a murder hobo, my power is far superior—he's just a cub. But a deadly, murderous cub that you'll be living with!"

"*Mmert!*" Aphrodite poked her head out of the car seat.

"Oh, Aphrodite." The Paragon scooped his pet up—she was wearing what looked like pink baby pajamas. "I'm sorry, are you cold?"

"I think this whole thing is the best thing that's happened to the Court in decades." Lord Dion laughed as he flopped down on the couch, looking much freer than I'd ever seen. "It'll be good for Rigel—and it's hilarious!"

The Paragon gave Lord Dion a withering gaze. "You're an idiot."

Lord Dion shrugged. "I was prepared to do my duty and marry her because you asked me, but I think this is a far better outcome. I mean, who is going to mess with her now?"

The Paragon turned back to me. "Is that why you asked him?"

"Yes, tell us, my Sovereign," Indigo drawled as she eased herself into a chair. "We're all dying to know your thought process."

Chase and Skye stood behind her—Chase with his arms folded behind his back and an expectant look in his eyes that said Indigo was right. Skye was still chewing on antacids—I don't think she'd stopped taking them since the receiving line finished the previous night.

That can't be healthy. Maybe I should send her to a doctor?

"I asked Lord Rigel to marry me because you, Paragon, told me to marry someone who didn't have split loyalties."

"Yes," the Paragon agreed. "But I was talking about Dion!" He gave the young lord a dirty look when he laughed again.

"Except Dion has political loyalties."

The Paragon peered at me over the rim of his spectacles. "To whom?"

"You."

The Paragon made a strangled noise, and Aphrodite patted at his face with a paw.

"Lord Rigel is the only one with virtually no connections—he couldn't have any or he wouldn't be trusted as an assassin," I said. "Which means I can do what I want, and I don't have to worry about the political baggage he'll bring with him."

It was around then that it occurred to me the genius of my idea might backfire if Lord Rigel stopped getting work as an assassin because he married me, and he got angry as a result.

But he'd be untouchable by the Court. From his point of view he'd still be escaping political games...right?

I glanced at my fiancé, who was still brooding in the shadows.

"Perhaps." The Paragon put his cat back down in her car seat, then adjusted the tie of his bathrobe. "But I still think you're nuts. And why are you concerned about political ties? I thought your greatest aspiration was to survive?"

"I'm still very much concerned with that," I assured him. "But my marriage is a long-term thing. And once I can finally convince the Night Court to follow me, I'll still be living with the consequences of it."

"Humph!"

The Paragon sat next to his cat, who affectionately purred and rubbed her head against his arm.

His reaction reminded me I had other people to be concerned about. I twisted, the skirts of my mermaid gown flowing around me. "How is the Court reacting, Skye?"

Skye set her tablet down and folded her hands in front of her. "There is *anger* to be sure, but acceptance as well."

"That's about what I expected," I agreed. "Everyone was sure when I got married they'd know exactly how to control and move me." I smirked. "Joke's on them!"

"Lord Linus seemed...upset," Chase said.

I waved it off. "Lord Linus frequently acts like a child. He's probably just mad that Rigel isn't the kind of person he can beg for money from."

"Perhaps, but he left shortly after you announced the engagement and hasn't been seen since," Chase said.

I wonder what new level of debt he's getting himself sunk in. Ugh. "It's fine," I breezily said. "He'll drag himself back eventually."

"The Court is mad and still can't make a move, Rigel got himself a fiancée, and I'm free," Lord Dion summarized. "All in all, I think this is the best possible outcome! And something tells me socials are going to be *a lot* livelier in the future!"

"Some of the lords and ladies who had previously signed up to enter the annual derby are threatening to drop out." Skye picked up her tablet again and peered down at it. "Which may become a problem. A minimum of six entries from a Court are required in order for the Court to enter."

"And we can't skip it?" I asked.

"Not if you want to keep the tiny scrap of respect the Night Court still has to its name," Indigo snorted.

"The results of the race—" Skye started.

"Wait, wait—let me guess!" I declared. "They greatly affect the always fluctuating balance of power between the Courts?"

"Yes."

"Thought so." I plucked my prism from my clutch and rolled it between my fingers—a habit that had become weirdly soothing. "Only fae would see power plays in a stupid thing like a race."

Lord Dion popped out of his chair. "Now seems like a convenient time to tell you that I'd love to be the royal lawyer, should the need ever occur." He handed me a business card, which was fancy with gold embossed font.

I studied it for a second before passing it off to Skye. "Are you seriously implying you think we're going to get a divorce before we even get married?"

"No, not at all!" Lord Dion flapped a hand at me. "Rather, you are planning to marry a fae lord with a rather unique career that may one day lead him to cross paths with the law and—how to say it with refinement—get pressed with a murder charge."

"And you would try to get him off?"

"Of course! My motto is 'I may not be able to lie, but that doesn't mean I have to tell the whole truth!'"

"Yes, you do—it's in the oaths!"

"Ah-ah-ah—witnesses take that oath! That's my second motto, 'follow the law to the letter, not the meaning'!"

I squinted at Lord Dion. "Wow. I am really glad I didn't end up choosing you."

"You and me both," he assured me. "Because this is going to be hilarious—and relaxing—for me!" He meandered up to Lord Rigel and slapped him on the shoulder. "I still can't believe it. Rigel, married! And becoming the consort, no less!" he laughed. "So much for skipping Court functions!"

Chase was writing up notes. "We will have to make adjustments for additional security for Lord Rigel."

"I will arrange for the suite connected to Queen Leila's to be cleaned out," Skye said. "But I expect Indigo will take point on having it redecorated?"

"Yep," Indigo said.

"Wait—*what?*" I stopped fiddling with my prism.

"As queen and consort you two obviously require connecting rooms," Skye said.

Oh. I didn't know about that.

I wasn't afraid that Lord Rigel was going to try anything inappropriate, or bust in on me swimming in my giant tub. No, the bigger danger was that he could now super easily murder me in my sleep!

I'm going to have to do something about that.

"He'll need a wardrobe," Lord Dion added. "He's only got black and gray clothes. He needs some variety!"

"Noted." Indigo dug her smartphone out and tapped away on it.

The Paragon let out a long, agonized sigh like an overdramatic actress. "When will the wedding be?"

"It's scheduled for a week after the Midsummer Derby." Skye said. "The first week of August. I imagine we should be able to achieve all of this."

"A moment, Queen Leila?" Lord Rigel asked in a low voice.

I jumped—he'd somehow moved across the room without me noticing and was now standing close enough I could almost *feel* the deepness of his voice. "Ah, sure."

The others were busy talking about wedding preparations, but Chase and Indigo both noticed when we started to leave.

I waved to them to stay put, but was thankful when Chase started typing away on his phone—probably letting the on-duty guards know we were on the move.

"What's up?" I asked Lord Rigel once we entered the hallway and he shut the door of my study behind us.

"I believe you owe me an explanation."

"Ah. Right. Okay—follow me."

I found the closest door to the outside and led him all the way to the stables.

The sun was already high above the horizon, and my eyes felt like they were filled with bits of gravel. Thankfully, half way through the night, Indigo had slipped me a pair of flats that were way more comfortable than my heels, but I was getting a little tired of the tight fit of my dress as I elbowed the stable door open.

I knew from experience Dusk and Dawn would have already been at work for hours, so the night mares were fed and their stalls were clean.

The siblings were actually in the open area at the front of the stable by the tack room. They were feeding the four glooms and seven shades that had elected to stay here.

"Queen Leila!" Dawn said. She and Dusk bowed, carefully balancing the bags of cat and dog kibble they were holding.

When they both glanced at Rigel, they each simultaneously dropped leaves from their hair.

I have such cute employees.

"Good morning, Dusk, good morning Dawn. We're going to go in by the night mares. Let us know if we get in your way, okay?"

"Y-yes, Queen Leila."

The glooms and shades wandered up to me. I stopped long enough to give everyone a pet before Rigel and I stepped into the stall area.

"Hello, my beauties!" I called.

A variety of screams—the night mares—a hee-haw—that was Bagel—and a polite nicker—Fax, the sun stallion—greeted us.

I led Rigel to Bagel's stall. The stall door was so high the little donkey could only get his chin up on the edge. "Are you going to do the bubble thing again?"

I jumped when I noticed he had a dagger in his hand, then relaxed when the sound bubble grew around us and he put the weapon away. "Talk."

I shrugged. "It's mostly what I told the Paragon. You don't have any political ties—which is what I wanted. Well—what I would have preferred would be to not get married at all. But since that's not an option, I wanted the fae version of a rock—someone who wouldn't affect my plans or give me extra junk to deal with. You're the only one like that."

Lord Rigel blinked. "There's more to it than that."

"There is?" I frowned. "I hadn't really thought of more than that. I mean, you know my goal is to crush this competition for power and end it."

Lord Rigel watched me with narrowed eyes. "Do you think you can order me to eliminate your enemies if you marry me?"

I'd been reaching over the stall door to pet Bagel so he didn't have to strain his little neck trying to reach me, but at this suggestion I thumped my hand into the stall door with enough strength to make my knuckles sting. "*What?*"

"I am an assassin. You may believe that the fastest way to end this all is to eliminate the most powerful players."

"What? *No!*" Taken aback, I leaned against the stall door and properly looked up at him. "First of all, killing everyone would just mean a new crop of power-hungry fae would pop in. Secondly, *I don't kill people!*" I scowled at him.

"Then I don't think you're ever going to achieve your goal," Lord Rigel bluntly said.

"No, when I say I want to crush this game I mean end the stupid competitions! Not become a power-hungry tyrant and make everyone do what I want!" I slapped my hands to my eyes—I'm sure badly smearing my makeup. "I'm doomed," I muttered.

"This stupid game is so entrenched into fae culture they can't even fathom any other way!"

"I more meant that someone will murder you before you can achieve this utopia you desire if you wish to abstain from killing."

I shivered. "Whatever, it's fine. The point is, no, I *never* will ask you to kill anyone for me! Got it?"

He flashed his dark eyes at me—and I had to admit when he wasn't being purposely creepy, Lord Rigel was possibly one of the best looking supernaturals I had ever met.

If she gets the courage, Indigo is going to have fun dressing him up.

"Then you intend to use my name to threaten the Court."

"Possibly?" I squinted up at him. "But probably not in the way you think. Like, I'm not going to tell people if they don't agree with me you're going to off them, if that's what you mean."

"In what other way could you use my name?"

"Hmm." I thought for a moment, then snapped my fingers. "I've got a good example! If an annoying noble keeps yacking my ear off, I can tell them they're fascinating and that I should call you over to hear what they have to say. I'm pretty sure that would make them run off."

Lord Rigel stared at me.

"Oh! Or if someone is complaining about a change I'm making, I'll tell them they'll need to convince you it's the wrong thing to do." I clapped my hands in glee. "Or when the chef tells me he'll only let a coffee machine in the kitchen over his dead body I'll tell him *you* like coffee, too!"

"I only drink tea."

"Please, Lord Rigel. I'm having a moment. Just give me this fantasy."

One of Lord Rigel's silver eyebrows might have moved the tiniest bit. "In other words, you intend to use my presence as an intimidation factor to pull yourself from unwanted interactions."

"Yeah, pretty much. Would that be okay?"

He shrugged. "If someone attacks you in their anger, I'm not going to defend you."

"No worries. That's why I have Chase." I rubbed one of Bagel's ears, and the donkey leaned into the gesture. "Are we good?"

"This is a rather one-sided bargain," Lord Rigel said. "I'm not getting anything out of it."

Whoa, there is danger here.

This next conversation could put me heavily in Rigel's debt—which was dangerous beyond words—or I might be able to smooth things out and get off easily if I was careful.

CHAPTER TWENTY-FIVE

Leila

I made myself casually shrug. "Life as a consort won't be too bad. You can sit around and do whatever you like. You don't have to study, or get cornered by annoying lords, or sit through meetings with really unpleasant people and smile."

I paused. "This is getting depressing. The point is, you can do what you want—although I won't lie, I'm hoping that's going to include a lot less murdering, and maybe a new hobby or two instead. And you can stay as uninvolved with politics as you are now. Maybe even less involved—because no one is going to voluntarily drag you in."

"Except you."

"Except me," I agreed. "Which, newsflash, I'm not too keen on, either."

"I'll agree," Lord Rigel said. "Not for any of these reasons, but because I still cannot ascertain what kind of a threat you are to the fae, and if I marry you I will find it easier to end you if you *do* become a threat."

Hmmm, will that count as an even balance between us? I'm going to say yes because it's my life he's threatening.

It was a warning more than a promise, but I took it to heart with a wince. "Yeah, I should have expected that. For the sake of curiosity, what do you consider a threat?"

"Destroying the Night Court beyond what it already has, to the point where the Night Realm has crumbled."

"Oh." I paused. "That's not too bad. I think I'd have to actively try to make things worse. And I'm not going to do that because my beauties already look terrible." I frowned as I peered across the aisle at Eclipse, who had her head hanging over her stall door. "Speaking of which, they're on a fat supplement. Why do they still look an inch away from death?"

"Then we have a deal?"

"Yes," I absently said. "Crap—wait, no! Rules of surviving with fae: never make deals or bargains! This isn't a deal, it's a business agreement. No take backs—that doesn't count!"

Lord Rigel stared at me. "You are a strange creature."

"Yeah, Indigo and Skye say that a lot, too," I agreed.

"Very well, it's an agreement, not a bargain or deal," Lord Rigel said. He snapped, and the bubble burst. "I'd advise you to take care not to expect anything from me. You're never going to see my wings."

"Uhh...yeah?" I said, kind of confused. "Good for me?"

Why would I care about his wings?

Wings were a part of fae culture that I hadn't looked into because—as far as I could tell—I didn't have any.

All members of fae nobility had wings—it was another expression of their great power—but they were secretive about them and apparently only showed them to those they really cared about.

I had no desire to see *anybody's* wings. Skye probably didn't have them either, Chase was a werewolf so he didn't have any, and since Indigo was a brownie, she wouldn't have them.

Lord Linus was the only member of my inner circle who had them, and if that doofus ever even *tried* to show me his wings—or talk about if he showed my mom his wings—I'd strangle him with my bare hands.

"Oh," I said when it clicked. "You're warning me not to fall in love with you. How very melodramatic and proper for a brooding fae like you. No worries, bucko. Murderizing snobs aren't my type."

I meandered back up the aisle, calling to the night mares. "I'll be back later today, boys and girls! I need some sleep—and I've got to get out of this dress!"

Lord Rigel quickly caught up to me with his longer legs. "I will be surprised if, by the end of your reign, you haven't offended every noble in your Court."

"Ohhh, now that sounds like a challenge. I accept!"

"It was an observation."

"I still accept!"

"If you anger so many people, there will be repercussions."

"Hah—none I care about!"

Rigel glanced down at me. "What are your other rules for surviving with fae?"

"Don't eat or drink anything a fae has made to avoid getting spelled. Pay attention to the way fae phrase things because even if they can't lie, they will manipulate until the horses go back into the barn. Oh—never put yourself in a fae's debt. And mind your manners since fae value them greatly."

"And this summer is an example of you minding your manners?"

"I'm queen. That rule shouldn't apply to me."

"Shocking."

"Hey, I do all the little speeches and stupid events and dinners—that ought to count for something!"

"Certainly, if your small donkey counts as a night mare."

"You're just jealous you have to use your brooding looks to get out of this kind of thing."

"*Brooding?*"

"You say that as if you don't do it on purpose—hah!"

"The last rider dropped out this morning, and all requests for new derby participants among the Night Court have gone unmet," Skye said.

"These are the repercussions for getting engaged to my dashing assassin, I imagine," I said.

"Most likely."

I shrugged and looked around Magiford—the "race track."

The city was cleared for the occasion. Lots of barriers were erected to block out pedestrian areas, keeping humans from accidentally wandering into the course—which was marked out by colored flags.

The Midsummer Derby wasn't like your typical race—oh heck no.

It started on the north west side of the city and ended on the east side, but there were all kinds of different ways to get between the two spots, and the riders decided where to go.

The areas marked out for the course included several parks, downtown, and even the lakeside boardwalk. Technically two of the lakes were included in the area we could ride through, but neither water nor flying mounts were allowed, so that was a bit of a moot point.

There were pockets of spectators—this was one of the Curia Cloisters' "good will" events that trotted us fae out for the humans to see, but I wasn't convinced it actually bought us much popularity since all the downtown shops had to close for almost the entire day.

Skye fiddled with her tablet. "The derby begins in twenty minutes. We need to scratch our entries now."

Lord Linus—yes, he'd returned from whatever hole he had crawled into after my engagement announcement—frowned and scratched Bagel's head, then adjusted his hold on the donkey's lead rope. "That's not going to look good. Even under Queen Nyte, the Night Court has always managed to enter the derby. It's going to make our reputation suffer even more."

"Actually, it won't, because we don't have to scratch." I held up my helmet and gestured to my riding clothes. "I came prepared."

"You're one rider, Queen Leila," Skye said. "We still need five more."

"No we don't, because I have six night mares," I said.

"What are you talking about?" Lord Linus asked.

"I read all of the race rules in excruciating detail. It says six horses are required per Court, but it never actually says each mount has to have a rider. And I've been working with the night mares—they'll race with me. That's why I insisted we bring Bagel and Fax, too."

I gestured to Lord Rigel, who was holding Fax's lead rope, and hadn't said more than two sentences since we arrived here via a portal from the night mares an hour ago. The older sun stallion didn't seem to mind, though. He pressed his giant head into Lord Rigel's shoulder and happily exhaled.

Lord Linus stared at me for a long moment. "That's it, you need to take a six pack of healing draughts. First you get yourself engaged to that *assassin*, and now you want to ride in a race that is famous among the supernatural community for its cut-throat competition! And you want to do this without anyone from the Night Court backing you up?"

"Frankly, the people of the Night Court have been trying to kill me. I'll feel a lot better if they're *not* there to 'back me up,' as you said."

"Chase, talk her out of it," Lord Linus said.

The werewolf gamely stepped up, his yellow eyes bright in the afternoon light. "It will be an unnecessary risk, Queen Leila."

"Maybe, but as much as I want to quell the game of power in my own Court, I'm aware I need to give in to some of their traditions. This is something I'm actually *good* at, and I have an advantage with the night mares," I said.

Chase, Skye, and Lord Linus exchanged glances as I strapped my helmet on, then whistled.

The night mares slunk out of the shadows. Blue Moon was the only one with a saddle—an English style one that Dusk and Dawn had pulled out for me—and a bridle.

"You've been planning for this," Lord Linus said. "That's why you've been practicing with all of your night mares."

"I figured something like this would happen eventually, but I didn't think it would with this specific race. I guess I underestimated my ability to annoy my own Court!" I winked.

Skye looked ready to pull out her hair. "Queen Leila, the possibilities of you getting injured are immense. You are an untested rider—the Court can survive another season even if we don't enter the derby."

"Hey—you know I can ride!" I protested. "And I'll be with the night mares. They'll make sure I'm safe." I patted Blue Moon's neck.

"The riding here is on a different level from letting a night mare take you for a stroll around your trails," Skye said.

"*Why* do you want to do this?" Lord Linus asked. "You don't have to."

"I don't," I slowly agreed. "But I feel like my Court underestimates the night mares, and me. And I want to show them I don't care what tactics they use."

"*All entries, report to the start line for opening ceremonies!*" a man declared through a megaphone.

Skye sighed. "I'll make arrangements for us to meet you at the end of the line."

Chase narrowed his eyes at me. If he were in wolf form, I was pretty sure he'd have his ears pinned, but he bowed. "I'll bring the security around."

"Thanks, you two. Come on, beauties." I started in the direction of megaphone guy, and my night mares followed behind me.

"You are such a willful, awful child," Lord Linus complained as he followed me. "You're going to send me to an early grave!"

"Yeah, yeah."

I glanced at Lord Rigel who joined me, walking side by side with Fax happily prancing along.

"Thanks for watching Fax for me while I ride."

Lord Rigel glanced at me. "I, too, think this is a mistake."

I pressed my lips together in irritation. "If you say it's because you think I'm a bad rider, I'm going to tell one of the night mares to bite you."

"No. I'm fairly certain you are a great deal better rider than everyone believes," Lord Rigel said.

"Oh?"

"When I was staking out a place to hide and then kill you, I saw inside your barn." He ignored Lord Linus when he squawked like an angry seagull. "Based on the kinds of equipment I saw, you've been riding a long time, and in a variety of styles."

"Excellent observation."

We followed megaphone man—who was repeating the announcement as he made his way to the starting point.

When we got closer, I could actually see more of the contestants, all preparing their mounts—which were mostly sun stallions.

I'd bet the Day or Night Courts founded this race since they were the only two Courts with magical horse mounts—I'd say it was that annoying jerk of a Night King, because as a first class fun sucker it seemed like it would totally be his thing. Regardless, talk about stacking the deck in your favor!

Of course, there were winged horses and unicorns, but neither of those animals were exactly common, and they didn't readily allow themselves to be ridden. Plus, it was extremely rare that anyone could successfully domesticate one of them, so even if there was a domesticated unicorn or winged horse trotting around, their owner wasn't going to risk entering them in a potentially dangerous race.

There were a few regular-ish horses—those were mostly owned by the less powerful seelie and unseelie Courts. And I say 'ish' because a lot of them still gave off a faint aura of magic—I was guessing they'd been stabled in the fae realm long enough to pick up some of the place's natural magic, or they had a fae on staff that—like me—had some natural animal magic.

It was pretty easy to pick out the riders representing the Winter, Autumn, Summer, Spring, and Day Courts.

Day's riders all wore golden robes and had gorgeous suns emblazoned on their tunics. Autumn's wore crimson shirts swirled with shades of orange and red, and had extravagant tack emblazoned with brightly colored leaves. Spring's sun stallions all had wreaths of flowers tied around their necks and twined around the tack, while Winter's tack were all a stark white that had shades of blue in it. Finally, Summer's people wore brilliant shades of blue and orange, and their sun stallions had brightly colored ribbons braided into their manes and tails.

The monarchs were nowhere to be seen on the bustling city street.

"The other Courts didn't bring any of their magical mounts?" I asked.

I think the Autumn Court has griffins? I don't remember what the others have.

"Only equines can be used in the hunts and races," Lord Linus said.

"Yeah, I'm well aware of the rules," I sourly said. "I meant why wouldn't the kings and queens ride their mounts here?"

"Not everyone treats their Court's magical creatures as pets," Lord Linus said. "Or, more correctly, the creatures don't always trust their Court enough to establish the bond needed to be a pet."

"*It's time for the opening ceremony!*" megaphone guy shouted. "*Here to mark the festivities are our venerable rulers of the Midwest region. Queen Rime of the Winter Court!*"

The representatives for and the fae from the Winter Court howled like wolves as Queen Rime—eye catching with her white hair, pale skin, and stark white clothes—stepped out of a fancy car, sunglasses covering her eyes.

"*King Fell of the Autumn Court!*"

A handsome fae who looked just a little older than me casually jogged down the stairs of a store, holding out his hands and smirking as his people cheered loudly for him.

He had perfect, brunette hair and a classically handsome face, but his clothes were...*unusual*. He wore a sort of gold-plated breastplate that just covered his upper chest—leaving the lean muscles of his waist uncovered—fitted red pants, gold wrist cuffs, and a red cloak that draped over one shoulder.

He looked like the kind of guy I just *itched* to punch—cocky, smug, and *annoying*.

"*King Birch and Consort Flora of the Summer Court!*"

I couldn't spy the Summer monarchs—judging by how far off the cheers for them were, I was guessing they were farther up the street, closer to the starting line.

"*King Solis of the Day Court!*"

All the sun stallions in the area—regardless of who owned them—raised their heads and neighed in tribute to their true owner as King Solis waved from where he had emerged at the base of the street with a few additional riders.

"*Queen Verdant of the Spring Court!*"

Queen Verdant—clothed in a gauzy green gown—laughed as she rode in on a sun stallion, her long, curly blond hair cascading over her shoulder, barefoot, and a crown of flowers with a set of white antlers on her head.

Her people cheered for her, making her smile bigger, as she waved like a royal attending a ball.

"*And Queen Leila of the Night Court!*"

I was perfectly prepared for zero noise. None of my people were here at the start line, and my riders had all backed out. So I was shocked when there were whoops and cheers behind me.

"Our Queen!"

"You get 'em, Queen Leila!"

"Night Court, Night Court!"

"Go angry demon horses!"

I spun around and was shocked to recognize Landon, the barista from King's Court Café, the two girls I had taken the selfie with, and about a dozen other humans, cheering and bouncing on the balls of their feet.

I laughed and waved to them, making them cheer louder.

It was around then I felt eyes piercing my back. I suspiciously turned around, expecting to see Lady Chrysanthe or Lord Myron.

Surprisingly, it was Queen Verdant who was flashing such a hostile glare at me, it made her beautiful facial features drawn and almost evil. She turned her back to me and enthusiastically chatted with her riders.

What was that about?

"Queen Leila!" King Solis—handsome, golden, and warm—strolled up to us, a smile gracing his lips. "How good it is to see you here today—and you, too, my fine fellow." He extended his hand and Fax nickered, then rested his muzzle in King Solis's cupped fingers.

"It's good to see you, King Solis," I said. "I'd say I wish your mounts luck, but it seems like most everyone is riding a sun stallion."

King Solis laughed. "They are beloved—speaking of which, I heard from the Paragon I am to offer you and Lord Rigel my congratulations." He was the first person to look from me to Lord Rigel without any open sign of anxiety or fear. Which meant either he was a very good actor, or he didn't care who I got myself hitched to as long as I didn't run the Court into the dirt.

"Thank you," I said.

"Lord Rigel is a very strong, respected warrior—a good choice. Surely he'll be able to protect you," King Solis said.

"Aha," I laughed weakly. "Maybe. Are you participating?"

"No—rulers traditionally don't risk themselves in this sort of manner," King Solis said.

"See! I told you!" Lord Linus glared at me over Bagel's head—the donkey was grinning as King Solis rubbed his forehead.

"You can't mean to imply Queen Leila is participating?" King Solis said.

"Me and the night mares," I confirmed. "I should probably get up to the lineup."

King Solis frowned. "Are you certain you should enter? It can be very dangerous."

"Yep. All my riders backed out—and I'm not looking to win," I said. "I just want to get through it."

"Even if you only wish to come in last, it still is folly," King Solis said. "It's an unnecessary risk."

"Listen to the Day King," Lord Linus echoed.

"I trust my night mares," I said. "Besides. Everyone seems to forget—I'm human. I grew up in Magiford."

King Solis's frown deepened. He glanced away from me, his eyes going to the other monarchs, before he leaned in and spoke in a quiet tone. "Very well, then I must warn you to stay away from the Fall riders—they're the most brutal, and will attack with weapons if it means securing a front position. Also look out for Lord Umer from the Summer Court. He's won every year for the past five years. It's a given that he cheats, but the area is warded against portal magic for the derby, and no one has been able to catch him in the act. He's avoided disqualification thus far, but he won't react well if you try to follow him as a result."

"Don't worry, I intend to go on a less traveled path," I assured him.

"Ahh, you're going for a longer route then? Good choice," King Solis said.

Lord Linus relaxed and dangled an arm over Bagel's neck. "If you do that, the danger factor will drastically decrease."

I conveniently remained silent, letting Lord Linus and King Solis make their own assumptions.

In reality, I was planning to push my knowledge of Magiford for my benefit. In this case, there were a few paths that would be a great deal faster, but also extremely dangerous for a regular horse and rider—those paths traditionally went unused as a result. Or so Skye told me when I walked the exterior of the course with her and asked her about a few of the alleyways and paths I knew of.

I glanced at Lord Rigel. *I wonder what he assumes I meant by a less traveled path? Ah, wait, I think I can guess. He's already probably lining it up with his conspiracy theory that I'm out to destroy the Court and frame it as losing on purpose.*

"A participation trophy is enough to keep your current level of influence and power," King Solis continued. "Even if you came in last, you'd be fine—and, as long as you finish, you won't be last. There are always some riders that are hurt and are removed from the field before they can finish."

A frown twitched at my lips. "You said some riders are hurt, how about the horses?"

King Solis gave me a blazing smile edged with the promise of pain. It betrayed the kind face he showed me and revealed the wildness within him. "Given that the majority of the mounts are sun stallions, no," he said in a voice that crackled with power like a fire. "No one would dare harm or hurt one of *my* creatures."

Ohh, now that was a promise of death. Fax, please be in good health for the sake of my *health!*

"The Midsummer Derby begins in five minutes. Contestants, please make your way to the starting point!" megaphone guy announced.

King Solis returned to his sunny self. "I suppose that's our warning to get to the transportation that will take us to the finish line. Lord Linus, Lord Rigel, would you like a lift?"

"We'd love to, but unless you have a trailer in your pocket, we can't." Lord Linus patted Bagel for emphasis.

"Oh, most of the other monarchs arrived in cars because they're putting every last sun stallion they have in the race." King Solis smirked. "But I have far more, so my escort and I arrived mounted. My stallion will open a portal to the Day Realm and then another to the finish line."

"In that case, wonderful! I didn't know how we were going to get these two to the finish line. I don't know that Fax would be willing to open up a portal for us and leave his little friends." Lord Linus nodded his head to the night mares, who flicked their tails.

"Splendid. This way, then. Queen Leila, I wish you all the luck I can spare—stay safe," he warned.

"I will do my best," I said.

"Yes, listen to him." Lord Linus nodded sagely. "And his wise words."

I rolled my eyes. "Good day, Lord Linus."

Lord Linus sighed melodramatically. "It's fine. I know children must one day separate from their parents!"

"*You*—" I started to hiss, but the nutcase was already gone, sweeping after King Solis with Bagel and leaving me alone with Lord Rigel and Fax.

He stared at me. "You're planning something."

"Only sort of," I said.

He shrugged. "Don't bring ruin to our Court." With that "beautiful" and "touching" advice, he left.

I shook my head. *He was my choice. My choice—I have to remember that.* I turned the night mares in the direction of the starting line. *Besides, it could have been worse. I could have gotten myself hitched to Lord Dion without knowing his personality is crooked!*

CHAPTER TWENTY-SIX

Rigel

The finish line was the same as I remembered it from the times I'd been unable to avoid coming to the derby as a child, and my teenage years when Dion had dragged me along because he thought it was exciting.

The derby ended in a park, with a long stretch of green to give the horses room to slow down after crossing the line, which was hemmed in by the temporary seating arrangements that would be torn down once this all was over.

Giant TV screens had been erected around us, allowing us a view of the race. All of the contestants were followed overhead by drones. Or they tried to—some contestants purposely lost them in forested areas in parks so they could then cheat or perform illegal maneuvers.

The only thing that had changed was that I now stood close to the finish line in a reserved seating area for the monarchs and their families with Lord Linus—and the donkey and sun stallion Leila had charged us with.

King Solis had inexplicably elected to stand with us, his face tight with concern as he watched the black blob at the starting line that marked out the queen and her six feral night mares. They were easy to spot in the sea of white, gold, and crimson sun stallions.

"I hope she manages to get through this," King Solis said.

"She's a fighter," Lord Linus said. "As long as no one ticks her off and hurts an animal in front of her, she'll be fine."

King Solis clasped his hands together and draped his arms over the chest-high wooden fence erected for safety.

It is strange he has such concern for the Night Court monarch.

King Solis's gaze skated past me and lingered on Fax and Bagel. "I assume Queen Leila was not planning to ride either of these fine mounts?"

I let Lord Linus answer—I had no desire to speak to the Day King.

"No." Lord Linus rubbed Bagel's head—the donkey leaned into it with glee. "She said we had to bring them as 'emotional support' for the night mares."

King Solis wrinkled his forehead in confusion. "Emotional support?"

"That's what she said."

"Must be a human thing."

"Yeah."

I watched on the screen as one of the derby officials raised a massive white flag, then swung it down.

"It's started," I said.

The horses were off like a shot, tearing down the streets in a dangerous crush, except Leila and the night mares.

They stayed far behind, grouped in a tiny pack, obediently standing at the starting line for no apparent reason.

I nearly frowned as the drone assigned to Leila zoomed in on her.

What is she planning?

CHAPTER TWENTY-SEVEN

Leila

I watched as the rest of the contestants disappeared down the broad, paved road. If the previous races were any indication, they'd all stay on this road as it traveled south, until it turned and went east.

From there it varied hugely as the riders branched off into what they thought were the best streets—or the secret places where they could cheat, like the Lord Umer whom King Solis had mentioned.

But I planned to turn off immediately.

Even though we were completely hemmed in on the east by lakes, there was *one* way out. One way that nobody took because they either didn't know the area, or because it'd be too terrifying for any horse to travel.

But I know the night mares, and I believe in them. Let's just hope they believe in me, too.

Once the last rider and mount passed about three blocks in

front of us, I gathered up the reins. "Okay, my beauties. Let's show everyone just how amazing you are. Group up!"

I cheekily waved to the drone as the night mares rearranged themselves into two rows of three. Eclipse was on my right and Solstice on my left with Blue Moon and me in the center. Behind us, Comet, Twilight, and Nebula guarded our backs.

I nudged Blue Moon into a trot, which the rest of the night mares copied, and immediately turned off the road, following a side street that circled back behind the stores, restaurants, and cafés that lined the lakeside and opened into a long but thin parking lot.

The night mares clattered across the parking lot, and I fought to keep my breathing steady even though my palms were fast getting sweaty.

We reached the lakeside, which—although it had a boardwalk—didn't have a beach, just a steep dropoff since the lake was about ten feet lower than the street.

But bridging over the gap and arching down to the water was a sturdy boardwalk the city had put in about a decade ago thanks to the funds the Curia Cloisters had dropped into a gigantic city beautification project—AKA one of the supernaturals' efforts to buy goodwill among the people when humans were still unsure if supernaturals were safe or not.

The lake—the horribly named Fairy Lake—actually only started a few blocks north, and at this portion the lake was pretty narrow. So narrow, in fact, the boardwalk cut straight across the water and bridged the lake to connect to a bike path that sliced between Fairy Lake and the other lake that pressed against downtown Magiford. Following the bike trail would drop me off in the downtown area—just a few blocks up from the finish line—and it would cut a significant amount of distance off the ride while providing a safe area and good footing for my night mares to gallop down.

But first we had to get there.

The boardwalk was narrow—made for foot traffic and bikes—but it was passable by horse...if you could get any horse out to the middle of the lake without it losing its mind.

I took a deep breath. *We can do this. I know them.*

"Single file—space yourselves, and walk *carefully*. Blue Moon and I will lead."

I clicked to Blue Moon, and he obediently walked up to the wooden bridge that marked the start of this water-crossing boardwalk. His hooves thudded dully on the wood as he took the first few steps.

When we reached the part of the boardwalk that started to tilt down toward the water, Eclipse started, breathing loudly as her footfalls added to the boardwalk.

This thing should be able to hold us all, I thought as Blue Moon tossed his head. *I've seen the city bring multiple bobcats and four-wheelers out here for maintenance. The bigger issue is if the night mares can stay calm.*

Blue Moon obediently marched on, and when I twisted in the saddle to look back, Solstice had already entered the boardwalk. He tossed his head, and his movements were tense, but he followed. Behind him, Nebula got on, her ears pinned but her head slightly lowered with a mulish sort of stubbornness.

We're doing it. We'll make it, and as long as we get good time on the bike path, we'll make it.

CHAPTER TWENTY-EIGHT

Rigel

"She is insane!" Lord Linus hissed. "What is she *thinking*?"

King Solis gaped in silence, though he gripped the wooden fence tightly enough to make it creak.

I stared at the TV screens, the least shocked as we watched Queen Leila lead the night mares—by all accounts uncontrollable beasts—out over the water, taking them far away from land against all their instincts.

"*Mmert!*"

Recognizing the sound, I turned and was not at all surprised to see the Paragon standing next to us, cradling a basket that held his overweight and bald cat.

"Those are the night mares? *Those* creatures?" The Paragon shook his fist at the screens. "I spent hours—no—*days* corralling you uncooperative monsters, and with just a flutter of her eyelashes Queen Leila can lead you out over open water? Like a bunch of peaceful lambs? That's not fair! You rotten ingrates!"

Fax struck the ground with his hoof, and I set a hand on his neck as I watched the screens.

Leila and her deadly pets were almost to the halfway point of the boardwalk.

The drone fluttered down to get a better shot, and from this angle you could see how nervous the night mares were.

They tossed their heads, swished their tails, and their ears were ever moving as sweat streaked their hides. They were so nervous, the sweat had created a froth on their legs, and a few of the animals drooled red and snorted sparks.

I hope you know what you're doing, Queen Leila.

CHAPTER TWENTY-NINE

Leila

The night mares were terrified.

Behind me, they snorted and tossed their heads. Sweat dripped off their necks, shoulders and chests, and at one point Comet charged a few steps, barely stopping before she slammed into the rail.

We were in the middle of the lake now, as far away from land as we'd get.

My stomach had numbed in my fear, and I knew that if the night mares didn't calm down, we'd be in a very dangerous position.

Blue Moon's hide twitched, but when I put a hand on his shoulder he calmed, his ears perking.

"It's okay, buddy," I murmured to him. "We're going to be fine."

He exhaled deeply, and his steps became surer.

Relieved, I twisted around in my saddle to look at the others.

Nebula stopped. She planted her front feet, and her whole body shook as she was unable to take another step.

Behind her Twilight rolled his pale yellow eyes and shrieked; his breathing was twice as fast as it should have been as something white dripped from his nostrils.

The others weren't faring any better.

I have to reassure them.

My heart twisted at the sight of my scared horses. "Eclipse, Solstice, Comet, Twilight, Nebula, we're going to be okay, I promise."

The night mares perked their ears as they listened to my voice.

"I will *never* let anyone harm you. I will never send you off without me," I vowed. "I'm here with you, and I promise we're going to get through to the other side. Don't look at the water, watch *me*."

Nebula exhaled hard, then rocked forward into a shaky walk.

Up and down the line, the night mares tucked their chins, their eyes fixed on me as they followed.

It was then that I really understood the depth of their intelligence—and the intelligence of fae creatures.

They were trusting me. They'd listened to my words and were choosing to override instinct because I asked them to.

I don't deserve them.

They clopped across the boardwalk, and I talked to them the whole way, my voice getting stronger and surer the closer we got to land.

Blue Moon shuddered with relief once he stepped off the wooden boardwalk and onto the dirt walking trail.

Eclipse tucked her butt under her and scurried after us, Solstice just a few steps behind her.

The horses breathed easier once they stepped on to land, and they inspected the bike trail. Wide enough for one car, the trail traveled both north and curved to the south and east—the portion we wanted to travel.

It was walled in with shrubs and a little wooden fence, but it was a much wider and more secure path. And—most importantly—it was a long, abandoned stretch of good footing.

"This is it, my beauties!" I called to them as the last night mare reached land with a relieved huff. I glanced up at the drone hovering above us, which emitted a high-pitched whirl as it buzzed around us. "Let's show everyone what you have!"

I cued Blue Moon into a canter, and he *ripped loose*.

I swear I felt a dark and wild magic ripple around us as he lengthened his stride, his hooves thundering against the dirt path.

I leaned low over his neck, every muscle in my body tightened. I squeezed Blue Moon with all the muscles in my legs and pushed down in the saddle stirrups as wind ripped at my clothes.

Eclipse galloped at our side, her body long and lean as she ran wilder than the wind.

As we galloped, there was something *silvery* about the moment.

It was like the night mares were glowing from within. The bony, malnourished look blurred and faded, and between the tears from the wind and the weirdness of the moment, it was like a silvery shadow enveloped them, and I felt a beauty beyond words.

I blinked, and the feeling was gone, but the night mares pounded along, their hooves tossing clods of dirt and turf as we raced between the blue lakes, closing in on the end of the path.

Soon, we'd rejoin the other racers.

I only hoped we could scoot to safety before they started fighting.

CHAPTER THIRTY

Rigel

"There goes Lord Umer into the park—he's just used his cheat," King Solis grunted. "He rides a sun stallion—I'm almost certain he uses a portal to jump from this park to the one farther east, but I don't know how he does it with wards."

"Look!" Lord Linus pointed to the queen.

Leila had gotten the night mares off the boardwalk, and they were now galloping down what appeared to be a small walking trail or bike path.

But galloping wasn't a strong enough word—the night mares were moving so swiftly they were streaks of black rippling through reality.

The drone was struggling to keep them within sight, they were moving that fast.

Murmurs of surprise broke out through the crowd, and when I looked at the largest TV screen—which marked out where the participants were on the map—I joined them.

"By the holy—she's in the front," I said.

The night mares—moving at speeds no other mount could ever catch them at and using a path that cut off a great deal of the distance the other riders had traveled—were closing in on the finish line. *Fast.*

Their black dots skipped across the screen, visibly faster than all the other participants.

They're going to win. Because the night mares love her—they're going to win!

CHAPTER THIRTY-ONE

Leila

The night mares slowed down to a trot when we crossed a wooden bridge and the walking/bike trail melded with the boardwalk, and then we crossed into one of the small, city run beaches, that was just off main street.

I exhaled, and glanced back at my night mares. "You guys are amazing!" I praised as we crossed the five parking spaces marked out in front of the beach and stepped into the main drag of downtown Magiford. "We just have to go due east, and we're finished!"

The night mares started to adjust their strides—getting ready to rock into a canter—when the feeling of magic slammed into me, and I slumped over Blue Moon's neck.

It was a confusing mix of sensations—the unforgiving hardness of metal, but the wild abandon of vines of ivy slowly taking over a garden. It was the edge of the sword, and the softness of feathers.

This wasn't fae magic, or any kind of wizard or shifter magic.

It was something I had never felt before. And whatever it was, it felt old and beyond my reckoning.

What is that?

"Hold up." I held my arm out to stall the night mares as I twisted wildly in my saddle, trying to track down the sensation as I peered up and down the empty street.

I didn't see anything, except for a spot of shadows that seemed weirdly placed. Or maybe it was that it didn't sit quite right.

I narrowed my eyes and pulled my prism from the pocket of my breeches. What scared me was that the familiar flood of magic that flowed through the prism didn't bring the usual reassurance.

Instead, it seemed to amplify the weird shadow.

As I watched, the shadow moved, crawling toward us.

It stopped, and I heard a sniffing noise that made the hair on the back of my neck stand up. Then, a creature popped out of the shadows, jumping into the human world.

Its torso was shadowy and incorporeal, as it swung short but thick arms tipped with hands that had too few fingers and ended in claws. Smoke seemed to swirl around it and trail behind the tips of its claws, leaving black gouges in the air. Its legs were long and spindly with too many toes, a gross contrast to its head—which seemed to flicker back and forth between the smooth head of a bird with a jagged beak, and the flat, smashed face of something uncomfortably humanoid but eerily alien.

It raised its head to the sky and roared—or, at least, I think it did. Rather than exhaling a sound, air, debris, and even I felt pulled in to the creature as if by a vacuum.

Solstice—the largest of the night mares—charged it with a glass-shattering scream.

"Solstice—*no!*" I shouted.

He ignored me.

"*Astrum!*" I shouted, activating my prism.

Purple magic flowed from the glass crystal. I snatched the magic up as fast as I could and forged a ward that glowed around the gelding's hooves. I finished—creating a barrier taller than Solstice—just before the creature jabbed a clawed arm at him.

My barrier held, but it fizzled and sparked as the creature tried to claw through it with another soundless shriek.

Is this one of those attacks King Solis talked about? But I don't see anyone around here, or feel any fae magic—and I'm standing directly beneath a drone!

"We've got to get out of here!" I yelled.

That drew the thing's attention to me. It switched from its bird head to its flat face and sniffed, slowly turning in my direction. It blinked its tiny, slitted eyes at me, then abruptly froze.

"Come on!" I shouted.

Before any of the night mares moved, it launched itself at me, using its powerful arms like a gorilla and pushing off the ground.

The point of my prism bit into my palm as I forged a ward, which quickly bloomed into a barrier and protected Blue Moon and myself.

The creature smashed into my ward, leaving a smoky residue on the surface when I pulled back.

To my horror, the residue seemed to eat through my ward, weakening it.

It smashed its fist into the barrier, then hooked its claws into the surface, slicing straight through.

I nudged Blue Moon, who finally launched into a canter. But before he'd taken more than three steps, the monster's fist broke through my barrier, and it grabbed onto the back of my neck, ripping me off the saddle and throwing me to the ground.

I slammed into the paved road with a pained wheeze, and the creature was on me, its fingers tightening around my neck as its claws bit into my skin.

One of the night mares screamed, and Nebula and Twilight charged it. They each bit it on the elbows, their jagged teeth digging into its flesh and their yellow eyes gleaming with a wild frenzy as they bit chunks out of its arms.

The creature screamed, but the smoky haze that curled around it settled over the wounds, restoring it.

Comet joined Nebula and Twilight, scraping her hooves down the monster's side.

It let go of me long enough for me to flip so I was belly down. I tried to scramble to my feet, but it latched onto my lower back, its nails digging into my muscles. It slammed me to the ground, and I whimpered.

Worse than the pain, I briefly opened my hand, and my prism fell from my grasp and rolled down the street.

"No!"

I heard hooves, and I saw a rider on a sun stallion come pounding down the street. The rider wore the crest of the Summer Court—a bird silhouette on a blue sky. This was probably the cheating rider King Solis had warned me about.

When he saw us he slowed his horse to a trot. The sun stallion snorted and tossed its head, frightened by the monster.

"Help—please!" I begged.

The rider smirked at me, then kicked his horse.

The sun stallion squealed and refused to go, but the rider ripped on the reins, painfully hauling the horse's head around, and he kept kicking the animal until it shot past us, leaving us alone.

Fae are the worst. They won't help, even if someone is in real danger? Why do I even care about these people?

CHAPTER THIRTY-TWO

Rigel

"Send someone to help her!" Lord Linus had a derby official by the collar of his shirt, and his voice had lost its usual happy tone for a darkness that promised death.

"W-we can't interfere!"

Lord Linus shook the employee. "This isn't allowed by the rules—there's a *monster* attacking her! And it's not a fae monster! Get. Her. Help!"

King Solis was pale as he watched the screen—where Leila screamed in pain while the monster dug its claws into her back. "Escape, Queen Leila. Escape," he whispered, as if he could will it. His eyes flickered to the monster she was fighting, and he shivered at its grotesque features.

One of the night mares rammed into the monster—the smaller mare named Eclipse, if I properly remembered the queen's stupid names.

The monster staggered, then ripped its claws higher up Leila's back so it could keep her pinned to the ground by stepping on her lower back and stand up straight to face the night mares.

Leila writhed in pain, and the creature shook when the mare charged it again, then clawed at her neck, raking its claws deep into her neck.

The mare stumbled and screamed.

The monster looked up, straight into the drone's camera. It picked a decorative rock from a bunch piled around the base of a tree on the sidewalk—keeping Queen Leila pinned—then flung it at the drone.

The TV screen turned black as the feed was dropped, the camera—or drone—destroyed.

Something in me twinged, and a foreign emotion twisted in my chest.

...Leila...fight back.

CHAPTER THIRTY-THREE

Leila

It hurt Eclipse.

It *hurt* Eclipse!

Even in my pained, pinned position, I saw the red of blood on the night mare's coat as she cried out in pain.

Even as the creature slammed its foot into my lower back, sending pain wracking through my body, I barely registered it. I was too angry.

This monster—and whoever sent it—had harmed *my* night mare.

No.

I stretched, the muscles in my arm protesting as I reached for the small tree and landscaping bed artfully arranged on the edge of the street. The creature twisted its claws, slicing the skin of my lower back, but my fingers brushed the small rocks dumped around the tree trunk.

I grabbed a fistful and flung them behind me, pelting the monster.

It leaned back, putting its weight on its other foot, giving me the chance to slide out from under it.

It badly tore my shirt as it tried to stab its claws into my side, but I rolled and jumped to my feet.

Aware it was right behind me, I darted behind a public garbage can—one of those pebbled concrete ones.

The monster chased after me, following me right up to the garbage can. Not expecting the concrete's solid heft, it slammed into it and practically flipped over the plastic top.

I jumped an empty bike rack and ran up the street, scooping up my lost prism that sat in the middle of the road. *How am I going to defeat this thing? I didn't bring my gun because of derby rules, and I don't know much fast-casting offensive magic—just wards!*

My prism was still activated, and I yanked more magic through it. I didn't know what I was gathering it for—my thoughts were scattered, like the night mares that screamed and ran around me.

Comet and Nebula charged the monster together. But even with their jagged teeth, whatever damage they did disappeared as the spell-powered creature's shadowy flesh regenerated.

Wait—this monster is obviously a spell. Otherwise I wouldn't be feeling this weird magic, and it wouldn't be able to regenerate like this. That means the easiest way to fight it is to destroy whatever magic is powering it, which should be held in a core somewhere.

The monster turned to me, and I automatically forged a ward, which glowed at my feet before erecting a barrier that briefly flickered with runes.

I studied it, trying to see if there was any part of it that looked more concentrated or different. Most likely the spell powering it was not in a limb—those would be easy to chop off.

Eclipse—even though she was hurt—charged it, and Twilight

kicked out at it, his hooves passing straight through the monster's disconcerting, ever-changing head.

It didn't bother the monster—which was intent on trying to break through my barrier.

That probably means its core isn't in its head. Which means it's most likely in the chest. But how can I destroy it when I've only been practicing wards! Wait, unless...

I skidded to a stop and whirled around.

The creature was right behind me. It reached for me, and I ducked under its arms, barely avoiding its claws.

My mouth dried up as I shoved my hand into the monster's shadowy torso and used the one magic I'd practiced endlessly for the past few weeks.

I made a ward.

Not around me or my night mares, but around the monster. Or—rather—in it.

When I'd poured all the magic I could muster into the spell, I released it, and the ward grew, expanding into a purple shield that vertically sliced through the monster's body.

I held my breath, afraid to hope.

The creature stopped flailing, split by the barrier.

A moment passed, and its chest cavity glowed white hot before the light. I heard a snapping noise, and whatever spell it was that forged the creature crumbled. Its body and limbs turned into thick clouds of black smoke.

A flower dropped from the haze before the smoke dissolved into the air.

Blood oozed down my back as I stooped over and snatched up the spotless, white flower. It was a chrysanthemum.

Lady Chrysanthe.

The muscles in my back ached, and my legs shook as I shoved the flower into my pocket. "Everyone okay? Eclipse?"

Eclipse called to me—she was already farther up the street,

pawing at the road and charging a few steps east. Toward the finish line.

Solstice, Nebula, Comet, and Twilight joined her.

Only Blue Moon waited at my side, swiveling so I could conveniently hop on.

"Really? We're just going to keep racing like nothing happened?" Despite my grumblings, I hurriedly tried to mount Blue Moon—and only succeeded in flopping on his back like a landed fish. "You're all crazier than I am." I kicked my leg over and pushed my foot through the saddle stirrup before I grabbed his reins.

Blue Moon snorted, took a few prancing steps, then fell into a rolling canter. We blazed past the other night mares, who caught up with us within a heartbeat.

Just as they had on the walking trail, the night mares stretched out, galloping at an insane speed that blurred sights and sounds.

I'd just fought a monster, and it wasn't a good thing that the magic my prism channeled had slowed down drastically during the fight, but that didn't matter right now.

We're going to win—to prove to the fae who underestimate us how wrong they are about the night mares, and to show them I'm not going to back down from their stupid games. I'm going to end this obsession with power in my Court, and show them just how a half human/half fae rules!

I clutched my prism, tangling it in the reins, and a smile crawled across my face as my night mares thundered around me.

CHAPTER THIRTY-FOUR

Rigel

"*Lord Umer has entered the final stretch!*"

I ignored the announcement—which indicated that he'd entered the park and was not far from the finish line—and watched as the new drone that had been sent after Leila and the night mares investigated the area where the previous one had been wrecked.

There was nothing there. No monster, no horses, no Leila. A bunch of trash cans had toppled over, but nothing more.

"Look!" a human shouted, pointing down the length at the park.

At the very back—where cement barriers had been erected to keep the riders and mounts from crashing into the park and making them bottle neck in the stretch—a black horse jumped the barrier.

A second followed, then a third, and a fourth, and a fifth.

She couldn't have pulled this off—not with a monster attack. It's impossible.

And yet, that impossibility—mounted on the back of a dappled night mare—jumped the cement barrier.

Six night mares streaked across the park, fast catching up on the unsuspecting Lord Umer like wolves closing in on prey.

If she catches up with him, he's going to attack her.

CHAPTER THIRTY-FIVE

Leila

"Line up!" I shouted to my night mares.

They pulled out of their scattered formation, forming a long, horizontal line with the faster horses—like Eclipse and Blue Moon—holding back to keep pace with the slower horses—like Solstice.

The line broke in half as we closed ranks on Lord Umer and his sun stallion, with me and Blue Moon and Nebula pulling up on either side of him.

When Lord Umer saw us, he cursed. He slipped his foot out of the stirrup and tried to awkwardly kick me, but Blue Moon nimbly dodged him.

Next he leaned out of the saddle and grappled with me, trying to yank me from my saddle. Apparently Lord Umer didn't give up easily.

Nebula, running shoulder to shoulder on the other side of Lord Umer's sun stallion, bit the fae on the thigh, making him jolt in his saddle and yell.

I took the opportunity to swoop down and yank the stirrup off his foot, straightening just in time to avoid being smashed when Blue Moon and Nebula shoulder checked the sun stallion.

Moving in tandem, they cut in front of the golden horse, cutting it off.

It reared up, and Lord Umer toppled over the side with a yelp.

I wanted to shout some kind of taunt—like he should have worn a helmet, or I hope he landed on his head—but the night mares took off after we passed him, bearing down on the finish line within seconds.

"Hold the line!" I shouted. "Hold it!"

Up and down the line the night mares held, and together, with all six mounts, we crossed the finish line as one.

The humans who had cheered for me at the start of the race must have hopped in cars and looped around to the finish line, because they were screaming and cheering for me and the night mares as we thundered down the open stretch of the park, slowing down and eventually stopping.

"Night Court, Night Court!"

"All hail the queen!"

"No one crosses the demon horses!"

The night mares, elated with the win, shrieked and reared up, pawing at the sky.

I laughed as I clung to Blue Moon, who tossed his head and pranced with the rest of them. "You were amazing!"

At the very end of the park I slipped off Blue Moon. Instantly I was crowded by six night mares, pressing in on me.

I laughed and kissed their scratchy muzzles and cooed words of praise to each one of them. I lingered over Eclipse, stroking her neck—which was whole and unharmed without a single mark.

How the heck did that happen? Do they have healing powers I don't know about?

It was something to ask Dusk and Dawn later.

"You're okay." My shoulders dropped in my relief, and I felt light headed. "We're okay."

"Queen Leila! Can we take your picture?"

The human observers crowded as close as they could behind the erected barriers.

Before I could respond, the night mares headed in their direction. I laughed and followed after them. "Yes, of course."

I posed for the picture—my night mares surrounding me—and tried not to fidget as I felt blood crust on my back.

I didn't think I was bleeding anymore, and I wasn't feeling light headed, but I wanted to disinfect the claw marks on my back as soon as possible—who knew what kind of dirt got in them when I was rolling around the street?

Landon peered at me over the barrier as the rest of the humans kept taking pictures of the night mares. "I guess it's good you've got demon horses with enemies like that," he said.

I felt for the flower I'd stuffed in my pocket. "I guess."

"Leila!"

Recognizing the voice, I turned around, then wheezed when Indigo slammed into me, hitting my gut.

"You idiot!" Indigo hiccupped. "We were so scared for you!"

"It was an unnecessary danger, Queen Leila," Chase said as he and Skye approached us.

"Yeah, but we swept the race!" I grinned. "The first six places *all* go to the Night Court!"

I saw Skye's tight facial expression, and for a moment my heart froze. "Right?"

"Lord Umer is contesting that the night mares should count as one entry since you all crossed the line together, but the placings for the top ten have been posted, and the officials granted you first through sixth," Skye said.

"That's great! But why do you look so grim?"

Indigo smacked my belly. "Oh, I don't know. Maybe it was because you almost got yourself killed, and the drone cut off! We didn't know what was happening!" Her voice went higher and higher until she shrieked at the end.

Skye started to circle around behind me, but she paused long enough to pull a sealed fae healing potion from the messenger bag she had slung over her shoulder. "How badly is your back injured?"

"I don't think too badly—it doesn't hurt a lot right now. Oh, but, Chase, I have something for you." I dug into my pocket and pulled out the chrysanthemum—which was now a little crushed. "The monster had this infused in its core. I'm not sure why—whatever that creature was, it was *not* made of fae magic."

I handed the flower over, then took a swig of the healing potion as Skye tried to discreetly look at my back.

I choked on the flavor—usually fae healing potions tasted pretty delicious, like coconut or chocolate. This potion tasted like a pulverized cabbage and kale. "This is awful—what is this?"

"A healing potion—one that is less pricy because of the foul flavor," Skye said.

"Why would you buy these?"

"Because they're cheap." Skye narrowed her dark eyes at me. "And because I intend to force-feed them to you whenever you recklessly put your life in danger."

"Negative reinforcement—a good plan." Indigo gave Skye a thumbs up.

Chase held the flower up to his sensitive nose and sniffed it. "It smells of Lady Chrysanthe."

"For real?" I asked.

Chase tilted his head as he delicately smelled it. "Your scent is stuck to it as well, but her smell is predominant. She must have worn this in her hair for a full day."

"Huh. Wow." I took another sip of my healing potion and grimaced. "I thought it might be hers, but I didn't think she'd be stupid enough to use a flower she'd worn when creating whatever that monster was. I'd like to find out how she did it—that weird magic was not fun to go up against."

"She is here today," Chase said. "I'll gather my men and bring her in for questioning."

"The Paragon is here, too," Skye said. "It might be worthwhile to have him look over the flower."

Chase bowed slightly. "A worthy plan."

"Leila!"

Indigo plucked the potion bottle from my fingers as I stupidly turned around. "What—"

Lord Linus stopped just short of crashing into me. He set his hands on my shoulders and forcibly turned me in a circle, checking me over. "Did you give her a healing potion?"

"Yes—though her back is no longer bleeding."

"She still needs to get looked over," Lord Linus said.

"I agree."

There was an ear-splitting hee-haw, and the night mares turned as a group and trumpeted in happiness to Bagel and Fax.

Lord Rigel was leading Fax, but King Solis had apparently taken temporary custody of Bagel as the donkey happily trotted at his side.

"You're alive—and you won!" King Solis grinned at me. "Congratulations are in order!"

"Thank you!" I beamed at the Day King, then hesitated as Lord Rigel drew closer.

He ignored the night mares that twined around Fax like pleased cats, and looked me over from head to toe. "You survived."

"What, disappointed?" I asked.

Lord Rigel was silent for several long, awkward moments.

Oh, nice. He really was *disappointed!*

"It was...illuminating," he said.

I frowned. "Illuminating? What's that supposed to mean?"

"No matter, you can flirt with your fiancé later. Drink this."

Indigo pushed the nasty potion back in my fingers. "And get ready."

"For what?" I asked.

"Justice," Skye said. "Because that flower should be all Chase needs to prove Lady Chrysanthe is responsible for all the recent attacks on you."

"Lady Chrysanthe is guilty of conspiring against Queen Leila." Skye gestured to Lady Chrysanthe—who was being led toward us by Chase and a squadron of guards.

We were in the gardens of the Night Realm—apparently fae justice needed to be meted out in the fae realm. It made sense, sort of?

I was seated in a large chair that had a massive, circular back that was sculpted to resemble the full moon.

A structure that was faintly reminiscent of Greek architecture with its classical columns and open ceiling surrounded the platform I was seated on.

Flags bearing the Night Court crest—a crescent moon with a spattering of stars—were hung between the pillars, and silver bowls bearing silvery globes of light illuminated the area.

When I glanced up, I could see the beautiful cosmic twists of blue and purple, and thousands of glittering stars we didn't have on earth.

Both Skye and Lord Rigel stood at the base of the platform, and past them spread my Court.

Though it was mostly the same party goers that had attended my engagement ceremony, there was a vastly different feel to it.

Apparently my triumph at the race had caught them all off guard, as did Chase's arrest of Lady Chrysanthe.

A few of the lower noble houses had started wearing clothing with the Night Court crest—which Indigo told me was a compliment and a sign they believed in me. I didn't believe her until she said a pixie had made a pin of my personal seal—yeah, the ruffled looking pigeon-raccoon-griffin thing—and apparently it had sold out among the common fae in the two days since the derby.

As if sensing my thoughts, a live pigeon-raccoon-griffin landed on the top of one of the pillars. It bobbed its head and stretched out its neck before regurgitating on a flag.

Yeah, it's fine.

I planted my elbows on the arms of my chair and pressed my fingertips together as Lady Chrysanthe—surrounded by guards—blearily stopped a few feet away from Rigel and Skye.

"We have witnesses that have placed Lady Chrysanthe at the scene of two attempts against Queen Leila's life, as well as witnesses—and evidence—that she designed the creature that attacked Queen Leila during the race," Chase said.

"These charges are false!" Lady Demetria shouted. "My granddaughter loves this Court and only wishes to aid it!"

The crowd murmured, and from my higher position I heard some of the whispers.

"*—she always was jealous of the queen.*"
"*Fancied herself the next ruler, I am certain.*"
"*She should have done better hiding her acts.*"
"*Shameful.*"
"*Disgraceful.*"

I studied Lady Chrysanthe as Kevin and Steve—who sat near my feet—growled at her.

Her beautiful blond hair was limp, her eyes were red, and she listlessly stared at the stairs of my platform, though she shivered when Muffin—skulking somewhere behind my throne—hissed.

Huh. I would have expected she'd go down screaming and spitting.

"Moreover, she threatened Queen Leila's companion in public," Chase said. "As such, she has been brought before Queen Leila for judgment."

"Lady Chrysanthe," Skye said. "Do you have anything to say in regards to these charges?"

Lady Chrysanthe opened and closed her mouth twice before she managed to speak. "I did not kill Queen Leila."

"No," Chase agreed. "You only attempted; you didn't succeed."

Lady Chrysanthe frowned, and a bit of her fire returned. "I never—" She was unable to speak, proving she'd been about to speak a lie.

I knew she plotted against me. She never hid that. But...I agree with Chase.

My director of security had presented me with his initial findings in the early hours of the morning—apparently the guards had scared Lord Myron into confessing, and he'd spilled the beans that Lady Chrysanthe had mentioned a plan to spike my food and had—in his sight—lingered around the base of the giraffe statue, and then given the bespelled golf ball to the fae who had hit the statue.

But Chase felt we didn't have quite enough evidence to convict her, and some of the details didn't match up. I had suggested we hold a public hearing to see if we could uncover the rest of the story through some bits of trickery. Chase had reluctantly agreed.

Let's see if we can get this to pan out.

"Do you have any questions regarding the cases, Queen Leila?" Skye asked.

The Court was quiet as it waited for me to speak.

"Yes." I squeezed the edges of the arm rests. "I have a clarification I'd like from Lord Myron."

Lord Myron stepped out of the crowd and bowed deeply to me. "My heart moves that I might help you, Queen Leila."

"Yeah, right," I said with zero belief. *Probably moves with anger.* "In the submitted report, you say Lady Chrysanthe looked into using an artifact to cast a creature that would chase and attack me if I dared to ride in the Magiford Midsummer Derby."

"That is right, Queen Leila."

"I didn't send it," Lady Chrysanthe whimpered.

I narrowed my eyes and studied Myron. "And you never joined Chrysanthe in her efforts to kill me?"

Myron held his hand up. "I swear upon my family name that I have never attempted to kill you, Queen Leila."

"But you were there when Chrysanthe made her attempts."

"I was present, yes."

There's something off about that. How can he make that vow when—or rather if—Chrysanthe really did all of this and he was with her? Shouldn't he be guilty by association?

I pressed my lips together as I chewed on the idea. Even when Steve rested her head on my lap, I only absently patted her.

"If found guilty, Lady Chrysanthe will be stripped of her title, exiled from the Night Court, and sent to live in the human world," Skye said. "As will her family."

Lady Demetria wailed. "How can you punish the family for the sins of the children?" She made a show of dabbing her eyes. "My kin and I had no idea of the viper we harbored in our family! We are not at fault!"

So much for believing she's innocent.

Lord Myron bowed his head at the pronouncement as I carefully watched him.

I felt something behind me stir in the shadows. A discreet glance, and I saw Twilight peering at me from behind the column. Perched on top of the column—nearly invisible in the darkness of the Night Realm—was Whiskers.

I'm not standing alone. Not anymore.

My gaze flicked from Indigo to Skye to Chase and—yes—even Lord Linus.

We can do this.

I stood up and slowly approached the edge of my platform, Kevin and Steve following behind me as Muffin padded in front of me.

"Lord Myron, am I correct that you *heard* her express a desire to poison me, and to set a creature to chase after me, but you didn't *see* her do anything?"

"Yes, Queen Leila." Lord Myron bowed again.

"And you saw her around the base of the giraffe statue, but you didn't actively see her cutting the bolts on the plates in its feet, or doing anything to it?"

"Yes, Queen Leila—though I did see her give the bespelled golf ball to the lord who accidentally hit the statue," Lord Myron said. "One can only imagine that if she announced her plan to us, her comrades, it was she who followed through with it."

Ugh. Fae—one can imagine, one would think, blah, blah, blah. They love leaving the important bits out...They love to leave the important bits out? Hmm...

I glanced speculatively at Chrysanthe. "I didn't do it," she whispered.

She's neatly pinned—she can't say she didn't want to harm me or try to harm me because she's been open in her dislike. Myron, though, can claim he didn't, even though the scheming jerk has been with this the whole time. Did he betray her just because the tide is turning in my Court and his family thinks it's time to try currying favor with me?

I studied Lord Myron, who gave me that same sneery smile he'd shown the day I arrived, and an idea slowly spawned in my head.

I think it's time to teach the Night Court that a half-blood sits on their throne. I have refrained from using some of my greatest advantages. But it's time to change that.

"I am relieved you chose to speak up, Lord Myron." I gave him my best smile. "I know you are trustworthy, and I believe you are such a good friend to me," I lied. "It's obvious you are blameless and share no fault—though Lady Chrysanthe was your friend. We can't control the actions of our friends, after all."

"I am honored you agree, Queen Leila." Lord Myron smirked again.

Yep, as I thought. He has no idea I can lie. I glanced out at the Court and saw all of them were taking my lies—hook, line, and sinker. *None of them know. They think I really believe what I'm saying!*

A smile twitched on my lips—this could be fun.

"It scares me to hear that Lady Chrysanthe planned to send a creature forged of magic after me in the derby." I theatrically shivered, then glanced at Myron.

He was relaxed, and his smile was stronger still.

Just a little more, and then I can hit him with a bluff.

"I'll have to reward you with jewels, land, money, whatever you want as a thank you for revealing this." I dismissively waved a hand, even though this lie produced a real chill in me.

As if I would ever willingly give anyone in this Court money when we are broke!

"I have just one more question for you." I turned back to him with an innocent smile.

"What is it, Queen Leila?"

I glanced at Chase and gave him a slight nod. He didn't appear to move, but—like magic—I saw a few extra guards step out of the crowd.

"The creature in the race that attacked me *wasn't* made by fae magic," I said. "But by something ancient that I've never felt before—which means Chrysanthe didn't set it on me. But *you* did, Lord Myron, didn't you?"

CHAPTER THIRTY-SIX

Leila

He fishmouthed, and I almost hooted.

I was right! Hoo-boy, talk about a gamble that paid off!

"I have never intended to kill you!" Lord Myron pleaded.

"Answer the question, Lord Myron. Did you set the creature to target me?"

"Who could imagine—"

"Answer the question," I said.

Steve and Kevin stepped out of my shadow, their lips curled back as they stalked up to him. Muffin had circled around behind him, and she growled deep in her chest, making him jump.

"I-I-I—" Lord Myron's gaze wavered from me to the Court.

"You never intended to kill me because your target never was me," I said. "It was Lady Chrysanthe herself. You were setting her up."

Chrysanthe jerked to attention, her eyes wide. "No, he

couldn't—you said together we could change the Court! You hated Queen Leila, too!"

"Oh, he hates me," I assured her. "He just hates you more."

Chrysanthe stared at him, her pretty features molded in shock.

I watched her for a moment, then turned my attention back to Myron, who was staring at the ground. "Start explaining yourself, Myron."

Murmurs swept through my Court as they gawked at the unfolding drama.

Myron took a step backwards and shook his head.

"*Now*," I ordered in an unforgiving voice of iron.

"I was only aiming at her, Queen Leila!" Myron blurted out. "It was never in my mind to kill you." His eyes widened, and he slapped his hands over his mouth to quiet himself.

"No," I agreed. "You believed enough of my staff would catch each attempt before you masterminded them. But I don't take kindly to being used as bait, and I *despise* anyone who seeks to harm another just for political reasons. And that's what this was, wasn't it?"

I could see the muscles in Myron's neck pop as he clenched his jaw. Against his will, he opened his mouth. "Her family needed to be brought down!" he said. I could see by the panic in his eyes that he hadn't meant to say that—didn't want to say that.

Vaguely, it reminded me of the time I stopped the fae guard from slicing through the pasture fence back at my parents' place. *Is this...am I doing this to him? I can feel magic, but I'm not pulling anything through my prism.*

Unrelenting, Myron continued, "Before you were found, they floated around—so *certain* she'd be picked. As if she was the brightest of the Court—hah!" He glared at Chrysanthe, who shook her head in denial.

"You, you told me I would change the Court," Lady Chrysanthe said.

"For the worse!" Myron scoffed. "Your family is nothing but a puffed-up bunch of nobodies who don't know their place or acknowledge how little power they actually have. And you really thought you had what it takes to be queen? You haven't even the guts to plan an assassination, much less a freak accident. You were never going to move—just complain how you and your festering family have been wronged and denied an honor none of you deserve!"

I was momentarily distracted from my worry about my magic to observe the fight. *Woooow, this Court is messed up.*

Chrysanthe's eyes were glazed with tears. "You set me up. You handed the golf ball to me before I put it on the spot." She paused, standing straighter with each passing second as she recalled the events. "You told me we should see the pitiful spread of food that had been prepared the night of Queen Leila's first social function. *You* were the one who took one of my chrysanthemum hair flowers!"

"You only just *now* noticed?" Myron spat. "The *human* noticed before you!"

Myron looked too furious at Chrysanthe to be under the influence of my magic anymore—I was going to have to ask Skye about that—so I decided now was a great time to end things.

"I'm glad the two of you have reached an understanding," I said. "But I don't like drama—it is an unnecessary use of energy, and it's *boring*. I'm finished here. Myron is guilty of plotting against a fellow member of the Night Court and will be punished accordingly. Chrysanthe is innocent," I said.

"What?" Myron whirled around to face me, his perfect dark hair slick with sweat. "Y-you said you thought I was trustworthy, blameless, and a friend to you," he stammered. "You were going to reward me!"

I shrugged. "I lied."

A smothering silence swept through the Court, and they stared at me in horror.

I grinned broadly and climbed the stairs to stand on my platform again. "Although you all *love* to imply that I'm inferior because of my human blood, and obsess over the idea that I can't be a good ruler because of it, you've completely forgotten: because of my human blood I share *none* of your limitations."

The night mares stirred from the shadows behind the columns, stepping into the magic-made light, as Kevin and Steve howled at the sky. The other five stable-dwelling shades slunk onto the platform, and Whiskers jumped down from the top of the columns where he'd been hiding with the remaining two glooms.

Ringed by my animals, I pressed my prism into the skin of my palm and felt wispy fae magic slip from it.

Later, Indigo told me my eyes glowed, and a silvery light ringed my temples like a crown as the night mares, shades, and glooms peeled back their lips and snarled in eerie silence.

"Remember that the next time you are tempted to scheme against me. Recall it the next time you think to hurt another Night Court member. Noble, fae, or creature—I won't tolerate *any* of it. And I'll come for you with all the power and will I have."

I flicked my eyes to Chase. "Take him away and have him questioned."

Chase bowed as his men converged on Lord Myron. "And Lady Chrysanthe?"

"Release her."

Chase took off Chrysanthe's metal cuff—a precautionary measure that sealed her ability to use magic. "You're free to go."

Chrysanthe flicked her gaze from Chase, to Myron. Her eyes were unfocused—she still seemed shocked by the turn of events. "You said I deserved to be on the throne more than Queen Leila."

"*Anyone* deserves to be on the throne more than Queen Leila, you imbecile!" Myron snarled as a soldier snapped a metal cuff on him.

"Ahhh, yes." I smiled as I sat back down on my stone chair,

doing my best not to show my reluctance—because, yeah, stone chairs are *not* very comfortable to sit on for long periods of time, and my butt still hadn't recovered. "I have one last reminder should anyone else from my *darling, adorable* Court get ideas. Rigel?"

When the assassin looked at me, I waved him up. *I really hope he doesn't kill me for parading him like this, but I'm gambling my entire life on ending these Court games. I need every advantage I can get.*

Rigel climbed onto the platform and took up a spot next to me when a gloom moved to make room for him.

I smiled at him, and wondered if I was daring enough to take his hand. When I glanced up, his eyes were glazed with that dead look, sealing it.

Nope, definitely not brave enough!

I settled for turning my smile on my Court and flashing my teeth at them. "Rigel and I marry *tomorrow*. Which means if I happen to die...the *Wraith* becomes your next king."

The tension and horror were so thick, I could almost squish it between my fingers.

The Court gaped at me with horror, their eyes flicking from me to Rigel as they lost their stuffy expressions and manners in their terror.

I had to hold in a laugh—hadn't this occurred to them?! I'd figured it out the night Rigel accepted me that this was one of the advantages I was going to push *hard*.

I mean, who would they rather have as their ruler? A half human queen who does a few crazy things, or a straight up *assassin* king who knows their every seedy dealing and is infamous for his spotless record?

"This is what you meant when you said you intended to use my name," Rigel said—somehow managing to sound normal even though his voice was barely louder than a whisper.

I risked glancing up at him and was relieved to see his expression didn't appear bothered.

I mean, he never really wore *any* expression, but I thought I could detect a faint tilt to one of his eyebrows, and his eyes didn't look glassy.

"Yep," I agreed.

"It's not at all what I thought you meant."

"But it is the best use of it!" I grinned to myself, increasingly giddier the longer my Court stared at me with horror.

Rigel didn't reply immediately. I assumed this meant he wasn't going to say anything else, and it took me by surprise when he answered after a few more minutes. "It is," he agreed.

We stood together at the throne even after a few of my Court members, apparently lacking any brilliant ideas, started clapping as Lord Myron was taken away by Chase's men.

It's over. I didn't let myself relax, but I did smile. *I gave them the first smack down and warning. The next time they start playing games with each other, I'll come down even harder on them. And those who don't play games will be rewarded.*

It had bothered me that through sheer will, just by being queen I could make them do whatever I wanted—as I suspect I just had with Lord Myron.

But I'd just be extra cautious not to do that. I shouldn't have to, since the magic already did its best to assure they couldn't straight up murder me, and it just didn't feel *right*.

I smirked, unable to hold back my delight. *And then I'll train you—every last one of you*, I promised myself as my eyes scanned my Court. *You'll stop playing this stupid game of power out of sheer self-preservation, and I'll destroy this awful tradition once and for all!*

When I stood at the front of the massive ceremony room, out to lunch even though it was the middle of my wedding ceremony, I was stewing and in a foul mood.

Not because I was getting married when I didn't want to.

Okay—not *only* because this stupid monarchy had backwards, ancient rules that seriously needed to be overturned, but because Skye and Indigo had banned Chase from giving me an update on Myron and his motives when I was getting ready.

Weddings take forever! *And this is a fae wedding. Of course it is going to take 2,364 hours to say all the useless prattle and everyone and their neighbor will come give me their carefully worded, insincere congratulations and unhappy wishes.*

To make it worse, I was getting officially crowned *during* the wedding ceremony. For real, an official pronounced us married, and then I had to turn around and thump my rear down in a chair so they could pop a crown on me and say more long-winded speeches that were uselessly vague so they could contain half truths and keep a bargain/contract from being struck.

For real, there should be a fae debate team. They'd win just because they would bore everyone to death!

Indigo discreetly coughed.

"Yes," I said automatically once I realized the stuffy fae marrying us was looking expectantly at me.

Are we through with the vows? Or did he just pronounce us married?

It seemed like it was the vows. He nodded, then shifted his attention to Rigel standing at my side.

"As Queen Leila's consort, do you swear your heart, body, and mind to her?"

I smirked at my reluctant fiancé, wondering how he was going to get out of this.

Indigo had been unable to stuff Rigel into a tux. Even though I wore a gorgeous wedding dress with a train I was definitely going to step on before the day was over, Rigel just wore one of his fancy black buckled shirts. He even had a sword strapped to his side, and I was pretty sure at least one dagger was hidden in each of his bracers.

Rigel glanced down at me. "It seems unfair to have this vow when you can break yours with no consequences."

"I have faith in you." I switched my flowers to my other hand and patted his muscled forearm. "I know you'll find a loophole!"

For a heartbeat, I thought I saw humor in his usually glassy expression.

It made his eyes more like a summer night sky than an endless void, and it cranked his icy good looks from brooding hero to the hottest supernatural I'd ever seen.

Holy cow! What was that?

I was still marveling over the change even though he went back to staring at the fae with his dead eyes. I wasn't fooled, though, I'd just learned I'd accidentally bagged myself a real looker as a husband!

Now if he'll just refrain from killing me, I think we can coexist.

"I will give to her as due her station," Rigel finally said.

Ahhh, there it is. Phrasing it so if I ever displease him as a monarch he can still off me. Plus, he didn't swear it—which is as bad as a contract. Nice work!

I twisted slightly to look back at Indigo who was standing a few steps behind me to see if she'd seen the change in Rigel too. She just scowled at me, crinkled her cute nose, and raised her eyebrows.

Skye stood next to her, holding her bouquet of flowers at about chest height. I could smell the peppermint sprigs she'd tucked into her flowers from here, and when she sighed, the scent mingled with the candied ginger she'd been chewing on.

Apparently she couldn't gnaw antacids during weddings. It wasn't "proper." She'd resorted to trying other methods of calming her stomach—sniffing peppermint and chewing ginger beforehand. Based on the way her eye was twitching, I doubted they were working.

Past her, filling the massive...ballroom—for lack of a better word—was my Court. Or, rather, all the nobles, and even more common fae.

Dad and Mom were sitting in the front row, and with them—

to my great fury—was Lord Linus, lounging next to Dad and looking way more pal-y and at home with him than he had any right to be.

The Paragon sat next to my mom, dabbing his eyes with a tissue as if this was a deeply moving event, and on *his* other side was Lord Dion, grinning like a fiend at his best friend.

The Day King was present—he was the only fae monarch who had accepted my invite—he was all smiles, and oblivious to the fae ladies sighing longingly behind him.

I thought I saw Lady Chrysanthe for a moment, but she looked *different*; I wasn't certain if I'd really seen her or if my eyes were just playing tricks on me.

And at the far back of the ballroom—standing with Dusk, Dawn, Azure, and Eventide all playing attendance for them—were my six night mares, four glooms, and seven shades.

When Kevin noticed I was looking, he happily wagged his tail at me.

"Queen Leila?" the fae performing the ceremony asked.

"Yes?" I turned around and smiled angelically.

"All fae traditions have been observed and followed," the fae said. "Thus, it brings a close to this most blessed of occasions. I pronounce Queen Leila and Lord Rigel mar—"

The enormous window behind the fae official burst, showering us with glass.

Two spiders, both the size of small ponies, crawled in through the broken window.

They parted their enormous fangs as their hairy legs—which had an unnatural number of joints—clicked when they scuttled closer. Their bloated bodies were covered in a hard shell, and each spider had eight eyes that glowed in the light of the ballroom.

I recognized them in an instant—it was the same kind of spider that attacked me on my parents' farm.

I slipped my prism out of my flowers—as much as people looked down on me for the small artifact, I was finding it was delightfully easy to hide in all sorts of unexpected places. I opened my mouth to shout a warning, but Chase beat me to it.

"Protect the queen!" Chase drew a hand axe from his belt and threw it at the closest spider.

The axe made a whooshing noise as it cut through the air, hitting its target with deadly precision. It sliced through the spider's head like butter—a testament to Chase's werewolf strength.

The spider dropped to the floor, its legs twitching as it proceeded to ooze green goo everywhere while it died.

The second spider bowled over the fae official, its many eyes fixed on me.

"*Astrum*!" I shouted, powering on my prism.

I heard footsteps as Chase's people closed in on us, but I doubted it was possible for them to hit the spider without getting me since it had closed in on me.

I took a few steps backwards as I funneled magic through the artifact and created a purple ward on the ground.

Before I could finish the spell and make the ward grow into a barrier, the spider jumped the short distance between us.

It stretched out its front legs, attempting to wrap them around me so it could scoop me in toward its fangs. The wiry hairs on its legs barely brushed my arms, and then the spider jerked to a stop.

Silence pressed down from every corner as I slowly flicked my eyes to the side.

In the span of a heartbeat, Rigel had yanked out his hidden bracer daggers and stabbed them into the spider's head, killing it instantly.

I stared, unable to believe what I was seeing—unable to fathom that Lord Rigel had saved *me*.

The spider collapsed, its legs giving out, and the glowing light of its eyes dimmed and went out.

Rigel stepped back to his place next to me, casually wiping his daggers off with a cloth he'd pulled out of his bracer. He stared at the ooze covered cloth and tossed it on top of the spider, then sheathed one of his daggers.

Unexpectedly, he turned toward me and slipped his freed hand down my back, stopping at my waist. His touch felt a little stiff and awkward—as if *he* was the uncomfortable one.

Maybe he's not used to touching others?

He then looked over his shoulder at our Court as he lazily twirled his remaining dagger, rotating his wrist as he changed his hold on it. The action passed along a message I never thought he'd do for me.

A part of me was almost afraid to interpret what he meant. If it were anybody else and in any other case, I'd have said he was saying he'd protect me, and come after those who harmed me.

But that couldn't *be!*

It seemed my Court didn't share my reluctance.

Pandemonium broke out as my terrified nobles started screaming.

"It wasn't us!"

"Who dared to betray our queen in this manner?"

"I and my family vow absolute loyalty to Queen Leila!"

I glanced at my parents. My mom had her hand over her heart, but Dad was patting her hand, and Lord Linus—seriously *why?*—was passing her a silver flask covered with elaborate etchings.

The Paragon was smirking at me, and when I met his gaze he raised his hands in a polite clap I couldn't have possibly heard over all of the shouted vows. "*Checkmate,*" he mouthed.

I tilted my head, still very much aware of Rigel's hand draped on my lower back. "*What?*"

"*You won over your Court.*" The Paragon knowingly tapped his nose, then sat back in the bench.

Aren't they just afraid of Rigel? I glanced up at my fiancé/husband—I wasn't quite sure which it was at this moment. He'd returned to looking bored, despite the frenzied fae.

"Quiet," I said.

Instant silence fell over the room.

Every fae stared at me with absolute attention, and I realized the Paragon was right.

They feared Rigel, but they thought I held his reins. I had shocked them when I swept the top six spots of the Midsummer Derby, unsettled them when I revealed Myron's actions and Chrysanthe's innocence, and now they believed I had the *Wraith* under my control.

They really are my Court.

There was a pain in my heart as I saw the terror on their faces. I didn't *want* them to be afraid of me.

I smiled a little, thinking of my pigeon-raccoon-griffin emblem. *I think I can teach them to laugh. It will be a fight of a different kind, but it will be necessary to grind the power plays out of existence.*

"Um, yes." The fae official stood up and brushed himself off. "We shall conclude the ceremony…"

It passed by quickly—Rigel and I didn't even pretend to kiss, we just stared at the official after he declared us married—and sooner than I thought any fae ceremony could go, I was plunked on the royal throne, and Skye was placing a gorgeous crown on my head.

The base was a silver circlet studded with opals and tiny intricate chains that ended in little diamonds threading from gem to gem. At the center of the crown, over my forehead, was a large, silver crescent moon that was reminiscent in shape and style to the original king's staff, except it had a giant diamond at the tip.

It was heavier than I expected—I actually had to forcibly keep my chin up so my neck didn't tilt awkwardly.

And as I looked out over my Court—which was applauding me—I realized I'd only gotten through the first round of this game.

I still had to face the other Courts and try to restore the Night Court's reputation.

Really, I'd only just begun the fight.

That's okay. I got farther than anyone thought I would. I glanced at Rigel, and then Skye. *And now I'm not fighting alone. We can do this. We'll change this region—because I'll never, ever give up.*

And as my Court—which had once hated me—cheered and shouted for me, I stood and took my first few steps as the crowned Queen of the Night Court.

EPILOGUE

Rigel

About three days after we were married, I found myself in the unlikely position of standing in the shadows of Leila's office, watching her bury herself in a veritable blanket of papers and documents as she splayed out over her couch.

"Hey, Rigel," she casually said.

My lips twitched—how had she known I was there? I had slipped in without her steward or companion noticing, and they'd left roughly two minutes ago.

She looked right at me and grinned. "Whiskers and Steve saw you." She petted the large gloom—which was draped over the back of the couch she was lying on—then fondly rubbed the ears of the shade curled up between the couch and a coffee table.

I stepped out of the shadows and reluctantly approached her.

"Did you finally realize I wasn't going to try to *ravish* you or something just because we're married?" Her grin morphed into a smirk as she flipped to a new sheet of paper.

"I did not disappear because I fear you," I said.

"Oh? What horrible thing pulled you away, then? It couldn't have been Lord Dion. He visited *every day* hoping to see you."

Leila glanced at me when I didn't reply, but let it go. "Chase gave me Myron's official confession, and the report of the spider attack during our wedding."

"What did he find?"

"The spider was the same kind that attacked me when Eclipse first found me. It's a predatory arachnid that is found in multiple fae realms, but it is not native to the Night Realm. Chase picked up its scent and confirmed it wasn't from the Night Court or the human realm."

"Which means it's unlikely a fae from the Night Court sent it," I said.

"Yeah—mostly because the first spider found me when no one in the Night Court knew where Eclipse had disappeared to. The Paragon helped Chase try to track what realm it came from. He said he'd stake Aphrodite's favorite bed that it was sent by another monarch—as a sort of warning."

"He found out what Court it came from, then?"

"He wasn't certain, but he thought Autumn."

Autumn—the second most powerful Court in the region, just behind Winter.

But while Queen Rime ignored the other Courts and typically only deigned to spend time with her siblings—the other Winter Kings and Queens of North America—King Fell delighted in throwing his weight around.

Leila frowned as she stroked her gloom's head. "I find it worrying that the first attack on me was from another Court. That means the biggest threat to my life is still out there."

"And Myron?" I prompted.

"My hunch was right—he did everything to set up Chrysanthe. His whole family was in it—they were attempting to overthrow them and get them kicked out of the Night Court.

Apparently they'd been longtime rivals, and they thought I was stupid enough that they'd be able to get me to do their dirty work for them."

I was silent.

She glanced at me again. Her eyes—a swirling mix of purple and blue that was uncomfortably enthralling—were bright with curiosity. "You knew?"

I blinked. "He did a shoddy job of covering it up and was overconfident because Lady Chrysanthe eagerly accepted his false attention. He thought you'd be just as easy to fool."

Leila grunted. "Yeah, that was one advantage I had that I won't have anymore—at least not within my own Court. Oh well!" She flipped to a new packet. "Chase hasn't been able to figure out what that weird shadow-creature-thing from the derby was. Myron won't talk about it." She paused. "Actually, Chase thinks he *can't* talk about it."

"He's likely under a geas."

She peered at me with more interest than she'd shown since she called me out. "A what?"

"A geas—a binding line in a contract. Likely, Myron agreed to a geas that would keep him from speaking."

"Hmm. Did you ever have to have a geas when you were... um...working?"

I had, actually, on the contract I'd taken to try to kill her.

While the contract was canceled, the geas was still in place, which meant I could never speak a word or indicate who had hired me for the job.

I stared at her, unable to say anything.

She narrowed her eyes. "I'm going to take that as a yes." Without a moment's hesitation, she returned her attention to her papers.

I lingered awkwardly behind one of her couches.

"You know," she abruptly said. "If my raw charm scares you

that much, you can use the lock installed on the door between our rooms to lock me out."

It occurred to me then I had married a feminine version of Dion in a far more attractive variety.

"Your sense of humor is not as witty as you think it is," I flatly said.

"I'm not the one who disappeared for three days after we got married," she laughed. Her eyes darted in my direction and she added, almost reluctantly, "I'm glad you're back."

I sighed and finally sat down in a chair. "Because you have the official ball that will recognize you as Queen of the Night Court in front of the other monarchs?"

"And I don't want to host it alone—*yeees.*" She shuddered, then tossed her papers aside. "The Day King should be fun, but I'd rather go to the dentist and get some teeth pulled than invite the other monarchs to the party. The King of the Autumn Court I would especially love to avoid—though that does remind me, I have some thank you notes I need you to sign."

I was so confused, my forehead actually wrinkled. "Thank you notes?"

"Yes. For all the wedding gifts we received?"

"You are the Queen of the Night Court. I'm your consort. We don't have to thank anyone."

"Yes, we do. It's good manners. And I don't want anyone holding a wedding gift over our heads."

I stared at her, dumbstruck. *Does she really not understand that she holds the ultimate power over everyone in our Court? Given that her marriage to me lacks any kind of political connection and that everyone has sworn themselves to her, they are at her mercy, not the other way around.*

Leila misunderstood my silence. "Don't worry—I have most of them written. The only one I'm going to make you write is for the Paragon—I think my insincerity would show through in that note. He got us a fancy tea maker, and I'm bitter because the chef has it put in a place of honor in the kitchen but *still* won't let me get a coffee maker!"

As I observed my very unlikely wife, it occurred to me that I was lucky she easily accepted what she referred to as my brooding silence. If not, Leila would have pushed and insisted on hearing why I had abandoned her, and I wasn't quite ready to tell her.

I'd spent the past three days trying to sort out what I felt about her as a queen.

I'd agreed to become her consort because I really wondered if she'd try to destroy the Court.

But in my absence, she hadn't acted like a tyrant or started beheading nobles. Rather, she'd carried on—business as usual.

Based on what I'd heard, the most tyrannical thing she had done was inform the Court she was cutting the number of social events in half to make up for a budget shortage.

No one dared to nay say her.

She won't willfully destroy the Night Court...but her idea of ending the struggles for power is madness. She's a threat to the Court still, because she's going to change the game one way or another.

If I were a more idealistic fae, I'd dare to hope that she could save us all. But it's too late for that.

"Rigel—are you listening?"

"You want me to thank the Paragon for the tea maker."

"Precisely!"

I watched her organize her papers with a bunch of fuss, and something in me prickled. Before I thought twice about it, I said, "You don't want me to kill anyone for bad wedding gifts?"

"*No!*" She gave me a reproachful look. "You are a bloodthirsty lion, aren't you? You should drink some tea. I hear it's calming."

"Perhaps you ought to try it, then."

"*I would rather die!*"

My lips shivered in an almost smile.

Yes, I married her to stop her if necessary. I never wanted it—neither did she, apparently—but at least she'll be an amusing person to tease from now until it's over.

THE END

To be continued in Crown of Moonlight: Court of Midnight and Deception Book 2

For free short stories and more information about the Court of Midnight and Deception Series, visit kmshea.com!

HOW TO TRAIN WITH VAMPIRES

A Court of Midnight and Deception & Hall of Blood and Mercy short story

"Good. Now slightly tilt the gun so you have the leverage to press down on the magazine release with your thumb," Josh said.

I stared at the handgun I held in my right hand and flicked my eyes to my left hand. "Can't I just use my free hand to press the button?" I asked.

"No. Your free hand needs to be reaching for your filled magazine which should be hooked on your belt," Josh said. "You want to make magazine replacement as swift as possible so you don't give your enemy time to strike."

I tilted my handgun as instructed, pressing down on the magazine release with my thumb. The emptied magazine slid out of the gun and fell to the ground while I grabbed the pre-filled magazine from my belt—where Josh had made me clip it when we first started my refresher course on what I meant to be target practice, but had somehow turned into giving me the gun skills of a super spy.

I shoved the new magazine in, which effortlessly clicked into place.

"Good. That's the basic movement. Now you just need to get faster," Josh said. "Practice it again."

I pressed down, releasing the filled magazine, and hooked it on my belt again before I squatted to pick up the empty magazine. "While I appreciate that this will make me look super cool, are you sure we shouldn't do more target practice? I don't intend to have to shoot so many bullets that I need to be reaching for refills."

I only had one week before the Paragon would return to my parents' farm to take me to the Night Court. I had to make my practice time count.

Gavino shook his head and folded his arms across his chest, making the impressive muscles of his arms bulge in his suitcoat. I have no idea how the hot afternoon sun wasn't roasting him. "You're going to be Queen of the Night Court, Leila. It's better for you to be prepared to protect yourself than be caught unguarded," he said.

"Besides, you are already a fair enough shot." Josh tapped the paper target he'd removed from the hay bale we'd hauled from my parents' farm and set up outside at the end of one of the outdoor shooting ranges on the Drake property. "While you have plenty of room for improvement, the effects of practice will have diminishing returns for you, particularly because if you're resorting to shooting it doesn't matter if you merely maim or kill as you are now a royal," Josh said. "We're better off teaching you methods that will allow you to stay active in combat longer, until your guards are able to reach you."

My shots riddled the paper target—which Josh had taped to the table he'd carried outside to hold some necessary items, like a cleaning kit, extra magazines, and more cartons of bullets than I'd use in the whole week of practice.

Based on the target, I wasn't a sharp shooter by any means, but my aim hadn't rusted as much as I feared. I was actually pretty likely to be able to hit anyone at close range. "That's a fun thought," I said.

Josh shrugged. "It suits your temperament."

I set my shoulders and practiced tilting my gun and releasing the empty magazine while I reached for the full one clipped to my belt. "What do you mean by that?" I slammed the full magazine into place, relaxing when it clicked.

"You are a fighter. You will fight to survive," Josh said. "If it were the average half-human half-fae that had been chosen as the new Night Queen, I would suggest meditating and cleansing your mind so that when death inevitably enfolds you—likely a gift from a hateful subject—you might kick off from this mortal coil in peace."

"Thanks?" I released the full magazine and prepared to practice the move again.

"He means it as a compliment," Gavino assured me.

"Leila, back again for some more practice?"

I set the gun on the table—Josh had endlessly drilled me when he first taught me how to use a gun to never hold or point one unless you were willing to shoot whatever you were aimed at, so there was no way I was holding it when greeting any of the Drakes. "Hello, Celestina! Yes, I'll be coming over as often as you guys don't mind it this week."

The Drake Family's First Knight—essentially the second in command and one of Killian's two most trusted vampires, the other being Josh, the Second Knight—beamed at me.

While Josh and Gavino had pasty pale skin—a typical mark of a vampire—Celestina's brown skin had retained some of the warmth she had in life, giving her a brighter appearance, even though she shared the same ruby-red eyes all vampires had.

"Don't be silly. We're happy to be of assistance to you as you prepare for the battle ahead of you." She swerved around a waist high shrub and stopped at Gavino's side, offering me a smile.

Celestina—tall and model like—wore a pair of high heels I'd

never be able to manage without breaking an ankle, and looked like she'd stepped out of a high-power board room with her impeccably fitted suit.

If I had her air of competence and power, I'm willing to bet the upcoming fight for my life would be a little easier.

As if aware of my thoughts, Celestina propped her hands on her hips. "Have you thought about my offer of giving you more advanced personal defense training?"

"I still believe you ought to learn how to fight with a knife," Josh said. "There is a simplistic elegance to stabbing an opponent."

"Considering it's fae she's facing, a gun is her fastest and best option for close range personal defense," Gavino said.

Celestina briefly puffed her cheeks. "Maybe, but it's empowering to know you could toss a grown man over your shoulder."

"It would be pretty awesome," I agreed. "But I don't think I have the right base for you to teach me stuff like that. The only self defense class I took was a gym class elective in college, and it was pretty bare bones."

Celestina sighed. "True. If only we had a month to get you into fighting shape—you already have decent strength and stamina given the daily chores you complete for your farm."

"What are you all doing here?" A red-haired vampire strolled around the shrubbery Celestina had dodged. His name was Rupert—he was pretty recognizable as he was the most sour-faced of the Drake vampires. I hadn't interacted with him much, but I got the feeling he didn't like humans—or at least that he *hadn't* liked humans, until Hazel Medeis and all the wizards in House Medeis had become the Drake's live-in allies.

"Afternoon, Rupert!" Gavino grinned at the slightly shorter vampire. "Ready to return to House Medeis tomorrow?"

Rupert scoffed. "Never. I dare say I despise the place."

"Is that so?" Celestina nonchalantly inspected her nails—which were painted a pretty coral-orange color. "I suppose we could add you into the patrol rotation here at Drake Hall so you could stay here."

Rupert shoved his nose into the air. "No need. I am willing to make great sacrifices for the Eminence." He peered from the target-less hay bale to the gun on the table, to me. "Why are you all out here fraternizing with the dog trainer?"

Josh—the shortest of the vampires present and, honestly, the least intimidating based on appearance alone—casually reached up and grabbed Rupert by his necktie, yanked him forward so he folded over into a bow, and cuffed him upside the head in a smooth, seamless movement that had Rupert choking on his shirt collar.

"I would advise you to watch your manners, as you are addressing the new Queen of the Night Court," Josh said.

"The what?" Rupert was red faced when Josh finally let him go and he stood up straight.

"I don't think he heard the news yesterday," Gavino said. "He was too busy playing bridge—cards, that is—with Great Aunt Marriane last night. He wasn't present at the debriefing meeting."

"I was not *playing*!" Rupert adjusted his tie. "That old bat had me captive!"

"Oh, yes. It would certainly make sense that one wizard would be able to hold you, a Drake Vampire, against your will," Celestina said.

"It was more than just Marriane!" Rupert huffed, then glanced at me and bowed his head. "Congratulations on the position, Queen Leila," he said stiffly, but with genuine respect. Rupert wasn't the type to lower his head easily, but he'd become a lot less muleheaded since the Drakes and Medeis wizards started intermingling more.

Josh patted him on the shoulder like an older brother rewarding his toddler brother. "Well done, Rupert. You are learning."

Rupert eyed him. "Since when did you become so worried about how I address others?"

"I am always concerned with your social manners," Josh said. "It is my greatest fear that they shall one day prove to be the reason you escape to death due to your propensity to speak impertinently to important supernaturals."

As he rearranged the cleaning kit, Josh looked anything but anxious. But I was smart enough not to question the Second Knight, so I fiddled awkwardly with the magazine clipped to my belt.

Gavino coughed into his elbow—probably to hide a laugh, and Rupert looked increasingly sour, so I scrambled for a new topic.

"Ah, Celestina! I love your nails—did you get another manicure?" I asked.

"I did!" Celestina excitedly held out her hands. "Hazel, Momoko, and I went to a spa—it was so delightful! I got a pedicure, too." The vampire smiled down at her fingers, the picture of feminine grace. "And best yet, I asked for a gel nail polish this time, so they shouldn't chip even when I'm reduced to hand to hand combat. I broke a nail last week when I disarmed a mad vampire."

"Disarmed?" I asked.

Celestina elegantly waved her hand. "He only had a sword, and was a very old vampire so he had very traditional views of dueling. It was an easy thing to break his sword with a few well-timed strikes and shake him senseless."

"A few well-timed strikes of what?" I asked.

Celestina's smile was a bright white against her warm skin. "My fists, of course."

Knowing Celestina's strength, it wasn't *too* surprising to hear just what she was capable of, but it was still hard to fathom. "Way to go," I said. "I hope next time you get a recording—I'd like to see something like that!"

Celestina tapped her lip. "I suppose it would be useful for

training purposes." She glanced over at Josh, who was straightening the boxes of ammo.

"I will not volunteer, unless we buy several boxes of cheap blades," Josh said. "I have already lost far too many of my deadly life companions to your strength."

"But the cheap swords shatter easily," Celestina argued. "Even Rupert could break them!"

Rupert angrily sniffed. "I rank high in the Drake family. Naturally I would be strong enough to break a mere sword."

"No," Celestina said. "You're ranked high in the Drake family in terms of deadliness, but if we're going purely on strength, Gavino would beat you."

"That's nonsense!" Rupert scoffed.

Gavino shrugged. "I can't break blades like Celestina—I'm not fast enough to track the motions. But I dare say I have the strength."

Rupert pressed his lips into a thin line. "You're just saying that because the wizards are forever hero-worshipping you for your weightlifting abilities."

"Oh-ho-ho—is that jealousy I hear?" Celestina chuckled as she prodded Rupert's cheek like an affectionate older sister. "You've come to finally admit your love of the wizards, have you? Little Rupert is growing up!"

"Hardly," Rupert scoffed.

At that moment, I heard a male voice call out over the gardens. *"Rupert! Where'd you go? We're going to start our Mario Kart Tournament and you said you wanted in!"*

The flair of magic in the air assured me the speaker was a wizard.

Rupert took a step towards the voice, then scowled when Celestina and Gavino smirked. "It's not what you think!" he said.

Gavino's smile grew.

Celestina draped an arm over Rupert's shoulders. "I don't know if it's the wizards' influence over me, but you've become increasingly more adorable and markedly less annoying—which is all you used to be. Come on—let's go see your little friends." Celestina hauled Rupert a few steps, then paused long enough to look back at me. "I'll be back in a bit, Leila. I'll let Hazel know you're here."

"Thanks—have fun!" I said.

Celestina chuckled. "Oh, we will."

Rupert grumbled under his breath as she hauled him through the expansive gardens.

Josh sighed morosely as he watched them go. "I had hopes of attending the next time there was a Mario Kart Tournament."

Gavino pushed his eyebrows together and studied the shorter vampire. "Because Momoko likes those tournaments?"

"Partially, yes," Josh said.

I squinted as I stretched my memory. "Isn't Momoko one of Hazel's childhood friends?"

"Yes," Josh said. "She is a very deadly wizard—practically poetry in motion with the careful precision of her strikes. She can kill quite easily—it's very beautiful."

Unsure of what to do with a seemingly love-struck Josh, I looked to Gavino for help.

He very *not* helpfully shrugged.

"Ah. I see. She sounds lovely," I said. "So, time for target practice?"

"No," Josh said. "You should practice switching magazines for several minutes. Then we'll move on to something fun."

I picked up my gun—carefully pointing it towards the hay bale—and tilted it so I could press the magazine release button. "And what would that be?" I asked.

"We'll take you into the downstairs shooting range, blindfold you, and then have you attempt to shoot Gavino and me so you start learning how to use your other senses to pinpoint targets," Josh said.

Gavino slightly bowed his head to the Second Knight. "A wise idea. Considering you are to be the Queen of the Night Court, Leila, it is wise to learn how to shoot in darkness."

"That's...great," I said.

I switched out my magazines—I had to admit I was a lot better than I had been when I'd been practicing just a few minutes ago—and settled in for a week of extremely *interesting* training from the Drake Vampires.

Odd training or not, I'd do whatever they told me. I trusted the Drake vampires a million times more than I trusted anyone from my Court. I was thankful for their friendship, and even though I hoped they were wrong about needing practice in all these areas, I wasn't overly optimistic.

They'd trained Hazel—who had become the fiercest wizard in the Midwest and returned to train a house of combat-ready wizards.

If they thought I needed to know how to shoot in the dark, I would.

I'm going to survive. I promised myself. *Assassins, hatred from my own people—I'll make like a cockroach and outlast it all!*

Several months later I was going through the cards and gifts sent to me—and Rigel, technically—congratulating us on our marriage and my official crowning.

I was pleasantly surprised when I opened a boring, white envelope and found the card inside was emblazoned with swords and guns. The card was signed by all the Drake vampires I knew best.

> *Congratulations on this strategic and wise marriage,*
> **Gavino*

Good luck not dying,
Rupert

I'm so excited for you! An assassin will make the PERFECT husband!
- Celestina

Seducing your enemy is an excellent way to reduce your number of foes. Well done. Remember to practice switching out full magazines, and try to avoid the sweet call of death.
Josh

I LAUGHED AT THE NOTES, but truthfully, they made the tension in my neck ease a little bit.

Marrying Rigel was the right thing to do. I'd followed my instinct, and if the Drakes approved, that meant it was the best choice I could have made.

Now I just have to survive meeting the other monarchs...

THE END

OTHER SERIES BY K. M. SHEA

The Snow Queen

Timeless Fairy Tales

The Fairy Tale Enchantress

The Elves of Lessa

Hall of Blood and Mercy

Court of Midnight and Deception

Pack of Dawn and Destiny

King Arthur and Her Knights

Robyn Hood

The Magical Beings' Rehabilitation Center

Second Age of Retha: Written under pen name A. M. Sohma

ADDITIONAL NOVELS

Life Reader

Princess Ahira

A Goose Girl

ABOUT THE AUTHOR

K. M. Shea is a fantasy-romance author who never quite grew out of adventure books or fairy tales, and still searches closets in hopes of stumbling into Narnia. She is addicted to sweet romances, witty characters, and happy endings. She also writes LitRPG and GameLit under the pen name, A. M. Sohma.

Hang out with the K. M. Shea Community at...
kmshea.com